MYTHS AND
Shadows

LIZ ANDREWS
LENA MATTHEWS

ELLORA'S CAVE
ROMANTICA PUBLISHING

Myth of Moonlight
Lena Matthews & Liz Andrews

Kimberly Brenin has been plagued by nightmares. Dreams of being chased by someone or something—the petrifying face of a Werewolf. Most would chalk up the image to that of a scary story, but Kimberly knows the truth. Werewolves are real. She knows because she is one.

Being orphaned at an early age has left Kimberly woefully naïve when it comes to Were rules.

As *Benandanti* of his pack, Nico is furious that Kimberly would dare come to his land. Every Were knows it is against Lycan Law for any Werewolf to come into another's territory without first gaining permission or making an offering, and Kimberly had done neither.

The feisty beauty is a handful and much to Nico's amazement completely unknowledgeable about the world they live in. Even more astonishing, Kimberly has no idea that she is coming into her heat...

Shadow of Moonlight
Lena Matthews & Liz Andrews

Remington is a solider first and a woman second. She's fought hard to earn her place as *Venator* for her pack. The safety of her *Benandanti* comes first, even before her own wants and desires. There isn't a Were alive who can make her feel any differently. Then again, Jace McClellen isn't an ordinary Werewolf.

Thanks to the roll of the genetic dice, Jace possesses all the strength of a Werewolf but not the ability to change. Instead he's been given the annoying talent to dream a fortune-cookie future. A future filled with more questions than answers and a dream sidekick who aggravates more than he helps. The one thing he doesn't need his visions to tell him is he and Remington are meant to be together. Now the only thing he has to do is convince Remington.

An Ellora's Cave Romantica Publication

www.ellorascave.com

Myths and Shadows

ISBN 9781419957413
ALL RIGHTS RESERVED.
Myth of Moonlight Copyright © 2007 Lena Matthews & Liz Andrews
Shadow of Moonlight Copyright © 2007 Lena Matthews & Liz Andrews
Edited by Mary Moran.
Cover art by Syneca.

This book printed in the U.S.A. by Jasmine–Jade Enterprises, LLC.

Trade paperback Publication January 2008

About the Authors

&

Lena Matthews spends her days dreaming about handsome heroes and her nights with her own personal hero. Married to her college sweetheart, she is the proud mother of an extremely smart toddler, three evil dogs, and a mess of ants that she can't seem to get rid of.

When not writing, she can be found reading, watching movies, lifting up the cushions on the couch to look for batteries for the remote control and plotting different ways to bring Buffy back on the air.

Liz Andrews is an Ohio native who loves rooting for the home team. When she can manage to unlock herself from the ball and chain that connects her to the Internet, she enjoys reading, going to the movies and hosting dinner parties for friends. In the real world, Liz has an MBA and works in the hospital business. However, she much prefers to escape into the world of books. She has admired and read various writers for many years and is happy to have finally joined the rank of author. She loves to hear from readers.

Lena and Liz welcome comments from readers. You can find their website and email addresses on their author bio pages at www.ellorascave.com.

Tell Us What You Think

We appreciate hearing reader opinions about our books. You can email us at Comments@EllorasCave.com.

MYTHS AND SHADOWS
ଌ

MYTH OF MOONLIGHT

Lena Matthews & Liz Andrews

ജ

Trademarks Acknowledgement

∞

Chapter One

శు

There was something wild out there, dark and overwhelming, like the black starless night. The rapid pounding of Kimberly's heart obscured the sounds of crickets chirping and a night owl's hooting. Eyes wide, she turned and looked around. The surroundings were the same as before.

Deep within a forest she had only visited in her dreams, she was surrounded by an overwhelming sense of foreboding that made her hesitant to take another step. Whatever was out there was waiting for her. Stepping back slowly, she nervously jumped at the loud snap of a twig breaking under her bare feet. Immediately the wild sounds surrounding her came to a halt.

Easing her foot back quietly, Kimberly tried to make her way out of the darkness of the forest. The rustling of the bushes caused Kimberly to hold her breath in nervous desperation. He was back, just as she knew he'd be, but worst of all, he was back for her.

Afraid for her safety, she turned and began running through the dense forest. Uncaring about the sharp stabs to her cold bare feet, Kimberly ran as if her life depended on it. Trying to dodge as many objects in her way as possible, she kept fluid and low to the ground. It was impossible to avoid every obstacle and her eyes began to tear as the branches lashed at her face. Kimberly raised her hands to try and protect herself but she didn't slow down because she knew he was gaining on her.

Suddenly Kimberly tripped over a protruding tree trunk, falling to her hands and knees. The underbrush dug into her and she lay stunned for a moment. Realizing she was wasting precious time, she scrambled up. Disoriented from the fall, Kimberly looked around wildly, trying to gather her bearings. From her right, Kimberly heard the crackling of leaves and immediately took off in the opposite direction.

Time seemed to slow as she continued to run. Her pursuer was relentless, never giving her time to stop and catch her breath. The forest seemed never-ending, as great an adversary as the one pursuing her. Kimberly began to grow tired and realized it was only a matter of time until he caught her. She couldn't think—she didn't know what to do. Tripping and falling a second time she lay on the ground, breathing harshly from her exertion. Abruptly, Kimberly realized she could hear breathing behind her as well. He'd found her. Turning, she gazed into glowing eyes and screamed.

Kimberly jolted upright. Perspiration drenched her body as she flopped back down on the bed. Her heart was racing.

It was only a nightmare. Even though she was safe, home alone in her bed, the thought did little to appease her. If her dream had been a one-time occurrence, she might have been able to blame it on the bad Chinese food she'd had the night before. But unfortunately, it was becoming a chillingly familiar nightly routine. The nightmares began a few months ago and had become progressively disturbing. At first, she dreamed someone was watching her. Later, it had turned into someone chasing her. Tonight was the first time she had seen him.

Yet she wasn't able to get a clear picture of him because all she had really seen were his glowing russet eyes. Kimberly knew what that meant—her pursuer was a Werewolf. Kimberly knew because she was one too. Although she knew what she was, she just didn't know what it meant. She'd never lived with the Pack, her family had broken from them before she was born. The only connection she had to that part of herself was the beast lying dormant within her and bedtime stories she had heard as a child from her parents.

Getting up, Kimberly walked into the bathroom, flipping on the light to study her ashen face in the mirror. The phantom stalker was beginning to wear on her. Dark bags underneath her eyes made it appear as if she had lost a fight instead of merely tossing and turning all night.

Deep down, what frightened her most was her dreams weren't always terrifying. Sometimes she wanted to stop, turn around and see who was chasing her. But to do so would leave her open to a reality she knew she wasn't ready to face. Her fear was neck and neck with her curiosity and Kimberly wasn't sure which part of her consciousness would win. Shaking her head at the thought, she hopped into the shower to get an early start on the day.

* * * * *

Stepping into her office, Kimberly hung up her coat and headed toward the break room to grab a cup of coffee. She enjoyed early mornings like this when the office wasn't too busy yet. Even though the law office was small, Lewis and Sinclair had a vibrant practice and she usually worked nonstop.

Work hadn't always been so exciting, but since her recent promotion from file clerk to paralegal, life had become so much more interesting. It was exciting for Kimberly to finally be making her own money. It was just further proof she could live on her own, despite her brother's vehement protests.

Even David couldn't complain about Bayside, except that it was a few hundred miles away from him, which to Kimberly was a plus in itself, besides the many other perks that came with the beautiful, picturesque town. A quiet little city right on the edge of the redwood forests, Bayside was filled with open-air markets and shopping galore. It wasn't so "small town" that everyone knew everyone else's business, nor was it too large that it was an impersonal metropolis. It fit Kimberly just right, much as her new job did.

Walking into the break room, Kimberly stopped short and muttered under her breath when she noticed the crowd. Maybe she wasn't the only person having nightmares. The doors didn't officially open until nine, yet already there were people bumbling about. Turning, she paused when she caught the earthy scent in the air. Nose flaring, she turned back to scan the faces of her coworkers. The musky odor had recently become as familiar to her as the back of her hand. Her senses were heightened because of what she was, but her youth prevented her from being able to home in on those abilities.

Kimberly's lip tensed and curled up a bit at the edge but she bit back the emotions clawing from inside her. There was someone impinging on her territory. Narrowing her eyes, she had to force herself to relax and refrain from giving the warning growl tickling the back of her throat. Kimberly wouldn't give in to her beast. She was not an animal, despite her split DNA.

Caffeine, all she needed was a shot of java and she could get through the day. Trying to ease closer to the coffeepot, Kimberly rocked from one foot to the other for several seconds, trying to patiently wait her turn before giving up and turning away. Halfway out of the room a voice called to her, freezing her in her tracks.

"Cream and sugar, right?"

Kimberly would recognize Nico Cassamonti's sultry, sexy voice anywhere. He was one of Lewis and Sinclair's very high-profile clients, which was one of the reasons he had access to parts of the building other clients did not. The Powers That Be wanted to keep him and his money as happy as humanly possible, and for some odd reason it seemed to please Nico to mingle with the underlings. She had only become aware of him when she started her new paralegal job and finally allowed in the break room on the third floor. Prior to her promotion she'd been tucked away in the file room and never had the opportunity to meet any of the clients, and now it seemed as if she couldn't go three feet without bumping into them, Nico especially.

Not that it was a bad thing though, because Nico was a walking god. He was tall and muscular, with thick black hair and eyes so dark she couldn't tell exactly what color they were. Although she secretly lusted after him, in her heart she knew he was way out of her league. He was worth more than some small countries and she was barely scraping by on her salary. Kimberly seriously doubted they had much in common.

"I'm sorry, were you speaking to me?"

"No need to apologize, Ms. Brenin." He turned with two coffee cups in his hands and tried to hand one of them to her. Kimberly hesitated and took a step back.

"Thank you, but no, Mr. Cassamonti," she murmured, her gaze darting around the room, hunting for the nearest escape.

Nico shook his head mockingly. "What have I told you? Please call me Nico."

"I really don't think it would be wise," she stammered, avoiding the cup as if it were poison instead of coffee. Kimberly always seemed to stammer around him and she had no idea why he made her uneasy. It could have had something to do with the fact Nico towered over nearly every other man in the room. Or it could have been the way he always seemed to look directly into her soul, but either way, she was never comfortable being in his presence for too long. And it was one reason she shied away from him.

"But I insist." Nico held the cup firmly out in front of him, daring her to refuse. Aware of everyone eyeing them speculatively, Kimberly cautiously reached out and took the cup, not wanting to give the group more reason to stare.

Just then, two of the firm's associates walked into the room addressing Nico and starting up a brief conversation about business. Kimberly breathed a sigh of relief and quickly escaped. Even though she didn't dare glance back, she could sense Nico watching her. His gaze caused a tingling sensation down her spine. She didn't know what to make of it. Maybe she was imagining something where there was nothing.

Of course she seemed to be doing that a lot lately. Her late-night dreams and the lingering musky scent were beginning to wear on her nerves. The odd scent was becoming more frequent and pronounced, but unfortunately, she still couldn't pin down the source. As she approached her desk, Kimberly heard the phone ringing. Hurrying over, she picked up the phone, "Lewis and Sinclair, Ms. Reynolds' office, Kimberly speaking, how may I help you?"

"Come home for a visit."

Closing her eyes, Kimberly said a silent prayer for patience before opening them slowly and letting out a calming breath. It had only been a few days since she had last talked to her brother, yet he insisted on trying to keep long-distance tabs on her. "David, why are you calling me here?"

"What, a brother can't call his sister for a chat?"

"David, I can't talk at work, please understand."

"Then come home for a visit so we can talk."

"I can't. I've been working a lot of long hours since I was promoted to this new job. I need to be here for a while." Kimberly knew her boss Cassandra would give her the time off if she asked, but it was a great excuse and she just didn't want to go home for a visit right now.

"Kimmie." Kimberly grimaced at the hated childhood nickname. "I need to talk to you about something important. I have been trying to reach you for a while now."

"How many times have I told you *never* to call me Kimmie?"

"Stop trying to change the subject." The irritation in her brother's voice rang over the line loud and clear.

"Look, my boss just came in, I've got to go." Kimberly crossed her fingers as she told the little white lie.

"Kimberly, please listen—"

"Sorry, David, bye." Kimberly quickly hung up the phone before he could continue the conversation. Putting her face in her hands, she took deep breaths, trying to find her center.

"Man trouble?"

Startled, Kimberly looked up into her boss' sympathetic face. She had only been working for Cassandra a little over a month, but what she'd seen from her time there she liked. Cassandra straddled the line of professionalism and friendliness carefully, but she never seemed cold or distant. Always willing to listen, she would have been someone whom Kimberly confided in, if she could have. But she doubted her boss, no matter how sympathetic she was, would understand her issues.

"You could say that."

"Men can be such animals sometimes."

Kimberly smirked at the irony. "You don't know the half of it."

"I don't know, I've had my share of horrible suitors."

"What about smart-ass older brothers?"

The pretty blonde leaned against the corner of Kimberly's desk with a smile. "I've dealt with older brothers but I was never blessed with one."

"Trust me, it's not a blessing." Kimberly felt horrible for saying them the minute the words left her mouth.

David, in all his protective glory, loved and cared for her very much. He had been her rock after their parents died and she didn't know what she would have done without him. But that was eleven years ago and Kimberly was no longer a child. However, instead of letting go, David still clung to her, eventually forcing her to move hundreds of miles away just so she could breathe. He was caring and supportive for sure—but a blessing, hardly.

"Oh it can't be all that bad."

19

"You're right, I do remember lots of good times when we were kids. Too bad he can't accept I've grown up."

"Sounds as if your brother needs a new hobby."

"What he needs is a girlfriend." Kimberly looked at Cassandra speculatively, wondering if she could fix them up. Nah, it would be career suicide, she decided in the next instant. If they broke up, it would make things awkward, but if Cassandra found out they were Werewolves, it would really spice up the office gossip mill.

Cassandra stood abruptly with a look of exaggerated fear. "I saw that look and you can forget it, girlfriend."

Kimberly laughed, glad her bad mood had been broken, if only for a few moments. "You better run before I start picking out songs for the wedding."

Cassandra smiled warmly before warning, "Get to work and *maybe* I'll forget you ever said anything."

"Aye, aye, captain."

Laughing, Kimberly turned back to her desk and tried to focus on work. Just as she was getting in to the flow of things, Kimberly looked up and spotted Nico standing in the doorway, watching her intently. He didn't say anything, just watched her for a few seconds before turning and walking away.

His stare didn't creep her out as much as it filled her with a sense of foreboding, driving home the fact she didn't want to run into him again, if she didn't have to. With that thought in mind, Kimberly threw herself into her work, mindful of the passing hours until she could escape to her home, safe away from Nico and his overpowering presence.

For the first time in a long time, Kimberly was one of the first people out of the office. Although she usually liked to work late, she felt mentally exhausted. Worrying about the increased sensations she'd been experiencing, the constant nightmares and the unsettling aura of Nico Cassamonti were wearing her down. The only thing she wanted was a strong drink, a hot shower and her bed, not necessarily in any particular order. Breaking away from the crowd, Kimberly headed toward the rear of the garage where she'd parked her car.

As she neared the car, Kimberly felt a strange sense of déjà vu. Just as in her nightmare, she felt as if someone were watching her. She glanced around, didn't see anyone, but it didn't deter her from slowing down. A familiar scent wafted in the air, the one she'd decided today was only in her imagination.

Deciding she didn't care if she looked like an idiot, Kimberly began running toward her car. She wasn't afraid of who was following her—well, not entirely—but it was hard to control the beast when her adrenaline started pumping. Controlling the beast was one of the main reasons she took yoga, so she could learn how to maintain her calm. The last thing Kimberly needed was to change in front of someone looking for some fast money. Unfortunately her heels were her downfall and she couldn't run very fast in them without twisting her ankle and falling. Heart racing she stopped, refusing to move a step farther. She had to calm down and calm down now before she gave the security cameras something good to look at.

The air stilled around her. It was there again, like in her dreams, and a feeling more powerful than her fear and her beast combined called to her. Kimberly felt a powerful force directly behind her getting closer and closer. Dropping her bag, she balled her fists and abruptly turned, coming face-to-face with not only her dream but with Nico.

Her gasp slipped from her mouth as Nico stepped toward her, closing the gap between them. Unexpectedly Kimberly was overwhelmed by the scents and sensations around her. She swayed, reaching out to steady herself. Looking up, she realized she had grasped his arm and jerked back. His dark eyes glowed down at her and his lips tilted up at the sides, bringing his canine teeth into view. The familiar musky scent was heavy in the air and her eyes widened as she realized not only who he was but what he was.

"It's about damn time you recognized me," Nico growled.

The fear in her eyes did nothing but heighten Nico's awareness of her. He could smell it on her, just as he could smell her heat, strong and deep and very, very spicy. Nico had known from the first moment he saw her at Lewis and Sinclair who she was. No—what she was. In fact, he had waited patiently for her to come to him but she seemed to shy away, forcing Nico to take matters into his own hands.

Biding his time, Nico gathered as much information about her as he could, wanting to see what she was up to. So far, he'd come up with zilch about who she was or where she came from and it didn't make any sense. It was against Lycan Law for any Werewolf to come into another's territory without first gaining permission or making an offering, and Kimberly had done neither. He could have her head if he wanted, but he wanted something more.

"Of course I recognized you. You're a client—"

Snarling, he tightened his grip on her arm. "That's not what I meant and you know it. Talk fast."

Awareness caused her eyes to light up, but she continued to protest. "I don't know what you mean."

Pulling her closer to him, he growled low in his throat and watched in approval when she lowered her eyes as was custom. "Who are you and why are you here?"

Kimberly licked her full lips nervously and tilted her head farther down. "I didn't know, honestly."

"Lies!"

"No, I swear. I didn't know there were others here." Her pulse tattooed against his fingers pressed hard on her wrist, but despite her nervousness, Nico could tell she was telling the truth. Lies, like fear, omitted a scent as obvious as darting eyes.

"Whom do you belong to?" His comment brought her head up fast. The deference he saw only moments before was gone and in its stead was an arrogance and will as strong as he'd ever seen. Nico preferred it to her submission.

"To no one."

"You're a rogue?" he asked astonished.

"No. I'm my own."

That was impossible. There were no unprotected female Weres anywhere. Even the other Were-animals never left their females alone. Ever since the Purification War, female Weres had become protected and cherished. Were births had dropped off dramatically in the last few generations and female Weres even more so. It was why the female Weres were treasured as much as they were. The survival of their species depended on it, especially these days. "Now I know you're lying to me."

Pulling her arm free, Kimberly step backed and widened her stance. Her body warned of her fight-or-flight mentality and part of Nico—a very large part—hoped she would choose the latter. Nothing was more exciting than chasing prey. "I'm not lying. I'm on my own."

"Where's your mate?"

"I don't have one." From the bittersweet smell radiating off her like heat, Nico knew that at least was true as far as logistics were concerned. Virgins had the sweetest scent of all. Especially when they were about to enter puberty, a later stage for female Weres, a precursor to going into heat, as Kimberly was.

Her heat wasn't the only thing that attracted her to Nico. From the first time he spotted her, she captured his attention. Smaller than a pup, Kimberly appeared as delicate as a flower, but up close, Nico could see the storm brewing in her hazel eyes. Skin as smooth as silk with a splatter of freckles across the bridge of her small nose, she resembled a pixie instead of the wild animal he knew she could be. It was hard for Nico to reconcile how anyone could let her wander about freely. If she were his, he'd have her marked, mated and heavy with his child before she blinked.

"Impossible."

"Look, I already apologized. What else do you want?"

"What do you mean, what do I want?" Nico was incredulous at her total lack of knowledge about their culture. "You should be making proper retribution to the *Benandanti*."

"And just what would proper retribution be and what the hell is a *Benandanti*?"

Nico stared at Kimberly for a moment before answering. *Was she kidding*? He had never experienced a female Were so totally unfamiliar with the Werewolf life. Were pups were taught from a very early age how proper retribution was to be given to all elders in the Pack, not only by age but by rank. And the fact she didn't know who or what a *Benandanti* was, was terrifying. What kind of Pack did she grow up in that was without a leader? Who'd looked out for her before she wandered onto his land?

"Let's start with the most important answer. A *Benandanti* is the leader. The head Were in charge. And he's the one you owe the retribution to, which can be anything from a fresh kill for his Pack, to monetary compensation or a mate."

"Well, since I'm in the know, I'll head straight out and slaughter a deer worthy of his forgiveness. Do points get taken away for roadkill?" Kimberly's annoyed tone amused Nico. If he didn't sense her sincerity, he would have had a hard time believing she was a Werewolf. Kimberly was the most un-intimidating wolf he had ever seen in all his life. Nico had known pups with fiercer growls.

"It's not only you who owes the debt," he added, trying to get at the truth. "Everyone must be held accountable."

"There isn't an 'everyone'. That's what I've been trying to tell you." Her voice echoed in the empty parking structure, causing her denial to ring even clearer.

"You're lying. I can tell." And it was pissing him off.

"I'm not lying," she argued, her scent rising off her like steam.

Confusion muddled her hazel eyes, making her irises appear darker and deeper than possible. "If I can speak to this *Benandanti* person, I can clear this up."

Who did she think she was talking to? Anyone else would have recognized him from the get-go, but his sheltered pup had no idea just who she was dealing with. "So far you haven't been doing a great job of clearing anything up."

Awareness dawned, widening her eyes with shock. If he weren't so pissed off at her, Nico might have found the whole situation funny as hell, but she was too close to danger for him to laugh it off.

"I didn't know."

"As was apparent from your total lack of respect." Nico stepped closer, forcing her back against the car behind her. Finally reassured Kimberly wasn't a threat, he allowed his canines to retract. Nico didn't want to frighten her, because if she were too scared to talk, he wouldn't ever find out what she was doing there.

Kimberly growled low in her throat, protesting his dominant move, trying to warn him away. The steel was back again, this time spreading from her fiery eyes to her backbone.

"Free lesson, *Zingaro*. A threat is only viable if the person is willing to go through with it."

"If you want me out of town by nightfall, consider it done," she shot back, offering the one thing he refused to consider.

Damn it! This wasn't the way he had wanted to approach her but she'd resisted all his efforts up to now to get her alone. Nico could tell she was frightened, any normal person would be in this situation, but he couldn't shake off his feelings of frustration. Kimberly wasn't normal, and as a Were, she should be more experienced in shielding her emotions. By not doing so, she was situating herself as a target for every creature under the moon.

Nothing attracted animals as much as fear and weakness, and Nico could tell Kimberly hadn't yet embraced her beast. She was afraid of it, and her fear, coupled with her heat, called to him. He didn't know whether to chase her or fuck her—both thoughts made him hard as hell. "You're not going anywhere until I tell you you can go somewhere."

"I'm not your problem." Her hand nervously went to her neck and she gave a slight scratch at the reddening area just above her collarbone.

"In a few nights you're going to be more than my problem."

"What are you talking about?"

"You can't be serious, *Zingaro*." No Werewolf reached puberty without being aware of the dangers of full moons and mating season. "You're in heat and there won't be a Were for miles around who won't be able to sense it."

"You're out of your fucking mind." Her denial vibrated in her words.

"And you're either naïve or dumb," he growled. Kimberly didn't know what she was doing. She wasn't only endangering herself, she was also endangering their very existence. No Were alive would be able to resist her call. Female Weres gave out a mating scent when they went into puberty, a way of announcing to male Weres they were ready to accept a mate. It wasn't only wolves attracted to the scent, any second-nature man within smelling distance would also be drawn to Kimberly. She would be marked and mated in a matter of minutes and she would have no one to blame but herself. Even if she didn't understand the how, she damn sure needed to know the why. "Come with me and I'll explain everything."

"I'm not going anywhere with you."

"Lycan Law."

"I'm not in your Pack."

"That's where you're wrong. According to Lycan Law, *Zingaro*, if you're unmated and unclaimed and you're in my territory, you belong to me." It was officially Nico's new favorite law. Anything to put Kimberly under his watchful eyes worked for him.

"Stop calling me that!"

"What?"

"*Zingaro* or whatever. My name is Kimberly."

"I know very well what your name is, Kimberly." He said her name as if it were a caress. "But *Zingaro* is fitting as well. It means 'my little gypsy'. My Were without a home."

"I have a home but more importantly, I don't belong to you. I don't belong to anyone."

She was such an innocent. It was rewarding and annoying at the same time. Nico couldn't imagine who would have let her leave without warning her about the ways of the world. "Not up on your rules and regulations?"

"Are we beasts or are we goddamn democrats?"

"Everything has laws, even in nature. The strong survive, that *is* the law of nature."

"If you say Lycan Law one more time, I'm going to scream."

"Prepare to scream," he warned, and to his amazement Kimberly opened her mouth to do so. Moving quickly, Nico covered her mouth with his hand. There was no doubt about it, her meekness didn't carry to the bone.

Threading his other hand through the auburn curls hanging loosely at the back of her head, Nico gripped the silky strands and used them as an anchor to hold her in place. Kimberly's eyes widened, not with fear as he thought they might, but with something closer to passion. The fever was upon her, and if she didn't submit soon, there would be hell to pay.

"Not only do you need a keeper but you also need a history book."

Eyes narrowing, Kimberly reached up and pulled his hand away from her mouth. "They have books on this?" she asked in wonder.

She kept surprising him. Shaking his head, he asked in shock, "Where were you raised?"

"Around." The squeal of tires swung both their heads toward the entrance as a white Volkswagen Bug pulled into the parking garage. "This isn't the place for this conversation."

Finally, she said something he could agree with. "Fine. I'll follow you home."

"That's not what I meant."

"For as long as you're in my territory, you'll do as I say. Unattached female Weres need all the support they can get. My Pack will help you through this."

"Through what?"

"You really can't be so naïve?"

"What are you talking about?" The irritation in her tone nearly matched the level of his frustration.

"Don't you wonder why I knew who you were? Why you're so antsy and can't keep still."

"You're the *Benandanti*, you can sense things."

"Yes," he said, nodding his head slowly, "and one of the things I can sense is you're in heat."

"What!" The smell of fear rolled off her in waves. The engaging scent actually overpowered the aroma of her heat, an amazing feat when she was this close to her time. The look of shock and despair on her beautiful face made Nico feel horrible. He hated breaking this to her so abruptly, in the middle of a parking garage, but she wasn't leaving him much choice. Her safety was on the line and she was running out of time.

"Your body is readying itself for mating. How could you reach puberty without knowing these things?" Whoever her *Benandanti* was, he needed to be skinned and mounted on a wall. It made absolutely no sense that Kimberly was so unprepared for the world.

"I'm a slow learner," she replied snidely, scratching again at her neck.

Nico's eyes narrowed on her neck and he had to bite back a curse. Her time was upon her and she was in no way prepared. "It's time, Kimberly. You'll need my protection. If you're not linked by the time of the full moon, you'll have every Were sniffing at your door. I won't have my territory tarnished."

"Then I'll leave." The hell she would and Nico was getting damn tired of her threatening to run away from him.

"The only place you're going is home with me. You need me—us—and you need us now."

"It will go away. It has before."

"No, it's only simmering below the surface, waiting for the right time to come out." Shaking his head, Nico picked up her hand and held it out in front of her. "Look at your pulse, *Zingaro*, practically beating out of your fragile flesh. Your nerves are raw, you're shaking and I can smell the moisture gathering between your thighs."

Nico's tongue felt heavy in his mouth. He wanted to delve between her legs and drink the juices beckoning him. Kimberly wasn't even in full force yet and she already had him feeling like a randy dog. There was no telling what would happen in six days when the moon was full and her heat blossomed. He could have a WWE riot on his hands. "It's only going to get worse. I can ease your pain."

Licking her lips, Kimberly asked nervously, "How?"

Herbs, meditation and the right amount of control were methods taught to Lupas when they were young, but nothing could be done for Kimberly now that didn't involve long hours of fierce loving. She was becoming prime and ready for her mating, and Nico was beginning to feel as if he were the Were for the job.

There would even come a point, once she was in tune with her beast, when Kimberly would be able to control her need to mate altogether. If she had been raised right, brought up right, her needs wouldn't even be an issue. But she wasn't and therein lay the real problem. "Come with me."

"No," she said again, refusing to give in. "I can handle this on my own."

Cursing in Italian, Nico turned from her, trying to calm his libido and his temper. As *Benandanti* he had the right to assert his wants over hers, as a wolf, he had the desire to force her to her knees and take what was rightfully his, but as a man, he knew he couldn't. The hardest part of being all three was trying to find the even plateau.

Turning back, Nico looked her steadily in the eye. He wanted to give her the option to come to him willingly, even if he knew she couldn't do it herself. Sometimes the pretense of control over one's destiny was just as good as the real thing. "You have four days to bring this to an end on your own. By nightfall on the fourth day, if you haven't cooled the fever, then I will come for you."

"Four days isn't enough time."

"It's all you have." Nico wasn't risking her health or wellbeing. If Kimberly made him, he would play the Alpha card and to hell with the plateau.

Chapter Two

Kimberly was still unsteady when she walked into her apartment. Leaning against her closed door, she sighed and shook her head in disbelief. Nico Cassamonti, the hottie she had been secretly lusting after, was a frickin' Werewolf. Oh yeah, and by the way, she was in heat. Unbelievable. It was too much to take in all at one time. Just when she thought she was getting the hang of her dual existence, something jumped up and bit her on the ass, or wanted to from the look in Nico's eyes.

For the first time since leasing her apartment, the familiar scent of home did little to warm her. Normally when Kimberly had a bad day, the first place she wanted to run to was her apartment, the place she had made her own private sanctuary. She had painstakingly decorated each room on a shoestring budget, furnished mostly from secondhand stores but enhanced with love. Each room represented Kimberly's own interpretation of the forest and it was a haven for when she wanted to escape from the real world. Yet now, Nico had messed that up for her as well. Instead of the instant feeling of relaxation she normally experienced, Kimberly was more tense than when she had woken up from her dream.

Tossing her briefcase onto her dining room table, Kimberly quickly kicked off her shoes, needing to release everything confining her. Opening the fridge, Kimberly sighed with relief as she noted half a bottle of Chardonnay. Maybe her day had sucked but this evening she was going to enjoy a glass of wine, read a good book, go to bed and forget this day ever happened.

Looking across the room, Kimberly groaned as she saw the red blinking light on her answering machine. She hit the button to play messages then headed toward the cupboard for a glass. Much to her dismay, David's agitated voice boomed over the speaker.

"Kimberly, you're being immature. We really do have to talk and you can't keep avoiding my calls."

"Gee, I wonder what you've got to tell me," Kimberly called out to the empty room. "Maybe I'm in heat and there's more to being a Were than you ever told me." While she had been voicing her frustrations, Kimberly had missed a portion of David's message but it didn't stop him from talking.

"We have so much to talk about." Kimberly snorted as she filled her glass, her frustration level rising with the wine. "There are things I...things I should have explained to you before now."

"You think?"

"But I refuse to do it over the phone, so call me."

"Dream on."

"Or I'll do something we'll both regret."

"Too late," she shouted at the phone. Taking a big gulp, Kimberly tried to calm her nerves. She hoped her hormones were acting out, otherwise she was in a world of trouble because not only was she in heat, Kimberly also seemed to be on the verge of mental collapse.

The chilled wine instantly began to take effect, calming her with a false sense of security. Kimberly knew better than to drink alcohol this close to the full moon but if ever there was a night to indulge, it was tonight.

She was not going to think about Werewolves, being in heat or her four-day deadline. It was only a big deal if she made it one. She had controlled this "heat" thing before and she could do it again if she had to. It was all an issue of mind over matter.

Opening the refrigerator again, Kimberly took out a ham she'd cooked the night before and cut off a generous slice before heading back into the newly decorated living room. The ivy painted walls, chosen because of its resemblance to underbrush, did little to soothe her shattered nerves. The living room, normally her favorite room in the apartment, now seemed like a cage. Her beast wanted to break free and run, but this was neither the time nor the place.

Kimberly closed her eyes, chanting softly to herself, trying to calm her wayward chi. It was a meditation trick she'd picked up in yoga and surprisingly it went a long way to appeasing her. After taking a deep breath, Kimberly opened her eyes again, feeling a shade more in control.

Despite what Nico said, she was her own person and she would handle the heat in her own way and in her own time. Now a bit more at ease, Kimberly walked across the room to her secondhand oak bookshelf, perusing it for an old favorite. She chose a book she hadn't read in a while and retired to her room with her meat and wine in hand. It wasn't a balanced diet but it would have to do.

After changing into one of David's old shirts, she climbed onto her four-poster bed and slid beneath her cotton sheets, ready to lose herself in the story. An hour and a completely empty glass later, Kimberly realized she'd reread the same paragraph three times. Sighing in frustration, she gave up, put her book down on her nightstand and turned off the lamp. The wine and the lack of rest from the night before soon lulled her to sleep and she sank into the dark abyss pulling at her.

As soon as she closed her eyes they opened again, but this time instead of her bedroom she was in a familiar forest, yet for once she was not running from someone. Instead of the previous panic feelings, Kimberly oddly anticipated what was to come. She began walking through the forest with a sense of purpose.

The forest seemed serene and although it was still night, she felt warmed as if by the sun. Kimberly looked around as she stepped into the grassy clearing, lush and full, almost tropical. It made her want to lie down and roll in the grass, letting the sharp, cool blades of grass comfort her like a downy quilt.

Looking down at herself, Kimberly saw she was wearing a sheer gown, something she would never wear in real life. Kimberly ran her hands down her body, enjoying the feel of the silk against her skin. This wasn't how the other dreams had started. In fact, Kimberly couldn't remember ever feeling this calm in her dreams before. Instead of panicking and running away, Kimberly decided to sit down next to a trickling brook running through the clearing. It was as beautiful as it was peaceful, another oddity for her nightmare.

All of a sudden a brisk wind picked up, rippling the water with its presences. And just as quickly as it had come, it disappeared and the earlier restlessness was back, bringing with it the sense of the unknown Kimberly had come to associate with the nighttime terrors. But still she wasn't scared, just anxious.

Suddenly she caught a familiar aroma and glanced around. A large gray wolf strode toward her on padded paws. It walked with a steady stride reminding her of someone. As it drew closer, the wolf gradually transformed, smoother than Kimberly had ever seen a wolf do in real life. The transformation didn't seem to require any concentration on the wolf's part. It happened so quickly and went so smoothly, the change almost appeared theatrical. With every step, segments of the beast disappeared and her wolf took human form.

Jumping up quickly, her eyes widened as she realized the same tawny eyes of the wolf were still possessed by the half-dressed man in front of her. His muscular chest was firm and smooth, a complete contrast from the animal he'd just transformed from. Kimberly was having a hard time tearing her eyes away from the sight of Nico shirtless before her but he seemed to have no such qualms.

Standing before her, strong and bold, his gaze slid down her body. He gave a low, appreciative whistle. "Nice, much more attractive than the bunny T-shirt."

His words brought her out her silent reverie. "The bunny T-shirt…oh my God. It's been you this entire time."

"So surprised, *Zingaro*?" Nico slowly walked around Kimberly, absorbing the full effect of her sheer gown. He brushed his hands along her back and shivers danced down her spine. Either she was going crazy or she was having the most realistic dream in her entire life.

"How are you doing this?" she questioned, her voice tinged with awe. The surreal dream was cool and creepy all at the same time. Nico was taking stalking to a whole other level with this freaky dream stuff.

"Which part?" Facing her again, he skimmed his hands slowly up her arms, coming to rest on her shoulders. Her flesh felt heated by his touch while she shivered with anticipation. Kimberly was afraid of the emotions rushing through her but she also wanted more. Nico slid his fingers under the thin spaghetti straps and toyed with her skin.

Shrugging her shoulders, Kimberly stepped back and looked around the meadow. It was practically a scene out of *Bambi*, all she needed was a cute little deer and a bunny with seizures. "Stop it, Nico, I'm serious."

"So serious," he teased, reaching out to touch her again.

Slapping at his hand, she frowned. "How are you doing all of this?"

"I'm surprised you haven't figured it out yet." Chuckling, Nico pulled back his abused hand and shook it as if it were hot. "It's a dream."

"Whose?"

"Does it matter?"

"Well, if it's my dream…" she snapped her fingers and the black pants he was wearing disappeared. Looking down at his engorged member, Kimberly wondered how much of his cock was her dream and how much was reality. A damn fine reality. "Mine. For sure."

"Now that's not fair." Snapping his fingers, Nico frowned when her gown didn't disappear. "Definitely your dream."

For the first time in a long time, Kimberly felt like smiling. "A girl could get used to this. I like the fact I can make anything I want happen."

"What else do you want to happen, *Zingaro*?" Nico's eyes were as predatory as when he was in his altered state. The air hummed around them, singing with electricity and desire. The hair on her arms stood on end and her womb felt heavy with need. "This is your dream. I'm at your command."

"I bet you don't say those words often." Kimberly licked her lips in anticipation. She felt as if someone had just given her the keys to a candy store and told her to dig in. Nico was like all her favorite treats combined into one. Every commandment broken, every sin committed, he was the epitome of bad and she couldn't wait to indulge.

"No, that's why you better act fast." Chuckling deep in his throat, he stepped behind her and pressed against her. Kimberly could feel every inch of him and her body shuddered in response. Her animal called to his, howling out to be mated and claimed. "*Zingaro*, you are trembling with your need. Let me help you."

It was less of a question and more of a demand, but it was exactly what Kimberly needed to hear to finally give herself over to him. It was just a dream, she reminded herself as she shimmied her shoulders and allowed the straps of her gown to slip down over her arms. Nico tugged from behind her and the gown slid down her frame, dropping to her feet like a puddle of silk.

Kimberly joined her gown on the cool grass. The ground was softer than she remembered but after all, it was her dream and she could control all the elements. Looking up as Nico dropped down in front of her, Kimberly had a hard time keeping the fact she was in control front and center. Despite what he said, she doubted very seriously if Nico would—let alone could—ever give up control.

Nico leaned over and nuzzled her collarbone, gently kissing and rubbing his face against her neck, covering her body with his scent and vice versa. Kimberly dug her nails in the grass as he nipped at her with his canines before slowly lowering himself down her body.

Pushing Kimberly's legs open with his knee, Nico slipped between her parted thighs. He moved up, pressing down into her, rubbing his cock against the juncture of her wet opening. His cock was scorching her pussy, hard as steel and just as heavy. Kimberly arched up into him, aching to have him fill her, but Nico didn't answer her advance. Instead, he took his time, kissing down her throat to the hollow between her breasts before turning his head to the side and capturing one of her aching peaks between his lips.

Kimberly cried out in pleasure as Nico teased her other breast with his fingers, rolling her nipple gently and then pinching it, bringing it to a taut peak. When she thought she would go mad, he moved his hand from her breast and stroked down her flat stomach to the wet heat of her entrance.

She sucked in her breath, waiting for the touch of his hand on her heated core. Nico surprised her however by moving his hands to her thighs, pushing her legs up and spreading them wide before sitting up and crouching on his haunches before her. Kimberly lay open before him as Nico's hot gaze viewed her hidden treasures.

"I wonder if you taste as good as you look."

"How do I taste?" Kimberly asked breathlessly.

Taking one finger, Nico stroked along her slit, causing her to jump at the unexpected touch. Sucking his finger into his mouth, Kimberly saw him savoring her essence.

"You taste like warm cream poured over succulent peaches soaked in brandy."

Stroking her again, Kimberly whimpered as Nico pulled his finger away from her arching hips.

"Taste yourself," Nico urged, spreading her juices along the seam of her lips. Kimberly sucked his finger into her mouth, running her tongue along the digit.

"Enough," Nico declared, pulling his finger out her mouth. "Appetizer is over, it's time to dine."

With that, Nico buried his face between her legs. Licking lightly along her opening, he reached up and spread her pussy lips, exploring with his tongue to learn her secrets. Kimberly arched into his mouth, trying to push his tongue deeper into her core.

She had never allowed herself to be so blatantly sexual with a man before because of the fear of her beast coming out. But with Nico she was liberated, and the feeling of letting go and allowing Nico to do whatever he wanted was so freeing. Of course it was only a dream, which meant she could do anything with no consequences.

Kimberly sobbed as Nico pulled back slightly and then gasped as his tongue circled her clit. She had been worried he was leaving her. He couldn't leave her when she was so close. His rasping tongue was driving her to distraction, building her to a fevered pitch before backing off, leaving her panting with need.

"Please, I need…"

"What do you need?"

"I need to come, please." The pleasure Kimberly felt was so much more intense than when she touched herself. She masturbated, but she had never felt that if her orgasm didn't come she would just spontaneously combust, as she was feeling right now.

Nico smiled wolfishly before returning to his teasing of her aching folds. But still he didn't finish her off.

"Now, please."

Nico smiled at her demanding tone before bending and sucking her clit hard into his mouth, nipping it slightly with his teeth. The surprise hint of pain was all it took to finally push her over the edge. Her body felt as if she had just jumped off a large cliff, heart racing and breathless with anticipation all at the same time. Kimberly cried out with her orgasm, her pussy contracting almost painfully before shuddering as the wave washed over her.

Collapsing back against the cushioned ground, Kimberly sucked air in in an attempt to regulate her breathing. Slowly opening her eyes, Kimberly gazed at Nico still crouching between her thighs. If the state of his arousal were anything to go by, Kimberly wasn't the only person who had enjoyed their little encounter. His cock jutted from his tan body like a third limb. Hard and thick, it glistened with the evidence of his arousal. Without realizing it, Kimberly licked her lips much in imitation of how she wanted to lick his cock.

This was a dream right? Why shouldn't she live out all her naughty fantasies?

Nico followed her gaze down to his member and chuckled. "Like what you see, *Zingaro*?"

The heat from her embarrassment rose high in her cheeks. "If you've seen one, you've seen them all."

"Then let me do something to ensure I'll stand out in your memory." With a wicked smile, Nico grasped his cock tightly in his hand and slowly began to caress himself much to Kimberly's surprise.

He pumped his cock with sure, long strokes. She had never witnessed a man masturbating before. Hell, she was still shy about pleasuring herself, yet Nico seemed to have no such qualms. It was a wonder he was able to get his hand all the way around his thick shaft.

His measured caresses were slow and steady, causing Kimberly to bite her lip in order to silence her desire to urge him to move faster. She shifted restless from where she sat, her longing making her feel the need to move.

When Nico ran his thumb across the slick crown of his cock, Kimberly almost died. He was so unashamed in his arousal, in his thirst for pleasure.

Even as he squeezed his thick cock, Nico intently kept his gaze on her. It was almost as if he were sharing his pleasure with her. And pleasure it was. Kimberly's pussy trembled under his watchful gaze. It was almost impossible to believe but it was true, she was getting turned on again, just from watching Nico touch himself.

Yet she wanted to caress his cock, to move his hand out of the way so she could learn the feel of him for herself.

He was sexy.

He was hot.

Reaching toward him, she was shocked when she grasped at empty air, her arms sliding through him as if he were made of mist. Nico smiled down at her and pushed away from the ground. Confused, Kimberly sat up and reached toward him again.

"No, no, *Zingaro*, if you want me, you're going to have to wake up."

"But I like the dream," Kimberly complained petulantly.

Nico started to fade, becoming more and more translucent.

"No, wait, come back," she said, pushing up off the cool, soft grass.

"I am waiting for you, *Zingaro*, you just need to ask."

Struggling to stand, Kimberly fought with an invisible shield preventing her from going to him, and in the process she shook herself awake and looked down to find herself tangled in her sheets.

Goddamn it. Frustration filled her soul as she labored from under the mounds of blankets. For the first time in a long time, Kimberly felt close to something real and it had all been a dream. A passionate, exciting dream, but a dream nonetheless.

It was worse than any of the nightmares ever were. Worse because it felt so right, as if his arms were the exact place she was meant to be. Groaning, she plopped back down on the bed, feeling frustration as she had never known before. Kimberly had to fight the urge to kick her feet against the bed in frustration.

"Why me?" she muttered aloud, punching her fist into her damp pillow. Sighing in disgust, she rolled over on her side and froze. A dark shadow loomed in front of her window. Thrusting her hand out, she flicked on the light beside her bed and stared in shock. Nico was standing outside her bedroom on the balcony.

* * * * *

The light shining from the television gave the darkened room an eerie look. If it weren't for the familiar smell of the Pack and the wailing of Paula Cole blaring from the television, Nico might have been alarmed, but since he knew only one person who had the balls to invite herself into his home and touch his precious remote control, he reined in his temper and gave a slight smile. "What are you doing here?"

"Cable's out at my place."

Dropping his jacket over the arm of the easy chair, Nico walked around and sat next to his childhood friend and second-in-command Remington. Snatching the half-filled bowl of popcorn out of her lap, he slouched next to her and grimaced at the TV.

"And it will continue to be out until you pay the bill. Companies are really weird when it comes to getting paid." A snort was her only reply. "Do we have to watch this?"

"Yes."

"What's with you and teen TV? I think it's illegal to salivate over prepubescent boys once you reach a certain age."

Remy tossed a handful of kernels at him without turning from the show. "I'm not salivating. I'm researching."

41

"Researching what?"

"Human interaction."

Snorting, Nico shook his head. Anyone else he might have disbelieved, but when Remy said it, he knew it was fact, not fiction. If there was ever anyone who was the embodiment of the Lycan way, it was Remy. After her parents' deaths, she had been taken in by the Pack elders and raised completely void of human contact. She was the only one of them who never went to regular school and who took the Lycan Law to heart. She could recite it as well as a fourth grader could recite the Pledge of Allegiance.

"This isn't human interaction, it's television. Nothing's real on television. Do you think teenagers could really afford those clothes?"

"I'm not looking at their clothes." Turning, her dark eyes narrowed on his and she gave a slight sniff and frowned. "Where have you been? I've been waiting here for over an hour."

"For?"

"For my health," she commented snidely, grabbing the bowl back from him. "The impromptu meeting you called earlier today. You know, wandering Weres, the elders. Any of this ringing a bell?"

"Shit, I forgot." And he truly had. Blood was a requirement for the brain to work but all of his had rushed straight to his penis when he cornered Kimberly in the parking garage. The dream-walking took every last ounce of sanity right out of him. Just the thought of Kimberly spread before him as she had been in the dream was enough to get him hard. It had been agony to tear himself away when she awoke and saw him on her balcony. Especially since all he'd wanted to do was to burst into her room and take her right then. But he had promised her four days and he was a Were of honor.

Dream or no dream, their encounter had felt real to him. It was the first time Nico had ever used his channeling power

42

for something so erotically charged and it had left him drained, yet still in need. Unlike Kimberly, Nico hadn't gotten off from their encounter and his balls were paying for it in spades. Shifting uncomfortably on the couch, Nico resisted the urge to push on his aching erection. One odd move and Remy would be all over him with questions.

"What were you doing?"

"Nothing of importance."

Remy grabbed the remote control from the side of the couch and pointed it at the TV, muting the morose whining coming from the show. "Let me rephrase my question. Who is it?"

He wasn't going to get into this with her. There was no reason to lie or even to pretend the scent looming around him wasn't another Were. Remy was too smart and he respected her too much to even try, but then again, it wasn't her business who he was with so he didn't attempt to fill her in on his night. His situation with Kimberly was one of those things Remy just wouldn't understand, so there was no use in bothering.

"No one of importance."

"I'm afraid you're going to have to do better, *Benandanti*."

Turning to face her, Nico raised a brow. No matter who he was with, Remy should have known better. Friend or no friend, Nico didn't answer to anyone. "As your *Benandanti*, I don't have to explain anything to you, *Lupa*."

The words lay between them like an uncovered secret. In all their years of friendship, Nico had never lorded his position over Remy. It was never necessary. Standing up, Nico walked around the couch and turned on the light switch. He headed into his kitchen with Remy right on his trail.

"Pulling rank?" she asked from behind him.

Nico turned to her and looked in the face of his childhood friend. With skin as smooth and dark as chocolate, the stunning woman before him in no way resembled the homely and scrawny kid he first met when they were seven but just as their bodies changed so had their roles, and despite their friendship, he was first and foremost her Alpha. "If I have to."

"She must be very serious if I'm not allowed to question you."

"I don't answer to anyone, Remington, including you."

"Uh-oh, I'm in trouble now, you pulled out the full name." Instead of anger as he would have expected, Remy was smiling at him. Russet eyes twinkling, she crossed her arms over her ample breasts and leaned back against the wall. "She wouldn't happen to be the reason for this meeting tonight?"

"Assuming it's a girl?"

"Please." Remy's smile widened, showing off the canines she never bothered to hide. She was wolf all the time, whether in human form or not. "I can smell a Were in heat a mile away. Just as you can, it seems. Anybody I know?"

If anyone else heard their conversation, they might accuse Remy of being jealous, but Nico knew better. Remy no more had intimate feelings for him than he had for her, but she took her job as *Venator* very seriously and never understood when to back down. It was one of the things that made her a great protector but at the same time, it made her a deadly adversary.

Nico refused to rise to the bait but sometimes being around people with heightened senses really blew. "No, now leave it be."

"You're going to have to come clean sometime. The Pack isn't going to take it too lightly if you try to bring in an outsider as your mate."

Raising a brow, Nico asked, "I'm sorry. Did I miss the part where the Pack picked and chose who I would fuck?"

"Fuck, no, mate with, yes, I guess you did."

"I'm sorry, but my mate is not an issue for discussion."

"Ah-ha, so she is your mate." Remy laughed gleefully. "When did you first know?"

Nico bit back the snappy retort, which was simmering on his tongue. Was Kimberly really his mate, as Remy seemed to think? It was a fact Weres could sense their true mates, spiritually and physically. If they were meant to be joined for life, the proof would be in the pudding, so to speak, once they made love. But in truth, he had been too concerned about finding out who Kimberly was and why she was alone, to think about something as trivial as mates.

Nico knew one thing though, whether they were mates or not, this was not a discussion he would have with anyone other than Kimberly. "All this sex talk is getting me riled. I don't need the whole Pack talking about my sex life. It's none of their business."

Remy made a clicking noise with her tongue and shook her head warily. "My job is to be your protector, remember? It's what I get paid the big bucks to do."

"I'm nobody's job, Remy."

"You're wrong, Sire, your safety is always my top concern." Remy's zealousness for her job was another bone of contention between them. His childhood friend had challenged and won the right to call herself his *Venator* and it wasn't a role she took lightly. He would have no other Were by his side in battle but his private life was a completely different thing.

Seeing his frown, Remy softened her voice as she continued with a smile, "And as your oldest friend, your safety isn't the only thing I worry about."

"The only person whose safety is in question right now is yours," Nico warned, taking a playful menacing step toward her. He knew her heart was in the right place.

Remy held her hands up in surrender. "Consider myself warned. But if you have any plans on attending this meeting, I suggest you shower first. If the wind blows the wrong way tonight, you might have a brawl on your hands."

"Trust me, that's what I'm trying to prevent."

* * * * *

The heavy scent of alcohol and pheromones filled the air as Nico walked through the crowded bar. The Howler, a local Were hangout, was also the place Nico and his *Elitario* met. It had been their meeting ground since Nico's ascension, allowing him to be surrounded by his brethren as he guarded them from within.

The Howler wasn't one of those new, upscale bars that had popped up recently in Bayside. Those places were filled with lawyers and business types making deals and young professional singles looking to make a love connection. The Howler was what Nico liked to think of as an old-fashioned kind of bar. It didn't serve food, unless bar nuts counted, and it didn't serve any fancy drinks with cute names. The Howler had been around much longer than Nico and his *Elitario*. The bar was not only a local hangout but a safe haven for Weres during the Great War. Yet despite its noble history, now it was a place Weres went to get drunk.

Ryan, the bartender and part owner of The Howler, appeared bored as he mechanically cleaned glasses behind the bar. He only showed signs of life when Nico sent him an inconspicuous nod. With a replying nod of his own, Ryan stepped forward and discreetly pressed the button hidden under the cash register, unlocking the door to a private room near the back.

Moving through the packed room, Nico followed behind Remy, taking in everyone around them. Scents, familiar and unfamiliar, filled his head as he eyed the room. More and more of late, different breeds of Weres had begun moving into their territory and for the first time in a long time, it wasn't about war, it was about survival.

Stopping at the door, which resembled part of the wall, Remy pushed against the hidden entrance and walked inside. Stepping in slowly at first, she checked the room for any danger that might be directed toward Nico before stepping out of the way to let him enter. As Nico walked into the room, he eyed the crowded poker table amusedly.

His *Elitario*, which consisted of his top security officers as well as the head of the educational arm of the Pack, never missed an opportunity to have a good time, no matter what the circumstances. The Weres were as close to brothers as Nico would ever have. He trusted them with his life, just as they trusted him.

"So many Weres, so little time." Remy smiled, eyeing the group warmly.

"There's nothing but time." Kellen stood as was his custom when Remy came into the room. The slight blush, which stole over his face, was only noticeable due to the paleness of his skin, which contrasted with his bright red hair.

"Down, boy." Remy winked, pulling up a chair and bulldozing her way into the game. It was common knowledge amongst the Pack that Kellen had a thing for Remy, but he didn't stand a chance in hell with her. There was only room for one Alpha in a relationship and Kellen, as loyal as he was, would never stand up to Remy. She would walk all over him and hate him for it, and knowing Kellen, he would take it with a smile.

"Any particular reason we're running behind schedule?" Derek placed his cards in front of him. "Some of us have lives."

"Speak for yourself," Kellen kidded, retrieving his chair and sitting back down.

"Oh I was." Derek's dark eyes twinkled as he smiled. Everyone chuckled because they knew out of all of them, Derek was the one who had the most social life. The Asian Were attracted more women than a pocket full of money and he never failed to exploit his exotic looks to their full advantage.

Some elders of the Pack expressed concerns to Nico about how much time Derek spent with humans, but Remy wouldn't think of having anyone but Derek and Kellen as her *Rahu*, bodyguard warriors. Nico had always thought it was because she felt a kinship with the two men, who like her, grew up slightly alone.

Looking around the now crowded table, Harrison asked, "Does anyone notice every time we go out as a group, we always end up looking like the goddamn Were rainbow coalition?"

Harrison's wide smile spread across his dark face, tempering his sarcastic words. With his large frame and bulging biceps, he too could have been a *Rahu*, but his heart lay elsewhere as *Cahalith*, teacher for the young Weres. In order to live among the humans, they had to learn how to control their natural tendencies and it was Harrison's job to make sure they did.

Remy snickered at the comment and even Nico had to bite back a smile. The only thing they all had in common was they were Weres. They were all from mixed human nationalities but they were Were-DNA related where it counted. Their human ethnicity was as unimportant as the color of their fur. It was the one thing the Weres had managed to overcome their human brothers had not.

"Yeah, I have a dream, one which will get me out of here in twenty minutes or less," Derek quipped, looking at this watch.

"Wrong speaker, dip." Remy smirked.

"What, you learned that from TV?" Derek teased, ducking his head as Remy threw a poker chip at him.

"The longer you taunt her, the longer we're here," Kellen came to Remy's defense as usual, causing the other men to smile.

"Speaking of here, exactly why am I here?" Jackson leaned back in his chair, the only Were in the room wearing a suit and glasses. He didn't need the glasses, it was just a little camouflage he used to take the attention off his yellow-tinted eyes. "Although I relish being included with the cool kids, I have to say I am a little out of my element with this group. No one needs me to buy a kegger or purchase any porn."

Jackson was the historian for the Pack and normally he wasn't included when Nico called a meeting of the *Elitario*, however with the way things were going lately, Nico felt he needed as many Weres on his side as possible. He was going to ask his Pack to trust him as he took them in a new direction and he had a feeling there would be a lot of resistance, especially from the elders.

"I don't know." Remy sat back, contemplating Jackson with a gleam in her eye. "You seen anything good lately?"

Nico watched them all, amused. They were like a bunch of big kids, armed, dangerous, well-trained kids, but juveniles nevertheless. Their banter wasn't new, even in wolf form they jumped and butted each other like playful pups.

Harrison socked Jackson playfully in the arm. "Ahh, Jackson, you know we love you."

"Considered me charmed," Jackson dryly replied. "But what's the deal?"

"The deal is," Nico walked to the table and Kellen immediately stood, giving his chair to him, "we have the opportunity to bring forth change and the only real question is, should we."

The laughter, which had been brimming around the room before, suddenly disbursed and everyone turned their attention to Nico. "I've been contacted by the representatives of Santana, the Alpha from the Morbauch clan, about a treaty."

"Morbauch?" Jackson asked, surprise filling his tawny eyes. "But they're coyote."

"Very astute, Jackson." Sitting up, Remy raised questioning eyebrows to Nico's. "And you said?"

"Well, we're here discussing it."

"Not that I'm not honored you feel the need to bring us into your decision, *Benandanti*, but you don't really need our say."

"A fact I'm well aware of, but looking around this table, I can't help but recall something you said just a few minutes ago, Harrison." Gesturing to the group, Nico continued. "We have African Americans, Asians, Caucasians, Latinos all sitting together claiming the other as family, yet none of us resemble one another or are truly related besides the Were DNA coursing through our blood. After the territories were set and the clans separated, we all put physical appearance to the side and started our lineage over again. And despite the elders' best attempt at assuring our continuing bloodline, every year fewer and fewer of our Pack are born."

Nico paused, letting his words sink in. The knowledge his people were becoming extinct lived with him every day, especially knowing those who had the power to change it did nothing about it. Although he was the *Benandanti*, the *Maggiore* were the ones who made and governed over the Lycan Law. Of course they hadn't actually changed the law in decades, much to the detriment of them all. They were bitter Weres, still held up on the ways of the past, unable to see the need for change even when it was facing them head-on. The *Maggiore* were comprised of Pack elders, many of whom held grudges against all other Were animals who weren't wolves. They allowed their prejudices to eat at them and their elitism was destined to swallow them all whole.

The majority of the *Maggiore* fought in the Great War, which had taken many lives. No one in the Pack walked away unscathed. In fact, no one in any Pack, wolf or otherwise, escaped without some sort of loss to their Pack. Previously the Were animals had only fought small skirmishes for territory, but when a few Weres decided they wanted more, war broke out, leading to the worst devastation their kind had ever seen. Unfortunately it was a bloodbath that ended with no true winners. Instead, it led to death and destruction more far-reaching than the Packs had ever realized. For some reason, their races were dying out and no one really knew the reason why. All they did know was the Packs were smaller every year and soon there would be no one to carry on the Were legacy.

This was why Nico's plan for survival was so important. "It's all a matter of genetics, boys. A half human, half Were mating with another half human, half Were has a fifty-fifty chance of conceiving a full human child."

"But what, half wolf, half coyote stands a better chance?" Derek questioned.

"Umm." Remy held up her hand, interjecting. "Am I the only one getting an image of cat-dogs in my head, because that's just nasty."

"The Were DNA is the common denominator, it's our shared beast. I've been telling you for years coyotes and wolves are compatible. In essence they are our long-distance cousins. We *can* mate with them. We just don't." Harrison sat back, templing his fingers as he spoke, ever the teacher.

Nico nodded his head. "Exactly, the possibility of extending both of our bloodlines is increased. Our chances are also increased if we mate with other Packs and take humans for mates."

"Humans." The surprise in Remy's voice was nothing compared to the looks on the faces around the table. "It has been strictly forbidden."

"It's a law, Remy, not a sacred oath."

"Are you suggesting we break the Law?" questioned Jackson, intrigued.

"No," Nico said firmly, looking around at everyone. "I'm suggesting we rewrite it."

Chapter Three

ை

The rash was getting worse. As were the many other heat-related elements wreaking havoc on her body. Just when Kimberly thought she could chalk everything Nico said up to lunacy, her body went all wacky and betrayed her. She was in heat. There was no doubt about it. The only real question was, what the hell was she going to do about it?

Nico's plans for her were as obvious as the crimson inflammation blooming under her blouse, but Kimberly wasn't ready to just drop to all fours for his sexual delight. She might be a Werewolf but she was a woman too. An independent woman who could figure this out on her own.

If only there were books about it.

Slipping behind her desk, five minutes later than she was supposed to, Kimberly sniffed the air, searching for any sign of Nico. She wasn't going to be surprised today or in her dreams anymore, if she had anything to say about.

"You're late." Kimberly jumped in her chair as Cassandra spoke. Damn it, so much for not being surprised.

"I know. I'm sorry. I couldn't sleep last night and then I overslept." Kimberly rubbed her hand over her eyes. "I'll stay late to make up the time."

"Don't worry about that shit, I'm worried about you. Is everything okay?" Cassandra spoke softly, intentionally keeping their conversation private.

Kimberly desperately wanted to confide in Cassandra. She felt so lonely sometimes, always having to guard her secret. It made it difficult to make friends because they inevitably sensed she was hiding something. And eventually, one by one, her friends would drift away.

Maybe she could just talk about the dream part, not so much about the Werewolf part. "I've been having these scary dreams of someone chasing me. Then last night it changed."

"Changed how?" Cassandra leaned in, engrossed.

"He wasn't chasing me this time, well, not really."

"Oooh, this sounds as if your dream turned sexy." Kimberly's cheeks flushed at Cassandra's words and the laughter that followed. "I'm right, aren't I? So, is it anyone I know?"

Kimberly didn't think she could blush any more, but with the heat upon her, she felt as if she were on fire. Looking around, she debated if she should mention Nico. It would be just her luck if he walked in right when she was talking. Thinking about it, she decided she just couldn't take the chance. "No, nobody you know."

Even to her own ears, she sounded as if she were lying. And Cassandra's face, animated and excited earlier, suddenly closed off. "Oh okay, sorry to pry."

"No, really, you weren't prying." Kimberly knew she should have never gone down this road. When would she ever learn? "I'm just a bit embarrassed."

"Embarrassed." Cassandra's eyes lit up at the word. "That must mean it's someone I know."

Looking down, Kimberly blushed harder. "Maybe."

"Oh it's definitely someone I know." Tapping her fingernail against her chin thoughtfully, Cassandra looked out her office door as if the phantom man would walk by. "It has to be someone worthy of the shame."

"I wouldn't say shame."

"Oh I know," Cassandra's voice rose with amusement. "It's the Swedish guy in the mailroom, isn't it? What's his name, Sven, Olaf—"

"Erik," Kimberly gasped in dismay. Was she kidding? "Good Lord, no."

Laughing now, Cassandra leaned against the desk holding her sides. "Can you imagine your kids? Bright red hair, taller than a tree…"

And with a tail. It wasn't a pretty picture.

"It wasn't Erik, all right, it was Nico."

Kimberly would prefer Cassandra know the truth than think she wanted Erik. The guy gave her the creeps, always leering at her. Something wasn't right with him and Kimberly seriously doubted it had anything to do with his home country.

"Nico, why in the world would you be embarrassed to have dreams of him? Hell, I'd be worried if you didn't." Cassandra wouldn't be so nonchalant if she knew what the dream was about.

The intercom on Kimberly's desk buzzed, startling them both. The receptionist's voice came across the speaker, "Ms. Brenin, you have a visitor at the reception desk."

"Oh my God, wouldn't it be funny if it were Nico?" Kimberly knew Cassandra was only joking but she was shaking in her shoes. What if it was Nico? Dear God, she wasn't so sure she was ready to face him just yet.

"Well, go on, find out who your visitor is." Cassandra pulled her from her desk and pushed her toward the door. Kimberly walked toward the receptionist as if she were heading for her final supper before execution.

Reaching the reception desk, she looked around in surprise. No one was there except Milla, the receptionist. "Where's my visitor?"

"Oh he must have decided to use the restroom." Okay, definitely a male. And since she didn't know many men, it narrowed the field considerably. "Oh there he is." Milla didn't have to finish the sentence for Kimberly to know whom she was talking about.

A familiar scent assailed her senses. Turning, she stared into hazel eyes, which were a mirror image of her own.

Suppressing the growl rising in her throat, she took a step forward. "David, what are you doing here?"

"I figured you couldn't hang up on me if I was standing right in front of you."

"Lover's spat?" Milla was the office gossip and Kimberly knew she better get David out of there before the conversation went any further. Grabbing his arm, she pulled him into the nearest available conference room.

"How dare you come to my job? I can't believe you would do this. I am not your baby sister anymore, David. I don't need you to take care of me, okay?" Kimberly blanched as soon as the words left her mouth. Why was she always saying the wrong thing? She had a terrible habit of letting her temper get ahead of her brain and then hurting the ones she loved.

"You may not need me to take care of you but I needed to talk to you, damn it. If you're so grown up, act like it." Kimberly bristled at his words but acknowledged the truth behind them.

"I think I already know what you're going to tell me. I'm in heat, right?"

For once Kimberly had surprised her brother. "What's happened?"

Of course he would know something had happened. He wasn't an idiot. The honor was reserved just for her it seemed. Deciding to change the subject back to him, Kimberly went on the offensive.

"Why didn't you tell me about this? I was totally unprepared."

David sighed and grabbed the nearest chair. Sitting, he looked at her before replying, "I know I should have, especially after you moved away from home. I kept thinking I could wait for the right time. But the right time never came."

Kimberly grabbed his hands in hers and sat next to him. "But, David, why didn't you tell me earlier? I don't understand."

"Kimmie…" Kimberly winced at the nickname and David quickly continued. "I was nineteen and raising my younger sister. It's not as if I knew a lot about female Werewolves. We weren't raised as Weres and Mom and Dad didn't prepare me. They had no idea they were going to be killed in a car accident. I just muddled along the best I could with the information I had. And I didn't want to talk to you about going into heat cause no brother wants to think about his sister in a sexual context, okay."

"It's not okay, David, because I'm not just your sister, I'm a Were—"

"Wait." David growled, jumping to his feet. Moving quickly in front of Kimberly, David faced the closed door as if death itself were on the other side.

"What's wrong?" Kimberly whispered, trying to grasp at the scent but unable to smell anything over David's raging pheromones.

"Someone's out there listening. I smell a Were." The door opened as the words left David's mouth and Kimberly had to put all her might into holding him back.

"Well, at least I can say his scent ability is better than his fatherhood ability." Nico stood in the doorway, an amused looked on his face. His stance was the polar opposite of David's, who looked ready to spring into action. "You must be the brother."

"And who might you be?" The energy in the air was electrifying.

The hairs on Kimberly's arms began to rise as her wolf began to respond to her brother's anger. A low whimper slipped from her lips as she gripped him tighter, trying to prevent the bloodbath Nico seemed to be instigating.

"It's just Nico, David."

Nico laid his hand over his heart mockingly. "Just? You injury me, *Zingaro*."

Strolling through the door, Nico firmly shut it behind him before making his way across the room and coming to a stop where they were standing. His outward appearance was one of a man without a care in the world, but his penetrating gaze told another tale.

"I'll do more than injure you if you don't identify yourself," David growled.

"Of course." Nico bowed his head slightly. "I'm Nicodemus Cassamonti, *Benandanti* of the Brachyurus and your sister's mate."

"What?" David uttered the words the second Kimberly gasped, "He is not."

"Okay, future mate. Details, details."

"Over my dead body." Kimberly could practically see David's hackles rising. Oh this was so not good.

"Easily arranged."

Nico's easygoing reply rankled Kimberly. "How dare you threaten my brother?"

"*Zingaro*, I do not threaten." His voice was warm but the words were measured and obviously not for her benefit.

"Kimberly, I don't need you to try and protect me." Addressing Nico, David bowed his head slightly in respect but he didn't lower his eyes to Nico. "*Benandanti*, I was unaware there was a clan in this area. My sister and I will leave your territory as soon as we are able."

"We will not," Kimberly shouted then clasped her hand over her mouth as both males turned to stare at her.

Nico looked amused while David looked pained. "No need to shout, *Zingaro*, you are correct. You will be going nowhere."

"You're being a bit presumptuous, aren't you?"

"Not at all. It is only natural my mate and I would live together."

"I am not your mate."

"Sorry to interrupt your little tête-à-tête, but this conversation is moot." David stepped between the two of them. "You are not my sister's mate and we *are* leaving town."

As Kimberly sputtered, Nico stepped forward, nose to nose with David. "I understand your need to protect your sister, although I doubt your ability to do so. But you are woefully uneducated about the ways of the Were."

David flushed with embarrassment at Nico's words but he didn't back down. "Maybe, but don't think I'll let some stranger who claims to be the *Benandanti* take my sister for a mate without a fight."

Kimberly had just about had enough. "Okay, guys, I don't know if either of you realize it but I am over twenty-one and I don't have to listen to either one of you. So there." Swinging open the door, she stalked out of the conference room and back toward her office. If the two of them wanted to have a pissing match, it was fine with her, but she wasn't going to stand there while her shoes got wet.

"Hey," Milla called over in a stage whisper. "What's going on?"

As if she would confide in the little gossip hound. "Family stuff."

Fucked-up werewolf family stuff, but family stuff nonetheless.

"Kimmie, get back here," David called from behind her.

Cringing, Kimberly refused to obey. She was past the stage where she listened to everything her brother told her to do. Resisting the childish urge to flip him the finger, Kimberly continued to her office, slamming the door once she passed through it.

The loud echoing of the door drew Cassandra from her office with an irritated expression marring her brow. "Erik?"

"No, worse. My brother."

"Kimberly, we're not through."

Spinning around, Kimberly faced David, angry as she had ever been with him. "This is my place of work," she growled.

"Kimberly, calm down." David's eyes were wide with fear.

Kimberly didn't need a mirror to know why. The change was coming over her, brought on by lack of sleeping and rising anger. Huffing, she tried to calm herself but she could feel her control slipping.

David grabbed her arms. "Fight it, Kim."

"Should I call security?" The fear in Cassandra's voice speared on Kimberly's beast.

"No." Her voice was becoming lower as she gripped her brother, trying to hold on with all her might. *Calm down, Kimberly. Get yourself together.* "I need to—"

"We need to use your office," Nico spoke as he came into the room. Without waiting for Cassandra's go-ahead, he grabbed Kimberly's hand and ushered her past the stunned woman.

"I'll come too."

Pushing Kimberly into the room, Nico turned on David, his anger raging. "Don't you think you've done enough?"

Nico slammed the door and locked it before Kimberly knew what was going on. Dragging her onto his lap, he lulled her with low purrs, stroking her tingling flesh. "Redirect the energy, Kimberly. You can fight the change."

Kimberly shook with the force of trying to control the beast. The only way she could describe it was the endorphins she experienced while exercising. She was reaching for the high only the beast could give her, but at the same time, she knew she didn't want to change in the middle of her boss's office.

Nico swore before she turned her head toward him. "Concentrate on me, Kimberly, only me." Bending his head, he licked at the seam of her lips, coaxing them open so he could slip his tongue inside. Kimberly moaned at the touch of his lips and feathered her fingers along his jaw.

His hand slid into the V of her blouse, his fingers moving in small circles around her aroused areolas. Kimberly's nipples tightened in response, heat pulling at her core as they stood, begging for his touch. She cried out in a mingle of pleasure and pain as his fingers pulled on her taut nipple. The heat inside her rose as the fire between her legs blazed hotter.

"Easy, *Zingaro*. I'm here for you." Nico's whispered words only made Kimberly more frantic. She shifted her legs restlessly, wordlessly begging for his touch.

Nico shifted her on his lap until she was sitting with her back pressed against him. Pulling her skirt up, he exposed her thigh-high hose. Kimberly could feel her beast pushing at her defenses, fighting to be free. But it was warring with her sexual energy.

Nico was whispering soft words in her ear but Kimberly could only hear his soothing tone. She pushed the beast back, concentrating on the sensations Nico was evoking. His hands slid inside her panties, pushing aside the restricting material. The cool air fired her senses, making her realize how exposed she was. The funny thing was, she didn't care. Kimberly just wanted his touch.

It took just the glide of his fingers against her engorged clit before Kimberly was coming, moaning his name. She gyrated on his lap as she dug her nails into his forearm. The fire in her body seemed to bank as her orgasm came to an end. She was tired, doused with sweat, but her beast was at bay.

This was so much better than the dream. Touching his warm, rough skin was heavenly. She wanted more but his clothes were in the way. Kimberly tore at his shirt, trying to find the buttons.

"Calm down, baby, it's okay." Nico ran his hands over her back, trying to soothe her fever.

Kimberly pulled at the knot in his tie, loosening it before Nico grabbed her hands, halting her motions. She stared at him, her heart racing. All she wanted was to touch him, learn his body, and she didn't understand why he was trying to stop her. "Kimberly, baby, much as I would love your sweet little hands on me, I don't think it's such a good idea."

Kimberly shook her head as if coming out of a dream. She realized Nico had distracted her with his kiss and the energy of her beast had been transformed into sexual heat. For the second time today, Kimberly could feel her cheeks burn with embarrassment. "Let me go, please." She struggled to get off his lap but froze as she realized her movements were rubbing her ass along his hardened cock. He probably thought she was some kind of slut the way she had attacked him.

"Now don't get all uptight on me now," Nico teased. "You were doing just fine."

Kimberly tilted her head back to look into Nico's eyes. His voice may have sounded amused but there was still lust shining in his eyes. And for the life of her, even though she didn't know why, she was proud. But she wasn't going to let him know. "Can you please let me go?"

Nico sighed before releasing her. "We need to talk, *Zingaro*, your deadline is looming ever closer."

"I know how to count," she grumbled, not willing to let him have the final say.

"And I know how to subtract, but the sooner you give in to me—"

"The sooner you'll go away."

"It will never happen, *Lupa*. Wolves mate for life."

"Insanity is for life too but you don't see people advertising the merits of it."

Chuckling, Nico stood. "You amuse me."

"Lucky me." Straightening her appearance, Kimberly tried to think of what she was going to say to Cassandra. Only God knew what her boss was thinking. "I've got to get back to work."

"You can run, *Zingaro*, but I will always find you. You're mine and I can't wait to tame you."

"In your dreams."

"No, my love, in yours."

* * * * *

Before Nico was out of the parking garage of Lewis and Sinclair, he'd already put the wolves on alert to stay close to Kimberly and her brother. He had almost lost his legendary cool when he'd seen them together in the conference room and if it weren't for the family resemblance, he would have torn David's hide to shreds for touching his woman. The exact moment when Kimberly became his wasn't quite clear in his mind, but for all intents and purposes she was his and Nico would have no other scent on her except for his own.

Turning into the parking lot of The Desert Sanctuary, Nico frowned as he spotted the elders' cars. The last thing he wanted to deal with right now was Pack bullshit he was sure they came to dish out. The *Maggiore* had a hard time letting go of the past and it was one of the reasons his Pack was in so much danger of becoming extinct. The old ways weren't working, but trying to convince them was about as easy as convincing Kimberly she was his.

His pack, the *Brachyurus*, was comprised of nearly all the Werewolves in the Southwestern states. There were many Packs all over the United States as well as the world, but Nico only concerned himself with that of his clan, which was made up from several different lineages that joined together after the Great War. They, like all clans, were self-sufficient with their own government and laws. Although most Were Law was the same, it was still left up to the individual ruling council to set and maintain them, which meant Nico had the right to veto and instate, within reason, any credo he felt necessary, much to the *Maggorie's* dismay.

Nico knew it had to be hard for the aging Weres to accept a younger leader as their Alpha, but unless the men had a way to go back in time, they'd better get used to it. Weres lived a long time, much longer than their human counterparts, and it wasn't unheard of for someone to reach their ninetieth year looking as fit as a man in his forties. Yet their longevity was a blessing and a curse, because the ones who lived the longest remembered the ways of the past, and they were reluctant to accept change, no matter what form it came in.

As he got out of his car, Nico spotted Remy lingering in the doorway. Her dark face was lined with worry and her frame taut with tension. When she saw him, Remy quickly headed down the stairs, trying to waylay him.

"We need to talk." The seriousness of her voice gave him pause more than her words.

Looking past her at the closed door, Nico frowned. "Who?"

Nico didn't have to say more, Remy was quick to understand the question. "I have no idea. All I know is, they know."

"And I'm assuming from your expression, they're not pleased."

"Are you surprised? You're trying to change our doctrine. It's the only thing they know."

"Change is a long time coming." To quote Kimberly, this wasn't a *goddamn democracy*. Nico had earned his right to lead his Pack and he would take them in the direction he chose. Their survival was at stake and he wasn't willing to sit back and do nothing to please a bunch of old men.

"You can't change them overnight, Nico."

"No, but I can change our future." Starting around her, Nico stopped suddenly and turned back to face his childhood friend. "There can only be one way, Remy. Mine or theirs. Where do you stand?"

Remy growled low in her throat, shooting him a stare he'd only seen on her face in battle. "Do I rip you a new asshole for questioning my loyalty now or later?"

Chuckling, Nico held his hands in mock surrender. "I had to ask."

"You never have to ask. I'll follow you to the end."

Nico knew, even if Remy had doubts, once she had given her word to have his back, he knew he would never need to worry. Now he needed to find out who his betrayer was.

The *Brachyurus* Pack chose The Desert Sanctuary as its official meeting place. After the Great War, it served as a haven for those pups who'd lost their parents. It had also acted as the first neutral meeting grounds for the different Packs. It was now a legalized animal shelter the Pack ran and organized, helping Weres all over the world. As the *Benandanti*, Nico acted as the president, overseeing all the ins and outs, and it was also where the *Maggiore* met for council meetings.

Walking into the building, Nico tried to evaluate each of the members of the *Elitario*. Even though they all seemed shocked by the idea of working with the other Weres, none of them had seemed too upset, once he explained his reasoning. However, someone was very good at hiding his true feelings since he knew the information from their meetings had reached the ears of the *Maggiore*. If he wanted to remain *Benandanti* and alive, Nico knew he couldn't wait too long to discover the culprit.

As he prepared to confront the *Maggiore*, Nico schooled his face into the emotionless mask that had served him so well in the past. He flung open the door to the observation room and all conversation immediately ceased.

Their reaction was no more than he expected. The taupe conference room was brimming with tension, seven men turning to look at Nico as he entered. Flanking the large marble table, each man represented a descendant of the regional Were leaders of the past, bringing with them several generations of traditions and ways, long forgotten in the Were youth of the day.

He was in essence the Commander in Chief to their Congress. Of course their situation wasn't as formal since the *Maggiore* obtained their positions through descendants from families of power instead of votes from the people. Nico respected them and their opinion equally but he didn't have time for their bullshit.

"So, do the *Maggiore* now meet without their Pack leader in attendance?" Nico walked into the room, Remy following closely behind him.

"*Benandanti*, glad you made it. There are some disturbing rumors we were hoping you could address."

"Rumors, really? Do tell." Nico walked around to the head of the table to take his place, glad to see no one had the audacity to sit in his chair at least.

"Ah well, we have heard, through reliable sources, you plan to contact...coyotes." The last was stated with disgust.

"Oh it's no rumor." Nico glanced around the room as he spoke, noting the reactions of the elders. "I have already contacted the Morbauch clan and have arranged a meeting with their Pack leader."

The gasps around the room were audible.

Immediately the room erupted with numerous voices, but one outraged shout in particular stood out. "You dare?"

Dare. He dared for the sake of his people. "I have contacted them and I will meet with them. This is not an issue for discussion."

"Nico, you cannot be serious. You disgrace us with just the idea of meeting with those vermin." Keith Laine, an elder from the *Roda* line, rose to his feet in outrage. "This is not a decision you can just make on your own!"

Nico looked at the elders with disgust. They wanted to be part of the process but they truly were just a hindrance to progress. Although they'd had this discussion many times in the past, he tried again to make them understand. "It is no disgrace to want to save our Pack. You all know the problems we have been experiencing, even if you want to bury your heads in the sand. Every year our numbers dwindle while you sit here like a bunch of old women wringing your hands in despair. We have the ability to save ourselves. I plan to do just that."

Everyone spoke at once, their voices mingling together to form one large roar of rage. Remy moved from her seat to his left, to stand directly behind him, presenting a show of force, which silenced some of the members. "Remington, you can't rightly agree with him?" Clarkson Vera from the *Cetyl* line was one of the most outspoken of the *Maggiore*. His outrage shined brighter than his auburn hair, which was receding with age. "You of all people know how important the Lycan Laws are."

"I follow our *Benandanti* in all things."

Eyes of fury faced Nico from Franklin Russell of the *Polda* line, the Were who had taken Remy into his home when she was just a child. Nico knew, out of all the *Maggiore*, he would be the one who felt the most betrayed by Nico's plan. Franklin, along with several of the Weres in the room, was a founding father of the bylaws and codes they lived by today. He was a smart man but not a strong Were, and it had always been his downfall. He could never rule and he hated anyone who could.

"This is a disgrace. The council will never abide by this."

"According to the laws you've established, *Maggiore*, they don't have to." Remy's words did something Nico had been unable to do. It silenced the room.

No one could deny the truth of Remy's words. The power given to the *Benandanti* by the very men in the room was coming back to bite them in the ass. Nico smiled at the irony of it all. It was poetic justice.

"I've extended a *Pax Pacis* to Santana and I have every right to believe he will accept my offer of truce. We don't need to continue to die to prove we are superior. It's a futile battle in itself. The only thing in a hundred years we've managed to do was to prove we're expendable and I will not have the blood of our youth on my hands so you can have pissing rights."

Looking around the room slowly, Nico let his words sink in. "No longer will my Pack be ruled by egos."

"Only for as long as you rule." Franklin spoke quietly, but with a room full of Werewolves, it wasn't likely anyone hadn't heard him. Nico knew whoever was plotting against him had Franklin in their corner. He only retained leadership of the Pack as long as he remained the Alpha. Anyone could challenge him at any time for the right.

"This will never work." All eyes turned to Heath, one of the oldest Weres of the Pack.

"And why not, pray tell?" Remy jumped in on Nico's behalf.

"Because, it is a show of weakness to the other Weres, and none of their Packs will be any more willing than we are."

"I think you're wrong." Nico couldn't believe they were actually letting him talk about his plans for a truce when in the past they had always refused to have the conversation. Their resistance to it was one of the reasons he had gone ahead without their input. "The other Weres are in a worse situation than we are. Their numbers have been decimating for decades, they're on the brink of extinction and they were open to our discussion of a meeting."

"Probably only to discover our weaknesses." Nico was convinced Franklin was the most negative Were he had ever met. It was a shock Remy turned out as well as she did.

"We aren't exactly opening our doors and inviting them into our homes. I plan to take precautions."

Heath nodded his head, full with snowy white hair. "It is good you are being cautious, Nico. I was afraid you had forgotten all the lessons of the past."

Nico was pleased Heath wasn't totally against him. He was one of the elders Nico admired, a mentor of sorts when Nico was moving up the ranks. Nico looked into his eyes and knew although it initially sounded as if he were against the plan, Heath was really giving Nico the opportunity to argue his case.

"We cannot continue to hold grudges to the detriment of our own Pack."

"You will be the downfall of us all." Franklin stood and stormed out of the room.

"*Maggiore*, I tell you this is the road to our survival. Give me the chance to prove it to you."

"You'll get your chance to prove it, let's just hope it doesn't ruin us all." Clarkson pushed back away from the table and followed Franklin out of the room.

One by one the elders rose, exiting the room quietly until only Heath remained. Standing, he walked toward Nico and Remy, pausing when he was in front of them. "You know they will never stand for a treaty. Are you prepared for the fallout?" Unfortunately Heath wasn't saying anything Nico didn't already know.

"Can you truly ever be prepared for dissension amongst the ranks?"

A small smile flitted across Heath's face before he patted Nico on the shoulder. "I hope you know what you're doing, son."

Nico watched in silence as the last elder left the room.

"Well, that went well." Remy dropped back into her seat.

"Better than my ascension ceremony." Nico's dry comment made Remy laugh as intended. In all actuality, it had gone better than he expected, but it also happened sooner than he expected. "So, looks as if we have a mole."

"Yes it does."

"Any ideas?"

Leaning back in her chair, Remy kicked her feet back on the table, crossing her arms over her stomach. "I have a hard time believing anyone would betray you."

"Believe it or not, someone did."

"Jackson, of course, would be the first suspect, seeing as how he's the new guy and all."

"Well, let's get someone on him."

"It might be kind of hard to do."

"Why?"

"Because you have them all tied up with your love life." Remy shot him an amused look.

"Remy—"

"You have got to learn to take a shower. I don't even know this *Lupa* and her scent is beginning to make me horny."

"If you concentrated on your own sex life instead of mine, this wouldn't be an issue."

"So you have a sex life now?" she teased, standing and stretching her arms above her head.

"Not yet, but now that I am done with this council mess, maybe I can get back to seeing about my little problem."

"Awww, it's little? I see now why you haven't had a sex life." Remy danced away from him before he could make her pay for her words.

"I am going to ignore your comment for the moment since I need you, but just wait. Paybacks are a bitch."

"I'm sorry to interrupt, *Benandanti*, but I have a message for you."

"Thank you, you can go." Nico dismissed the Were as he slit open the manila envelope.

"Anything good?" Remy was the best second-in-command around, but she was also extremely nosy and always wanted to know what was going on.

Nico read the missive with interest before answering her query.

"Yes, actually, something very interesting. It seems Kimberly and her brother David were raised by a mated pair of Weres who left the Pack after the Great War."

"That was kind of quick news."

"Yes, it seems as if someone recognized the family name and after a quick review of the history was able to come up with a brief account for me."

"Why did they leave the Pack?"

"That part isn't quite as clear, but it may have something to do with our friends, the *Maggiore*."

"Man, they do get around, don't they?"

"Yes, and I don't want their involvement to ruin what I'm trying to accomplish with Kimberly."

"You're going to have to present her to them eventually, especially if she truly is your mate."

"You're right of course, but I hate to expose her to them before she even knows what being a Pack Were is like, let alone the mate of the *Benandanti*."

"What exactly are you trying to accomplish?"

"I need to convince her that her heat won't abate without me."

"You're working awful hard just to get some trim."

Nico stood, bristling with anger. "Don't *ever* talk about her with such disrespect."

Instead of retorting back with an angry comment of her own, Remy seemed to brim with amusement. "You are so gone. This isn't just a sex thing, she's the one, isn't she?"

Nico sat back down, his anger dissipated. "Perhaps. I will know for sure when she stops being so obstinate."

"When she stops or when you stop. You're like a dog with a bone, pardon the pun, and if she were just another pretty tail, we wouldn't even be having a conversation."

Nico contemplated her words, knowing she was right. He would never be this tied up in knots if Kimberly weren't truly his mate. Although difficult to admit, she had gotten under his skin as no one else and he enjoyed it.

"Come on, lover boy, enough mooning over your mate. Why don't you go run for a bit and get her smell off you," Remy advised. "You haven't been out in a while and should probably make your presence known, know what I mean?" Remy glanced at the closed door the *Maggiore* had recently left.

"Probably a good idea." Nico knew if he went to Kimberly now, in his current state of mind, with the agitation of the day beating at him, his beast would take over and he would lose the control he was barely holding on to. Going for a run would allow him to exert some of his energy before he saw her.

"Let's go." The best part of having their meetings at The Sanctuary was it was the perfect place to run after a heated discussion. They owned approximately a thousand acres of land, enough so the Pack could run to its hearts' content.

Heading outside, Nico sniffed the evening air. The beast in him yearned to run free, to be released after the tension of the meeting. Impatient to join the other Weres already running with the night, Nico shed his clothing and with the image of the wolf in his head, he instantly shifted to his natural form. Sitting on his haunches, Nico glanced over at Remy who had also changed. She was slightly smaller than the average male wolf and her coat was an almost silvery gray.

Let's run. Taking off, Nico headed out across the open plain, already scenting the other wolves. Heading in their general direction, he heard Remy sprinting closely behind him.

Their run was as fluid as the wind. Passing through brush, jumping over limbs, it was the most natural feeling in the world for Nico. He was one with the earth. He was a son of nature. He was free. It wasn't long before the other wolves running the land joined Remy and him. Not all of them were Were, but they all were family.

Nipping at his heel, Remy toyed with him. Running with one another, butting noses into hides, they played as carefree as pups, pinning one another to the ground. Tackling Remy in midair, Nico held her to the ground by the fur on the back of her neck. Giving her a playful shake he released her, but not before yapping at her to follow. They ran until the sky darkened and the air grew chilled, dodging each other through the brisk night air.

Time was irrelevant as they played, but soon another need began to fill Nico that had little to do with games. Trotting to a small lake, which was hiding by a dense brush of trees, Nico lay on the ground. Slowing his breathing, he began to rise, his fur receding inside as his male form began to take place. It only took a matter of seconds for him to return to his human state but already he missed his connection to the land.

Soft fur brushed against his bare legs as Remy came to stand by his side. Reaching down, he caressed his friend's flank. "Stay and enjoy the night," he murmured when she started to whine. "It's bedtime for little Weres."

Or one Were in particular whom Nico couldn't wait to see again. The run had cooled his hunger but nothing would sate the desire he felt for Kimberly.

Chapter Four

ဆာ

The sound of running water did little to calm Kimberly's already fried nerves. She'd had some bad days at work before but today was really going to take the cake. Her boss was watching her as if she were a freak, which by being a Werewolf, she might actually qualify as one. And everyone at the office was talking about her.

Milla, the little bitch, had run off and told everyone Kimberly had two men fighting over her and one of them was Nico. It wasn't true of course, but Kimberly knew it wouldn't be long before the head honchos stopped by and had a little talk with her. She was so fired. Fired and in heat. A condition she couldn't deny anymore, even if she wanted to. Really, Nico was hot and everything, but under normal circumstances she wouldn't have ever dreamed of humping his leg in her boss's office. It was taking the whole "bitch in heat" thing a bit too far, even for her.

After adding bubbles to her rising bath water, Kimberly began to undress. If there was ever an evening for Calgon to take her away, it was tonight. Hopefully, the soothing suds would calm her ragged nerves and ease the ever-present ache from between her legs. Arousal wasn't supposed to hurt this bad. It wasn't supposed to be a constant, incurable ache that had her seething for a man she hardly knew. And yet, here she was, wet from her own desire and quickly running out of excuses for not taking Nico up on his offer.

The knocking on her bathroom door roused Kimberly from her musings. Leaning over the tub, Kimberly shut the running water off.

"Kimmie, ahh, Kimberly, you okay in there?" David sounded worried. She ought to make him suffer some more but she just didn't have the energy right now.

"I'm fine, David, really." Kimberly dipped her toes into the water to test the temperature.

"Are you sure you don't want me to stay?" David had wanted to stick around town for a few days, but instead of staying with her, Kimberly had asked him to get a hotel. One of the reasons she had only rented a one-bedroom apartment was to avoid houseguests. Plus, she really didn't feel up to a bunch of questions and confrontations right now.

"Yeah, I think it's best, don't you? As soon as I'm done here, I am off to bed."

David sighed heavily before replying. "Let's get together and have brunch tomorrow, okay?"

Kimberly knew it was only a matter of time before they had the big confrontation they avoided this afternoon. Might as well make it tomorrow. "Okay, sounds good."

"I'll lock up when I leave." David walked away from the bathroom and a few minutes later Kimberly heard the front door shut.

Slipping into the warm bath, she stifled the urge to moan aloud at the soothing sensation of water caressing her heated flesh. As she sank lower in the oversized tub, Kimberly surrounded herself with the bubbles until only her head was exposed. She closed her eyes and allowed herself to drift off.

If she could have breathed underwater, she would have sank deeper. Kimberly just wanted to disappear into the bubbly goodness of the water. The heat soaked into her tired muscles, soothing her aching joints. The almost change today had taken a toll on her body. After work, David insisted they go for a run but so far Kimberly hadn't found a place safe enough to change. Her beast was running her ragged. Kimberly needed to change and she knew it.

Of course she also needed to relieve some of the sexual tension she was experiencing before she started to hump the furniture. *That would make her really popular with the people she worked with.*

Slipping her hands over her soap-slicked body, Kimberly caressed her breasts, cupping them in her hands. Kimberly felt a warm sensation traveling throughout her body and the smell of the Pack surrounding her. Scents, familiar and strong, began to cloud her senses as she felt a calling from within.

"Come out and play."

Startled, Kimberly sat up, splashing water everywhere. It was Nico's voice. But how was this possible? She was awake, wasn't she?

"Are you?"

Kimberly wondered if she were going crazy or if he was reading her thoughts. She knew he wasn't there, not really, but she could still sense him, as if there were a connection between them. Maybe she really was dreaming. Dreaming of Nico wanting her wasn't such a bad thing to think about when she was alone, naked and wet.

Kimberly again cupped her breasts, flicking her thumbs across the nipples, bringing them to life.

"That's right, baby, touch yourself for me."

Kimberly wasn't as surprised this time by the voice. It was a bit disconcerting to have someone inside her head, knowing what she was doing. Of course it was also a bit naughty, almost as if she knew she was being watched but didn't care.

"Do you enjoy it when a woman touches herself?" Kimberly felt odd speaking to someone in her head, even if she were dreaming.

Nico chuckled. *"I like anything you do to yourself."*

"Big shocker you're into watching. The closest you'll ever get to seeing it is in my dreams."

"*Do you really still think you're dreaming?*" Nico sounded affronted she would dare to talk back to him.

Kimberly froze. Opening her eyes, she quickly released her breasts and grabbed for a towel.

"*Awww…*" Nico's voice was filled with humor. "*Just when you were getting to the good part.*"

"Pervert," she said, but this time out loud. "I'm awake, aren't I?"

"*I've been trying to tell you all along, Zingaro, don't get mad at me because you didn't catch on before you began your little show.*"

Good God, was she going mad?

"*No, you're as sane as —*"

"Stop doing that."

Nico's chuckle resounded in her head. "*Doing what?*"

Dragging the wet towel around her body, Kimberly climbed out of the tub. She didn't know how Nico was doing what he was, but she wasn't going to give him more of a show than she had to. "You're beginning to freak me out. Where are you?"

"*I'm closer than you might think.*"

"How close?"

"*I'm outside your door.*"

Turning, Kimberly grasped her towel to her chest, trying to calm the beating of her heart. She could sense him. He was near. Pulse pounding, she walked slowly to the bathroom door. Nervously she gripped the handle and pulled the door open quickly, hoping to surprise Nico on the other side, but the surprise was on her. He wasn't there.

"Liar."

"*I never said which door, Zingaro.*"

"You are a menace."

"*I'm your mate.*"

"I think the two words might be synonymous."

"Let me in, Zingaro. I will ease your pain."

"You are my pain." Shaking her head, Kimberly walked the few steps to her bedroom to get dressed.

Pausing in the doorway, Kimberly looked over her shoulder toward the front door. Nico's scent was rampant in the air. He was there.

"I'm not going to invite you in."

"I'm not a vampire. I don't need an invitation."

His comment brought her up short. "Are there vampires?"

"There are many things that go bump in the night. I'm one of them, as are you."

Tossing the towel on the floor, Kimberly grabbed her nightshirt and slid it over her damp body. Stalking to the front door Kimberly wrenched it open, glaring at Nico lounging against the jamb.

"I can't believe you can do this."

"Really, I thought you would have discovered by now I am capable of doing all types of things." Nico stepped through the door, pushing Kimberly back so he could close it.

"You must be the most arrogant, pigheaded man around."

"It's not an arrogant thing, it's a mate thing. It's just one more reason I know we're meant to be together. Only mates can communicate through telepathy."

"You're lying."

"You wish I were, mate."

Kimberly wanted to scream. He was just so infuriating. As far as she knew, he could be pulling the mate shit out of his ass.

"You know what, it doesn't even matter. The point is you have no right to barge in here!" Kimberly poked him with her finger to emphasize her point. "And how dare you intrude during my bath? That was private, damn it!"

Nico laughed at her bravado and Kimberly narrowed her eyes. He wasn't taking her seriously. "Yes, I am, *Zingaro*, I take you very seriously."

"Stop answering my thoughts. In fact, stop reading my thoughts. It's really starting to piss me off."

"Too bad, *Zingaro*. As your mate, my first priority is to please you. I can do no less. And since you do not talk to me, I have taken it upon myself to find out what your needs are by any means I have. If it means reading your thoughts, so be it." Nico reached out and stroked her arm, putting her off balance. It wasn't fair he was all concerned and loving when she wanted to be mad.

"I am not your mate so you can stop that shit right now." Kimberly decided to go on the defensive and maybe she could stop thinking about how she really wanted to throw herself into his arms. Before the thoughts had barely formed, Kimberly was groaning to herself. He probably was still reading her mind and just heard everything she had thought.

Nico pulled her in close, tilting his head toward her. "Yes I did, mate. And I must admit I am pleased you want me as much as I want you. Even if you have decided to fight it."

"I think it's an invasion of privacy and rude."

"I'll stop if you promise to stop hiding from me." He dropped a quick kiss on the tip of her nose. "But I do say I will miss it. You have the most amazing fantasies. Vivid with details and imagery."

"Oh my God. You should be stuffed and hung on a wall."

"But then you'll miss me."

"I'll adapt," she grumbled, her irritation fading. Damn it, even when she wanted to stay mad at him she couldn't. Her body wouldn't let her. Just standing next to him had caused the havoc in her body to return.

Kimberly felt as if she were on fire. Her nipples were hardening, her labia was saturated with her juices, her body was trembling. How the hell could she want him so bad and want to wring his neck at the same time?

"Because you're in—"

"Damn it, I thought you said you would stop reading my mind."

"You haven't promised to stop hiding from me yet."

"Fine." Pulling away from him, Kimberly stalked across the room and flounced onto her couch. "I won't hide from you and you stay the hell out."

"I agree."

"I don't believe you."

Laughing, Nico walked to Kimberly, dropping in front of her when he reached her side. "Then why have me promise, *Zingaro*?"

Nico was kneeling in front of her, mere inches away from her tingling flesh. Kimberly longed to reach out and pull him to her but something was holding her back. Fear and desire were terrible bed partners. As if sensing her uncertainty, Nico reached out to her, brushing her bare legs with just his fingertips.

"You don't have to be afraid."

"Stop reading my mind."

Cupping her legs in his hands, Nico stroked her shivering flesh. "I wasn't, *Zingaro*. I was reading your face."

Kimberly felt Nico gently tugging her legs apart but she did nothing to stop him. She didn't want him to stop. "What do you see?"

"I see passion mingled with fear and uncertainty. I see a beautiful, desirable woman. I see my mate."

Kimberly didn't want to acknowledge his words. She just wanted to feel what his hands were doing to her body. Nico started to caress her calves, slowly moving up her legs as he pulled them wider apart. When she pulled on her nightshirt she hadn't bothered with panties and now she was trying to decide whether or not to regret her decision.

"I am regretting my decision." Nico's words had her jerking her head up, eyes wide as she stared at him. Hadn't he promised to stop reading her thoughts? The liar!

"I can see by your face you are angry but I am not doing it." Nico stroked her inner thighs, distracting her from her anger. "I was only commenting about how I was regretting my promise to stay out of your head because I so wanted to know what thoughts were making you look so sexy and vulnerable at the same time."

Kimberly's face flamed at his words. No one had ever spoken to her in this manner before. It was hard to know how to handle all his compliments.

"Will you tell me what you were thinking?" Nico's hands moved closer to the curls covered with her desire. One swipe and he would know how wet she really was.

"I was wondering if it was such a good idea to forget my panties." Kimberly decided to throw caution to the wind.

Nico chuckled, pulling her toward him until her ass was just on the edge of the couch. "You have been very naughty. What if I had been the big, bad wolf, coming to eat you up?"

"Isn't that what you are, the big, bad wolf?" Kimberly trembled as Nico pushed her nightshirt over her hips, exposing her to his hot gaze.

"And do I get to eat you up?" Nico hooked her legs over his arms and leaned in close. Kimberly was dying to have him touch her, do something before she melted all over the floor.

"Yes, please." The words hung there in the air between them for a scant second before Nico smiled wolfishly and bent his head.

"Your scent has been driving me crazy since before I walked in the door, *Zingaro*. You smell of freshly cut flowers and musk."

Nico followed his words by burying his face in her folds, licking at her essence. The second his tongue touched her engorged clit Kimberly was lost. Lost to the pleasure of his mouth finding her as no man had before. Lost to the pain of her beast roaring to life inside her. Lost to the power that was Nico's alone.

Pulling her closer to him, Nico feasted on her tender flesh. His tongue tasted and touched every inch of her quivering pussy, drawing deep, ragged groans from Kimberly's parched mouth. She had pleasured herself many times, but never before had the sensations been this intense.

Clichéd as it was, Kimberly truly felt as if she were going to explode in a million pieces. Her body was as taut as a bow, she dug her hands into his hair to pull him closer. The dream in no way compared to the reality of Nico's talented tongue. She wanted—needed—more.

"Please," she begged, her body arching toward his as Nico's tongue darted inside the slick depths of her body. "Please, don't toy with me."

Pulling back, Nico slipped his hand between her legs, inserting two probing fingers into her tight channel. "I haven't begun to toy with you, *Zingaro*."

"Bastard," she cried, pumping her body onto his tortuous fingers.

"You have no idea." Nico removed his hand to pick up where he'd left off seconds earlier. Fucking her with his tongue, Nico drove her wild, alternating his tongue thrusts with laps against her aching clit. Drinking her juices as they poured from her body.

He was punishing her, she just knew it. No one could survive this much pleasure at once. Just as she thought she couldn't handle any more, Nico enclosed her clit between his lips and sucked. Screaming out as her body convulsed beneath him. "Yes, oh God, yes."

Her beast roared with her, the howl mingled with her own cry of pleasure, bringing goose bumps to her already shivering skin.

With the sweet taste of Kimberly still lingering in his mouth, Nico sat back on his haunches, pleased. Never before had he seen someone give in to their passion so completely. The aroma of her pleasure lingered in the air between them, teasing Nico's senses with its spicy smell. It was a scent he knew he would carry with him to his grave. The scent of his mate.

"Good Goddess, that was great." Kimberly said it as if she were shocked.

"It's only the beginning."

"There's more?"

Smiling, Nico stood, pulling a lethargic Kimberly into his arms. "There's a world of more."

Kimberly wrapped her arms around his neck as Nico swept her into his arms and headed down the hallway to her bedroom. Pushing open the door, Nico dropped Kimberly to a kneeling position on the bed.

"Let's get this off of you." Nico pulled her shirt off and tossed it over his shoulder before kneeling on the bed.

"Wait." Kimberly held her hand up as she began to move back on the bed.

"What?" Nico growled. He didn't think he could stand it if she changed her mind now.

"Off the bed."

"Kimberly—"

"No, I want to see you naked too."

Easing off the bed, Nico smiled. "But you've already seen me. In your dreams, remember."

"That doesn't count." Licking her lips, Kimberly eyed him hungrily. "I want to see you naked and in Technicolor."

Throwing his head back, Nico roared with laughter. "Your wish is my command, *Zingaro*."

Nico stood at the foot of the bed watching Kimberly stare at him. Knowing she wanted him was the best aphrodisiac in the world. With his eyes focused on hers, Nico began to slowly undress.

As he bared his chest to her watchful eyes, Nico tossed his shirt onto the floor, stepping closer to the bed until his knees touched the mattress. "Don't you want to help?"

Kimberly dropped to her hands and knees and crawled across the few feet of bed separating them within seconds. Reaching out, her warm hands slid over his chest, caressing him with her hands as she had with her eyes.

"I feel as if I've dreamt of this moment forever."

"I know I have." Nico brushed his hand through her thick auburn hair. "I've waited years for you."

"You don't have to wait any longer." Kimberly slid her hands down his chest to the buckle of his pants.

Nico thought he was being tortured while Kimberly fumbled with his buckle and zipper. Her fingers brushing against his heated cock drove him insane with the need to feel her hands on his bare flesh. Nico changed his mind about the torture and felt as if he had died and gone to heaven when Kimberly finally released his engorged member.

"Touch me, *Zingaro*, learn the feel of me," Nico encouraged, pushing himself into her soft, cool hands.

Kimberly measured his length with her hands, stroking him from the head to the root before cupping his balls gently. "Oh my, this is so much better than in the dream."

Nico couldn't agree more. In the dream he wasn't able to feel her hot breath caressing his skin. All she would have to do would be to lean over and her mouth would cover him. Nico jerked with anticipation of such an event and as if reading his mind, Kimberly leaned forward. Nico held his breath as her tongue peeked out from between her full lips and swept across the head of his cock.

Pulling back, Kimberly looked at him. "I've never done this before."

Nico chuckled hoarsely. "There is no wrong way to do it, *Zingaro*."

Unable to resist the sweet temptation of her mouth, Nico slid his fingers through her thick hair and nudged her gently forward. When Kimberly took him into her warm mouth, Nico almost died. Her mouth was heaven. A novice, Kimberly started off slow, barely taking his thick member completely. The more she got into it though, the bolder she became. Wrapping her hand around his length, she stroked him as she suckled his cock. Groaning, Nico tightened his hands in her hair, fucking her mouth with steady strokes.

Nico knew if he didn't stop his little temptress now, the evening would be over before it really started. "No more, love."

Pulling away quickly, Kimberly looked up in alarm. "Did I hurt you?"

"Not in the least, but my body hungers for more than your sweet mouth." Instead of looking eager, Kimberly looked a bit worried. "What's wrong, *Zingaro*?"

"I want to have sex but I don't want to get pregnant."

If she hadn't looked so serious, Nico might have chuckled. They would be extremely lucky if she got pregnant at all, let alone on the first night as she feared. "You won't get pregnant."

"I know I won't because you're going to wear something."

"Something?"

"You know, a condom."

This time Nico couldn't hold back, he chuckled. "When they make one to fit me, I will."

"I know you're large and all, but you're not that large."

"It's not the length or girth, my naïve one, but because of the knotting."

Kimberly blushed. "I didn't think of that."

There was no doubt in Nico's mind that if he didn't pull out, he would knot inside her. Knotting only occurred in mates and even Kimberly's denial of their status would not change who they were to one another.

"I'm not going to lie to get you to have sex with me. You want to stop, we will, but if you're just worried about pregnancy you don't have to be."

"Why, do you have some sort of special pregnancy prevention cure?"

"Unfortunately, the Weres are suffering from infertility. The females are rarely getting pregnant, even mated pairs. Our race is dying, *Zingaro*, although I am fighting it at all costs."

"I didn't know it was so serious, Nico." Kimberly bit her lip, regret and uncertainty upon her face. "But I'm still not willing to take the chance that this will be the one time when a female Were conceives. I'm just…not ready. I'm sorry, Nico."

"It's okay, *Zingaro*. I will pull out before I knot so there will be no chance at pregnancy." Nico's beast roared with dissatisfaction but he tamped down his disappointment. He would make this promise to Kimberly and woo her to accept him as her mate.

"No chance?"

"A better chance."

"Those are odds I can live with." Smiling, Kimberly lay back on the bed, spreading her arms out seductively, she invited him to take her with every movement.

"We will take this slowly, *Zingaro*," Nico promised as he lay beside Kimberly and gathered her into his arms.

"Don't take it slow on my account." Kimberly reached over to stroke his jaw and Nico turned to press a kiss into her palm. "I'm on fire for you, I don't think I can wait."

Nico chuckled at her enthusiasm. "But, *Zingaro*, I want to make it last for you. This is your first time and the beginning of our relationship as true mates. This is not something you rush."

Rolling over, Nico pinned Kimberly beneath him, stretching her arms out above her head. He could feel every inch of her skin touching his and groaned as she opened her thighs, allowing him to settle his body into hers. She was making it hard for him to carry through with his promise to make it good and slow for her. What he really wanted to do was push himself into her and take her like the beast he was.

"I can't touch you," Kimberly complained, trying to pull her arms out of his grasp.

"That's the point, *Zingaro*. I would go up quicker than a torch if you were to touch me now. Just let me love you."

Kimberly gave a frustrated nod seconds before Nico took her mouth with his. He kissed her slowly, tentatively at first until Kimberly relaxed under him, opening like a flower before the sun. Her lips were as sweet as honey and her tongue was even tastier. Nico could have kissed her forever. Delving into her moist cavern, learning her taste by heart.

It took an act of God to pull away from her lips but Nico did. There was so much more of her to taste. Giving Kimberly a pointed look, Nico released her hands, daring her silently to move. When she stayed as he wanted her to do, Nico began his pilgrimage down her soft, curvaceous body.

Pausing at her beautiful breasts, Nico cupped the full twins in his hands, praising them with his lips. Lavishing them both one at time with his tongue, he toyed with the mauve erect peaks, biting them gently between kisses.

Kimberly squirmed beneath him, her need as obvious as his own. "Please, Nico."

"I want to please you, *Zingaro*. You must be ready before I take you."

"I'm ready," she growled, raising her head to stare heatedly into his eyes. "If I were any more ready, we'd have a river on our hands."

"I want more than a river. I want an ocean."

Deciding to test her bold pronouncement, Nico stroked his hand across her body and between her legs, combing through her damp curls to the sodden folds hidden there. Slipping his finger easily into her, Nico tested her readiness for his cock.

"More, Nico, give me more." Kimberly arched her hips toward his thrusting digit.

"Slowly, remember?" Gradually parting her tender flesh, Nico eased another finger inside. She was so tight.

"You're killing me here."

"No, *Zingaro*, I am preparing you. You are a virgin and there is no way you can take my cock without some stretching." Nico wasn't teasing since as a Werewolf and an Alpha male, he was much larger than the average human male. Of course Kimberly's body would eventually accept him, he knew she just needed to be primed.

Pressing a third finger inside, Nico brushed his thumb across Kimberly's engorged clit. She gasped at the whispered touch and arched her hips, begging without words for him to take her.

Nico could no longer ignore her wants or his desire. Taking his cock in his hand, he coated his thick length with her sweet juices, lubing himself in the nicest of ways. Centering his cock at her entrance, Nico looked into Kimberly's eyes, needing to watch her as she became his.

With a control he didn't know he possessed, Nico pushed into her slick body, biting back a growl as he felt her body stretch to receive him.

"Nico..." His name was a whisper on her lips. Back arching, Kimberly cried out softly as he pushed past her hymen and deep inside her body.

Nico's canines descended as the faint scent of blood wafted between them. "Mine," he growled low in his throat, surprising himself.

He had to get a hold of himself. Nico knew although Kimberly would adjust to his girth, he still had to be careful with her. He could hurt her if he let himself go. Even though she was aroused and wet from her desire, she was still a novice when it came to making love. And her inexperience alone kept him focused on her. It had to be pleasurable for Kimberly. Nico would have it no other way.

Pulling back slowly, Nico paused at the precipice, wanting to enjoy every thrust inside her tight little body.

"Please." Kimberly closed her eyes as she wrapped her legs around his lower body. "Don't stop now."

"I don't want to hurt you."

"You won't. You can't."

Nico knew better but his beast had been given permission and took over his calmer thoughts. Pulling back, he gazed at her desire-filled eyes before plunging into her body, burying himself balls deep inside her. His hips thrust wildly, meeting her frenzied movements.

The beast inside seemed to wake from its slumber. The need to change came over him quickly but he fought it. For every thrust Nico made, his Were growled in approval. Nico could feel his senses expanding as he and the Were became one. His eyes dilated and his skin began to tingle the deeper he powered into Kimberly's body.

And his mate responded in kind. Nico could feel the changes coming over her. Her groans were mingled with growls, her nails digging into his back felt sharper. She was his mate. There was no doubt about it in his or his beast's mind. She belonged to them.

"So good, so good." Kimberly's chants were sending Nico to the edge of any control he ever thought he possessed. He pushed Kimberly's legs up, opening her wider to his driving body. She sobbed her satisfaction, begging him incoherently for the ultimate pleasure. His beast roared with the need to mark her, claim her as his mate. But he had promised he wouldn't knot inside her, so for tonight, he would have to disappoint his beast. Bending over her, Nico sank his canines into the soft valley of her neck, drawing blood and signifying his possession of her, marking her as his mate for all to see.

Nico knew Kimberly was on the brink and he could feel his own release pending. Reaching between them, Nico rubbed her clit furiously, sending her into orgasm. As her body clutched him, Nico powered into her one last time before roaring with regret and pulling his cock from her welcoming warmth, spilling his hot seed over her soft belly. His canines withdrew from her tender flesh, leaving an imprint of his teeth on her skin as she shivered in the afterglow of their loving.

"Shh…" Nico whispered, bending to run his tongue around her bleeding wound. The metallic taste filled his mouth and his senses. Never before had he had a sweeter release.

"Hmmm…" Kimberly moaned.

"Are you okay?"

"Never better." Kimberly lifted her head and kissed him tenderly before lying back on the bed.

Nico felt on top of the world. He had found his mate and claimed her. He could feel his beast clamoring to take her again and ensure his line by planting his seed. Nico had to fight his urge. He knew Kimberly was tired and would want to sleep. She was sated for now, but the heat was still upon her and she would be begging him to fuck her again soon.

"I can't believe how great I feel," Kimberly murmured as he cleaned the evidence of their lovemaking from their bodies before joining her on the bed once more. "I never thought I would ever be done with being in heat."

Nico chuckled at her words. "*Zingaro*, you are not done with 'being in heat' as you so easily put it. The heat is a cycle that will not abate until the full moon when it finally culminates."

"You are fucking kidding me, right?" Kimberly stared at him, disbelief clouding her face.

"This is no joke, Kimberly. Yes, the heat is gone for now but it will return. We will make love long and often before the full moon comes in four days' time."

"You mean I have four more days of this?"

Nico frowned. "It won't be as bad as before now that we've made love but it won't go away."

"Fuck."

"You don't have to make it sound as if you abhor the cure."

Sighing, Kimberly sat up and ran her hands through her tussled hair. "What I abhor is not feeling as if I have a say in the matter."

"I would never force you."

"You would never have to. My body craves your touch."

Nico turned over on his side and brushed his hand against her spine. "And your heart?"

Kimberly gave a very un-Werewolf-like snort. "Let's leave my heart out of this."

Nico chuckled as he pushed himself up, trailing tiny kisses up her spine. "It's too late, *Zingaro*. Your heart is already involved."

He knew his was.

Chapter Five

ဆာ

"So I guess I'm a little too late to try and give you the 'birds and bees' speech." Sniffing the air, David shut the door behind him with a loud slam. "About six hours too late."

"Actually more like twelve, if you want to count from the first time." Kimberly continued running the vacuum, refusing to allow David to sully her wonderful night.

"Did he hurt you?"

Did he hurt her? Far from it.

"No more than necessary."

"Damn it." Running his hands through his hair, David sighed in frustration. "This is not the way I wanted things for you."

Kimberly shut off the vacuum and turned to look at her brother with a frown. "No, you wanted to keep me ignorant and sheltered. I can't say I'm not sorry your plan didn't work out."

"No, the plan was to protect you at all costs. The Were Machiavellian bullshit is what drove our parents to leave the Pack in the first place. And the first thing you do is run straight into the arms of a *Benandanti*."

"That's not the way it happened. Wait, why am I explaining myself to you anyway? This is my life, David, and I'll live it how I choose."

"Last time I checked, Kimberly, I was part of your life too."

Kimberly sat on the couch and fought to keep from strangling her brother. She loved him but sometimes he could be so stupid. "Of course you are a part of my life, David. But it doesn't mean I want to be wrapped in cotton and kept on a shelf."

"I don't do that," David protested, flopping on the chair.

"Bullshit. You never let me make my own mistakes or learn the lessons of screwing up. You decided what I should know and not know and how I should live. It's why I moved away."

"I never wanted to see you hurt, Kimberly. And I certainly never wanted to push you away." David's face was bleak and Kimberly could see all the hurt there but she knew she couldn't back down, not now. "You might have forgotten but I was only nineteen when Mom and Dad died. No way was I prepared to handle a fourteen-year-old or automatically equipped with the rules and regulations of raising a kid sister let alone a brand-new Werewolf. I had hardly mastered my change and you had just begun yours a year earlier, so forgive me if I left out some hows and whys. When they died, all I was left with was a million unanswered questions and you, and I did the best I could."

"You know sometimes I think they hated what they were."

David snorted. "You think."

"We weren't exactly the fuzzy Waltons."

"Hell, we weren't even the Addams, but looking around at what they left, I can see why they wanted to run."

"Running is one thing, David." Kimberly chastised him gently. "But as you said, they left us very unprepared for this life without them."

"I doubt they knew the car was going to roll off an embankment and I would like to think I didn't do that shitty of a job taking care of you. I kept us together and I kept us safe."

"I know, David, but you have to let go. I mean, come on, aren't you tired of taking care of little sister? Don't you want to have a life for yourself?"

"Right, not all of us can find a mate at work."

"A mate, I don't think so." Kimberly enjoyed sex with Nico but it certainly didn't mean settling down with a litter of puppies. At least, she didn't think she wanted such a commitment. Although the thought of spending the rest of her life with Nico wasn't as scary as it had once been. God, she was driving herself crazy thinking about this stuff too much. "Speaking of work, when do you have to get back to yours?"

"No time soon," David hedged.

"How not soon."

"Ever. I quit."

"Quit." Shocked didn't even begin to explain how Kimberly felt. David had always prided himself on the fact he was able to take care of them. He wasn't one to walk away from his responsibilities. "Why?"

"There were lots of reasons."

"Like?"

"Like we're wolves." David met her confused gaze with his steady one. "We're not meant to be alone. As small as our family was, it was the only Pack I've ever known, and with you gone, I'm...I'm missing the connection."

Kimberly shook her head in amazement. "In one breath you're talking about how horrible the Pack is and in the next you're longing for Pack life. I just don't get it."

"I never said I made sense, sis. I still think a Pack this big is too political for me to feel comfortable, but I can't be the lone wolf anymore."

"So, is this why you're so interested in talking about mates? Are you interested in anyone in particular?"

"We aren't talking about mates for me. And not you either, if I could help it."

Kimberly wasn't too keen on exploring the mate question too deeply right now. Unfortunately that left the only other topic currently on her mind, work and her boss.

"I don't think I'll ever be able to look Cassandra in the eye again." After the incident in Cassandra's office, Kimberly wasn't sure where she stood with her boss. Nico had hustled her out of there and David had taken her home so quickly she hadn't had time to talk to Cassandra.

And now she was afraid to talk to her. How would she explain everything? Kimberly knew it was childish but it was just easier to call off sick and worry about it another day. Plus, after her morning with Nico, she wasn't too motivated to get out of bed early.

"If you aren't going to work, do you want to go for a run?"

"A run? In daylight?"

"Yes, I think it's exactly what we need. To be one with nature, to feel the wind whipping through our fur—"

"To be hauled to the pound."

"Ha, ha." David tossed a pillow at Kimberly. Finally, the tension was gone. They were finally getting back into the brother and sister routine of the past. "Your boyfriend is the president of one of the largest natural wildlife preserves in the state of California. I'm sure he won't mind if we trespass on his land."

"He is?" The minute the words left her mouth, Kimberly wished she could call them back. The last thing she wanted to give David was more firepower.

"You didn't know?"

"We really haven't talked a lot."

"How long have you known him?"

"David," Kimberly warned. "We're not going to get into this."

She had seen him around the office but they had never engaged in more than office pleasantries until the fateful meeting in the parking garage. And now, even though she could honestly say she knew him physically, Kimberly

94

couldn't say she really "knew" knew him. She knew how he was in bed but she would be hard-pressed to answer if someone asked her a simple question such as his favorite color or his birthday.

"I'm just asking."

"Well, don't." Standing, Kimberly stretched her body, still tender from last night. She hadn't known it was possible to make love so many times in one evening. If it were a Were thing, then hallelujah for advanced DNA, if it were a Nico thing, then thank God for comeback power. The man was wonderful.

"So, what do you say—you, me, trespassing?"

"Maybe," Kimberly hedged, "but I want to be back before dark."

"Before dark, why, are you going to turn into a vampire?"

Laughing, Kimberly shook her head. "You're incorrigible. No, I'm expecting Nico to call."

"And you want to be here like a good little wifey?"

No she didn't, did she?

Kimberly growled menacingly. It was better to attack David than examine her own feelings too closely. She had been so determined to gain her independence from David and then make sure she held on to it, she had pushed Nico away at the first sign of him trying to claim her as his mate, too afraid to give up her freedom.

"David, I really don't want to have to hurt you."

"Ha, as if you could. You know..." Pausing, they both turned to the front door at the same time. A light floral scent permeated the air.

"Shit, it's Cassandra." Kimberly groaned. She was amazed how acute her senses had gotten, especially since last night. "I really don't want her to see you here. It'll just stress me out more, trying to talk to her with you listening."

"Okay fine, I'll go back to the bedroom but hurry up. It smells like sex in there."

"Just go, she's going to get suspicious and take this stupid vacuum with you." Kimberly tried to calm her shaking nerves. She had dreaded this confrontation, which was one of the reasons she called off this morning.

The knocking continued and Cassandra called through the door. "Kimberly, are you in there? Is everything okay? Please answer the door."

Kimberly pasted a smile on her face before pulling the door open. "Hi, Cassandra," she started weakly, before being pulled into a hug.

Stunned, Kimberly stared at Cassandra as she pushed her way into the apartment. "Oh my God, Kimberly. I thought you were dying or something. Is everything okay?"

"Ahh, yeah. I'm sorry I called off today, I just wasn't feeling too hot when I woke this morning." Kimberly followed her into the apartment, confused as she watched Cassandra look around.

"Oh Kimberly, it's okay. I just was worried that maniac had done something to you."

"Which maniac?" Kimberly felt as if she were in some surreal dream. Cassandra was acting so oddly. Kimberly gestured to the couch, silently inviting Cassandra to sit even though she really was just hoping she would leave. Unfortunately, it didn't look as if she would be leaving any time soon.

"Nico Cassamonti." Cassandra sounded annoyed, as if Kimberly should know what she was talking about. "I mean, after yesterday when he pulled you into my office, I didn't know what to think."

"Ahh, well, umm, sorry. I was feeling a bit faint and he thought he would just help me out." Oh yes, here it was, the dreaded "What the fuck were you doing in my office yesterday?"

"When you told me you were dreaming about him, I had no idea it was because the two of you were together."

"Well, we weren't, not really." Oh boy, Kimberly didn't like where this conversation was going at all. She didn't want to look like a slut in front of her boss, but if she denied a relationship with Nico, he would have a fit and she wasn't so sure she wanted to deny it.

"That's past tense. Do you mean something is going on now?" Cassandra looked embarrassed and Kimberly wondered if she had been attracted to Nico.

"Something...I..." Blushing, Kimberly couldn't think of the best way to explain what exactly was going on with Nico and her. For some reason she seriously doubted Cassandra would understand how the moon cycle had her in heat and she had to fuck Nico constantly or go mad. Her crazy life couldn't be explained in eight words or less.

"We're kind of seeing each other."

Cassandra's eyes looked as if they were going to pop out of her head. "Wow, and the other guy was..."

"My brother. David just got into town and he and Nico aren't exactly hitting it off."

"Brother." Cassandra grinned. "Well, that takes a load off my mind."

"It does?"

"Yes, I was imagining some strange S&M ménage a trois. I actually thought I might have to come untie you from your headboard or something."

"Ewww."

Laughing, Cassandra stood up. "Since my mind is at ease, I can go back to work with a clear conscience."

"I'm really sorry about today, I just felt horrible this morning."

"Say no more. We all have bad days. Just don't make it a habit."

"I won't." Guilt assaulted Kimberly. She hated lying to Cassandra, especially when she took time out of her day to make sure Kimberly was all right. "I promise to be there bright and—"

"Oh my," Cassandra's face lit up as she stared toward Kimberly's bedroom. "That's the cutest dog I've ever seen. What is he, an Alaskan Malamute?"

God no! Turning around quickly, Kimberly saw her brother trotting into the room and wanted to die. "David!" she hollered before she could stop herself.

Surprised, Cassandra looked over at Kimberly with a confused look on her face. "You named your dog after your brother?"

Fuck! "Yeah, uhhh...he was a gift from David so it seemed appropriate."

David was dead. Deader than dead. And to make matters worse, he was edging his way over to Cassandra's extended hand.

"David," Kimberly growled, vowing to kill her brother at the next available opportunity. "Get back over here."

"No, it's okay. I love dogs." Bending over David, who was damn near grinning, Cassandra petted her brother behind the ear. "Aren't you a good dog? Such a good dog."

Kimberly groaned as David sniffled around Cassandra's feet before slipping his head under her skirt. "Oh my God, I'm so sorry," Kimberly apologized before grabbing him by the tail to pull him back. How dare he do this to her?

"Oh he's a friendly one," Cassandra giggled, but Kimberly's face flamed at Cassandra's words. She had to get him out of there and the sooner the better.

"A little too friendly," Kimberly muttered as she grabbed David by the scruff of the neck, intent on pulling him out of the room.

"Don't worry, I'm used to dogs. It's okay." Cassandra continued to protest, but Kimberly doggedly pulled David along as he whined and struggled in her grip. She leaned over and muttered, "You better stop it, asshole, or you're going to the vet."

Shoving him into the bedroom, Kimberly glared at David as he sat on his haunches, tongue lolling out of his mouth. "You are sooo in trouble right now."

Turning, Kimberly slammed the door before returning to the living room. "Sorry, he's very unruly." Kimberly thought her excuse sounded lame but Cassandra just smiled.

"Don't worry about it. I love dogs. Now that I know you have one, I'll have to drop by once in a while to see if he'd want to go out and play." Kimberly groaned inwardly. David was going to have to go to doggie heaven soon.

"Yeah...you'll have to do that."

"All right, I'm off. I'll see you Monday, bright and early."

"With doughnuts," Kimberly promised, trying her best to fix today's faux pas.

As soon as shut the door behind Cassandra, Kimberly yelled David's name. The bastard. How dare he?

"You rang?" David strolled back into the living room, pulling his shirt over his head.

Grabbing the pillow off the couch, Kimberly jumped on her brother's back, beating him on the head with the pillow. Laughing, David tossed her over his shoulder and dodged behind the recliner. "Calm down, Kimmie."

"Calm down? Calm down! That was my boss you were molesting."

"I wasn't molesting her and besides she liked it. She's used to friendly dogs, remember?"

Kimberly jumped up, intent on beating her brother into next week. "But you're not a dog. You're a pig."

"She liked it." He grinned, making sure to keep something in front of him. "And she smelled fucking great. I wonder what that was."

"Her crotch."

"Who are you telling? Think she might be into bestiality?"

Gasping, Kimberly grabbed the lamp from off her side table and threw it at her brother, ripping the cord out of the wall in the process. "You're a sick, sick individual."

"No, I'm a Werewolf, sis. We're ruled by our beast. You've just never experienced it before but you'll learn soon enough we answer nature's call and there is only so much we can control."

"If you or your beast go within an inch of my boss, I'll make a throw rug out of you."

Raising a brow, David crossed his arms over his chest. "Didn't you just get through telling me to stay out of your love life?"

"Yes, but, David—"

"No buts. I'll stay out of yours and you'll stay out of mine."

"She's human, David." Kimberly couldn't help but warn.

"So am I, half the time."

"I don't want to see you get hurt."

Smiling, David came from behind the chair. "Welcome to my world."

* * * * *

"So let me get this straight." The anger in Kimberly's tone resonated over the phone line. "You're not coming over tonight, because you have to hang out at a bar and meet some friends."

"Not friends, *Zingaro*, allies."

"Allies…I see."

Nico seriously doubted it. "If it were my decision, I would be there."

"I'm sorry, *Benandanti*, I thought it was."

Swearing under his breath, Nico tried his damnedest to keep his temper in check. "I'm not going to have an argument with you about this, Kimberly."

"You're right. You're not."

The threat in her voice wasn't difficult to detect. "Don't you dare hang up!"

"I just want to point out it was you who pursued me. I never wanted to have sex with you in the first place—"

"I beg to differ, love."

"And now that we are having sex, you should at least keep your end of the deal and come over here and—"

"Fuck you." His words cut her off in midstream. There was a very long pause before she spoke again.

"Goodnight, Nico."

"Kimberly," he called before the dial tone greeted him. The stubborn little minx didn't know whom she was messing with.

If it were any other night, he would be there, in her arms, between her legs, wherever and however she wanted, but tonight they were meeting with the *Benandanti* of the Morbauch clan and Nico couldn't miss it. No matter how much he might want to.

The meeting came up at the very last minute. Unfortunately, he was informed only a few hours after he made plans with Kimberly and she didn't take it as well as he'd hoped.

Trying to shake off their argument, Nico attempted to focus on the upcoming meeting. Until this point, Nico had only spoken through emissaries. Although he believed in his plan for a truce, until he met face-to-face with Santana and could size up the man, Nico wouldn't know if he could trust Santana's character.

"Trouble in paradise?" Remy spoke from behind Nico, interrupting his thoughts.

"Where have you been all night?" Nico ignored Remy's question.

"That damn *Rakshasa* has been following me around all day." Remy snorted, and glanced back over her shoulder, as if her words would conjure him to appear. "You know, if you hadn't put us all out on the street protecting your new girlfriend, I wouldn't have to spend time with him."

Nico was a bit taken back by Remy's hostility toward the Pack's *Rakshasa*, Jace McClellan. As a seer for the *Brachyurus*, Jace held a certain level of authority with Nico and the *Maggiore*. His word was sacred and his insights were valid.

"Remy, where is your respect? You know the *Rakshasa* have given great service to the clan, warning us of upcoming troubles and plots. They were invaluable during the Great War."

"I've read the history books but I get tired of all the cryptic bullshit." Remy rolled her eyes. Nico knew she didn't hold much stock in the abilities of the *Rakshasa* to predict future problems, but Nico had heard too many stories of their powers to not hold them in high regard.

"So should I ask why he was following you around all day?" Nico knew sometimes it was hard to get to the point with Remy when she got off on a tangent and he had to rein her in.

Remy sighed heavily. "I know you are going to take this all wrong. It's one of the reasons I've been avoiding you."

"Okay, spill it." Nico hated it when Remy decided she was going to protect him from himself. The one bad thing about having a bodyguard was it made a person seemed childlike somehow.

"He says there's something off about the meeting tonight but he can't pin it down. He is so fucking useless."

"Remy, I don't ever want you to say anything like that again." Nico knew he sounded harsh, but if anyone had heard her speak and not known it was a personal issue, they might believe she was one of those Weres who felt the *Rakshasa* were an abomination. "Now tell me more about what's off about the meeting tonight."

Crinkling her nose at him, Remy put her hands on her slim hips and eyed him sarcastically. "I know technically you are the boss of me but don't go thinking you're the boss of me. I'll say what I want about that nuisance anytime I please."

"Excuse me." Startled, Nico stared at his friend. Never before had she ever addressed him with so much disrespect.

"No." Sighing, Remy ran her hand warily through her chocolate locks. "Excuse me. I'm just tired and pissy."

"Why?"

"Have you ever tried walking around with a talking fortune cookie? I mean if he were any more cryptic, he'd need a decoder. He's fucking driving me insane."

"It can't be that bad."

"Fine, let's switch jobs, you hang out with him and I'll get fucked all day."

Bursting out laughing, Nico pulled Remy into his arms. Their banter could always make him feel better, even when he was still thinking about pulling Kimberly over his lap. Growling, she batted at him a bit before giving in to his embrace. Her familiar scent brought a smile to his soul. No taller than his shoulder, Remy fit with ease in his arms, a place she had been many times. Sometimes there was nothing as comforting as Pack. And Remy was a Were who had needed comforting a lot growing up. "I'm sorry Jace has been giving you a hard time tonight."

"Tonight," she grumbled, pulling back. "Try all of his life."

"But we need him for tonight."

"Well, can I make him into a nice ball of yarn tomorrow?"

"If he could shift, I would say yes, but since he can't, I'll say no. A human ball of thread could get very messy."

Snickering, Remy looked at him with a smile. "Messy but tasty."

"Very." A car pulled into the parking lot, shining its bright headlights onto the pair. Turning to look at the familiar black Hummer, Nico slipped his hand in his pocket and waited for Derek to join them.

"I still say he's overcompensating," Remy teased as Derek jumped out of the vehicle.

"I heard that, Remington," Derek teased back, walking across the lot to meet them. As usual the Asian man was dressed all in black, blending in with the dark night sky. "And I'm more than willing to prove you wrong."

"Yeah, but if I sleep with you, then technically I've slept with everyone you've slept with and I refuse to go into triple digits. A girl's got to have her standards."

"Ouch, that was not nice."

Leering, Remy teased, "Neither am I."

"Let's take this party inside," Nico directed, turning to go back into the bar. If he didn't stop them, Remy and Derek would be at it all night.

But Derek was the least of Nico's concerns because as soon as they entered the establishment, Remy spotted Jace sitting at the bar, flirting with a pretty, young Were.

"Aww," she moaned. "Who invited him?"

At the sound of her voice, Jace turned toward them and smiled. Even though he wasn't a shifter, he was built similar to one. The DNA he shared with his Were kin made him lithe yet muscular but he wasn't able to turn as they did. His premonition was a double-edged sword. It granted him mystical powers but held back his basic Were gifts. Nico always thought it was a bit unfair he shared their strengths but not their beasts—it was the best of both worlds.

Standing up, the blond *Rakshasa* made his way across the room, arms opened wide. "Sunshine, aren't you glad to see me?"

Jace went to hug her but was held back by Remy's hand held out in front of her.

"Touch me and die."

Her words seemed not to affect the boisterous man. "Ahh, I thought we had a great time this afternoon?"

"Who told him he could come?" Refusing to answer the question, Remy turned accusing eyes toward Nico, who was having a hard time keeping a straight face. It was amusing to see Jace get under Remy's skin. Normally she was as cool as they came, but there was just something about Jace that rubbed Remy the wrong way. Everyone knew it, especially Jace, who went out of his way to antagonize her at every opportunity.

"I did, Remy. We might need him," Nico said.

"Like we need a hole in the head," she grumbled, taking a seat at the bar. "This is supposed to be sacred ground."

"It's a bar, Remy," Jace teased.

"It's a bar, Remy," she mocked in a high-pitched tone. "I know it's a bar, but it's *our* bar."

"And without me, there wouldn't be a sacred place for you all to go."

"Think awful highly of yourself don't you, watcher boy?"

"Stop it." Shaking his head, Nico didn't have time for this. "Jace is just as much a part of our Pack as every shape-shifter you call kin. He's part of the club, Remy, so deal."

"If he gets a secret decoder ring, I'm resigning."

"There's a secret ring?" Jace's eyes twinkled as he tried but failed to look innocent.

"Shut up." Remy leaned over the bar and grabbed a beer from the bartender, acting as if she were completely ignoring the rousing greetings as more of the clan members began to arrive. Nico knew she saw and heard everything that was going on. Her job as *Venator* would allow her to do nothing less.

Nico pulled Jace away from the bar, intent on following up on this "bad feeling" he had about the meeting tonight. Nico was not interested in having this evening fucked in any way. The clan could not afford it and neither could he. It would be just the kind of ammunition Franklin would use to turn everyone against him.

"What's up?"

"Remy told me about the premonition you had about this evening. Any hints you can give me about what it all means?" Nico would love it if Jace suddenly gave him a word-by-word rundown of the evening but of course, it never worked that way.

"All I know is it's not dangerous, but the Morbauch clan is definitely hiding something." Damn it, Remy was right. This cryptic shit sucked sometimes.

"And no idea what it might be?" Nico was struggling to keep the sarcasm from his voice.

"Sorry, man, I just sense they're hiding something but I also sense this evening's outcome won't lead to tragedy. It's the best I can do." Jace looked upset that he couldn't give Nico more.

"It's okay, we're all frustrated." Nico clapped Jace on the shoulder and they returned to the bar to await the Morbauch Pack. The emissaries had set the time at midnight so they would be arriving any minute now.

Kellen, who had been outside standing guard, stepped into The Howler and headed straight for Nico. His normally jovial face was set in a serious line. Everyone was on guard tonight. Whether they needed to be or not. "Hey, boss, I think company has arrived."

With a nod of his head, Nico headed to the rear of the bar to a set of tables sectioned off tonight especially for them. He didn't know the Morbauch clan well enough to have it in their private room, and if they were smart enough, they wouldn't want to go into a secluded spot with their former enemies either.

Nico situated himself in a chair that faced the entire room, putting the wall at his back. It was the best seat in the house and the safest. Remy, who stayed at the bar, was now leaning close to the bartender, delivering the message Nico had instructed her to. He wanted the bar cleared of all civilians. If things went wrong, and they so often did, Nico didn't want any bystanders to get hurt. Too many Weres had lost their lives as it was.

The door flew open the second the clock struck midnight, as if the coyotes had been waiting for the exact moment to make their presence known. And as they walked in, Harrison began to shepherd people out. Yet even in the confusion of the crowd, the Morbauch clan stood out.

The air around them had a stronger scent, like the air of the sea, salty yet crisp. Their bodies seemed bulkier, not as lean as the wolves, but there wasn't a person out of the eight of them who stood under five-nine.

Remy sidled over to Nico, taking her place behind him, her hands close to her side. The energy around her hummed with electricity as she faced their opposition head-on. Nico could almost smell her excitement. She was ready for anything.

"Is it just me or do they all resemble fucking Ken dolls?"

Nico bit back a smile as he eyed the blond group. Leave it to Remy to crack a joke at a time like this. "Or as if they're going to a neo-Nazi rally."

"Nazis, the other white meat."

Clearing his throat, Nico stood as the Morbauchs headed in their direction with Kellen and Derek flanking their rear. The bar had cleared in record time, leaving just Nico's clan and their guests.

The two emissaries he spoke to earlier led the group, followed by a number of guards. What Nico didn't see was anyone who resembled a *Benandanti*. Great, maybe this was the thing Jace had sensed, their leader wasn't going to attend. Sure, it wouldn't end violently but it wouldn't end well either.

"Welcome to The Howler, gentleman, please join us." Nico was playing the gracious host but inside he was seething. He had had such high hopes for this meeting, thinking it would lead to more alliances with the other Weres.

One of the Weres from the Pack stepped forward and began to speak. "Thank you for inviting us, Mr. Cassamonti. I've looked forward to this meeting with much anticipation." Nico could tell the quaint little speech had been scripted, but still, there was some interesting information there.

"Please, call me Nico. But speaking of your leader, where is he?" Nico looked around, knowing there was no true Alpha from the Morbauch clan present. This was becoming more curious by the moment.

The Morbauch clan glanced at one another apprehensively, before looking back at Nico. His own clan began to sense their unease and came to attention, wondering if they were going to have trouble after all.

Just then the door of The Howler opened and a young female Were-coyote entered. Harrison stopped her at the door, glancing at Nico for a decision. Nico sensed no threat and nodded to allow her entrance. The Morbauch clan all reacted by moving to her side and surrounding her as she moved toward Nico. He wasn't sure what was going on but this night was beginning to feel similar to one of those bad *Twilight Zone* episodes.

"I am sorry to have deceived you, Nico, but my clan was protecting me. I am the leader you have requested to meet. My name is Rachel Santana."

Nico stood in shock, staring at the young woman as his mind tried to wrap around the image he was seeing. "Would someone care to explain what's going on?" Nico realized this was what the Morbauch clan was hiding but he also knew he wanted the whole story before he made any decisions about allying with them.

"May we sit? I think I can clear up everything." Nico nodded in agreement to Rachel's request and the clan leaders both took their seats.

"This wasn't an attempt to deceive you in any way. But since my husband's death, keeping my throne has been as difficult as keeping my head attached to my body."

"I wasn't aware your husband had passed."

Raising a brow, Rachel nodded. "There was no need for you to know. Until six months ago, we weren't on speaking terms."

Nico nodded, still a bit amazed this delicate-looking woman was leader of a brutal clan such as the Morbauchs. Killing first and asking questions later seemed to be their only creed. Many casualties from the Great War were attributed to the Morbauchs. It was only in the last few years the vicious Weres had appeared to be willing to put the bitter past behind them. The coyotes were as secretive as they were deadly. It had only been recently he had learned the name of their *Benandanti*. "And once we were?"

"I had to be sure you could be trusted before you were told."

"And you trust me now?"

"No, but I'm intrigued by your offer. We've been at war for years. Why does our mortality interest you now?"

"Because our mortality depends on it."

"And if I agree to your proposal, what then?"

Nico had been waiting for this moment for years. "Your survival, because it is as important as ours. Then your enemies become our enemies."

"But I know my enemies." Tapping her nails on the table, Rachel looked questionably at him. "Who are your enemies and why would we would want to cross them?"

Narrowing his eyes, Nico leaned forward. "Because crossing me would be worse."

"I'm not sure we want to get involved at all." Nico was starting to get pissed off by the cat-and-mouse game.

"Bullshit." Rachel looked startled by his reaction. "You damn well are interested, otherwise you wouldn't be here. You know no Weres can continue to survive as we have been. We both want the best for our clans. Don't be stupid and throw this opportunity away."

Rachel smiled and nodded. "Yes, I had heard you didn't often take no for an answer, and you are right, we are dying. I still don't like the idea of taking on more enemies, on the other hand, we could always use more friends. So tell me more of this grand scheme of yours to save all the Weres."

Nico knew she may balk at some of his plans but he had just gained a major foothold and a new ally.

Chapter Six

೫

Kimberly knew she was being a brat but she wasn't going to be one of those women who fawned all over their man, jumping at his every request. She refused to allow him or any other man to ever walk all over her, and if it meant frustrated nights with a vibrator, trying to alleviate the heat by herself, then so be it. She had rushed back like a good little girl, much to David's amusement, just to be stood up. It was humiliating and degrading and she wasn't going to put up with it. That's why when Nico came to her apartment, she decided she was going to hold firm and not let him come in.

"Come on, *Zingaro*, open the door. I'll tell you all about the meeting." Nico had started out forceful but now was dangling these little tidbits in her face, just daring her to open the door.

"I don't really care, Nico. I was asleep as you damn well know." Kimberly yelled through the closed door. "And if you don't stay out of my dreams, I'm going to get you neutered."

"I wouldn't have to dream walk you, *Zingaro*, if you would answer your phone."

"Me not answering the phone should have told you something."

"It did. You want me to kiss it and make it better." Nico's smooth voice floated around her, caressing her senses like a lover's hand. Of course it wouldn't have mattered a damn if she didn't feel as if she were being singed alive from the fire roaring inside her.

Kimberly had really thought the heat thing was going to disappear, despite what Nico had said. But it hadn't, and she was as horny as ever.

And the worse part was…the bastard knew it.

"*Zingaro*, stop torturing us both. I can sense your need. Let me in and I'll make you feel all better."

Kimberly's resolve began to waver as the cream pooled between her legs. His voice was a siren's call. It made Kimberly's insides turn to mush and she peeked out the peephole to see what he was doing.

As if he could read her mind, Nico straightened and stood back from the door so Kimberly could see his entire body. Even through the peephole, she could discern the outline of his cock through his jeans. Kimberly moaned as she felt a gush of wetness between her legs, imagining his hard cock thrusting into her.

Leaning against the door, Kimberly tried to calm her breathing, which had gone into overdrive. Damn it, she had no willpower at all. Kimberly wanted him just as much as he wanted her. She would just let him in, have her wicked way with him and then throw his ass out after they were done.

"You can come in, but only for sex."

"It could never be just sex between us."

"Yes it can," Kimberly lied. "Because I'm still mad at you. You stood me up."

"It was not my intent." Nico's voice held a hint of humor in it, much to Kimberly's dismay. "But I'll make it up to you. I'll tell you all about what happened when we're in bed together. After we make slow, sweet love and you are so sated you can't even move, I'll wrap my arms around you and tell you a bedtime story."

"What if I don't want you to make slow, sweet love to me?"

"I can do it hard and fast too, *Zingaro*, whatever way you like." Nico's words were a beacon to her beast. Resting her forehead on the door, Kimberly waged a silent war with herself. What was happening to her? With just a few words, she was surrendering to him again. She didn't know what falling in love felt like, but she was beginning to wonder if this was it. It couldn't be just the heat because her heart was too involved.

"*Zingaro*, have you made up your mind? Is it going to be sweet and slow or hard and fast?" Kimberly could just imagine him licking his lips as he spoke, or better yet, licking hers.

Throwing caution to the wind, Kimberly whipped open the door to confront Nico leaning against her doorjamb looking sexy as sin. "How about hard and fast the first time and then sweet and slow?"

Nico slowly pushed himself away from the doorjamb, smiling a wicked little grin. "Just twice? Oh no, *Zingaro*, you will have to consider all the other ways in between."

At his words, Kimberly yelped and turned, intent on running back to the bedroom. Although his words were spoken quietly, Nico had a hungry, predatory look in his eye that made her fight-or-flight instinct kick in. And she was definitely going for the flight. Unfortunately she only got a few steps in before he harnessed her around the waist and pulled her to a stop. He wrapped his arms around her, bending his head to sniff her neck.

"Running from your mate is a punishable offense. Lucky for you, I am a forgiving Were. Especially since I can smell your arousal." Kimberly moaned as Nico ran his hands lightly over her breasts before moving them between her legs. She would have collapsed to the floor if he didn't hold her tightly in his arms.

"Of course, I can't let you get away with such disobedience entirely." Nico turned Kimberly quickly before throwing her over his shoulder, her ass in the air.

Kimberly had a pretty nice view from this angle. Reaching down she tried to pinch Nico's ass, which earned her a swat. She wanted to be indignant but instead broke out into giggles.

Nico began walking toward the bedroom as he spoke. "You're in big trouble now, *Zingaro*. I will have to make love to you all night to cure you of this need to tease and torment me."

Kimberly laughed as Nico tossed her onto the bed. The teasing glimmer in his eyes did little to corral the lust brimming in hers. She would have never guessed he could be so playful. Kimberly was willing to bet Nico didn't know either.

Her Alpha Werewolf was doing a little playful striptease for her. Slowly removing his shirt, Nico winked at her before tossing it toward her.

Laughing, Kimberly caught the shirt and brought it to her face, inhaling his animalistic scent. His smell was, for lack of a better word, like catnip to her. Kimberly could roll around in it all day.

"Are you going to make love to my shirt, *Zingaro*, or me?"

Embarrassed at being caught molesting his clothes, Kimberly tossed his shirt to the floor much to Nico's amusement and got up on her knees.

Hands on hips, she faced him with a mock frown. "I thought we were going to discuss the meeting."

"I said after we made love we would discuss the meeting."

"What if I want to discuss it now?"

Unbuckling his pants, Nico slid the zipper down slowly, his grin spreading as Kimberly's breathing intensified. When had she become so cock crazy? "Do you really want to talk?"

Talk, hell no. Kimberly could think of many more yummy things for him to do with his tongue. "If I say yes, what are you going to do?"

His pants shimmed past his hips at the same time the words left her mouth. "To do, hmmm, let me think on that."

Apparently, Nico already had a plan. He began to palm his rigid length, his strokes long and sure. Words faltered on Kimberly's tongue as she watched him. Part of her wanted to run from the bed and replace his schooled hand with her mouth, but another part wanted her to watch Nico bring himself to orgasm.

"You are such a tease," she finally got out, dragging her gaze from his erection up to his eyes.

"Me…tease you, *Zingaro*? I wouldn't dream of it."

Heart pounding, Kimberly felt as if there were a flood bursting from her quivering mound. Principles aside, she wanted Nico inside her.

"Come here." Her voice was even hoarse to her ears.

"Where?"

Grabbing the hem of her nightshirt, Kimberly pulled it off, tossing it somewhere near his shirt. Naked underneath, she spread her legs, slipping her fingers down to her dew-coated slit. Her moans weren't the only ones loose in the room. Nico had paused in his teasing to stare hungrily at her.

"Come here," she murmured again, this time tapping her pussy with each word.

Nico released his cock and stalked to the bed. All traces of humor had bled from his eyes. Now they shined with passion and power. "Hungry for me?"

"Starving."

Climbing onto her bed, Nico mirrored her stance, his cock brushing against her middle, damp with proof of his own desire.

"You're not the only one who wants to eat, *Zingaro*. Feed me. Give me your sweet pussy."

Although his words were of her pussy, his lips claimed her mouth. Surrendering to his touch, Kimberly folded into him as his tongue danced with hers. The taste of barley and hops mingled with his natural flavor, intoxicating Kimberly as if she had been the one drinking.

Nico slipped his hand between their tightly entwined bodies, his fingers combing through her damp curls, parting her swollen lips.

Kimberly tore her mouth away and cried out with passion as his fingers slid deep within her body, his thumb caressing her swollen clit. He stretched her, fucked her with his fingers as if they were an extension of his cock. And like the hungry beast she was, Kimberly pushed down on his hand, arching her back, begging for more.

Much to her dismay, the pleasure didn't last long. Just as she felt ready to explode, Nico pulled his hand from between her legs, chuckling when she growled in protest.

"Get on all fours, *Zingaro*. Welcome me into your body."

His words sent a bolt of lightning straight to her core. Unsteadily, Kimberly turned and lowered herself until her hands were flat on the bed and her ass was in the air. "You want to mount me?"

Nico rubbed his hands lovingly over the slope of her rear, his fingers dipping between her lips, coating his digits with her cream. "I want to claim you."

"Same rule as before applies. You have to…"

"Pull out. I know."

Kimberly was unsteady at his touch, but his words almost sent her into a tailspin. She was ready to be his in every way, even if she didn't know exactly what it meant yet.

Nico growled and roughly pushed her legs apart. Kimberly trembled at his touch and his hands slid over her flanks, gentling her nervousness. "Easy, *Zingaro*, I would never hurt you."

The head of his cock nudged at her slick opening, searching for entrance. Kimberly pushed back against him, urging him to fill her. "Steady, there is no need to rush."

"Yes, there is. I need you inside me, Nico. Please stop teasing me." Kimberly didn't know how much longer she could wait to feel him filling her body.

"No more teasing, *Zingaro*." Nico increasingly pushed his cock inside her pussy, stretching her open. Kimberly's fingers curled into the comforter below her as he pressed inside.

"More, I want all of you." Kimberly was crazed with desire, her beast calling at her. This position only increased her frenzy, making her want to bite and scratch and impale herself on his cock.

Nico paused for a moment, pulling back before thrusting forward again, pushing deeper inside her aching sex. Setting a steady rhythm, Nico began to fuck her pussy with deep, firm strokes. Kimberly met him stroke for stroke, pressing back against him.

Pressure built to an unbearable height. Her pussy pulsed around him, her nails dug into the comforter, the fabric ripping in her grasp.

He was so deep. She felt him against her womb as if he were begging entrance.

"*Zingaro*." His words were hardly recognizable.

But then again, neither were hers. They were both too far gone. Too lost in the rapture to hold on for longer than a few syllables. "Fuck me. Fuck me. Fuck me."

As he pulled out and powered forward, Nico thrust so hard Kimberly's arms nearly gave out. Digging his nails into her side, Nico ground out her name, pushing into her with rapid speed. A loud buzzing filled the room as energy slithered across her skin.

Kimberly felt as if she were about to combust. It was too much. It wasn't enough. Just as she thought her orgasm was imminent, Nico suddenly pulled from her body, leaving her empty and aching.

"What…don't leave me." Kimberly tossed her hair back as she tried to turn, gasping when Nico growled and pushed her head back toward the bed.

"I want to come in your body, *Zingaro*, one way or another."

Kimberly shivered, her body still thrumming from the pinnacle of her almost orgasm and the vision evoked by his words. She could hear his shallow rasping breath behind her and tried to anticipate his next move.

Nico's hands were stroking along her thighs, causing her to tremble in expectation as he eventually reached her quivering pussy. Kimberly groaned and pushed back against him as he cupped her mound, collecting the moisture gathered there. Drawing it back, Nico began teasing her anus, rubbing her essence around the sensitive rosette.

"I…I don't know about this." Kimberly groaned as Nico's finger penetrated her hole, igniting the sensitive nerve endings there.

Nico growled in response, pushing deeper into her body. "Take it, *Zingaro*, take it so you can take me."

Kimberly cried out at the invasion, the pain melding with the pleasure. Her pussy gushed in response as she pushed back against his probing finger.

"Yes, *Zingaro*, that's what I want." Nico pulled from her body, causing her to whimper in protest. Gathering more lubrication from her pussy, he immediately returned to her anus, pressing two fingers inside.

"I don't think I can take it." Kimberly grasped the sheets beneath her, her body clamoring for more as she protested the invasion.

"Yes you can." Nico was giving her no time to object, thrusting his fingers deep and widening them inside to stretch her body.

The painful fullness was beginning to recede, replaced with pleasure and the need to move. Kimberly pushed her hips back, causing Nico to chuckle in response. Kimberly felt her face flush from embarrassment at her response and tried to pull away from him, but Nico quickly disabused her of that notion, swatting her ass with his free hand.

"You aren't going anywhere."

Nico pushed a third finger inside her, causing Kimberly to cry out in pain. He stilled for a moment, letting her get used to the feeling. She could feel the sheets bunched beneath her hands and hear her heart beating madly.

"Shh, *Zingaro*, just relax and feel." Nico thrust gently, with short, shallow strokes. Kimberly tensed in anticipation of pain but was surprised that she just felt fuller. The thrusting was increasing and Kimberly began pushing back against his fingers once again. When Nico pulled his fingers from her body, Kimberly groaned in dismay, surprised at how she suddenly felt empty without them.

She didn't have long to miss the presence of his touch though. Nico grasped his cock and thrust inside her pussy, coating himself with her juices, before pulling out of her body once again. Then positioning himself against her anus, he began pressing forward, slowly pushing his cock inside. Although his fingers had stretched her, nothing could prepare her for the thickness of his cock.

"Nico…"

Nico stopped but didn't pull out, his breathing rough and shallow. Reaching around, he stroked between her legs, causing her body to awaken to pleasure once again. Plucking her clit, he quickly brought her back to the edge of her climax. At the same time he continued to gently thrust the head of his cock into her, slowly stretching her anus. Never pushing all the way in—but never pulling out either. The mingling of pleasure soon sent tingling shivers throughout her body.

"Push out, *Zingaro*."

Kimberly followed his direction and once again Nico pressed inside, the head of his cock pushing past the ring of muscle that had barred his way. Pausing, Nico gave Kimberly a moment to adjust to the fullness before pushing deeper. She breathed deeply, giving herself up to the multitude of sensations bombarding her body.

Nico began to thrust, pulling almost completely from her body before sinking deeply back inside. Kimberly caught his rhythm and pushed back against him with every driving plunge. His thrust pushed her from her hands and she collapsed to the bed, her head cushioned on the pillow and her ass still in the air.

Bracing herself with one hand, Kimberly reached between her legs and pressed her hand against her aching mound, her own touch causing her to moan appreciatively.

"Put your hand inside you, *Zingaro*. Feel my cock in your ass."

Flushed with the conflicting feelings of desire and embarrassment, Kimberly slipped her fingers inside her vagina as he ordered. She could feel the ridges of his cock through the thin membrane there and stroked him in wonderment. His speed increased at her caress, his fragile control finally at the breaking point. Her own control was flimsy at best, her clit on fire as she aroused herself with every movement.

"Come with me," he growled as he pulled out and powered forward. He thrust so hard Kimberly's arm nearly gave out. Digging his nails into her side, Nico ground out her name, pushing into her with rapid speed. A loud buzzing filled the room as energy slithered across her skin.

Kimberly felt as if she were about to combust. It was too much. It wasn't enough.

"Nico," she cried as her orgasm tore through her, her eyes dilating, her nails lengthening.

Nico joined her in ecstasy, thrusting one last time, before his cock swelled with the knot of his desire. His seed pumped out as he bit back a groan of ecstasy. Her body clenched

120

around his cock as Kimberly gasped when another orgasm tore through her. Kimberly collapsed on the bed as Nico fell over her, his cock still jerking, spilling his seed into her spasming body.

Panting, Kimberly lay on her stomach, staring at her nails in surprise. She hadn't fully changed nor had she stayed completely human. It was a conundrum. But she felt good. Her beast was curled up inside her like a sedated puppy. Fed and fucked at last.

As the knot eventually subsided, Nico gently pulled free from Kimberly's body. Standing, he left her room for a few minutes. He returned shortly with a moist towel that he used to tenderly clean them both before joining her on the bed.

"Nico."

"Yes, love?"

His words were slurred as if he were drunk from pleasure. It was a feeling Kimberly could well relate to. This was crazy, but it was much more than a heat thing to her.

"Now tell me what happened at the meeting."

Amused, Nico's body shook with laughter. "All right, *Zingaro*, all right."

Settling back against her headboard, Nico pulled Kimberly into his arms as he began to speak.

"The biggest surprise was the coyotes' leader. It's a woman."

"Really? Wow. I guess I shouldn't be shocked, but...wow. I never thought any Were Pack would allow a woman to rule them."

"She's the widow of the previous leader, but I can't imagine she wasn't challenged. She must be one hell of a fighter. And she certainly evokes loyalty in her Pack."

"Sounds as if you really admire her." Kimberly attempted to mask her feelings and put on a good face, but inside she felt her beast growl with displeasure. She couldn't be jealous, could she?

"She has a tough job on her hands controlling that Pack. And I thought I had it bad getting the *Maggoire* to listen."

"So tell me more. Were they agreeable to an alliance?"

"Time will tell, *Zingaro*. For now they're listening. Tonight was only the first meeting and we don't have a written agreement, but she is willing to call a truce and that's the first step. Now we'll have to see if she can enforce it with her Pack. As will I."

"Why wouldn't everyone be happy with peace?" She would never understand the quagmire of Were politics.

"Ah well, wartime breeds power for those who never would get it during peace, *Zingaro*. And some thrive in the chaos. But we will no longer survive if we don't begin to band together. Let's just hope that we both can convince our Packs of this truth." Nico fell silent and Kimberly mulled over their discussion. She just hoped the coyotes didn't betray them.

* * * * *

A constant ringing alternating with loud knocking woke Kimberly from her slumber. She rolled over in bed, groaning as she noticed how light the room was. Oh boy, she had overslept big time. Thank God it was Saturday and she didn't have to go into work. Glancing over, she noticed Nico was no longer in her bed. Grumbling, Kimberly pulled herself out of bed. Grabbing a robe, she shrugged into the cotton covering as she walked toward the front door.

"I'm coming already. Hold your horses." Opening the door wide, Kimberly was confronted with a strange woman standing before her, sunglasses shadowing her eyes. The woman was tall, five-ten or -eleven, with curly black hair and ebony skin. Muscular without being masculine, she had an attitude without ever opening her mouth.

"You know you should never open the door unless you know who's on the other side."

Kimberly realized the woman was probably right but she wasn't going to back down and act scared. "Who the fuck are you?"

The woman smiled slightly before finally taking off her sunglasses. "Remy, Nico's *Venator*."

"*Venator*?" Kimberly felt like an idiot because she had no idea who this woman was or what she was talking about. For all she knew, this Remy person could be Nico's wife.

Tsking, Remy shook her head. "Yeah, Nico told me about that."

"What?"

"About how you don't know much."

Fuck you very much. This chick was quickly getting on her nerves. "Well, that puts you at an advantage because he hasn't said a thing about you."

Instead of taking her comment as an insult, the woman grinned. "Frisky too, huh?"

"Can I help you with something?" Kimberly was getting more than a little annoyed at Remy's superior attitude.

"Not really, I just wanted to visit the land of Mecca myself."

"I have absolutely no idea what you're talking about."

"I wanted to meet you in person."

"Oh goodie. Should I feel privileged?"

"No need to get an attitude with me. As *Venator* I watch Nico's back. And if it means I get to come over and check out the new mate, well, I guess it makes me the privileged one."

Kimberly knew she shouldn't be mad at this woman, but damn it, Nico was starting to piss her off. How dare he leave her blind like this? Sighing, Kimberly stepped back into her apartment, holding the door open for her unwanted guest to enter. "I'm gonna brand his head in with a frying pan."

"It's a tempting idea." Remy walked in, looking around her as she entered. "But I'm afraid I'd have to stop you."

"Why?" Right now, it seemed like the best idea in the world to Kimberly.

"Because unfortunately, it's my job. I'm his guard. Second-in-command."

"You?"

"Yeah, don't let the breasts fool you." Remy winked. "I'm fierce."

Kimberly smiled, loosening up. "Yeah well, you won't be in the bedroom, so who will save him then?"

Remy laughed out loud. "I think I'm beginning to like you."

Kimberly gestured for Remy to sit and she joined her on the other end of the couch, curling her feet beneath her.

"So what all did Nico tell you about me?"

"Well, for one, he says you don't enjoy being stood up."

Kimberly blushed as she remembered last night.

"You blush too. Good Lord, where did he find you, out in the backwoods somewhere?"

Kimberly's face flushed further, embarrassed at being teased by Remy.

"Oh hey, I'm sorry. I suck at social situations. I just say what I think and I usually don't think before I talk so…" Remy trailed off, and Kimberly realized they were both sitting there in silence, too embarrassed to continue.

"So other than being stood up…" Kimberly quickly tried to change the subject and break the uncomfortable silence.

"Well, Nico told me you're a Were without a Pack."

Kimberly wasn't sure how much she wanted to reveal to Remy about her family so she waited to see if Remy would say anything else, but unfortunately it looked as if Remy had the same idea and the uncomfortable silence was coming back.

"So, how does it feel to be part of a Pack?" There, the question was general enough without giving away too much information.

"I was raised by the Pack so I've never known anything different. I live and breathe the Pack, which sometimes gets to be a pain, but for the most part it's cool."

"So, how long have you and Nico known each other?"

"We met when we were kids, both of us around seven, but even then he thought he was hot shit." Remy snorted. "I had to protect his ass back then too."

Kimberly couldn't help but to chuckle. The thought of Nico needing anyone, let alone Remy, to protect him was mind-numbing. "Well, thanks I guess. For the ass protecting and all."

"No prob. That's not to say he hasn't saved me a time or two. But I did it with more style. None of his dream-walking 'where are you' bullshit."

"Dream-walking." Kimberly gasped. "It's not just a mate thing."

Damn, now she was even referring to herself as his mate.

"Hell no, it's an annoying Nico thing. Weres of great power often have additional gifts. Nico's is dream-walking. It was one of the reasons he was chosen as *Benadanti*. The position, despite what others might think, isn't always about the better, stronger fighter. To be a true leader, a true *Benadanti*, a Were needs to possess extraordinary power, as well as the ability to see past their own selfish wants and desires. It just sucks that Nico's ability is so damn maddening. I mean, he's a great leader and all, but man, get out of my head when I'm trying to get busy with Will Smith."

Instead of feeling jealous it wasn't something he did with just her, Kimberly felt a kinship with the other woman. "It is a bit annoying."

"I know, as if I don't have something better to do in my sleep then play tag with him." Shaking her head, Remy gave

Kimberly a sympathetic look. "He's a pain in the ass. Are you sure you want him?"

"Very much so." Kimberly was surprised at the truth in her words. She wanted Nico, and she wanted him forever.

Remy sighed. "I guess this means I have to keep him alive for you then."

Kimberly bit back a laugh. Maybe they would get along after all. "I'd appreciate it."

"Think nothing of it."

* * * * *

"So where are you taking me?"

Sparing Kimberly a quick glance, Nico smiled before he turned his eyes back to the road. "It's a surprise."

"I don't like surprises," she pouted prettily.

"You'll like this one."

"You're such a tease."

Nico chuckled at her childlike ways, but refused to give in. He'd given in too much when it came to her and so far it had gotten them nowhere. Kimberly was no closer to admitting she was his mate than she was two nights ago.

It was pretty obvious she was afraid. He still wasn't sure of what though.

"So are you going to tell me what Remy was doing over at your house?" he asked, breaking the silence.

Kimberly looked over at him in amazement. "How did you—?"

Pointing to his nose, Nico laughed when she sighed in frustration.

"You know that is very annoying. And rude. I don't go around sniffing you."

"I didn't sniff you."

"Fine, sniff your apartment."

"I live in a house."

"You're such a little smart-ass," she fumed.

"And you're trying to pick a fight." Releasing his right hand from the wheel, Nico placed it on her thigh. "But I'm not going to fight with you, Kimberly. I'm done with fighting."

"See that's the problem right there, you're the one who thinks he has to be in charge all the time. What about what I want?"

Now they were getting somewhere. Pulling the car over onto the side of the road, Nico cut the engine and turned to face her. "What do you want, *Zingaro*?"

"I want to stop being in heat for once," she muttered, pushing his hand off her thigh. "Do you know how hard it is for me to sit here calmly next to you and not try to climb into your lap?"

"It's the same way for me."

"Sure it is."

Nico took her hand and placed it on his rigid cock. Her eyes widened as her fingers instantly tightened around him. "I've been hard since I was outside your door. Your scent drives me wild, your eyes and lips make me feel crazy. Trust me, *Zingaro*, it isn't just you."

"Why is it like this? I don't understand."

"It's the heat. The way we're built. You're my mate," he whispered as he leaned his head forward to rest against her own. Her hand was steadily stroking him, making it a bit difficult for him to concentrate. "If you would only accept it, things would go a lot better."

Kimberly squeezed him gently before pulling her hand away. "Maybe that's the problem. I'm not used to being a Werewolf, knowing about this kind of stuff. You just accept it because it's part of you. It's not a part of me and I have a hard time blindly accepting these changes to my body and my life."

Nico sighed heavily before adjusting his painfully hard erection. "I understand your reluctance, but just because you don't want it to be, it's not going to disappear. You're a strong Were and you can either struggle against the inevitable or accept your heritage and embrace it."

"Okay, so I'm trying to embrace it. Just don't expect me to jump into the deep end of the pool right away. I'm getting my toes wet in the baby end."

Nico chuckled. "Well, I don't know if I want sex with me compared to the baby end of the pool but okay, we'll take it slow."

Restarting the car, Nico pulled back out onto the highway. "So, back to our original conversation, how was your visit with Remy?"

"You know, you're like a dog with a bone. Do you ever give up?"

"Nope."

"Nope? That's all I get?"

"Call me curious."

"More like nosy," Kimberly muttered under her breath.

"Werewolf hearing over here," Nico reminded her sarcastically.

"Okay, curious, the meeting was fine. Other than the fact I had no fucking idea who she was when she knocked on my door and invited herself in. It might have been nice if you had told me you had a second-in-command."

"I wasn't sure if you were ready for the three foot part of the pool yet."

Kimberly smacked him for his smart-ass comment. "You ought to be a comedian, really, I mean it."

"So what did Remy have to say?"

"Oh my God, I get it. You want to know if Remy has been telling tales about you. Ooh, do you have some embarrassing fact you're trying to hide from me?"

Nico snorted in amusement. The last thing he was worried about was Remy saying anything embarrassing about him because it just couldn't happen. He was an open book and if Kimberly wanted to know anything about him, all she had to do was ask. But he was worried Remy might say something that might offend Kimberly. Sometimes Remy spoke without thinking and although he was used to it, Kimberly was not.

"Ask me anything, *Zingaro*, and I will tell you."

"Anything?"

The interest in her voice amused him. What had his little wolf being thinking about? "Yes, anything."

"This is going sound stupid."

"Go ahead."

"Do you like being a wolf?"

"Like being a wolf?" Nico couldn't keep the surprise out of his voice. Out of all the questions under the sun Kimberly could have asked him, this question shocked him the most.

"Yes." Her embarrassment tinted her cheeks. "Do you enjoy it? I mean, I know you can't help it, but do you mind it?"

"Enjoy and mind are two different things, *Zingaro*." Nico paused as if searching for the right word. "I am what I am. Being a wolf is as natural to me as breathing. I don't know how not to be it. I was raised with the Pack. I grew up with other wolves, running, chasing, living with it day in, day out. For me not to like it would be for me not to like myself."

Kimberly sighed and turned to look out of the window. "So I take that as a yes."

"Yes, I like being a wolf." A grin quickly came to his lips. "But there are times when I do mind it."

"When?"

"The heightened senses can be a pain in the ass on occasions. I would really prefer not to know who's slept with whom or hear conversations not meant to be overheard."

Kimberly smiled as he intended. "And the forced mating can't be all too much fun."

"Oh no. I happen to think it is quite a bit of fun."

Kimberly turned slightly in her seat to stare at him a moment before responding. "I guess maybe if I had been raised as you had, it wouldn't all seem so strange."

"Perhaps. It's the classic nature versus nurture. Will your wolf side overpower your human upbringing?"

Kimberly flopped back in her seat with a dejected sigh. "It's what I'm afraid of. Everything that made me who I am is going to be besieged until the only thing left is a raging animal."

"*Zingaro*, you're being dramatic. You will always be you, whether you are experiencing the mating heat or not. Do you seriously think you are going to start attacking men on the street?"

"Well, I started attacking you with no thought but getting myself satisfied." Kimberly's cheeks were tinged with pink and Nico couldn't help but laugh. "Damn it, Nico, I'm serious. I've never acted the way I have with you and it scares me."

Nico snagged her hand, gently brushing his lips across her knuckles. "Ah, *Zingaro*, I am very glad to hear I am the only man you've attacked. But you must realize this only happens with your destined mate. This is why I know we are meant to be together."

Kimberly pulled her hand away. "Oh come on, you were no virgin, Nico. You can't tell me you've never experienced passion before."

"Passion yes, but the kinds of feelings I have for you far surpass passion." Nico loved Kimberly but he was worried any major declaration after only three days would scare her further away. Nico had been looking all his life for her while she, on the other hand, had been running all of her life from herself.

Kimberly sat quietly for a few minutes and Nico wondered if he had gone too far.

"I never even knew I was a Werewolf until I was five years old." Kimberly's words, seemingly out of nowhere, caught Nico off guard.

He had gotten little follow-up information since the initial revelations about Kimberly and her brother. It seemed as if when their parents left the Pack, they had fallen off the face of the earth. There wasn't any evidence they had interacted with any other members of the Pack since then, and Nico was willing to bet that wasn't a coincidence. "And what happened when you were five?"

"I saw my father change in front of me."

Nico couldn't hide the surprise racing through his system. The image of a naïve five-year-old having to witness something straight out of a horror movie was hard to imagine. "How did it happen?"

"We had just moved — again — this time into the city and I think he was having a hard time adjusting to it." Kimberly gave a shaky little laugh before she continued. "I guess my father and I were a lot alike. Neither one of us handled stress well and one thing led to another and it happened. Of course looking back on it now, I realize he must have put off changing and the new environment must have taken a toll on him, but back then, all I could think was something very wrong was happening to my dad."

"Were you home alone?"

"No, David was there. He ran into the room when he heard me scream, only to do some screaming of his own."

"I can imagine." If Kimberly's father weren't dead, Nico would have killed him on the spot. The scarring the man had done to his children just because he wanted to escape from a war that ended two years after he left was irrepressible.

"No, I really don't think you can. Now I know it's normal, but seeing my father stand before me one second and seeing a big scary animal in front the next, tends to be a bit of a mind-fuck. The worst part, I think, was the not knowing if I was having a nightmare or a psychotic episode. Up until that moment in time, Werewolves weren't real. Monsters didn't sleep in the next room and we were your average normal family."

"What happened then?" Part of him didn't want to know, but at the same time, Nico knew she needed to speak of it. He was more than sure she hadn't spoken of it before. It wasn't as if her family could have taken her to a shrink. How could they explain to a doctor their daughter wasn't insane, she really saw her father turn into a Werewolf and when she turned thirteen, she would too.

"David hustled us into the closet and there we stayed, huddled together until my mother came home. I couldn't go near my father for months. I was scared of him and of what I was."

"And you still are."

"I'm not afraid."

Nico spared her another glance as he pulled into the driveway of The Sanctuary. Easing into his space, Nico turned the car off before he addressed her again. "Do you really believe that?"

"I do," Kimberly stubbornly replied. "Just because I have a hard time dealing with some aspects doesn't mean I'm a suicidal wolf."

"Nope, it just means you're a scaredy-cat," Nico teased.

"Okay, as a wolf, I take exception to your comment."

"As a wolf? Wouldn't you have to know what it means before you take exception to anything?"

Kimberly scrunched her nose as she spoke, defiance written all over her face. Nico was wondering if she would pick up the challenge he had thrown before her. "Fine, I don't know a thing about being a Werewolf. Okay, are you happy?" Before he could reply, she was barreling on with her tirade.

"But you know what, I'm going to learn and prove you wrong, so there."

"You are just like a spitting kitten," Nico teased as he jumped out of the car. He could hear her cursing him through the window as he walked around to open her door. Swinging the door wide, Nico jumped back as Kimberly shot out of the car.

"Are you deliberately baiting me?" Kimberly was stalking toward him before Nico finally grabbed her and pulled her into his arms.

"And if I am?" Nico bent his head to her neck, inhaling her musky scent. He could tell their banter aroused not only her ire but her lust as well.

"I might have to unsheathe my claws and scratch you."

"I might let you."

"Pervert."

"Don't you mean purr-vert?"

At Kimberly's good-natured groan, Nico chuckled and dropped a quick kiss on her neck. "Come on, I want to show you something."

"That's what all the bad wolves say."

Looking around them, Kimberly took in a deep breath, filling her lungs with the fresh forest air. "This place looks a bit different from this side of the forest."

"This side?" Nico tossed her a confused look. "You've been here before."

With a knowing grin, Kimberly nodded. "I guess you don't know everything."

"Remy?" Nico questioned as they walked across the grassy knoll.

"No, not Remy. David and I came over here for a run yesterday."

"Without me? On my land?"

"I didn't know I needed your permission, oh great one."

"Well, now you know." Nico stopped at the top of the hill and slipped his hands into the loops of her pants. Kimberly mockingly fought against him but it was no use. The sooner she realized it the better it would be. "You're walking a fine line, *Zingaro*."

"Am I?"

Nico raised a brow in lieu of commenting and turned Kimberly around until her back was pressed against his chest. This moment was too precious to wile away the moments bickering. They had come there for a reason. It was time Kimberly understood her place in the world.

"This land is ours. We live, fight and die to protect it and each other. Do you feel it, *Zingaro*? The connection to the land. To the earth we tread upon."

"I want to know. I want to understand." Kimberly turned her head slightly to look back at him. "You just need to be patient with me and give me time."

"You have all the time in the world, *Zingaro*." Nico felt Kimberly's body relax at his words. She was beginning to accept and understand her role in the Pack. His heart swelled with pride but it wasn't the only thing swelling.

"It's so beautiful here, the moonlight shining through the trees." Kimberly was gently stroking Nico's arms as she spoke. His beast was ripping and roaring to be set free.

"There is no moonlight, *Zingaro*, it's just a myth. The moon only reflects the light of the sun."

"Are you kidding?"

"No, it's all a part of your perception." Pausing, Nico glanced at her. "Similar to how you perceive your beast. You think it's a part of who you are, when in reality it's what you are. Just because you don't see your beast every day doesn't mean it doesn't shape who you are and what you do in your human form."

Kimberly stood silently for a moment before turning in his arms. "So are we going to go for a run now?"

Chapter Seven

After running from her beast all her life, Kimberly still felt ill at ease about embracing herself, no matter what Nico said. Despite what he'd believed, she didn't hate herself or her beast. She just wasn't sure how to be one without losing the other. And no matter how much they talked about it, she knew she would never get him to understand.

How could he? He was as comfortable in his skin as he was in his fur. It was an attractive feature. Kimberly even envied him a bit but she wasn't now or nor would she ever be him. A lifetime of hiding oneself wouldn't just dissipate because Nico growled at her. No matter how cute he looked when he did it.

Like it or lump it, it was the way things were. And as soon as she could stop staring at Nico's butt as he led them to the clearing, she would tell him.

"Are you ready?"

Glancing up from his ass, Kimberly tried her best to keep a blush from staining her cheeks. Even while giving herself motivating talks, she was thinking about sex. "For what?"

"To change, *Zingaro*."

Change, hell no. Fuck until she couldn't move, oh yes. "Tell me again when this heat thing will be over?"

A wicked gleam twinkled in his eyes as Nico began to unbutton his shirt. "In a hurry to be out from under my spell?"

Slipping her shoes off, Kimberly didn't reply. Her body temperature was rising and she knew from her experience in the office, if she didn't channel her energy, her beast would take over and make the decision for her.

"I didn't say I was in a hurry." Her actions belied her words as Kimberly quickly began stripping off her clothes, eager to be as naked as Nico seemed to be. She was sure she could convince him to fool around a little. Finally slipping off her panties, Kimberly stood transfixed as she stared at Nico. His sculpted body put the gods to shame. Kimberly's lips were dry as paper and she had to consciously close her mouth to keep from gaping at him.

"I guess not." Nico's words jumbled around in her head and Kimberly had to sort out what he was saying. Her body felt on fire and it didn't help to see he was responding just as eagerly to her.

"Umm, aren't we going for a run?" Although it had been the furthest thing from her mind initially, Kimberly decided since she had just made a big fool of herself, it was better to be in wolf form where her blushing wouldn't be so apparent.

Nico grinned and Kimberly knew he had caught on to her ploy. Dipping her head, she allowed her hair to fall forward, hiding her flushed cheeks. Concentrating for a moment, Kimberly gave herself up to the beast, allowing the animal to break free. It never hurt, in fact it felt quite freeing, but Kimberly knew from experience it wasn't pretty. From an observer's point of view, it would appear as if a monster were escaping from within her body, when in reality it was just the merging of bones, flesh and fur, bring life to a different form of herself. Suddenly she was sitting on the ground, staring at Nico standing before her. She stood and gently rubbed against Nico's legs, enjoying the tactile feeling of his skin on her fur.

Nico ruffled her gray fur teasingly before he suddenly was sitting before her. This was the first time Kimberly had seen Nico in his wolf form outside her dream. She sat back on her haunches, staring at him as hungrily as she had a few minutes ago. Kimberly couldn't believe the heat was just as intense in her beast form as when she was human. She thought the feelings would dissipate somewhat. Unfortunately she had been wrong.

Nico bumped his large snout against her shoulder, jarring her from her musings and urging her to stand. Loping ahead of her a short distance, Nico barked once, encouraging her to follow him. Kimberly took off down the hill, following Nico along the tree line.

The wind zipped through her fur as she sailed after him. For the first time in a long time, Kimberly actually ran joyfully. Not to exercise her beast, not to relieve tension, but for the pure fun of it all.

A sweet scent assaulted her senses, stopping her in tracks. Veering off the path Nico had made for her, she turned sharply to the left and into the deep forest. Nico's growl of annoyance spurred her on and soon the chaser was the chasee.

Fueled on by his warning snarl, Kimberly sped up, dodging branches and debris in her way. She could smell water ahead. The crisp smell of the spring urged her on.

If she could make it to the water ahead, she might be able to lose him. Of course, she hadn't figured into her deviant little plan how well Nico knew the area. Before she reached the woodland clearing, he was on her. They tumbled round and round before he landed on top of her, teeth deep in her flank.

Gotcha!

With a warning growl, Nico released her and pranced back. His gaze urged her on. Struggling to her feet, Kimberly hung her head as if in defeat, and when Nico stepped toward her, she turned the tables, pouncing on him, knocking him to the ground.

His yelp of surprise was reward enough. Jumping off, she took off through the bush, laughing as she reached the water's edge ahead of him.

Off into the water she went. Cavorting through the cool stream as if she were a hapless pup. Kimberly rolled onto her side, wetting her entire body before jumping back onto the bank. With a quick twist of her body, she shook the water from her fur with ease, still high from her pounce.

Looking around for Nico, Kimberly was surprised to see him stepping out of the forest in human form, his long legs eating up the distance between them. The heat immediately hit her deep in her belly and she knew she wanted him. With a quick decision, Kimberly focused her wolfish mind on her human form and transformed herself just as Nico reached her.

"You have been a very bad *Lupa*," Nico drawled, stopping just in front of her. Kimberly swayed as the scent of their combined arousal hit her. She raised her hand shakily, placing it on his chest. The beat of his heart and the heat radiating off him warmed her body and soul.

"Nico, I need you." Kimberly tilted her head and swiped her tongue over his chest, tasting the salty residue there. Nico growled appreciatively and pulled her close, pressing their bodies together. Kimberly could feel the evidence of his arousal. Snaking her hand between them, she grasped his cock, wrapping her fingers around him.

"Are you trying to tempt me?"

Kimberly laughed huskily. "Is it working?"

"Damn right it is." Nico didn't seem too worried. In fact, he was rocking his hips, encouraging her strokes.

"Good." Kimberly suddenly stepped back and dropped to her knees in front of Nico. Staring at him for a moment, she licked her lips invitingly. Nico growled back in response.

Kimberly's tongue swept across his cock, tasting the salty drops of pre-cum along the tip—slowly tracing the shaft with her tongue down to the base and then back up again. Circling her tongue around the mushroom tip, Kimberly licked his cock in slow, luxurious strokes.

Nico groaned his appreciation, spurring her on. Kimberly slipped the head of his cock in her mouth, gently sucking. Nico snagged his fingers in her hair, pulling her toward him. Kimberly struggled for a moment to open her mouth wider before she relaxed. Nico fucked her mouth tenderly, gradually quickening his pace.

Kimberly had never imagined sucking a man's cock could be so arousing. She had always believed it was strictly done as a favor. But here she was, Nico's cock in her mouth, and her pussy was wet and her nipples were hard. She knew if Nico touched her right now, she would probably come in an instant.

Suddenly Nico pulled back, staggering slightly as if under a large weight. "No, no more. I want to fuck you, Kimberly."

Kimberly dropped back to the ground, smiling at Nico. She definitely wanted to fuck him too. Nico dropped to the ground beside her, pushing her legs wide. Taking his cock in his hand, he centered it at her moist opening. "I don't think so," Kimberly murmured, pushing his hand away. "This is my coming-out party, remember?"

"As you wish, *Zingaro*." Nico chuckled, moving his hand innocently up in the air. "But it will be difficult for me to pull out of you when you're riding me."

"That's okay, I don't want you to." Turning the tables on him, Kimberly pushed him back to the ground and quickly straddled his body. "I want you to come inside me."

"You know what this means, *Zingaro*. If I come inside you, I'll knot. Your fear of pregnancy, however remote, may be realized."

"I know, Nico, but I don't care." Kimberly knew in her heart that she was his mate, even though she still wasn't sure what all it entailed. With one hand on his shoulder to steady her, Kimberly slowly lowered herself onto his rigid length. "Now I'm in charge. No more talking. I want to fuck you."

The words hissed from deep within her throat as his thick erection stretched her full. *God, he felt great.* It seemed as if days had passed instead of mere hours since he had been deep inside her.

"Ahh…" Nico closed his eyes, laying his head back on the ground.

Kimberly couldn't agree more. She felt powerful and vulnerable all at once. Nico felt heavenly inside her. His cock, hard and unyielding, thrust farther in her channel than he had ever been before. The pleasure mingled with hints of pain and the intensity made her want to cry.

Gripping him with her knees, Kimberly rose unsteadily before plunging down on his cock again. The grass-covered soft earth made for the perfect bed, seemingly designed by nature for their pleasure alone.

Her breath slipped from her parted lips like a whispered prayer. As she clung to his tense shoulders, Kimberly sank and rose with an unsteady rhythm. Her muscles milking his cock as she trembled with passion.

"*Zingaro.*" Nico's hands quickly moved to her hips, urging her, guiding her into riding him faster. His nails bit into her thighs as she moved to his pace.

It had been too long for Kimberly to hold back her passion. She had held it at bay for far too long and now with her beast sedate from their run, it was time for her to feast.

As much as she wanted to torture and tease Nico, she wanted to come even more. Nico seemed to be of the same accord. Working his hand up her thighs, Nico's wandering fingers centered on her aching bud and did some teasing of its own.

"Fuck...fuck..." he moaned, flexing inside her.

So much for being in charge.

With a circular motion, Nico quickly brought her to the edge. Kimberly's body trembled with pleasure as she gyrated her hips, fucking him with all the strength she had left.

"Nico...Nico..." she chanted as she exploded around him.

Nico wasn't far behind her. He pushed into her with frenzied pumps. His hands now returned to her hips, working her back and forth, forcing Kimberly to ride him to his own bittersweet end. Nico cried out her name as he erupted inside her.

Kimberly gasped as the knot Nico had warned her about blossomed, spreading inside her like a fist. The fullness had her gasping at its intensity.

"Breathe, *Zingaro*. It may be a while before we unlock." Nico stroked her back and hips, soothing her with his touch. Nico's cock continued to spurt as the knot locked them together, allowing his seed to find its way to fertile ground or what she hoped was fertile ground. The thought of kids before had always scared Kimberly, but as she felt her body welcome him into her own, she could almost imagine a little boy with Nico's roguish smile.

"What's this smile for?"

Kimberly knew she was probably grinning like a fool but she just shook her head. "Wouldn't you like to know?"

"Brat."

After several minutes Kimberly gradually felt the knot beginning to dissipate, but the aftershocks from the experience reverberated through her womb.

Groaning, she dropped her head forward onto his damp chest, exhausted from the inside out. "Wow. I should be in charge more often."

Nico guffawed at her bravado, gently squeezing her ass. "I don't think my heart could handle it."

"You'll just have to try."

"You're talking as if you're planning to stick around for a while."

Happy he couldn't see her face, Kimberly smiled. "I heard a rumor somewhere about wolves mating for life."

"It's not a rumor."

"Then I guess I'll have to stick around for a while."

His deep chuckle resonated in her ear. "As if you had any choice."

Kimberly rose and looked at him mockingly. "I can count, wolf boy. This whole heat thing should have run its course in two days."

"The heat will never completely go away, *Zingaro*. Besides that's not what I was talking about. I'm not letting you go, heat or no heat. My scent is in you now, all around you. Everyone will know who you belong to."

"You're not letting me go?" Kimberly had to fight the childish urge not to roll her eyes. He was so damn Alpha sometimes it was sickening. Lucky for him, this wasn't one of those times. "Just for the record, you can't just keep me, especially if I don't want to be kept, and I don't belong to you."

"That's the beauty of it, *Zingaro*. I have no doubt you do want to be kept and you very much belong to me, just as I belong to you."

Any second now, she was going to call him a liar. Yep, any second. Wait, who was she kidding, everything about this man did it for her, even the stuff that used to annoy her. She was in love and the damn fool knew it. Snorting, Kimberly eased off him and onto her side. "Conceited, aren't we?"

"Not this part of we," he teased, sitting up. "But I'm not so sure about your part."

"Ass."

"Brat."

"Caveman."

"Mate."

Narrowing her gaze, Kimberly crossed her hands over her chest. "As in checkmate?"

"No." Nico rose to his feet and then pulled her into his arms. "As in life mate."

Kimberly wrapped her arms around his neck. "Always have to have the last word, don't you."

"Yes, I do." Nico laughed before sweeping Kimberly into his arms and striding toward the edge of the lake.

"Don't you dare!" Kimberly wrapped her arms tightly around his neck, worried about being dropped into the cool water.

"I should drop you just for thinking such a thing." Nico began walking into the water, grimacing slightly at the cold. "A wolf cares for his mate, which means protecting her from harm as well as seeing to her comfort."

Kimberly hung her head in embarrassment. She was going to get a hold of this mate thing eventually.

Waist-deep in the water, Nico gently lowered Kimberly, allowing her time to adjust to the changing temperature. He swiftly washed away the evidence of their lovemaking.

"Don't brood, *Zingaro*, you will trust me soon enough." Kimberly smiled wryly, not surprised he had read her face so easily.

Splashing water at Nico, Kimberly laughed at his shocked look. "Hey, I stopped brooding."

"So you want to play, huh?" Nico began stalking after her. Laughing, she stepped back and lost her footing, sinking under the water. Coming up sputtering, Nico was immediately at her side, brushing her wet hair from her face. "Careful, *Zingaro*, you don't want to injure yourself."

"State the obvious, why don't you?" Kimberly ducked back under the water in order to sweep her hair back. Breaking the surface, she was surprised to see Nico turned toward the bank. Glancing over his shoulder she ducked behind him quickly when she saw three wolves on the shore.

"Nico, who are they? What's going on?"

"What's going on," he repeated stonily, "is exactly what I would like to know."

Nico couldn't remember last time he was this angry. It wasn't as if The Sanctuary were his private lovers' oasis, but the audacity Franklin and his cronies had to bother them when there was no emergency made him see red.

Just the way the Weres watched them as they walked out onto the bank, made his hackles rise. There was something predatory, more so than usual, about Franklin's stare, which thrust Nico's beast forward and he had to fight himself not to change.

Frowning down at the wolves, Nico held his hand out to Kimberly, who took it hesitantly.

"Don't be afraid," he warned her silently.

"Damn it," she growled back, tightening her hand in his. *"I thought you weren't going to pop into my head anymore."*

"Do you really want to have this conversation aloud?"

"Good point."

With noses in the air, the wolves stalked toward them carefully. Nico tensed as he waited to see what they would do. If they pounced, he would rip into them faster than they could howl. Part of him wanted the confrontation to happen, but the other part knew this was neither the time nor the place.

But there would be.

And it would be soon.

The wolves stopped a few feet from them and rapidly changed into their human forms. Franklin, flanked by Clarkson and Keith, two of the other *Maggiore*, stood in front of them with frowns marring their aging faces.

"Wow, I could have gone all day without seeing that."

"What?"

"Old Were penis. How gross."

Kimberly's comment was so unexpected, Nico burst out laughing, confusing the men standing before him.

"Benandanti, how fortuitous to find you here." Franklin's smarmy voice grated on Nico's nerves. Did the Were really

think Nico was so stupid he couldn't figure out Franklin and the Supremes had tracked him here?

"What do you want?" Nico decided there was no reason to be all politically correct and act as if he were happy to see them. And he especially didn't like the way Keith was eying Kimberly. He growled menacingly, causing the older man to step back hastily.

"Perhaps it would be better to speak to you privately," Franklin said, nodding toward Kimberly.

Nico could feel Kimberly pressed against his back and knew there was no way he was sending her away. The fucking *Maggiore* were just going to have to deal. "Sorry, but anything you say in front in me can be said in front of Kimberly."

Franklin sneered but Clarkson was never one able to control his temper. "*Benandanti*, this is completely unacceptable. How dare you bring a mutt into the Pack? You have no idea of her breeding or lineage. This is just another example of your utter lack of leadership."

Allowing his beast to break free, if only a little, Nico's arm shot out and he wrapped his hand around Clarkson's throat. "Never insult her again or so help me God, *Maggiore* or no, you won't live until the next full moon." Clarkson's hands were scrabbling at Nico, trying to break his grip on him.

"Enough," Franklin drawled. Nico found it interesting Franklin did the minimum he needed to defend his so-called friends. They were clueless, not realizing they were just lackeys in his struggle for power and domination.

Nico released Clarkson, flicking him like a bug. He landed on his ass, coughing and choking. Keith knelt to help him to his feet. "The rest of the *Maggiore* will hear about this, *Benandanti*. You can't abuse members of your own Pack in such a callous fashion."

"It is especially heinous since you are embracing such...degenerates as the Morbauch clan." Franklin had to add his two cents, but Nico noticed he was smart enough to keep Kimberly out of his insults.

"Gentlemen, you may not approve of me or my methods, but until I am dead, I'm the *Benandanti* and I will rule as I see fit."

Kimberly gasped from behind him. "*Dead? Nico, what you are saying? Don't give them any fucking ideas.*"

"*Don't worry*, Zingaro, *I'm not giving them any ideas they don't already have.*"

"*You're not making my feel any better.*"

"*Sorry, my love, I didn't know I was supposed to.*" Nico turned his attention back to the Weres in front of him. "If we are through, gentlemen…?"

"We are for now." Franklin shot a murderous look at Kimberly before transforming back to his lesser self. The other two quickly followed suit, leaving Nico and Kimberly alone once more.

"Wow, that was fun," she said aloud, coming from behind him. "So they're a part of the stellar clan you continuously brag about?"

Nico smiled at her remark. "Every family has their black sheep…or wolves, as the case may be."

"I think they're a lot more deadly than you give them credit for."

"Trust me, *Zingaro*, I'm not taking their threats or them lightly."

"So what should we do?"

"We?" Nico had to admit he liked the sound of the word *we* on her lips.

Shrugging her shoulders, Kimberly looked a bit sheepish. "Well, you're the one going on and on about you being my mate. I can't have you killed off just yet."

He was having a hard time keeping his smile at bay. "Not just yet. Well, we are going go back to the clearing and change. Then I'm going to contact Remy and call a meeting."

"And then what?"

"We're going hunting."

"Hunting?" Confusion flickered in her eyes.

"Yes." Nico looked into the thicket into which the wolves had disappeared. "For a traitor."

* * * * *

The loud music from The Howler resonated through the thick walls, filling the quiet meeting room with welcoming noise. This was the quietest it had ever been with them all together as a group but that was part of the problem. They weren't all together.

At least not as a group. One of them was working for someone else. It was just a matter of figuring out who it was.

There was a chink in their armor, an obvious missing entity that was replaced by fear and distrust, and if they didn't act quickly, it would devour them whole.

Everyone was on edge. They could all tell something was up and they sat as if waiting for the other shoe to drop.

"So…" Harrison started, the first one of the group who dared speak. "What's with all the cloak-and-dagger stuff?"

"What do you mean?" Nico countered, taking a drink from his beer.

"I mean, you call this emergency meeting and yet when we get here, we're all sitting around staring at one another. What's up with that?"

"Well, we're not all here for one."

Kellen looked around, bewildered. "Who are we waiting on?"

"Jace."

Remy's groan resonated throughout the room. "Jace?"

"Do you think that's a good idea?" Derek asked, glancing between Remy and him.

Nico's nostrils flared in irritation. "Would I have invited him if I didn't?"

Having to explain his decisions to them was rankling his temper. Truth be told, he was still irritated from his run-in with the *Maggiore* two days ago. Now he was sitting in a room with someone he treated like a brother but who was truly a traitor. It had him up in arms.

"There's a traitor among us."

His words drew everyone's attention to him. Suddenly everyone erupted with questions.

"What the hell do you mean?"

"Who?"

"What's happened?"

Remy walked over to the table, slamming her beer on the poker table, effectively silencing all the questions. "Let the *Benandanti* speak."

"I know someone has been revealing information from our meetings to the *Maggiore*. It's nothing they wouldn't have learned eventually but to know the discussions we have here are being leaked is a major betrayal to me and the Pack."

Ryan pushed the door open and peeked his head in. "Sorry to interrupt."

"What is it?"

"Phone call for you, Nico. It's Jace."

Frowning, Nico stood and made his way across the room. "What did he want?"

"Wouldn't say. All he said was he wanted to talk to you."

"Thanks." Nico took the phone and walked to the corner of the room. He knew everyone could hear the conversation, he just wanted the appearance of privacy, if nothing else. "What's up, Jace?"

"Something's coming up. I can't meet you there." Jace sounded rushed and a bit panicked. "I want you to meet me at The Sanctuary at midnight."

"Why? What's going on?"

"I can't talk about it now. Just come alone."

"Ja—" Nico's words were halted by the dial tone.

"Bad news?" Harrison was the epitome of the understatement.

"Jace can't make it. We're going to meet at midnight at The Sanctuary."

"Midnight? This is really fucking with my plans for the evening."

"Damn, Derek, don't you ever take a break?" Jackson shook his head in amazement.

"I'm no nerdy boy like you. I love the ladies." Derek ducked as Jackson threw a punch his way. "Missed me."

"No need to worry about your love life, Derek. I'm meeting him alone." Nico stared thoughtfully at the phone in his hand.

"I don't think this is such a good idea, Nico. Not with all the trouble we've been having." Remy was ever diligent in her role as *Venator*.

"I appreciate your concern, but it was at Jace's request."

"Fuck Jace." Remy gestured for Kellen to rise from his seat and sat in his stead. "I'm not going to let you go out there by yourself."

"I don't recall asking your permission." Nico's cool comment silenced the room, stunning everyone, including Remy, who was staring at him in shock.

"Nico, you can't be serious." Kellen said softly. "Questioning someone's loyalties is one thing, but to go by yourself would be just foolish. You're leaving yourself open to be assassinated."

"And if I take someone with me, will their presence guarantee I won't be assassinated?"

"You will, if you stop being foolish and take me with you," Remy stated with a frown.

"If you're not the traitor."

Eyes widening, Remy pushed back from the table, toppling her chair as she stood. "You doubt my loyalty?"

"Of course he didn't mean it the way it sounded, Remy." Harrison stood as did everyone else in the room who was watching the pair warily.

The tension was deafening as everyone waited for him to counter what Remy had said and set things straight. But he couldn't and wouldn't give them the satisfaction. Someone had betrayed them. "All I know is, three can keep a secret, Remy, if two are dead."

Remy took a step forward, stopped only by Harrison's grip on her arm. The other Were leaned forward and tried to whisper in her ear but was prevented by her hand, held up to silence him.

"Let her go, Harrison," Nico ordered, stepping around Derek, who foolishly moved to stop him. A low growl had Derek backing up as the room parted and Remy and he faced off. "Do you have something you want to say?"

Shaking Harrison's hand away, Remy moved until they were breaths apart. "Is the power going to your head, *Benandanti*, are the *Maggiore* right?"

"Do you really think I can't do this job without you?" he countered, steeling himself against the pain in her eyes.

"I'll guess we'll see." With her parting shot, Remy walked around Nico, pushing past Ryan who was standing against the wall in shock.

"Remy," Kellen called, moving to follow her.

"Leave her be," Nico said, sitting again in his chair. "We don't have time for her little temper tantrums."

"*Benandanti*, Remy is just concerned about your welfare." Harrison was attempting to be a peacemaker. By all rights, Nico could have her killed if he truly questioned her loyalty.

As he looked around the room at the faces of the men he had grown up with and fought with all his life, Nico could barely stomach the idea one of them was the traitor. It should show as clearly as the scarlet letter, but instead they all looked a little shocked and confused. All except for one. Nico paused thoughtfully before turning to Harrison.

"I will not continue to be questioned. I am your *Benandanti* and I refuse to constantly explain my decisions." Nico stood and stared at the group for a moment longer. "We will meet again tomorrow but not here, at Sanctuary. At which time I will reveal the traitor." Leaving them with his final thought, he exited the back room and made his way through the bar.

Stepping out into the cool night, Nico stopped for a moment then turned and smiled.

"So, did we get the reaction you were expecting?" Remy's voice drifted around him, although anyone looking at him would not have seen her. She blended into the shadows.

"Even better than I had hoped." Nico smiled as Remy stepped up beside him and smacked him in the arm.

"Just remember, you need me."

"How could I ever forget with you constantly needling me, ever-present, never-ending—" Remy shoved him then, cutting off his words.

"You wanna start something?" Remy danced around like a boxer, pretending to punch at him.

"As much as I would love to *dance*," emphasizing the word, "we both better get out of here before the boys decide to leave and see us chatting."

"You never let me have any fun." Remy pouted.

"Poor baby, guess I'll have to let you catch the traitor tonight."

"You have yourself a deal." Remy and Nico both silently melted into the shadows as the bar door opened and Kellen and Derek stepped out onto the empty sidewalk.

Chapter Eight

ഔ

"If he's not here in another ten minutes, we're leaving," David grumbled, plopping onto the barstool next to Kimberly.

"I don't recall inviting you in the first place."

"You didn't have to."

"So, I shouldn't have to listen to you grumble either."

Narrowing his eyes, David refrained from saying anything. Not as if it would do any good in the first place. Kimberly was past the time when she listened to anything he said. So headstrong and naïve, two qualities that were going to lead her straight into trouble and Nico was in it up to his scruffy little neck.

"What time did he say he'd be here?"

"Eleven-ish."

"He said eleven-ish? What a pansy."

Kimberly tossed him an annoyed look. "No, his secretary did."

"So wait a minute. He couldn't even take the time to call you himself? He had his secretary call and order you to show up here?" David was not liking this guy one bit. If the asshole thought he could order David's baby sister around, he had another think coming. And David sure as shit didn't like the idea of Kimberly taking those orders.

"He didn't order me. Jeez, you make him sound as if he's some kind of dictator. He's a busy man. His secretary called and asked me to come."

David thought he was going to throw up. The Nico lovefest was sickening.

"Don't give me that face," Kimberly chided. "Nico had a rough day. He was going to talk to the *Maggiore* and—"

"Fine, he's a wonderful guy." David wasn't interested in a blow-by-blow account of Nico's day. Picking up his beer, David took a swig and glanced around the bar. It was about three-quarters filled and most of them were Were. For all his good looks and sissy boy getups, Nico had shitty taste in hangouts. The bar, if that was what they could call this pissant of a watering hole, was lacking in several departments. Décor, drinks and dames, just to name a few. There were more Were-animals in there to suit David's peace of mind and the music sucked balls too. This was not his idea of a way to spend a Monday night, but he had come for Kimberly's sake. And boy did she owe him big time.

Even if she didn't want to admit it.

"Look, I'm going to the ladies' room to freshen up. I'll be back in just a minute." Kimberly slid off her stool and tugged at the short skirt she was wearing. David couldn't stand the more risqué clothing Kimberly was wearing now. In fact, it really pissed him off. His Kimmie, the kid he had practically raised, preferred denim and jerseys over leather and lace. The new half-dressed *Kimberly*, who was showing all her business to everybody, needed to be sent back to her room and in a hurry.

"So what, do you expect me to hold your purse or something?"

Kimberly rolled her eyes. "No, I'm taking it with me. No need to worry about the homo factor." Spinning on her heel, she walked to the back of the building. David turned back to the bar, catching the attention of the bartender.

"Get me another beer."

"Make it two."

David went as still as the night as an older Were made himself comfortable on the barstool next to him. The bar was filled but it wasn't overflowing. There were plenty of empty

155

seats available so David saw no need for the man to sit next to him. This Were's presence made him uneasy. He didn't growl that way.

The Were must have sensed his unease because he looked over at David and chuckled, "Hackles down, junior. I'm just here to enjoy a drink."

"There are plenty of seats for you to enjoy your drink on."

"Yes, but none next to someone who came in with Cassamonti's mate."

David turned to the dark-haired man and frowned. He hated when he was right. It was about to rain shit everywhere, starting with the son of a bitch next to him. "Can I help you with anything?"

"You're new around this part, aren't you?"

"Are you taking a survey?"

"There've been a lot of new faces popping up. I just like to keep track of them. It's nice to know who's on whose side."

"I wasn't aware there were sides."

Taking a sip of his beer, the man peered out onto the dance floor. "There're always sides, son. Always."

Everything about this Were rubbed David the wrong way, from the sour smell wafting from him to his presumptuous attitude. These were the bastards who were after Nico and if they were enemies of Nico, then they were against his sister. And anyone against Kimberly automatically became enemies of David.

"I suggest you take your beer and move on, old man."

Instead of heeding David's warning, the man smiled at him. "And I suggest you talk to your sister about the company she keeps. She's a pretty little bitch."

The blaring music did little to cover the growl David emitted at his threat. Several Weres turned in their direction, including the bartender, who quickly made his way toward them. "Is there a problem here, Franklin?"

"Not at all." Franklin dropped a few bills on the bar and stood. "We were just clearing the air."

"Yes," David said, committing the fellow's face to memory. "Consider the air cleared."

At the very first opportunity, he was going to wipe the floor with the bastard.

"I think you're through here too, mister."

"I'm not leaving until my sister gets back." The bartender sneered at David but turned back to the crowd to take an order.

"Miss me?" Kimberly hopped on the stool Franklin had just seconds earlier vacated.

"Yeah, I almost called missing persons." David knew he was being rude but this latest confrontation was just another example of why his family had left the Were community—too many politics. "Look, I think I'm going to get out of here."

"Is everything okay?" Kimberly was looking concerned and David didn't want to have to explain how her boyfriend had some mean-ass enemies and unfortunately they were a part of Nico's own Pack.

"Yeah, everything's fine. You were right. I never should have tagged along." David stood and began to shrug into his jacket.

"Hey." Kimberly tugged on his sleeve. "I appreciate you coming."

"Yeah, yeah, yeah." He rolled his eyes, much to her amusement.

"I love you, butthead."

David dropped a quick kiss on her cheek. "Call me when you get home."

"Yes, master."

"Kimberly—"

"Fine, I'll call."

With a final glance in the direction of the watchful bartender, David headed out of the bar. Just as he reached the exit, the heavy wood door flew open and Kimberly's boss Cassandra walked in, bumping right into him.

"Sorry," she laughed, backing up.

Good Lord, there was that sweet smell again. Looking down at the petite blonde, David felt his mouth go dry. He would recognize her scent anywhere. The smell of dried roses and sunlight drifted around him as she tried to step out of his path and David had to do everything in his power not to pounce on her like the horny animal he was. "No apology necessary, Cassandra."

Stepping out of the way of the incoming traffic, Cassandra lifted a brow questionably. "Well, well, well, if it isn't…"

What a flirt, David thought with a smile. "Ah, don't tell me you don't remember me?"

"Well, you do look familiar." And so did she. David remembered when he first laid eyes on her at Kimberly's office. Even as upset as he was, there was no way he could miss looking at this hot little package. She was the epitome of the California girl with blonde hair, sun-kissed skin and brilliant blue eyes.

David wondered if he dropped to all fours and shoved his head under her dress, if his name would come back to her. "We met a couple of days ago."

"We did?"

"At your office. I'm Kimberly's brother."

"David, like the dog." Her smile relaxed and appeared more genuine.

"The dog, yeah." David couldn't help but shoot Kimberly a murderous look, although he had to admit it was his own fault. But still, he would have thought she could have come up with a better cover.

"Oh I'm sorry." Covering her smile with her hand, Cassandra blushed under his wary stare. "How rude of me. God, what you must go through having a dog named after you."

"Kimmie has a sick sense of humor."

"I knew there was something I liked about her."

All of a sudden David was in less of a hurry to leave the bar. "So what are you doing here?"

"I was driving by and decided to stop in. I've always wanted to come in and tonight I thought, why not."

"Ahh, you don't want to drink here." Especially smelling and looking as good as she did. David would have to neuter a few Weres tonight if they did.

"Why not?"

"The drinks are watered down, the beer is overpriced and the company is definitely something to be desired."

"I don't know." She eyed him with a secretive little smile. "I think the company is just fine."

"Hey, didn't I tell you to get out of here?" The loudmouth bartender was heading in their direction and David's hackles were on the rise. Not only did this guy piss him off just for being an asshole, the way he was looking at Cassandra made David want to tear him limb from limb.

"Uh-oh, did you get into trouble?" Cassandra teased.

"Guess I pissed off the wrong guy." David silently cursed his bad luck. Just when he thought he might be able to get to know Cassandra, he was getting thrown out in the cold and this dickwad was going to be coming on to her.

"I ain't gonna tell you again. It's time you left." The bartender had come out from behind the bar and the nearby patrons had stopped drinking and decided to enjoy the floorshow instead. But before he could retort, Cassandra surprised him by slipping her arm through his.

"Well, looks as if we better go. Come on." With a tug Cassandra headed back out the door, David in tow. Throwing a glance over his shoulder, David bared his teeth at the bartender.

Stepping out into the cool night air, David stopped Cassandra for a moment. "Hey, you didn't have to leave, you know. You never even got to talk to Kimberly."

"Oh it's all right. I think she'll understand."

David smiled, swelling with pride because this beautiful woman wanted to spend time with him. "Well, where do you want to go? The night is too young to end this early."

"Well." Glancing at her watch, Cassandra bit gently into her lip, something David desperately wanted to do for her instead. "I did skip dinner. I don't suppose you want to go grab something to eat?"

If he were eating between her legs, then David was all in. "I would love to."

"Any place in particular?"

"This is your city, you decide."

"Hmmm…a man who doesn't mind giving up control. I like that," Cassandra teased with a wink before walking away.

* * * * *

The dinner was great, conversation flowed and three hours after they left the bar, David was pushing Cassandra's pants down her thighs. If he said he hadn't planned for this to happen, he would have been lying, but he'd been around the block plenty of times to know his plans meant jack shit. Women, Were or otherwise, made the call when it came to sex and anyone else saying differently were liars or fools.

Without waiting for a word, David pushed her down on the bed and quickly began to undress. When his pants dropped to the floor, Cassandra's gasp of surprise halted him in his tracks. Fuck!

In his haste to finally get a taste of her, David had forgotten one of the reasons he had stayed celibate for so long.

He was well-hung.

For him it was more of a curse than a blessing. Human women didn't handle sex with a Werewolf too well. David vividly remembered his first girlfriend who literally fainted at the sight of his cock. Normally a guy might think it was a good thing, but in his case, he knew it was a problem.

Hard as hell, David eyed her warily. Gone was the uncontrollable lust swimming in her eyes mere moments earlier. Now Cassandra stared at him with a look of awe and trepidation on her pretty face. "Wow."

"I was just thinking the same thing," he teased, trying to lighten the mood.

"You're huge."

"Because of you."

Cassandra chuckled roughly. "I'd say because of Mother Nature."

"You can handle it."

"You think?"

David wiggled his brows leeringly. "I know, but just to be sure." David dropped a kiss on her nose before moving down her delectable body. "I'll make sure you're more than ready."

As he settled between her splayed thighs, he stared hungrily at her glistening mound. Never before had such a delicacy been presented to him for his enjoyment. Sure, David had pleased woman with his mouth before but he could tell, just from the sweet scent of her arousal, that this time it would be entirely his pleasure as well.

Cassandra's bare pussy beckoned him forth and David was quick to answer its call.

She tasted as great as she looked. Her spicy flavor had his cock swelling even greater, desperate to enter hot pussy. David feasted on her luscious flesh, his tongue spearing into

161

her hot, tight channel as she undulated beneath him. Yet he couldn't get enough of her.

It was as if her fluids were a river of aphrodisiac. Every lick, every drink from between her luscious lips, was better than the one before. The more he tasted, the more he wanted her. She was addictive and she was his.

"David… Jeez…oh my…"

David growled in response, as his tongue drove deeper inside her hot pussy. Still it wasn't enough. He had to possess her. Moving his probing tongue from her hot channel to erect clit, David eased his fingers into her slick pussy, taking up where his mouth had left off. He pumped his fingers with a rhythm that matched that of his stroking tongue.

"God yes…" she moaned. "Fuck me. Fuck me."

He had every intention of fucking her, but on his time.

David could feel Cassandra's body tightening around his fingers as he thrust them into her clinching pussy. She was close to coming. Her pending release filled his nostrils with the sweetest of scents, but David wasn't ready for her to come. No, this way was too easy.

He wanted her to work for it. To feel as if her body were breaking in two. He knew what she needed. Even if she didn't.

David pulled his fingers from her body, much to Cassandra's dismay. "What…don't stop!"

The desperation in her voice amused him. "Who's in control here?"

"What?" she asked confused.

"I said." David moved his soaked fingers to the pucker of her anus, gently teasing it with feathery-light strokes. Her body tensed as he pressed against her resisting entrance, but he wouldn't be deterred. "Who's in control here?"

"You are."

"Your sweet pussy, your luscious ass, they belong to me. For as long as I say."

162

"Yes."

"Say it."

"My pussy and my ass belong to you."

"And don't you forget it." He quickly moved his head down as he tilted her ass up and swiped his tongue against her rosette, coating it with a mixture of her juices and his saliva. Cassandra's cry of pleasure rang out around him as he stiffened his tongue and pushed it inside her tight passage, preparing her there as he had prepared her pussy earlier. His fingers soon replaced his tongue, one at a time until he had three pumping digits inside her, spearing her ass as he feasted on her mound once more.

Cassandra let out a moan so loud it almost sounded as if she were baying. Her body trembled violently as she came, screaming his name, hands digging into his flesh, marking him as he wanted to mark her.

David's own animalistic growl soon accompanied hers as he pulled his fingers from her tight hole and reared up his to knees. His need to fill her now outweighed every other need in his soul.

"Do you trust me?"

His words startled her. "What do you mean?"

Reaching over to the floor, David pulled his belt from his pants loops and brought it to her view. He rolled the belt on his hand, buckle flat on his hand, buried under the mound of leather. When it was wrapped until only an inch or two was left hanging free, David ran it over her flat stomach. "Do you trust me?"

"To do what?" The curiosity overrode the fear in her voice.

"To bind you to this bed and please you until you go mad."

Cassandra's eyes widened a bit as her tongue sneaked out to moisten her lips. "You're asking for a lot, aren't you?"

163

"Just everything you have to give."

"And then some."

David leaned over and took her hands into his, moving them one by one until they were over her head. He watched her the entire time, waiting for a "stop" or a "no". When none came, he slowly began to unwind the belt. "If you don't want this, say so now."

Cassandra's deep breathing was answer enough as he bound her hands together. She looked so submissive trussed up before him. So vulnerable. Awaiting his every command.

"You're protected, right?"

"Yes."

"Are you sure you want this?" He knew what her body was saying but he wanted to her say it aloud.

"Yes, yes, just fuck me. Please fuck me."

"I do so love the sound of 'please' on your lips." David gripped his cock in his hand, angling it toward her hot pussy. Cassandra tensed when he pressed his thick head against her and moved as if she were bracing herself for his girth.

Despite being aroused out of his mind, David held himself back, knowing if he didn't do this carefully, he could seriously hurt her. "Don't fight me," he warned as he pushed slowly into her trembling body. "You were made for this. Made for me."

The words came out of nowhere, but they felt so true because he was right. Her body opened up and took him into her depths, and it was better than anything he had ever felt in his life. The nectar from her warm pussy had been sweeter than honey and it had taken willpower he hadn't known he possessed to keep his canines at bay as he sampled her delectable delights. Her bare lips had him salivating and her tender clit had him aching for more. With her legs spread around his shoulders, David had felt free to feast on her flesh, but now they were face-to-face, he had to forcefully keep his beast at bay. One glimpse into his changing eyes would have her screaming in fear and David had too many other plans for her mouth to let anything happen.

From the tight grasp of her body, David knew Cassandra wasn't a woman to give her favors lightly and it made his conquest of her all the more sweet, and when he sank his full length inside her, he felt as if he'd died and gone to canine heaven.

The soft, downy bed made for the perfect mating place, cushioning Cassandra's fragile flesh as David filled her. His speed was quicker than he wanted and his thrusts were deeper than he intended, but David couldn't stop his hips from plunging forward.

"You feel so good, baby. So fucking good." She gripped him as no lover or hand had. So tight. So slick. So…his.

He wanted to mount her as if he had fur instead of skin. To power into her from behind with her soft ass pillowing his pelvis. The desire to sink his teeth into her was even more alarming. She wasn't Were. He shouldn't want to mate with her and mark her for all other Weres to see, but he did.

"Holy…my…ohh…" Cassandra had barely uttered a complete phrase since he had entered her. Instead, her passionate cries resonated in the room and in his head.

David knew he couldn't hold out much longer. Cassandra had come already and was on the brink again. There was no way he had enough control to ride out another one of her orgasms.

Just as her body plunged over the edge, her climax hitting her head-on, David surged into Cassandra one last time, deeper than he had been all night and released a torrent of seed into her body, but his seed wasn't the only thing he released inside her. Much to his amazement and horror, David's cock knotted. Her cry of surprise was no match for his own. He had fucked women who were not Were before and never had this occurred.

As his cock jutted spurt after spurt of semen inside her, David fought his beast, praying to all that was holy that he wouldn't hurt her, but from the sounds radiating from her parted lips, pain was the last thing Cassandra was feeling.

"Oh my God. What are you doing?" She whimpered beneath him, pumping her hips up for more. "I've never...never..."

"Am I hurting you?"

"Yes, but don't stop."

He couldn't if he tried. Slipping his hand between them, David zeroed in on her engorged clit, frigging her bud until she came again for him. It was the least he could do for all the pleasure he was receiving from her. When he thought he would go mad from being inside her tempting flesh, his bulb shrank and he was finally able to pull himself from her tight little body.

Collapsing on her tiny frame, David fought to regain his breath as Cassandra's legs slipped around his hips.

"Cass, you okay?" Damn, he hoped he hadn't hurt her. Quickly unbinding her hands, he prayed she was all right. He had never been so fierce, so unguarded with a lover before, and he'd hate like hell for Cassandra to have suffered for his pleasure.

"Hmbjask." David realized he couldn't understand a word Cassandra was saying and gently rolled off her body.

"Thanks." Cassandra's voice sounded breathy and sexy as hell and David winced when he realized he was already getting hard again. Damn unruly dick. Didn't it know when to keep its head down?

Smoothing her hair back off her face, David asked her again. "You okay?"

"Hmmm, better than okay." Cassandra rolled over onto her stomach, stretching erotically.

Down, boy.

"Good." Okay, that was a lame comment if he ever heard one. David realized he had always sucked at after-sex conversation. Probably one of the reasons he never had a long-term relationship.

Cassandra rolled back to her side, smiling a wicked little grin. "Good thing I take yoga and Pilates. I'll need to be flexible around you." Cassandra blushed prettily as soon as the words were out of her mouth and she rushed to make explanations. "What I meant to say is… I mean…"

"Don't worry, Cassandra, I won't get offended if you want me to hang around." David couldn't believe his own words but it was the truth. He was actually looking forward to spending some time with her and getting to know her better, in and out of the bedroom.

"I think we're going to kill my diaphragm," she teased, running her hand down his chest to his raging, hard cock.

Groaning, David felt his eyes rolling back in his head at her strong grip. Human or not human, he might have just met his match. "Or die trying."

* * * * *

Nico sat in the dark of his office, contemplating the future of his Pack. Once the traitor was revealed and he defeated him, it would be Nico's job to guarantee the continuity of the Pack. This schism could not continue. He needed to ensure his Pack survived and continued. Which meant more alliances with the other Were animals.

Thoughts of the future made Nico think of Kimberly. He was so pleased she had finally allowed her beast to run wild. Kimberly was accepting her life as a Were and hopefully accepting her role as his mate would soon follow. He hated the idea of not being with her tonight, but once this business was done, he wasn't ever going to let her sleep alone again.

"Oh my God, is it midnight yet?" Remy stepped out of the shadows and began pacing in front of Nico's desk. He could tell she was struggling to rein in control of her beast. He'd had to talk her into the whole con game setup. Remy was more straightforward and confrontational.

"Remy, how are you supposed to be surprising the traitor if you're talking to me?"

"Come on, Nico, you can tell me. Who do you think the traitor really is? I know you have an idea."

"No, I won't accuse someone without cause. We will wait."

Remy flopped onto the couch and turned to stare at Nico. "So is Jace really coming tonight or what?"

"Yes, I told him he better come, in case the traitor is watching the compound. It's better to stick as close to the truth as possible."

They both turned at the sound of a vehicle pulling into the parking lot.

"Jace?"

"No, it's too early."

"Uh-oh, did we plan what we were going to do if the traitor showed early and decided to just shoot you in the back and not wait for Jace to get here?" Remy's sarcasm was evident in every word.

Nico threw her a withering look. "Will you give it a break? So I like to plan things."

Remy slipped back into the shadows, intent on surprising whoever walked into the office. However they were both surprised by a knock on the door. With a disgusted snort Remy flipped on the light and threw open the door.

"Oh look, it's Tweedledum and Tweedledee."

With sheepish grins, Kellen and Derek entered the room.

"What are you doing here?" Nico didn't know whether to laugh or be enraged. Did no one follow his orders anymore?

"*Benandanti*, forgive us. But we weren't going to leave you alone to meet Jace. Whoever has been betraying us might show up." Kellen's sincerity touched Nico even though he still wanted to kill both of them. If they fucked up this plan, they were dead.

"No shit, really?" Remy walked up behind the two of them and tried to knock their heads together. Of course she didn't try too hard because they easily eluded her.

"Hey, how come you didn't think we were the ones betraying you?" Derek dodged around Remy and she grabbed at him.

"Gee, I don't know. All the traitors I know are really polite and knock on the door before they kill their leader." Remy smirked.

Derek growled, batting her hand away. "I wasn't talking to you."

"What made you assume I didn't think it was either of you?" Standing up, Nico walked around his desk to perch on the edge.

"Well, we're not dead, for one." Kellen moved across the room to the couch against the wall. "And of course we knew it wasn't us."

"So you think it's either Harrison or Jackson?"

"Be careful how you answer." Harrison strolled in the room drawing everyone's gaze but Nico's, who was staring at Remy, bemused.

That about cinched it. No one listened to him. "Come on out, Jackson, I know you're there too."

Strolling into the room, the dark-haired wolf had the grace to look a bit sheepish. "I wasn't hiding. I was just waiting to make an entrance."

Remy snorted. "I told you no one would buy it."

"I bought it for a second," Derek offered, "but then you stormed out of the room."

"So…" Remy didn't seem to be getting the correlation either.

"You're too hotheaded. If you really thought Nico was calling you a traitor, you would have taken his head off."

"Or tried." Silence greeted Nico's statement. Fine, she would have possibly taken his head off but they all didn't have to act as if it were a given. "You're all fired."

"I haven't even gotten my first paycheck yet," Jackson grumbled good-naturedly, taking a seat next to Kellen.

"The pay sucks but the benefits are pretty good," Kellen added.

"You get paid? When did we start getting money?" Harrison asked with a mock frown.

"Will all of you just be quiet?" Nico shook his head in frustration. "I'm trying to catch a traitor here."

"And we're just here to make sure you don't end up dead in the process." Nico knew Derek meant well. Hell, they all did, but the trap wouldn't work with all of them sitting around bullshitting with each other.

"If it will help." Harrison pulled a small wire out of his pocket and presented it to Nico. "I think this will explain a lot. I did a little looking around after you all left and found this sitting as pretty as it pleased behind the mirror."

"Or you could have planted it." Derek smiled.

"I'm going to plant my fist in your face." He growled menacingly. "I'm no traitor."

"Of course he's not the traitor." Tired of the bickering, Nico snatched the wire out of Harrison's hand. "None of you are."

"Then who is?"

"The person who planted this for starters." Bringing the wire to his nose, Nico sniffed it carefully.

"Hey, why didn't you sniff it?" Kellen asked Harrison.

"At The Howler where there are fifty Weres a day stinking up the place?" Harrison shook his head before turning back to Nico. "So are you getting anything?"

"Just a confirmation." Nico was aware his statement had brought all the Weres in the room to attention.

"So you've known all along who the traitor is." Jackson sat back and slipped off his glasses, rubbing the bridge of his nose. "Are you going to let us in on the secret?"

"I haven't known all along but I had my suspicions. The clues continued to point to one person but it didn't seem to make any sense."

"Okay, I can't be diplomatic like the great scholar here. Please, I gotta know." Derek's earnest look caused the rest of the group to laugh, all of them knowing he loved to be in on the latest gossip.

"It's Ryan. He bugged our meeting room and he's been relaying our conversations to the *Maggiore*. I just need to know if it's all of them or just a select few."

Nico stared out at his closest comrades, watching the various emotions play across their faces. There was some surprise, anger and resignation, all of them realizing no matter what they did or said, some Pack members were not going to agree with the way Nico handled Pack issues.

"Okay, I've been the good little girl, sitting in the corner while you all played Detective Clouseau, running around like a bunch of morons. I want to know what we're going to do with the bastard when he shows up?"

"Chill out, Remy. We're still waiting on Jace." Nico looked at the rest of the men in the room. "I hope I can assume you all didn't drive and leave your cars out in the parking lot."

"Oh *Benandanti*, you are a laugh riot." Derek pretended to wipe the tears from his eyes. "Give us some credit."

"Speaking of Jace, where is he?" Kellen checked the time on his watch. "It's almost midnight."

Just then the door was pushed open and Jace came in, closely followed by Ryan with a gun to his head. "Here's your *Rakshasa*, boys." The Weres all jumped to their feet, suddenly alert by the threat in their presence.

"Hey, Jace, guess you didn't see this one coming, huh?"

Jace turned toward Remy with a disgusted look. "This is sooo not the time for your smart-ass comments."

"I think it's the perfect time. I mean you're always spouting doom and gloom to anyone who will ever listen. But have you once told us something useful? I don't think so."

As Remy and Jace continued to argue, Kellen and Jackson cautiously began making their way around the room in an attempt to get behind Ryan to ambush him. Nico knew as long as Ryan's attention was distracted, they had a chance to overtake him.

"Please, just because I can't give the name of your future mate you're pissed at me."

"Oh you are so dead if this asshole doesn't kill you first. As if I fucking care who my mate is. I don't even want a mate."

Jace snorted in response and Remy made a move toward him in retaliation, causing Ryan to back up suddenly. "Both of you shut the fuck up. Now."

Everyone froze in place, not wanting to put Jace in any more danger. The only person who wasn't completely out of sorts was Nico, who looked on amused. "A gun. You're using a gun. For that alone I should kick your ass."

Remy snickered, angering Ryan further. "You think this is some kind of game?"

"Do you really want me to answer?" Nico shook his head disappointingly as he pushed himself off his desk.

"Don't move."

"Or else what?" Nico countered, walking slowly toward the shaking Were. "You going to shoot Jace?"

"Move faster," Remy chided, her comment causing the other Weres in the room to laugh.

"Bitch."

"Arf. Arf."

Ryan pulled the gun from Jace's head and pointed it at Remy as he edged closer to Nico's desk. "Maybe I'll shoot someone you care a little bit more about. Maybe then I'll get your attention."

Stopping, Nico raised his hands in mock surrender. "Is this what you want, Ryan, my attention?"

"No, I want to prove once and for all you should have never been made the *Benandanti*."

"And killing all of us is going to prove what exactly?"

"I don't have to kill all of you."

"See you're wrong there," Jackson said, moving a bit closer to them. "None of us will follow you. Neither will anyone else, once the word of how you sabotaged the real *Benandanti* gets out."

"Then I'll have to make sure it doesn't get out." Ryan suddenly realized the other Weres were closing in on him and stepped back, pulling Jace along with him.

"The Pack is not full of idiots, Ryan. They'll realize something was going on here. Just as we did." Nico's words were condescending.

"You didn't figure out shit." Ryan snorted in disgust. "Do you know how often I sat and laughed at how dumb you all sounded at your little secret meetings?"

"Yeah, guess you didn't realize we were laughing right along with you." Harrison spoke up. Nico wasn't surprised the Were had figured out he'd been planting a false trail for the traitor.

Ryan narrowed his gaze. "Right, you guys aren't that good of actors. I was there and I saw the way Remy and Nico were fighting."

"Ryan, please, this is a fool's errand. You've lost. I knew about your betrayal, I set up this trap and you fell right into it. Now, be a good little Were and admit to your actions. Perhaps the Pack will only banish you, instead of calling for your death." Nico was matter-of-fact and he could tell he was irritating Ryan. Of course he had no illusions Ryan would just walk away. Not that Nico would have allowed him to anyway.

"Lost, have I? Well, I'm not as stupid as you think I am." Ryan nodded at Nico's astonishment. "Oh yeah, I always knew you thought I was dumb. But guess what? We've got your little mongrel mate and you've had no idea."

Everything went still in Nico's mind. Ryan's word washed over him like a cold tide and for a moment Nico couldn't think. All he wanted to do was to react. His beast growled inside him, fierce and deadly. They had dared touch Kimberly, dared to say her name. There was no doubt about it, Ryan was going to die.

The tightening of Nico's jaw was the only outward indication he had heard Ryan's declaration. Inside he was frantically trying to contact Kimberly through their mental link but he could feel nothing. He felt as if his heart were slowly being pulled out of his chest.

Remy must have realized the extent of Nico's rage because she spoke, filling the sudden void in the conversation. "How do we know you're not lying? You could just be saying all this because you know you've been beaten."

"Beaten! I'm not beaten. And I'll never be, no matter what you do. Do you think I'm alone? I'm not the only dissatisfied member of the Pack. There are members of the *Maggiore* who support me." Finally, they were getting somewhere. Now if Nico could only convince this moron to tell him who, he could snap his neck.

"But they're not here, are they?" Catching Jace's eyes, Nico sent him a message.

"Count to three and drop to the floor."

"She's still alive, Nico."

"I know. I refuse to believe anything else. Now count."

"You're all dead," Ryan growled, no idea his time on this earth was numbered.

Jace went completely limp, throwing Ryan off guard as Nico went for the gun. As the Were closest to Ryan, Kellen charged at him, catching the mad Were off guard.

"What the—" were the last words Ryan ever had the chance to speak.

Kellen tackled him, both of them falling against Nico's desk. Unfortunately for Ryan, he hit the hard wood neck first and his neck snapped like a twig in the breeze.

"Damn it, Kellen," Derek grumbled as he pulled his companion up. "You weren't supposed to kill him."

"Consider it a perk." Kellen kicked Ryan to the floor.

"I can't believe you decided to pick an argument when he had a gun to my head. He could have killed me." Remy shrugged her shoulders as she helped Jace up. "I was considering it a perk."

Ignoring the entire group, Nico found the phone, which had been knocked off the desk, and frantically dialed Kimberly's apartment. Although it was a futile hope, he prayed she would answer. When her machine picked up, Nico slammed the phone down in despair. The thundering noise silenced the bickering Weres.

"Nico, we'll find her. We'll all help." The Weres all nodded their agreement at Jackson's words.

"Her brother. Let's try to find him and see if he knows where she may be." Remy sent Derek and Kellen out to the streets to follow-up on their contacts.

"I'm going to her apartment. Maybe I can pick up a trail." Nico knew he couldn't sit idly waiting for a call, if one were even going to come.

"We'll take care of the garbage. Go find your mate." Harrison and Jackson hauled Ryan out of the office as Nico left for the parking lot, Remy hot on his heels.

Chapter Nine

❧

Kimberly sat back down on the barstool and watched David head for the door. When Cassandra came in, Kimberly almost jumped off to go over and greet her boss but something stopped her. She wasn't sure if it was the seductive look on Cassandra's face or the interested look on David's, but when the two of them left together a few moments later, Kimberly was wondering if she'd made the right decision.

Glancing at her watch for the hundredth time, Kimberly decided this entire night was going to be a bust. First David left, and with her human boss no less. Now it appeared as if Nico were standing her up—again. She tried to be realistic and reasonable, figuring Nico had gotten held up with business at The Sanctuary, but she knew he had a cell phone, but unfortunately she had forgotten hers at home and had no way of getting in contact with him. The pay phone wasn't working either, and the bartender had growled rudely at her when she'd asked to use their phone, proving once and for all the world was out to get her.

She had never wanted to be one of those women. One of those women who relied on their man to determine their happiness. But here she was, sitting at a bar—by herself—waiting for Nico to show up. And she just knew if he walked in the door that minute, all would be forgiven and she would be asking him about his day and telling him about hers.

"Enough of this Ozzie and Harriet bullshit," she muttered to herself. If Nico showed after she left, he would just have to wonder what happened to her. Standing, she threw some money on the bar to pay for her tab and gathered her coat, preparing to leave.

"Leaving so soon?"

Startled, Kimberly turned around and almost tripped into the arms of the very last person she wanted to see. With clothes on, the older Were from the lake didn't seem as imposing or amusing. In all actuality, if it wasn't for his familiar scent, Kimberly would have never known he was a Were. He didn't give off the same glowing vibe everyone else seem to. He was weak and anyone could tell, even a novice, such as herself. Even if she hadn't been in a bar full of people, she wouldn't have been afraid of him.

He wasn't flanked by his cronies now, but there was still a menacing look in his eyes that warned Kimberly not to trust him. "Not soon enough."

"I'm Franklin, by the way, one of the members of the *Maggiore*. Nico didn't introduce us." Titling his head to the side, the older Were watched her with amusement. "I don't remember you being so feisty the last time we met."

"Sadly, I was startled by all the wilting flesh."

His amusement quickly vanished as anger filled his face. "Bitch in and out of fur, I see."

Was this the best he had? Kimberly wondered amusedly. She'd seen puppies with bigger barks. "Wow, you really got me. I'm going to have to rush right out and have myself a good long cry."

"You're awfully bold for someone in my territory."

"I'm not." Kimberly raised a brow. "I'm in Nico's."

"It's only his for as long as I say."

The words were meant to sound threatening but to her they merely sounded sad. "Somehow I seriously doubt it."

"You don't know anything," he spat. His anger poured out of him on to her and she could feel his beast stirring.

Taking a step back, Kimberly eyed him warily. He was weak all right but he also seemed crazy. And crazy was more dangerous than strength.

The Were smiled menacingly as he saw her back away from him. "It's about time you showed some sense. You better learn to know who has the power around here."

Kimberly didn't reply as there was nothing she could say to him that would make sense to his diseased mind. Better to just sit tight, listen for a moment and then get the hell out of there as soon as she could.

"Did Remy ever tell you I raised her?" The sudden change in subject confused her for a moment. He seemed to stare at her expectantly and she realized he was waiting for a reply.

"Ah no, she didn't. Poor girl probably tried to hide it from people rather than brag about it. She may work for Nico now, but she knows what her place in the Pack should be. She'll prove herself a true daughter of mine soon."

Kimberly knew she was trying to keep her mouth shut but she was usually a pretty good judge of character. She had no doubt this freak probably had raised Remy, but she also knew Remy was loyal to Nico and she wanted to tell him so. It wouldn't do any good though, since it would only start an argument and she wasn't willing to get into with him.

Franklin's eyes were shifting back and forth as he scanned the room before he turned back to her. "You know, when the power balance shifts, you'll have to come to me for favors. If you want to stay with the Pack and keep our protection, you'll be talking to me about it."

"All right, I've tried to keep quiet and play nice but you're just too much. It'll be a cold day in hell before I ever come sniffing around your saggy ass asking for help, so just get the fuck away from me."

Kimberly grabbed her purse and started to leave. Turning back for a moment, she added, "And Nico is going to wipe the floor with you when I tell him you even suggested Remy is disloyal, let alone when he hears what you suggested about me." Turning back toward the door she headed outside, needing a breath of fresh air to clear the foul scent she had of the evil Were.

The crowd seemed to part as she stomped her way over to the door. Kimberly couldn't believe she had allowed the foul man to get to her. Just thinking about everything he said and implied made her spitting mad. Instead of threatening him with Nico, she should have eviscerated him.

Yeah…eviscerate him then dance on his spleen.

The vicious thought brought a smile to her face and a bit of a queasy feeling to her stomach. Not too queasy though, which kind of scared her. She was becoming more wolf by the day. But for the first time in her entire life, the thought didn't scare her.

It looked as if Nico were good for something besides multiple orgasms after all.

As she pushed the door open, a cool breeze drifted by her, filling her senses with the smell of Nico.

He was there after all.

Bastard. When she got her hands on him she was going to kick his ass…then give him a big kiss and a shove in the direction of Franklin so she could watch him kick Franklin's ass.

Damn, there it was again. Vicious and violent, would it ever end?

"It's all your fault, Nico," she called out as she walked out into the parking lot. "Hey, where are you?"

A quick rustle behind her, the entwining scent of Nico and another Were had her turning around to look behind her. But when she looked around, he wasn't there. Frowning, Kimberly tried to determine where the scent had come from when she felt someone at her back.

"Looking for me?" Before she could reply, a hand closed over her mouth and a sweet-smelling cloth was placed over her nose as her body was pulled back tightly against a chest.

Fear radiated through her body and she screamed in protest as she kicked out with all her strength. The cloth muffled her cries and her attempts at escape seemed to be made in vain. The grip on her didn't loosen, in fact her struggles only made her attacker pull her in closer to him.

Afraid, Kimberly could feel her beast rising to the surface, but before the change could take over her body, the fight went out of her and her body went slack. Her beast screamed in protest as she was swallowed whole by the darkness of unconsciousness, Nico's name a silent cry on her lips.

* * * * *

The pain in her head was unbearable as was the silence, which seemed to surround the night. From past experience, Kimberly knew it was never this quiet unless a predator was near, but try as she might, she couldn't smell anything or anyone.

Easing into a sitting position, Kimberly tried hard to concentrate on her surroundings, but she couldn't make heads or tails of where she was. It seemed vaguely familiar, as if she should be able to recognize this place, but at the same time, it didn't feel quite real to her. The night air was thick with the smell of impending rain and the fog circled the trees like a waltzing lover.

Suddenly it clicked in her brain that she had been here before in her dreams, and now just as then, Kimberly could tell she wasn't alone. The crackle of the underbrush brought a relieved sigh to her lips as she turned her head and looked into the russet eyes of her lover.

It was going to be all right, Nico was there.

Padding out of the dark, he made his way over to her. Nico nuzzled her, sniffing as if to ensure himself she was okay. Kimberly reached up to pet him, sinking her fingers into his fur. Even though she knew she was dreaming, she felt safe and protected. There was a sudden warmth beneath her hands and instead of petting the wolf, she felt Nico's tense muscles.

"Ah, *Zingaro,* I almost died when I couldn't contact you."

Kimberly wrapped her arms around him, too choked up for a moment to speak.

Pulling back from her slightly, Nico gently wiped away the tear Kimberly hadn't even realized she had shed. "I'm so glad you're here. Even if it is only in my dreams."

"I will always be with you, Kimberly, just look here." Nico tapped her chest and the heart he had indicated melted.

"I love you, Nico." Kimberly had held back the words, afraid of what would happen when she finally gave in, but she was no longer afraid of having Nico in her life.

Nico's eyes flared at her declaration and he bent his head to claim her lips in a bruising kiss. Kimberly could feel the heat he was generating spread throughout her body and was surprised at how easily she found herself lying back with him covering her.

Nico suddenly pulled back, running his hand through his hair. "You would tempt a saint. And unfortunately this is not the time or place for making love. But when I find you and get you home, be prepared…"

Kimberly laughed breathlessly and pushed herself into a sitting position. "I'll consider myself warned."

"We don't have a lot of time, *Zingaro.* I need to know where you are so we can come get you. David is beside himself—"

"David's with you?" Kimberly couldn't help the trembling tone her voice took on. She wanted to go home.

"Yes, honey, he's here with me. Now tell me what happened after you left the bar."

"I waited for you for over an hour—"

"I never called you."

"Well, not you, but your secretary."

The bleak look in Nico's eyes spoke volumes. "I take it the call wasn't from your secretary."

"No."

"Oh." Really, what more was there to say? She had been a fool.

"Did you see anyone you recognized?"

"Franklin, the Were from the lake."

"I'm going to kill him," Nico roared, anger rising from him like steam.

"But it wasn't him. It was you." The memory came flashing back as Kimberly rose to her knees. "I smelled you."

"Wait a minute. Back up the bus. We know it wasn't me, so tell me more about Franklin."

Kimberly was irritated Nico wasn't understanding her but she knew it would probably take less time to just go along with his thought processes instead of trying to argue with him.

"I ran into Franklin. He said some nasty things. I got nasty right back. And then I threatened him."

"Threatened him?"

"Yeah, with you." Kimberly smiled at the thought.

"So I probably don't want to know the details of the nasty things that were said?"

"Let's just say Remy and I both got insulted and leave it be."

"Remy is going to love hearing this story. And don't think you're going to get away with not telling me forever." Kimberly just nodded as he continued. "So what happened next?"

"I left the bar and went outside. I thought I noticed your scent and followed it to the parking lot but you weren't there."

"I can't understand why you would be getting my scent. It's been hours since I was at The Howler."

"I know what I smelled. But then there was this other smell too, something sickeningly sweet. I struggled against whoever grabbed me but…" Kimberly hated to remember how out of control she felt and helpless to do anything. "Anyway, the next thing was, I awoke here."

"Do you know who did this, *Zingaro*?"

Kimberly shook her head sadly. "No, I never saw his face."

Nico frowned at her announcement. "Try to replay the scene in your head. I want to see if there was something you missed."

Kimberly nodded slowly, not really understanding how this would help but willing to do whatever Nico asked. Closing her eyes, Kimberly remembered walking out to her car, thinking she smelled Nico's scent. Turning her head, she suddenly noticed a reflection in the car window of a man standing behind her. He swiftly pulled her toward him, covering her mouth with a cloth.

Scared, Kimberly opened her eyes. "No, I don't know."

Standing, Kimberly backed away from Nico. She didn't want to remember. She didn't want to ever see him again. "Just come get me."

"I need to know who he is."

"I can't… I just want to come home."

Nico jumped up and grabbed her arms. His fear and frustration wafted off him waves. "Show me then, *Zingaro*. Show me who did this to you."

Kimberly closed her eyes tightly, willing the image closer. She was there again, in the parking lot struggling for her life.

"God!" Nico's startled cry forced her eyes open. They were there. In the parking lot, watching the scene unfold before them. The image played out in front of them like a black and white vintage film but in three dimensions.

Kimberly could feel the breeze, the same one that had whipped her hair around as she walked through the lot. She could smell Nico's scent just as strongly as she had earlier when she had first walked through the parking lot. She could also feel the fear that had radiated from her body when she struggled in the grip of the mad Were.

"Show me," Nico urged. At his biding, the image pivoted before them from front to back, revealing not only her frightened face but that of her attacker. Nico's quick intake of breath startled Kimberly and broke the image before them. Turning she stared at Nico who was sitting with a look of shock and disappointment on his face.

"Heath."

* * * * *

Nico shook himself from the fog, which always surrounded him as he left the dream-walking state with a roar, allowing his beast to break free for a few moments. He was enraged with the knowledge that not only had someone from his Pack betrayed him, but it was someone he considered a friend and mentor.

Heath had been one of the only Weres of the *Maggiore* who had supported him in his bid for role of *Benandanti*. He had advised Nico at the beginning of his leadership, never pushing him but guiding him. Now to find out Heath was the traitor was especially infuriating.

With a rare show of temper, Nico jumped from the chair and overturned the coffee table, sending everyone around him running for cover.

"The bastard!"

"Who has her?" David's fury matched his own. The dark-haired Were had practically worn a path in the carpet waiting for word from his sister.

"Heath."

"Heath!" Remy stepped forward, her brow wrinkled in confusion. "Are you sure?"

"She saw him…I saw him." Explaining the vision would take longer than Kimberly had. Stepping over the rubble, which had once been the table, Nico headed toward the door.

"Wait," Remy called out, halting his escape. "What are you going to do?"

"Get back my mate."

"But you don't know where they are."

"I'll find her."

"We'll find her," David interjected.

Rearing around, Nico growled at him. "She wouldn't be in this mess if it wasn't for you."

"For me!" David roared. "This is your Machiavellian bullshit war she's entangled in. If it wasn't for you—"

"Boys, boys, boys…" Remy moved quickly between the two heated men. "This isn't helping matters."

"If they hurt my sister, I'm going to kill you."

"You can try—"

"Damn it, you two—" The door burst open just as David swung at Nico.

Acting quickly, Remy slammed her elbow into David's chest, sending him flying back into the wall.

"Don't make me kill…either one of you."

"What did we miss?" Kellen asked stepping into the room with Derek hot on his trail.

"Heath betrayed me."

"Heath."

"Yes, and we don't have time to go in to it again." Shoving her hand through her hair, Remy let out a frustrated breath. "Fucking men. We need to think, where would he take her?"

"Someplace he considers safe," Derek offered.

Kellen nodded his head in agreement. "Someplace reasonably close by."

"His estate." The answer was obvious, unlike the traitor himself. Nico could practically hear Heath advising him as a young wolf, "If there is to be war, better it be on your own turf."

Heath wanted an advantage. But he made a huge mistake when he took Kimberly—he left Nico alive.

David, recovered from Remy's attack, grabbed Nico's arm. "I'm coming with you."

Ignoring David, Nico addressed the room. "We're leaving now, let's go." As he headed out of the apartment building, the group of loyal Pack warriors behind him, Nico stopped short at the entourage he encountered on the sidewalk. For a moment he thought Heath had sent a guard to destroy him but realized it was the Morbauch clan who stood before him.

"Our *Benandanti* wishes to speak with you."

"Tell your *Benandanti* I don't have time for diplomacy right now." Nico tried to walk past them but they continued to block his progress. He turned on them with a growl. "Don't make me send you back in a box. Now get the fuck out of my way."

Just then, the leader of the Morbauch clan stepped from the shadows. "I come to you with an offering of peace and a show of our commitment to this treaty."

"As much as I would love to sit and chat about our treaty, I just don't have the time." Nico pushed through the two emissaries and headed toward his car before the words of the Morbauch *Benandanti* halted him in his tracks.

"We know your mate has been seized and we are willing to fight at your side. Will you accept my offer of assistance?"

Reacting quickly, Nico picked Rachel up and slammed her against the side of the stair railing. Her cry of surprise was no match for the growls and shouts from behind them as her

Pack moved in to protect her and his moved in to guard him. "Tell me what you know."

Without raising her hands to defend herself, Rachel spoke calmly. "We have been waiting and watching you ever since you initially contacted us. I've had guards stationed at The Howler and one reported a very unseemly incident, which occurred in the parking lot. When we heard on the streets your *Rahu* were looking for news of a missing female Were, I contacted your *Rakshasa* Jace and told him of what was witnessed."

"And I'm just supposed to believe you...believe this..."

"You can trust me."

"Or not."

"Or you can trust your *Rakshasa*." Rachel nodded her head in the direction from which she came. "He's in the car. How else did we know where to meet you?"

"I don't. But tonight, I'm not big on trust."

"Seeing is believing."

"And why now?" Nico asked, distrust rampant in his tone. "Why would you choose to join us now?"

"Because our mortality depends on it. We either fight together or die out altogether."

Releasing her slowly, Nico stepped back. "So you're not just another stubborn female after all."

"I have my moments." She smiled softly. "Now let's go get your mate back."

* * * * *

The drive to Heath's estate grated on Nico's nerves. Realistically he knew they would arrive faster by car but his nature wanted to allow his beast the ability to run free. It would have been somewhat easier if he were in contact with Kimberly, but he hadn't been able to make contact again since they had left her apartment. Nico was worried it meant Heath was keeping her drugged and didn't want to contemplate the possibility too deeply.

"How much longer?" Nico knew Heath's estate was only a half an hour out of the city, but time seemed to be creeping by at a snail's pace.

"Just a few more minutes." Remy turned onto a side road and cut the lights. Thankfully, with their superior night vision they didn't need to rely on them to see where they were headed.

"What's the game plan?"

"We're going to rescue Kimberly and kill Heath."

"You know he's going to use her as a shield. We need a game plan."

"I can't think strategically right now. I just need to get to Kimberly." He couldn't believe that only a week ago he hadn't even contemplated taking a mate. Now, he knew there was no way he could live without her. He had given Kimberly until the full moon to admit she was his, battling her fears and worries so she would finally accept herself and him. Tonight was the full moon, the night he planned to celebrate the beginning of their life together and he wasn't going to lose her to a madman.

Remy sighed heavily but Nico knew he could rely on her to maneuver and run the troops. They could handle everything else but he was going to handle Heath.

Remy stopped the car a few hundred feet from the house and the other vehicles pulled in behind. Nico stared at the house, his eyes flickering as his beast pushed at the control he was barely holding on to. The estate was ablaze with lights as if every room were inviting them.

The full moon rested in the heavenly sky, devoid of clouds and stars. It was the clearest night Nico had ever seen, and it would have been the perfect night for a run at The Sanctuary and the rendezvous he had planned for Kimberly. Instead of making love with his mate, he was on a mission to rescue her and kill his mentor. Not exactly the way he had originally envisioned the evening going.

"I'm going in. He's got to be expecting me so there's no need for me to sneak in there." Nico got out of the car, purpose behind his every step.

Catching his arm, David halted him for a moment. "Look, he may be expecting you and even the *Rahu* over there, but he's not going to expect me and he's certainly not going to expect them." David thumbed over his shoulder, indicating the members of the Morbauch clan who were currently exiting their car.

"David, you and Remy are going to have to work this out. I'm headed in to find Kimberly." Nico began walking purposely toward the front entrance of the estate, blocking out all the extraneous stimuli around him.

"Zingaro, *can you hear me?*" Nico had attempted to contact Kimberly every few minutes without luck so he was surprised when she answered him.

"*Nico, where are you?*"

"*I am here,* Zingaro. *Are you okay?*" Nico prayed Heath had not harmed her.

"*I'm fine. I don't think anyone knows I'm conscious yet.*"

"*Where are you being held, can you tell me anything?*"

"*I'm in a large room, similar to a library or den. I think it may be in the back of the house, because I don't see any lights outside the windows.*" Nico immediately knew the room from his previous visits to Heath's home.

"*I'm on my way, baby, just hold on.*" Nico had finally reached the front door and didn't even knock but kicked the door in. The Weres in the foyer all jumped to their feet, surprise written on their faces. Nico was a bit disappointed Heath had such inept guards.

And the sad part was he knew them. They were members of his own Pack, his own blood, betraying the brotherhood and their kin.

Nostrils flared, they faced off, ready to do battle. They had signed their own death warrants the moment they sided against him. The real shame was they wasted their last moments in life lounging around in the cheesy parlor decorated in outdated Eighties black lacquer.

"So you've finally shown yourself." Shaw, a cocky young Were with more hair mousse than brains, boasted. "Pity, I haven't had a chance to get to know the queen as intimately as I would have liked."

Before the words fully left Shaw's mouth, Nico pounced. With two swift punches, he snapped Shaw's head back and his neck, leaving the young Were dead before he even hit the floor.

The stunned silence was short-lived as the entryway spewed forth Nico's backup and the room around him erupted into rage. Wolves and coyotes filled the foyer with roars and howls as beast met beast.

It was more of a slaughter than a battle but Nico didn't take time to gloat as he pushed through the carnage in search of Kimberly. Not bothering to change, he darted down the hall as more of Heath's underlings came scurrying forth to join in.

With David and Remy covered in fur and fast on his heels, he charged up the stairway to the back of the house where he assumed Kimberly was kept.

The open door gave him pause for just a moment before he ran in and surveyed the room in his search for Kimberly. She sat tied to a chair, head lying limply to the side. And the man who had become his mortal enemy sat directly behind her.

"Nico, so glad you could join us. I must say I'm surprised you took care of the guards downstairs in such an effective manner. Ah well, perhaps it's best we leave this business to just the two of us." Gesturing to Remy and David, Heath added, "And your two loyal companions, of course."

"I'd love to sit and chat but I'm here to kill you, not have tea."

Ignoring Nico's comments, Heath continued his polite conversation. "I really must commend you on the loyalty you've drawn from the coyotes in such a short time. I would have never thought it possible. Of course, you approaching them was what precipitated these events in the first place."

"Okay, I'll bite, why?" Nico wanted to just transform and rip out Heath's throat, but as long as he was using Kimberly as a shield, Nico couldn't take the chance.

"I knew eventually you'd win them all to your side."

"Why is this such a bad thing?"

"The bloodline must not be broken," Heath spewed, for the first time showing real emotion. "We did not fight for you to sully our race with the blood of our enemies. It's a desecration."

"And you thought my brother had issues."

Nico's heart skipped a beat at Kimberly's sarcastic words. *"Zingaro, you're back with me."*

"I never left, the bastard came in before I could make it out of the room, so I acted as if I were still out."

"I'm going to get you out of here." Nico kept his face still as Heath raged, not wanting to give anything away.

"So how long are you going to let him rant before you kill him?"

"Bloodthirsty little thing."

"The bastard kidnapped me, hello."

"Don't worry, Zingaro, I just need to find out who's all in it with him."

Turning back to Heath, who had finally shut up about perfect bloodlines, Nico asked him, "You'd rather let us die out?"

"Yes."

"Then you're crazier than Franklin and the rest of your goons."

"Franklin." Heath snorted. "He is a weak old fool."

Remy growled low in her throat, inching closer. "I'd stay where I was, if I were you, Remington. Unless you want to see the insides of this bitch."

"I trusted you." Nico had considered Heath to be a surrogate father after his own was killed, so his betrayal was especially painful.

"*Got your answer yet?*" Kimberly's comments almost had Nico smiling.

"*Yes, I believe so.*"

"*Can we go home now?*" Kimberly sounded more bored than scared. She was a hell of a woman. It was no wonder he was in love with her.

"It was your first mistake," Heath sneered his reply.

"And my last."

"*Now, honey.*" Before Heath knew what was going on, Kimberly quickly tilted her chair causing it to topple to the side. It was enough of a distraction for Nico, who quickly ate up the distance between his mentor and him. Nico transformed instantaneously, knocking Heath down and pinning him to the floor.

If the old ways were what Heath wanted, then Nico would gladly give them to him. Unable to admit defeat, Heath roared and brought the gun between them, giving Nico the last little push he needed to do what was necessary.

Looking his mentor-slash-father figure in the eye, Nico tore into his throat, growling in satisfaction as his blood spewed forth.

It was a quicker, kinder death than Heath deserved but it was the last thing Nico could do for the man who help make him king.

Chapter Ten

ഔ

The stress of the last few hours was beginning to take its toll on Kimberly. After the anticlimactic death of Heath, Kimberly barely had time to greet her brother and to assure him of her safety before Nico whisked her into the car and out of sight. Normally his caveman-like behavior would have at least earned him a raised brow and snotty sniff, but she was just so damn happy to see him.

"Where are we going?" Kimberly was dead tired and just wanted to sleep, but she was almost afraid to close her eyes. Afraid the nightmare of being held captive would haunt her dreams.

"Home, *Zingaro*, home." Nico glanced over at her before taking her hand in his. The warmth of his body infused Kimberly and she scooted over, laying her head back and drifting off to sleep.

The next thing Kimberly knew, Nico was carrying her up a large flight of stairs. "Where are we?" she asked sleepily.

"Our home." Nico's clipped answer caused Kimberly to open her sleep-laden eyes and look around. Okay, it was a nice house and everything, but when did his house become her house?

"So when did I move in?"

"Today."

"So am I ever getting anything but monosyllabic answers from you ever again?"

As he walked into a bedroom Kimberly presumed was his own, Nico gently laid her on the bed.

"*Zingaro*, I know I'm being heavy-handed and I'm sure I'll pay for it in the future, but for now, if you were out of my sight, I don't think I would be able to control my beast and a lot of people might get hurt. So you're moving in here today and never leaving again."

Kimberly chuckled and reached up, stroking his jawline. "You're very lucky, you know. Because I think I'm going accept the offer to make you pay in the future. So I guess I'll be sticking around."

Nuzzling his cheek into her hand, Nico remarked, "Not enough, little one. I want to hear the words again."

"Once wasn't enough?" Kimberly had waited too long to tell him she loved him.

"Once will never be enough." Nico dropped a kiss onto her upturned palm.

"I love you," she whispered, thankful she had the opportunity to tell him face-to-face. They had been blessed with a second chance and Kimberly refused to waste a moment of it.

But apparently for Nico, her simple words were enough. "And…"

Kimberly raised her brows questioningly. "And what?"

"And tell me I'm the mate of your dreams."

His serious tone was ruined by the slow smile spreading across his full lips.

"Literally and figuratively." Kimberly pulled a chuckling Nico onto her. His solid weight was a comfort to her still scattered nerves. He felt like home. The seriousness of the situation they had barely escaped from came crashing back to her. "I was so afraid I would never see you again."

Nico's smiled slid away. "You're not alone."

"That man…he was someone significant to you, wasn't he?"

"It's not important."

"But he was…wasn't he?"

Nico sat up and turned, staring out into the bedroom. Kimberly gently stroked his back, silently urging him to talk to her.

"He was my mentor and friend. He helped me in my fight to become *Benandanti* and he was a surrogate father to me." Nico bent his head and Kimberly could sense the defeat he was feeling.

Getting swiftly to her knees, Kimberly slipped her arms around him and laid her head on his back. "He might have changed recently, Nico, but it doesn't mean he wasn't sincerely all those things at one time in the past. You have to remember those good times you had with the man you want to honor and not the man he later became."

"I'm beginning to wonder if it was all for nothing."

"Of course it isn't," Kimberly argued. "It wasn't just wolves I sensed tonight fighting with you, Nico. Whether your doubters admit it now or later, you've done the very thing you set out to do. You've taken the first step to unite the clans."

"To fight."

"To fight for their survival."

"You are too good for me, *Zingaro*."

Deciding this was the perfect opportunity to elevate the mood a bit, Kimberly laughed as she threw herself back on the bed. "Well, of course I am, silly. Now, what wonderful things are you going to do to me to make up for being so insignificant?"

Turning back to her, Nico's look smoldered. "Do to you? Don't you mean do for you?"

"You say tomato, I say tom-ah-toe." Spreading her arms, Kimberly invited him to do what he wanted. She had decided to embrace life fully, her life as a Were, as Nico's mate, everything.

"You know…technically the heat thing is over. We don't need to have sex anymore for my sanity."

"Fine, we can just do it for my sanity."

Kimberly giggled as Nico nuzzled her neck, causing shivers to rush over her. Twining her arms around his neck, she gently nipped at his ear.

"So you want to play rough, huh?" Nico ripped at her blouse, sending buttons flying.

"What big eyes you have." Kimberly reached up and unhooked the front clasp of her bra, slowly exposing her breasts to his hungry gaze.

"The better to see you with." Leaning down, he tongued her rapidly hardening nipples, bringing them to diamond points. Kimberly arched into his embrace, pushing the juncture of her thighs against his jeans-clad leg.

Palming her breasts, Nico pinched and tugged at her nipples. Kimberly let out a moan of desire as heat shot straight from her aroused tips to her now soaked center.

"I love to hear you enjoying my touch." Nico's rough whisper sent shivers down her spine.

"God, Nico, I'm burning up for you. Are you sure this heat thing is really over?"

Pulling back, he smiled wolfishly at her. "Oh it's over for now. You're just on fire for me, all on your own." Reaching down he unclasped her skirt and tugged it past her hips. Kimberly quickly kicked off her shoes as Nico jerked the skirt off and tossed it over his shoulder.

"What big teeth you have." Kimberly knew it was cheesy but she was enjoying the lighthearted lovemaking they were experiencing.

"Ah, the better to eat you with, my dear." Nico proceeded to divest her of her panties. Bending his head, he gently parted her folds and then swept his tongue along her soaked slit, ending at the tiny bundle of nerves and sucking her clit into his mouth. Kimberly's body jerked at the intimate kiss and she pressed her feet against the bed, striving to get closer to his teasing mouth. Nico alternated the licking and sucking, purposely driving her mad, never allowing her to come.

Nico's fingers slid inside her pussy, her juices coated them almost instantly. Kimberly's hips rocked slowly at first then harder with each thrust of his hand. She groaned with pleasure, urging him deeper.

"Nico, you're driving me mad. Please…" Kimberly whimpered with need as Nico removed his hand and abruptly sat up, pulling off his T-shirt. She reached up, sliding her hands along the contoured muscles of his chest.

"No more, *Zingaro*, I want to be inside you when you come." Nico stood and shucked his jeans. Kimberly pulled off her ruined blouse and slipped off her bra as Nico quickly rejoined her on the bed.

But Nico surprised her by rolling over on his back and pulling her atop him. "Ride me, *Zingaro*."

"Soon, my *Benandanti*, soon."

Sitting up, Kimberly straddled Nico's hips, enjoying the sensation of his hard, angular body beneath hers. As she reached between her legs, she gathered the cream there and coated his cock, mixing it with the pre-cum gathered on his purpled head.

"Stop teasing, *Zingaro*, and put me in your body."

"With pleasure." Grasping his cock firmly she guided it to her heated core and slowly lowered herself over him. Inch by inch, she took him until she was fully seated.

As she leaned forward to seize the headboard, Kimberly rocked her hips, slowly teasing them both. Nico took advantage of Kimberly's draped form and reached up to tweak her nipples. Kimberly moaned appreciatively at the attention and increased her rocking pace.

"Now who's teasing who," Nico whispered.

"I know, but it's okay because I'll get what I want."

"Without a doubt." Nico finally released her tormented nipples and clutched her hips, driving her to accelerate her speed.

Kimberly could feel the tingly tightening of her muscles and knew her orgasm was near. Reaching between her legs, she rubbed her clit, bringing herself over the edge. Nico growled and flipped Kimberly onto her back, driving his hips into hers. A second climax, close on the heels of the first roared through her body, leaving her limp. Nico's hoarse shout announced his own peak and his cock knotted inside her as he spilled his seed deep in her womb. He gently lowered himself to the bed, turning them both on their sides as their bodies remained locked together.

When Kimberly was finally able to regain her voice, she whispered to Nico, "What a big heart you have."

"The better to love you with, *Zingaro*."

* * * * *

Smoke rose from the burning estate, filling the night sky with haze and ash. Standing in the shelter of the forest, Franklin watched the ebbing war with a jumbled emotion of satisfaction and sorrow.

He knew Heath's plan would never work. It couldn't. Obsession mixed with craziness was a deadly combination, even in the greatest of minds.

Franklin was so focused on the howls and gunfire he almost missed the sound of the car pulling in behind him. Almost.

Without sparing the driver a glance, he spoke. "You're late."

"Was this your doing?"

"It didn't work, did it?" Franklin snorted, surprised she would even have to ask. His plans always worked. This cluster-fuck didn't remotely resemble the havoc he was planning to rain on Nico's head.

"But...but you knew about it."

Her distaste annoyed him. She had no penchant for violence. It was something they were going to have to overcome.

"There's little that escapes me."

"Funny, because Nico seems to do it on a daily basis."

Shooting his daughter an aggravated look, Franklin bit back his scathing reply. If anyone else had even muttered those words, he would have had their hide but she was the last link he had to greatness and he wasn't ready to ostracize her just yet. Even though she was human, she had to have some of his DNA in her, although her human half was suppressing it. Unfortunately this was the risk he took when he slept with her slut of a mother. Too bad she didn't produce the Alpha male Were heir he had been hoping for. At least she was easy to control.

He had plans for her.

"When I'm ready, he'll come to me."

"Just as I did."

"Exactly."

With a shaky sigh, she ran her hand through her long blonde hair, the locks shimmering around her shoulders in the moonlight. Nervousness radiated off her like steam, filling the night air with its bitter taste. "I want out."

Franklin knew the words were coming before she uttered them. He knew it just as surely as she should have known his response. "Not going to happen."

"I don't want anything to do with your demented plan. Nico seems happy with Kimberly and I feel nothing for him. Marriage is completely out of the question now."

"I never spoke of marriage."

Startled blue eyes sought his in the dark. "I beg to differ. You said you wanted us..."

"To produce an heir. A rightful heir. And it's not too late."

"Unless you're carrying his semen in a turkey baster somewhere, I'm inclined to differ. Kimberly might be a tad upset if I try to partake of her mate's juice. And seeing how she can turn furry and I can't, I'm thinking she has the upper hand here."

"I'll take care for her."

"If you harm her, I walk." The finality of her words penetrated through his vengeance-filled brain. She was serious. "But not before I pay Nico a visit."

"Threatening me, daughter?" She was as amateurish as she was beautiful.

"No, bargaining for my life. I'm not you, Franklin…there's nothing here worth dying for. Or killing for, for that matter."

"How about the life of your child?"

"I told you, your plan for Nico and me will never work."

"I'm not talking about his child, I'm talking about the child you're carrying now."

Her shocked gasp brought a smile to his face as his gaze followed her hand to her womb. "What are you talking about?"

Silly girl. She knew nothing about the wiles of wars. "A new life carries such a sweet scent. Even one only hours old."

Franklin reached out to touch her but she stepped out of his way. "You're mad."

"And you finally carry my heir. It only took a little planning and the right little fertility pills to ensure you'd conceive."

"Fertility pills. I haven't been taking any damn pills."

"That Milla makes a mean cup of coffee, doesn't she?"

The shock on her face was damn near amusing. If he taught her anything, it would be to trust no one. "Milla…"

200

"Of course now that we know the little pink pills work, I'll have to give Dr. Traven a raise. I can give my Pack the one thing they need without interbreeding with those mongrels. Nico's plan will fail and finally *my* Pack will have the leader it deserves."

"If you're right...and I'm not saying you are, I'm not letting you near him."

"I'm right, all right, and you will. Where else will you go?"

"Away from you." Turning, she raced to her car, hand firmly planted across her middle.

"Cassandra," Franklin called, halting her in her tracks. "Do you really think David or I will let you escape so easily?"

"David has nothing to do with this."

"It's his seed growing inside of you, isn't it?"

Cassandra's eyes widened comically in her pale face. "You're psychotic."

"I'm a grandfather now, thanks to you." He grinned as she dove into her car and started her engine. This was only the beginning for them. He would rule the Pack. It was just a matter of time.

SHADOW OF MOONLIGHT
Lena Matthews & Liz Andrews

ഔ

Trademarks Acknowledgement

ഇൻ

The author acknowledges the trademarked status and trademark owners of the following wordmarks mentioned in this work of fiction:

Barbie and Ken: Mattel, Inc.

Cliffs Notes: IDG Books Worldwide, Inc.

Domino's Pizza: Domino's Pizza PMC LLC LT

George of the Jungle: Ward Productions, Inc.

Hummer: General Motors Corporation

Metallica: Metallica

Wheaties: General Mills IP Holdings II

Chapter One

ഌ

On nights such as these, so dark and crisp, Jace McClellan cursed the fates for the path they'd laid before him. He was neither man nor beast, but an amalgamation of the two. He was cursed with their strength but not with their ability to shift. And to him, a curse it was. To be the anomaly within his own Pack, a brother in arms, but not where it truly counted. He was *Rakshasa*, a seer for his clan, and tonight his gift called to him.

As Jace walked through the dark forest, the sound of a babbling brook grew louder with every step. It was the only sound in the still of the night, the one constant that beckoned to him, leading him to where the future lay. Normally his visions weren't as intense, but as Jace neared the clearing, he noticed a naked woman bathing in the water. The water lapped at her firm brown thighs, showcasing her body in all its glory. Although she was turned slightly from him, Jace would have recognized her anywhere. Elizabeth Remington was unforgettable.

Even though he'd never seen her naked, he knew every curve and sinew of her body. Elizabeth, or Remy to anyone who didn't want to die a slow and painful death, was tall and muscular, but altogether a woman with high, rounded breasts and a curvy ass that evoked images in his mind of her kneeling before him as he pounded into her from behind. Droplets beaded on her as she knelt and sluiced the water over her body, being careful to keep her shoulder-length dark hair dry.

Jace sat on the grass, his back against a tree as he watched her. She looked like the Venus de Milo, rising from the water, as if she were some ancient fertility goddess. Remy stepped from the bank and knelt on the soft carpet of grass, staring at him but not really seeing. Her dark war-weary eyes saw right through Jace as she stretched out before him. Her body was riddled with scars and bruises, some fresh and some aged, yet every one was a wound to his soul. Remy was a warrior, a *Venator*, second-in-command to their Pack leader, and she'd earned her title the same way she earned her scars—by fighting.

Her strength and determination were just one of the many things he admired about her, along with her dark, spankable ass, an ass, thanks to her new position in which she faced away from him, was now within licking distance. Jace knew it was only a dream, but his cock didn't care—it hardened at the thought of Remy kneeling before him.

Stroking himself through the rough fabric of his denim, Jace pictured Remy reaching out to release him and cupping his cock in her hands before enveloping it in her warm mouth. Jace closed his eyes and imagined wrapping her hair in his hands as she licked and sucked him until he was wild with wanting her.

The purpose for his dream long forgotten, Jace began to unfasten his jeans, wanting to touch his flesh as he imagined it was Remy. The hand on his shoulder brought him to a halt and he turned to see who dared to interrupt him.

"It's not that kind of dream, *nipote*."

"You have the worst fucking timing, Vlad."

Vladimiro McClellan, Jace's ancestor guide, frowned in annoyance. "You know I dislike it when you shorten my name."

"Yeah, yeah, as if I care." Quickly refastening his jeans, Jace stood and ran a hand through his hair. He glanced over at the image of Remy still kneeling and now brushing her hair. Frustration burned in his gut knowing he would be unable to recapture this dream without first finding out what premonition was in store for him. "What do you want?"

"I wish you would be more appreciative of your gifts." Sighing, the blond man crossed his arms over his bare chest. With the same almond-shaped blue eyes, wavy dirty-blond hair and muscular physique, the two of them could have been mistaken for brothers instead of the great-grandfather and great-grandson they were.

Vladimiro, like Jace, had been cursed with the gift of sight, and it was he who appeared whenever Jace had a vision. A watcher for the watcher.

"I am appreciative. It's just damned inconvenient, you know."

"Stop thinking with that head and start looking around you. There is more going on here than you realize."

As if he could possibly see anyone or anything else when Remy was present.

"Go on, *nipote, see*." As if by Vladimiro's words alone, the vision grew more vivid. Almost as if someone or something had lifted a shrouded curtain and more of his premonition came into light. Jace glanced around the clearing and saw a number of wolves gathered around. Cutting his gaze back to Remy, she was now in her wolf form as well, her sleek silvery gray coat shining in the moonlight. Remy stood between two groups of wolves, an older Pack and a younger one led by Nico Cassamonti, the Pack *Benandanti*, and his *Elitario*, his top security officers, as well as other important Pack members. Into the clearing walked a human, a woman with long blonde hair and penetrating blue eyes, who appeared frightened and very, very pregnant.

"Who is she?" Jace didn't recognize the woman, but he realized there must be some significance to her presence.

"Keep watching." Jace should have known better than to ask Vladimiro any questions. His ancestor was only a guide and never answered an obvious question. Instead, Jace received all his premonitions in riddle form, which was very annoying. All the symbolism was sometimes hard to decipher, making Jace wonder why the fates had to be so fucking cryptic all the time.

The woman first walked toward the older group of wolves, who circled around her as if she were prey. They howled and jumped at her, their claws reaching for the child she carried within her. Crying, she covered her stomach and tried to keep the wolves at bay—as clichéd as it sounded—but she was merely human. No match against any of them. Turning toward Nico's Pack, Jace realized there was a strange wolf in their circle and the blonde woman kept trying to gain his attention, all to no avail. She looked downhearted at the rejection.

Jace noticed the older wolves were taunting the blonde woman now, pushing her off balance and pulling at her clothing. She looked scared and began to back away from them, only to have them circle her again and again, cutting off her escape. During this entire exchange, Remy continued to stand between the two groups of wolves, never moving, just observing the action.

Finally Nico howled, calling Remy over to him and Jace could almost imagine them speaking as they sniffed and nuzzled one another. Remy turned and headed for the blonde woman, and for a moment, Jace believed she was going to attack the human as well. But at the last moment Remy dragged her away from the group of older wolves, pulling her into the circle formed by Nico and his *Elitario*.

There was a loud scream as the woman dropped to her knees and Nico's Pack gathered around her. Everyone except Remy, who stood at Nico's back, ready to do battle. The scream abruptly broke off but was replaced by a loud wail, seemingly from an infant.

Annoyed, Jace turned to Vladimiro, who was watching him intently. "I get it. She's pregnant. Pregnant women give birth. See, I'm getting this dream reading down pat."

"If you weren't of my blood, I wouldn't waste my time with you."

"If I weren't of your blood, I wouldn't be seeing you," Jace reminded him as he turned back to the wolves. "You're dead, remember?"

"I live on, young Wolf."

"I'm not a Wolf." The words were as bitter as Jace himself was. "I ask you again, who is she?"

"It is something, *nipote*, you'll have to figure out for yourself."

Of course. "And the child?"

In an instant the clearing and the wolves were gone. The only thing left was the woman and child, who were standing on a lawn-sized chessboard. The mother stood with the child in her arms as Nico, now in human form and his wife Kimberly, walked behind her and took their position as king and queen. Next came Remy, who at first filled the spot as the knight to the king's right then she slowly took a step forward so she was even with the woman and child.

Confused, Jace stepped toward them as the older Pack of wolves once more came on to the scene. They stayed clear of the board, but snapped at the heels of Nico and Kimberly.

Undaunted by the angry wolves, Jace stepped onto the board and walked slowly around the human pieces. They were all in specific spots, and with the exception of Remy, no one had moved forward or backward, as if they were there for a reason. Nico, the leader, was the king, his wife the queen and the woman and child…

It couldn't really be so simple could it?

"The woman and child are pawns."

"So astute." Vladimiro moved next to Jace and gestured with his head toward Remy who was looking straight ahead. "But they are not the only ones on the battle line."

"Remy was in the knight's position."

"Yes."

209

"But she didn't move in an L shape. She stepped forward." Jace frowned, his brows furrowed as he concentrated on the scene before him. It didn't make any sense. A knight was unlike the king or queen. It could only move in one particular pattern. Circling her, he studied her position carefully. "It isn't right."

"How so?"

"She shouldn't be able to take this square."

"And why not?"

"Because she's a knight."

"Is she?"

Jace looked up sharply into Vladimiro's knowing gaze. "Isn't she?"

"You tell me."

Jace didn't want to believe what his vision was showing him. His Remy was a fighter, not someone to be used and discarded.

"You're thinking with the wrong head again."

"I'm not."

"Then tell me what she is."

"A pawn," Jace bit out. He wanted to pull back the vile words even as they slipped past his lips. "She's merely a pawn."

"Aren't we all?" Vladimiro clasped Jace on the shoulder and turned him until they were facing one another. The scene shimmered and vanished around them as the two locked gazes. "Sixty-four squares, *nipote*, which one will you stand on?"

Jace sat straight up in bed, sweat dripping down his back from the intensity of his vision.

"Fuck." The visions often exhausted Jace, but this one was one of the most powerful yet. If this were any indication, his gift was growing. Unfortunately it didn't mean the premonitions became any clearer. In fact, they were just as obscure as ever. Although this dream only had one conclusion. Jace needed to contact Nico.

Glancing over at the clock on the bedside table, he noted it was four-thirty. Nico certainly wouldn't thank him for the early morning interruption. On the other hand, Jace knew this message was one that couldn't wait until working hours. Jace had no idea who the blonde woman was, but she needed to be found. Her presence as a pawn on the chessboard meant if she wasn't protected by Nico, she could be a threat to the Pack.

Jace tried hard not to be reminded Remy had also been a pawn. He hated to think of her in such a way, someone to be used at a whim. At least as a knight she had power, but as a pawn, she was nothing.

Not true.

Although he rarely heard the voice of his ancestor outside the dream realm, the thought came through loud and clear. And then Jace recalled his childhood chess games. If a pawn were able to make it across the chessboard unscathed, it turned into a queen. Jace could only hope Remy would be so lucky.

Picking up the phone, he dialed Nico's home. The phone rang three times and Jace was wondering if the fourth ring would come and he would have to leave a message on the answering machine when the phone was finally answered.

"This had better be life or death." Nico's voice was scratchy with sleep and Jace winced at the fact he had to bother the *Benandanti* at this early hour, but he reminded himself it was for a good cause.

"Nico, it's Jace. I'm sorry to bother you but I had a disturbing dream."

Thankfully Nico didn't deride him. The *Benandanti* was instantly aware of the significance of the call and immediately got down to business.

"I'll meet you at the Desert Sanctuary within the hour."

Jace hung up the phone and slowly stood. His body felt as if he'd participated in a marathon race, his muscles screaming in agony as he moved toward the bathroom. He was going to need a hot shower and plenty of coffee before he faced the *Benandanti* this morning.

* * * * *

Over the course of Remy's lifetime, she had maimed, tortured and killed, yet there had never been a time she wanted to hurt anyone as much as she wanted to harm Jace. It was five-thirty in the fucking morning. *Five-fucking-thirty.* The bastard was going down.

With the flat of her hand, she shoved against the observation room's door. The latch gave way under her powerful strength and the door slung back forcefully, banging into the wall.

"I've said it before and I'll say it again—" Remy's voice roused the gathered men who all looked over at her and smiled. To say Remy wasn't a morning person would be like saying Beethoven's *Für Elise* was a snazzy tune to listen to. "Nothing short of the world's chocolate supply being held hostage is worth getting out of bed before nine."

"Good morning," Harrison Wood called out to her as he rose from his seat. He headed straight for the coffeepot where he quickly prepared a cup of coffee for her. "How many have you had?"

For such a muscular man, Harrison moved with grace. The dark-skinned man was as agile as he was handsome. Even though he preferred his role as *Cahalith*, teacher for the young Weres, Harrison had seen his share of battles and had the marks of valor to prove it, including a nasty scar that ran just shy of his left eye to the corner of his newly grown goatee. Instead of taking away from his good looks, the scar added to it, at least in Remy's eyes.

212

"Three," she grumbled as she made her way around the conference room table to her self-designated seat, directly to the right of Nico's, which flanked the head of the table.

Unfortunately for Derek Chow, he didn't move fast enough out of her chair, and he nearly fell on his ass as she pulled the chair from underneath him. Undaunted by her normal behavior, Derek laughed and moved to the chair next to her. "Morning, sunshine."

"Eat me."

"Maybe later." He winked, knowing it would drive her further mad. Remy knew he sat in her chair on purpose. For some reason the Asian man adored getting her goat. It was the only thing he lived for, next to pussy. And for Derek, that came in spades. Women were drawn to the handsome Were like bees to honey. With jet-black hair that hung past his shoulders and eyes the color of onyx, Derek was the epitome of exotic sensuality. Throw in his muscles and his charisma and he was a force to be reckoned with.

"In your dreams." Harrison handed the cup to her as he rounded the table and took his seat across from her. The other two men in the room also took their seats, following Remy's lead in the room just as they did in all things related to the Pack.

She'd known them all since adolescence. They'd grown up together in the Pack and met as young pups, just learning the ways of the Were. They were all outcasts in their own way and had banded together as a group. Luckily Nico was part of the group and when he became *Benandanti*, his friends continued to follow him.

Remy had fought by their side in battles past. Bled for them, tried for them. And she would die for them. They were her Pack. Her brothers, though the only one in the room who slightly resembled her was Harrison, and he only because they both shared the same skin hue.

Harrison and she were the only Weres in Nico's *Elitaro's* that shared African forefathers. Derek was of Asian descent and Jackson Young and Kellen Quinn, the other two Weres in the room, were of European descent. Yet to them, it didn't matter. Their human ethnicity was as unimportant as the color of their fur. It was the one thing the Weres had managed to overcome their human brothers had not.

"Does anyone want to enlighten me regarding what the hell we're doing here?"

"Jace," the men chimed in all at once, much to her annoyance. She wasn't irritated they spoke at the same time, but that they'd all spoken the dreaded name of her mortal enemy.

"I know that," she bit out before pausing to take a drink of her coffee. It was strong, bitter and black, just like herself, and despite the soothing effect of caffeine, Remy still was pissed off. "But do we know what Watcher Boy dreamt about?"

"You of course, princess."

Naturally he walked in while she was talking about him. With a heavy sigh, Remy closed her eyes and slowly counted to ten. When she finished counting and it hadn't done anything to relieve the tension coursing through her veins, she counted to thirty.

Jace, the never-ending yeast infection who haunted her nightmares. He was a pain in the ass, and not the sexy, sharp sting of someone's hand. He drove her crazy and damn him, he knew it. The unfortunate part was she was strangely attracted to the man. She could barely be in the same room with him for a few minutes before they started sniping at each other, but it didn't stop her body from responding to his presence.

"Who left the door open?" Remy opened her eyes but kept looking ahead. She refused to glance his way. He'd use it as an opening to annoy her further.

"Aww, your bitterness wounds me." His voice caressed her ear as he leaned over and spoke softly in her ear. Try as she might, Remy couldn't stop the way her nipples hardened under her bra. As irritating as she found him, Jace was the one man who could make her wet with a single glance. And he knew it. The bastard.

She didn't have to glance at him to know how good-looking he was. His image was burned into her brain and late-night fantasies. Jace typified the California surfer dude, with his sun-kissed blond hair and smiling blue eyes. He was tan and muscular, giving the appearance of someone who could handle himself out on the waves or in a back-alley fight. Why he couldn't look like a troll, she had no idea.

"Good, maybe you'll bleed out."

"How about you kiss it and make it better?"

Enough was enough. Remy slowly turned her head until her face was mere inches from his and growled low and deep. Her growl was a sound that frightened men to death, yet Jace merely smiled, as if the threatening sound amused him.

He wasn't too bright.

"If I were you, Jace, I'd back up." This came from Kellen, her champion and former lover. Former by her decision not his, and everyone knew it, even Jace, who didn't budge. At six foot two inches, Kellen's fiery temper matched his flaming hair. His eyes were a light blue that could sometimes make him look cold and unrelenting, much like now.

For someone who didn't get all fuzzy, Jace surely had balls of steel. Kellen could change in a second and rip out his throat before he drew another breath, but by the way Jace leaned closer in to her, moving back toward her ear, he wasn't threatened. In fact, he seemed to egg the younger man on.

"But he isn't me, is he, Remy? And that was the problem, wasn't it?"

His words weren't whispered but even if they were, with their keen hearing, everyone would have heard him anyway.

Jace's taunt didn't fall on deaf ears. Kellen pushed his chair back and stood, much to Jace's amusement.

Not everyone was amused though. Harrison jumped up as well and placed a cautionary hand on Kellen's arm. He shot Remy a "do something" look, but short of banging their heads together, she was clueless. She wasn't the type of girl men fought over, and it flattered and frustrated her all at the same time.

Fucking men.

"Could you fellas piss on her another time?" Nico stood in the doorway, eyebrow raised in annoyance. The *Benandanti* held a commanding presence, towering over everyone in the room. His thick dark hair matched his nearly black eyes, which swept across the room, catching everything in his intense gaze. "We have more important things to discuss."

Everyone except for Remy looked toward Jace, knowing he was the bringer of the doom and gloom. Remy long suspected their venerable watcher didn't know shit and often made stuff up just to piss her off. On the other hand, he'd come through when Kimberly, Nico's mate, had been kidnapped. So rather than make a firm commitment, she was staying neutral on the subject of his abilities until she had further proof. On his ability to heat her up, with anger or desire, she had no problem ruling him a complete pain in the ass.

"Okay, Jace, let's hear it." Nico was ready to get down to business.

"I'm going to Cliff's Notes it for you."

"Why?" Remy questioned, mainly just to get a rise out of him. It worked.

Jace shot her an annoyed look before letting out a heavy sigh. "Simply because I could go into details and since you're not in the know, most of it won't make any sense to you."

"Not in 'the know'?" Remy raised a brow at his a haughty answer. "I didn't realize it required a lot of skill and know-how to sleep."

"Remy," Nico warned.

"Sorry." She wasn't, but it sounded good.

"Basically, here's the deal. There's a human blonde pregnant woman out there and we need to find and protect her. For some reason she and her child are important and the *Maggiore* want her, bad."

At the mention of a human woman, the room turned en masse toward Derek, known not only for his womanizing but for his affinity for humans.

Holding up his hands, Derek laughed for a moment until he realized everyone was still staring him down. "Hey, don't look at me. I'm more careful than that—really. Besides, aren't we all supposed to be dying off because we can't reproduce?"

Remy remembered the conversation they'd had only a few months before in the Howler, when Nico first suggested they join with the *Morbauch* Pack, a group of Coyote Weres. It was the first time any leader had acknowledged their females were unable to get pregnant or have as many young as they'd had in the past.

Nico sighed and nodded. "It's true our females are having a harder time getting pregnant. But perhaps this woman has some answers for our problems."

"But Watcher Boy here said she was a human. How does that help us?" Remy held in the smile when Jace frowned at her nickname for him. She could give as good as she got.

"Good question. But a better question may be, who is this woman?" Harrison had the innate ability to boil a problem down to its lowest level.

"Sorry, Jace, but I think we're going to need a little bit more. Can you describe the dream?" Nico's request was a lot more tactful than Remy's would have been, which is one of the reasons he was the *Benandanti* and she was the *Venator*.

Jace ran his hand through his hair, a look of frustration on his face. Remy had to steel herself from wanting to comfort him. First, it would make her look weak in front of her *Rahu*, something she'd never allow herself to do. Secondly, he'd probably turn it against her, teasing her mercilessly.

"I don't know who she is. I didn't recognize her. In my dream, she stood between two Packs of wolves, the *Maggiore* on one side and you and the *Elitario* on the other. You sent Remy to bring her to you and she gave birth to the baby. Then the scene changed and both you and Kimberly willingly stood guard over her. I don't know why, but I can only can go by the feeling she knows you both."

Remy felt as if Jace were holding something back in his explanation, but she couldn't figure out why. There was no reason for him to hide anything from Nico. Jace was the one who asked for this meeting in the first place.

"Describe her to me." Nico's words cut off Remy's further musings.

"She's a beautiful woman, very petite, blonde hair and blue eyes."

"She sounds like half the women in California," Jackson noted, amusement spilling from his tawny gaze. The historian wasn't until recently part of the *Elitario*, but after Nico's power play with the *Maggiore*, he'd become as synonymous with the group as jokes and laughter. He wasn't much of a conversationalist, but there was very little the staid Were missed, which made him a great sounding board.

"She sounds like a fucking Barbie doll." Remy didn't enjoy the feelings she was having when Jace described the woman. She just about felt jealous, although she pushed the idea aside almost immediately. Hell, Jace didn't even know the woman.

But he was dreaming about her.

Kellen rubbed his chin thoughtfully. "Hey, didn't you call those *Morbauchs* Ken dolls? Maybe she's from their Pack?"

"Hello, human, duh. The *Morbauch* Pack may only be Coyotes, but they're still Were." Remy grimaced as she watched Kellen flush at Derek's words. Derek sometimes didn't think before he spoke, shooting everyone's ideas down whether they were good or not. Kellen was a good fighter and he didn't deserve Derek's derogatory comments.

"Enough. This is getting us nowhere. We need to discover who this woman is. The sooner the better." Nico's gaze swept the room as he spoke.

"Can't you nail down her identity any more than you have?" Remy's irritation came through her question, and Jace's response was just as frustrated.

"I can't fucking turn it on and off, you know. The visions come and they don't exactly make a hell of a lot of sense. For God's sake, I'm doing the best I can."

"We know, Jace. Everyone realizes the seriousness of this situation and we appreciate your contribution." Nico was trying to soothe over Remy's rudeness and she felt as if she were a child whose parent had to apologize for their unruly offspring.

"I don't think everyone does, *Benandanti*." His words and his gaze were pointed, and Remy fought back the urge to make him eat them. How dare he challenge her in such a manner? "This is serious."

Even though Remy knew the logistics of Jace's so-called talent, the why and how it worked still eluded her. It didn't help that he was the youngest watcher in two decades — the last, his great-grandfather had been murdered in the Great War. Leaving just Jace to lead the future watchers, a class of six young Weres, all with the same power he possessed. All just as clueless. It was the blind leading the blind. And it was annoying as fuck.

"Yeah, yeah, yeah." Remy waved her hand in a dismissive way toward Jace, already bored with the meeting. Did she really have to get out of bed for this crap? "Fine. We search for a pregnant blonde chick. We bring her with us, to the dark side. Shove her away in a stable so she can safely give birth. We win. Bad guys lose. Party and pizza at my house."

Her simplification of the situation brought forth laughter from everyone surrounding the table. Everyone but Jace, that is. "You think it's so easy?"

"For us, yes."

"You're just going to walk in and kill first, ask questions later."

Remy shrugged her shoulders as if his comment didn't faze her. "Dead men don't talk."

"What about dead women?" Jace leaned forward, his gaze intently focused on her. "Are they immortal? Are you?"

The room grew deadly silent at his words. The way he said it didn't come off as a simple question. "Are you threatening me, human?"

Jace flinched. Disclaiming his Were DNA was a direct shot. Remy was just as good at wounding with her words as she was with her hands.

"Remy!" Nico barked at her disrespectful tone and words. Even the other men turned shocked gazes her way.

Remy wasn't going to feel bad though. He had pushed her. But she couldn't exactly meet his eyes. "Look—"

"No, you look, Remington." Jace slammed his hand on the table. The force of the blow cracked the wood, and all eyes shifted to him in surprise. Everyone knew Jace was gifted with some of the strengths, but she had no idea he was so physically powerful. Impressed by his show of force, Remy didn't retaliate against his insolent action. She actually sort of admired him a bit now…but just a bit. "I've had it up to here with you."

"You have, have you?"

"Damn straight."

Now things were getting good. If there was one thing Remy admired, it was someone who didn't take her shit. It amused her. "And what exactly do you think you're going to do about it?"

Jace moved with lightning speed out of his chair and around Derek until he was at Remy's chair. Shocked, Remy stared at him as he pulled back her seat and picked her up, chair and all, until they were eye to eye. "Keep testing me, she-wolf, and you'll see exactly what I'll do about it."

Without another word, Jace dropped Remy's chair and strode from the dead-silent room. When her chair hit the floor the legs shattered and Remy was left sitting in a pile of wood.

"What the..." Remy bound to her feet, dusting off her rear in the process. Looking up, she noticed every eye was on her, and they all wore the same stunned expression on their faces.

Nico frowned, yet for some reason, Remy was sure it wasn't to her advantage. "Remington, you owe him—"

"An ass-kicking," Kellen offered, his face as red as his hair. "I ought to do it myself."

"No, I'll handle it." Glancing at the door, Remy knew just what she had to do. Damn it all to hell, she hated the taste of crow.

Nico stood, capturing the attention of the entire room with his gaze. "Good, now let's go find out who this woman is and bring her home."

Chapter Two

ॐ

The paper gown crackled as Cassandra Adams shifted on the exam table for what seemed like the hundredth time since she'd entered the room. Try as she might, she couldn't control the foreboding sense of dread hovering over her like a dark cloud.

Where the hell is the doctor?

Biting her bottom lip, she tried to still the thoughts bouncing around her brain. Unfortunately she hadn't been very successful up to this point, hence the restlessness.

Cassandra never thought she'd find herself in a "delicate" situation as the nuns at Catholic school used to say. But here she was, waiting for the obstetrician to return and give her the verdict. The same verdict five pregnancy tests, four months of missed periods or the word of her father hadn't been able to convince her of.

Of course her father—Franklin Russell—wasn't the most reliable of sources. The man was truly treading on the dark side. If it weren't for the DNA test telling her otherwise, Cassandra wouldn't have believed someone so evil or so…unnatural could be related to her. And it didn't get much more unnatural than dear ol' dad. He was a Werewolf.

If Cassandra hadn't seen him change right before her eyes, she wouldn't believe it herself. Lord knows, when she started her quest five years ago to find her biological father, she never expected to find proof of the supernatural as well. Now all Cassandra wished was she could go back to the safe, sane world of not knowing. Then she wouldn't have to deal with her father and his crazy plan to take over his Pack or any of the other Werewolf bullshit she had witnessed over the last year.

Then again, if she went back in time and changed everything, she wouldn't be here today. Unfortunately Cassandra wasn't too sure how she felt about it. Sure she hated everything her father stood for, but her distaste of her new four-legged friends would have to come to an end. Especially since the father of her child was a Werewolf as well.

David… No, she wasn't going to think about him. It was more than obvious he hadn't spent a moment thinking of her in the last four months. Hell, he probably hadn't given her a second thought once he climbed from her bed and walked out of her townhouse. Of course, it was no less than she deserved, sleeping with him as quickly as she had.

Although she'd never planned a future with the guy, she didn't think he'd turn out to be a "wham, bam, thank you, ma'am" type. But when she'd slyly inquired about him to Kimberly, her assistant and David's sister, Cassandra was surprised to hear he'd gone home.

Thankfully her thoughts were interrupted by a quick knock on the door and Dr. Felicia Osterman peeking her head around the door, smiling as she entered the room. She was a classic beauty with sable hair and big, beautiful green eyes. Cassandra always imaged her in a Rubens painting, frolicking in a garden.

"Your suspicions were correct, you are definitely pregnant. About four months along, I'd say." Cassandra wrapped her hands around her middle as the doctor spoke. "You're already starting to show, you really didn't think it was anything else, did you?"

Cassandra shrugged her shoulders. Yeah, she knew. She'd just been hoping for a miracle.

"Okay then. Am I to assume the father won't be involved and this wasn't necessarily a planned pregnancy? Maybe something you've been avoiding for a while?"

Cassandra snorted with derision. Since David wasn't living in the same city, she doubted he would be involved.

Felicia laid down her chart and took Cassandra's hands in her own. "Cassandra, this is me. We've known each other for the last three years, ever since you moved to Bayside. I didn't even think you were dating anyone. So what's going on?"

Cassandra just shook her head, knowing there was no way in hell she could ever explain this to anyone. "Nothing's going on and no, the father won't be involved."

Felicia pressed her lips together as if she wanted to say more but was holding back. "As your doctor, I feel I need to inform you you do have choices here. This is obviously an unplanned pregnancy. I can leave information for you or we can discuss your options."

"Wait a minute, are you talking about abortion?" Cassandra was surprised at her own shock. She never planned to become pregnant, and certainly not like this, with no father for the baby in sight, but hearing someone actually talk about terminating her pregnancy brought out her protective instincts.

"No, that's not going to happen. I'm keeping this baby. She's going to be all mine." Now that she'd actually said the words aloud, Cassandra realized she really believed them. She'd never let her crazed father get a hold of this child and she'd protect it with her dying breath.

"She?"

"Yes, I've decided to have a girl. You can make sure that happens, right?" Cassandra smiled at her own joke.

"Sorry, too late. It's already been decided. But by the twentieth week we should be able to find out for sure."

"I guess when it's all said and done, it doesn't really matter what the sex is. It's not as if I can send it back if it's a boy."

"So true." Felicia grinned. "I'm going to call for a nurse now and we're going to do an ultrasound."

"An ultrasound!" Cassandra's hand instinctively went to her stomach.

"Don't worry, Momma. It won't hurt your baby."

Cassandra wasn't so much worried about the ultrasound hurting the baby as she was of the doctor seeing something unusual on the screen. Wolf pregnancies weren't exactly covered in health class. "Is it necessary?"

"Necessary, no, but we usually do a baseline diagnostic at the beginning of the pregnancy."

"I'm not sure if I want to do one." In fact, Cassandra wasn't even sure if she was going to make any more doctor visits after today.

"Cassandra, I…" Felicia paused for a second, as if searching for the right thing to say. "You do understand whatever is said between us stays between us."

"Yes."

"And even if we didn't have doctor-patient confidentiality, I'd hope you know as your friend you can trust me."

"I do."

"Do you?" Felicia picked up the file she brought into the room with her. "So do you want to tell me why the pregnancy hormone wasn't the only thing we found in your bloodstream?"

Cassandra paled. "What else did you find?"

"You tell me." Felicia opened the file. "Why in the world would a woman who I personally fitted for a diaphragm less than six months ago, have a Clomid derivative in her system? I was under the impression you weren't trying to get pregnant."

"I wasn't. I don't even know what Clomid is. I met a guy and one thing led to another and here I am." Cassandra desperately tried to downplay the mention of fertility drugs, turning Felecia's attention to the matter at hand.

"Fine, don't tell me. I'll give you some names of obstetricians you can contact."

"What do you mean?"

"If you can't be honest with me, I can't treat you to the best of my abilities. It would be better if you found another doctor."

"I am being honest, Felecia. I don't know what is in my blood and I wasn't trying to get pregnant. But it happened and I'm here and I need a friend. I really do." Cassandra burst into tears.

"Shhh, it's okay. It's just the hormones screwing with you." Felecia wrapped her arms around Cassandra, offering the comfort she needed.

"Please don't dump me on another doctor. I don't think I could stand the rejection right now." Cassandra wiped at her face, knowing she probably looked atrocious. Her hormones must be messing with her since just a few minutes ago she was contemplating dumping the doctor.

"Okay, but you need to be honest with me during this whole pregnancy. I'm going to write you a prescription for some vitamins and I'll want to see you again in two weeks. And we will do an ultrasound then."

Cassandra nodded her head in agreement. Felecia left as Cassandra began to get dressed. Two weeks. She would have to decide what she was going to do by then. As she walked out of the building with prescription in hand, her cell phone rang.

Struggling to grab her phone, she frowned at the unknown number as she answered.

"Hello?"

"Hello, daughter dear. I hope the doctor confirmed my diagnosis." Franklin's words caused Cassandra to stop in her tracks and glance around at her surroundings. Although she didn't see anyone, he obviously had someone watching her.

"Why are you calling me?"

"To offer you congratulations of course. You surprised me, and I'm not often surprised."

"Oh yeah, how'd I do that?" Cassandra began walking quickly toward her car, wanting to get out of the open. She didn't like the feeling he could find her so easily.

"I figured you for a little rabbit who'd run away. But you didn't. Have you decided to embrace your destiny?"

Reaching her car, Cassandra struggled for a moment to open the door before she was finally able to gain entrance. Once inside, she locked the doors immediately.

"Listen to me and listen good. I'm not 'embracing my destiny' as you so aptly put it. In fact, I want nothing to do with you ever again. Leave me alone." Not waiting for his reply, Cassandra ended the call and turned off the phone.

Looking into the rearview mirror, Cassandra saw an overwrought woman staring back at her. She took a shaky breath, trying to regain her calm. She hadn't heard from her father since the night of the fire at Heath's estate when Franklin told her she was pregnant. Cassandra shuddered when she remembered the moment he revealed he'd been slipping her fertility pills.

That was the moment she knew for certain her father was insane. She had wanted to have a family so badly she initially did everything he'd asked of her. His stories of persecution by the Pack leader seemed legitimate until she discovered it was all based on lies. Unfortunately she didn't realize how far gone he was until that fateful night.

Placing her hand on the noticeable bulge of her stomach, Cassandra tried to imagine what was in store for this child. Even though she might have been ambivalent about getting pregnant, she knew now she would hold on to this child for all she was worth. And she'd do it without David or her father.

* * * * *

Jace jogged on the treadmill, his heart rate pumping as he tried to relieve the tension haunting him the entire day. A confrontation with Remy usually had a way of making his blood pump, but this morning's incident was still grating on his nerves even as the sun was going down. Her dismissal of his abilities and him in general stung like no other hurt.

Reaching down to increase the speed of the machine, Jace picked up his pace, running now, sweat dripping off his forehead. He'd long since removed his shirt, clothed only in socks, running shoes and low-slung jogging shorts. A shower was definitely going to be in order after this workout.

The ringing of the doorbell threw off his concentration and Jace stumbled for a moment before regaining his balance and slowly bringing the treadmill to a halt. Walking to the door, he swung open the heavy oak to reveal the source of his frustration staring him in the face.

"What do you want?" Jace wiped a towel over his face and down his body as he stared at Remy, unwilling to give even an inch.

"I came over to see if little Watcher Boy was okay after his temper tantrum today."

"You can be a real bitch, you know."

Remy pushed past him and walked into his living room. Shaking his head, Jace closed the door and followed her, wondering what her motivation was. She rarely did anything without a reason and he questioned whether Nico had ordered her over here to apologize. He certainly wasn't interested in accepting some half-assed forced contrition.

"Yeah well, she-wolves like me are usually wired that way."

"Don't try to make me feel guilty. You were out of line." He crossed his arms, mainly in an attempt to control his desire to take her over his lap and give her the spanking she was desperately in need of. "Did Nico send you?"

"I'm no one's lapdog."

"No, just a bitch." Instead of looking insulted, she grinned, as if she were pleased by his remark. "You know you're wired completely wrong."

"Why do you say that?" Remy dropped on his couch and propped her feet on his coffee table as bold as she pleased.

"First of all," Jace dropped his arms and walked over to her, shoving her feet off the table on to the floor, "you have no manners."

"Manners are just a façade people put on to hide who they really are."

"And you don't hide, do you?"

Remy held her arms out wide. "What you see is what you get."

"Yeah, right." Jace shook his head. He wondered if she really believed that bull.

"You say it like you don't believe me."

"I don't."

"Jace, you're going to hurt my feelings."

"Do you even have any?" His words were a low blow, and by the look that quickly flashed across Remy's face, she felt the hit.

Of course she quickly masked her emotions. "Surely you jest. Me, with feelings other than rage? It could never happen."

"That's what I thought."

"So are you going to offer me something to drink?" Remy asked a little too brightly.

"No."

"Why not?"

"Because it would imply you're a *welcomed* guest."

"Ouch." She laughed, her full lips spreading wide in a big grin. Remy's eyes sparkled with merriment and instead of standing and leaving as a decent person would have, she settled back as if making herself right at home.

Jace would never get her. If he was nice to her, she ignored him. If he ignored her, she seemed not to care. But when he gave her shit, she seemed to love it. She was twisted.

"So you've done your duty, made your appearance to make sure I'm all hunky-dory, so why aren't you leaving?"

"Damn, talk about manners. No drink, practically throwing me out the door ...you're the Emily Post reject." Remy bounced to her feet and headed toward the bar. Turning to glance over her shoulder she asked, "You want anything?"

Jace shook his head silently. He watched as she poured herself two fingers of his finest Scotch and drank it in one swallow. When she poured herself a second round, he decided enough was enough. Stepping behind her, he pulled the glass out of her hands and set it down.

"Enough with the delay tactics, spill it. What's the real reason you're here?"

"I told you, just stopping by to see if things were cool after this morning."

Fuck it. Picking up the glass, Jace downed the amber liquid as quickly as she had. "No, things aren't cool. I don't appreciate your attitude. In fact, it's detrimental to the Pack. Nico needs to take you in hand."

Remy laughed. "Nah, he has Kimberly for that. He likes me right where I am, guarding his back."

Jace grabbed her arm, pulling her in close. "Well, someone needs to take you in hand and maybe I should be the one to do it."

Instead of pulling away as he expected, Remy stared up at him silently, almost as if daring him to make a move so she could have the excuse to break his arm. "You think you can handle a she-wolf like me? Somehow I doubt it."

Jace took the dare without thought, pushing her back against the edge of the bar and leaning over her menacingly. "Don't push me."

"Awww, is little Watcher Boy gonna get mad?"

"You need your ass spanked."

Remy snorted derisively. "And you think you're the *man* to do it?" Her emphasis on "man" riled his nerves. She knew he didn't appreciate quips about his abilities as a Were kin and the words were too close to this morning's name-calling.

"That's it." Jace bent his head, capturing her mouth in a heated kiss as he tried to shut out her insults. His tongue dueled with hers as they both fought for dominance in the embrace. He wasn't willing to back down from this encounter. Although he'd lusted after Remy for years, always teasing and taunting her with sexual innuendo, they'd rarely touched, let alone ever kissed.

Pressing her body back against the bar, he let Remy feel the evidence of his desire. His cock was always semierect in her presence, but at times such as these, when she fired his blood, he became rock-hard at the thought of possessing her. Remy moaned into his mouth as he pressed against her, parting her legs slightly as if in acceptance of his body.

Breaking the kiss, Jace gasped for breath as Remy did the same. Her breasts heaved with the effort and Jace longed to see them bared, wanting to know the color and size of her nipples. Without thought, he reached out and began unfastening her shirt, slipping the buttons through the holes and slowly revealing her bare flesh to his gaze.

"What are you doing?" Remy's voice was low and husky, no longer taunting, it held a hint of wonder in her question.

"Exactly what I want to do." Jace pushed the blouse off her shoulders. He was shocked to realize instead of the utilitarian bra he expected to find, Remy was covered in pink lace. *Pink*. It was unbelievably girly and so unlike the *Venator* it made him smile. "Pink, Remy?"

Sweet hell, Remy had forgotten what she'd put on this morning. Of all the days to delve into her secret passion for lingerie, it had to be the day when she let Jace get to second

231

base. And of course, like the gentleman he wasn't, he would have to comment.

Remy grabbed at the lapels of her khaki shirt and tried to close it but was stopped by Jace, who took her wrist in hand. "It's not pink. It was white and I washed it with something red."

"Right." Jace all but choked on his laughter. The bastard. "And let me guess. This isn't lace, it's really cotton and that one night, in a fit of boredom, you decided to make snowflakes out of your bra and took your scissors to it."

Eyes narrowed, Remy smacked his hand away. "Which is exactly what happened."

"I think you're lying."

No, really. Remy gathered her shirt together so she could button it as she thought of all the different ways she was going to hurt him. "Well, it's just my word against yours."

"Is that the problem, she-wolf?" Jace once again took hold of her hands, but this time moved them down her shirt and behind her back. He gripped her hands together in one of his and pushed the shirt open again, exposing her breasts to his hungry gaze. "Are you afraid the boys will know Little Miss Big Bad is into girly things?"

At any time, Remy could have broken Jace's hold on her. Despite his strength, she had years of combat and martial arts training on him. With a single blow she could render him unconscious, even with her hands tied behind her back, and this was all without turning into her wolf form. Yet she stayed there, passive in his grip.

For the life of her, she couldn't figure out why. Despite that, she couldn't help egging him on. "I'm not afraid of anything, especially not you."

"I'm willing to bet underneath these jeans, you're wearing a *pretty* little pink scrap of lace that matches this bra."

"I am not." She so was.

"No?" Jace's brushed his fingers teasingly against her annoyingly erect nipples before sauntering down her stomach where they came to a rest on the waist of her jeans. "Do you want to bet on it?"

"As if you'd have something I want."

Jace cocked a brow, his lip spreading in a wide grin. "Oh, I think I do."

Now there was a point when cocky went from being cute to downright annoying and he was toeing the line. "Do you think you'll be the first man who'll say they've been to heaven?"

His smile disappeared and his grip tightened, causing her back to arch and push her breasts out. "No, but I think I'll be the first man who can say they've taken you to heaven."

Good Lord, the man could talk dirty. For the first time in her life, Remy felt lightheaded and it had nothing to do with the loss of blood. "You think you're God's gift or something?"

"No, I think I'm yours." Jace ran his fingers softly back and forth against the waistband of her jeans. The gentle teasing touch was a promise of more to come. Her stomach was taut and she felt almost afraid to breath. Afraid if she moved too quickly, she would lose out on discovering if Jace was as good as she hoped he was.

Remy licked her lips nervously as she stared back at him. She was more aroused by his mere words than she had ever been in her entire life. "Don't let the pink bra fool you, Jace. I'm a warrior first, a woman second."

"I don't think you know how to be a woman." Jace stopped his teasing caress and moved his fingers to the button of her jeans.

"And I guess you think you're the man for the job."

The button popped open.

"No." Her zipper slid down. "I think I'm the Were for the job."

And Jace's hand slid into the front of her lacy, feminine, pink panties and cupped her sopping-wet pussy. "Don't let the lack of fur fool you, she-wolf. I'm all the Wolf you'll need."

"If you think this proves you've taken me in hand, think again."

"I don't think it proves anything. Yet."

Remy gasped as Jace's fingers slid along her folds, finding her opening without hesitation. He teased her for a moment before slipping his fingers inside, his blunt digits making her rise on her toes for a moment at the thrust. His thumb brushed lightly over her clit and Remy bit her lip at the movement.

She didn't want to react, didn't want to let him know just how much his words and touch were affecting her. But it was as if she had lost all her bravado when he first kissed her and she was just a woman, longing to be taken by her man. Even when she and Kellen had been lovers, Remy had fantasized about Jace. She sensed he had a dark side, one she was eager to explore. But she'd always held him off until now. Her body was betraying her at every turn, pushing back against his questing hand, begging for more of his touch.

"I think you like me fingering your wet little pussy. In fact, I bet you'd spread your legs wide for me if I asked."

Remy whimpered as at his words, knowing he was right. She wanted Jace and maybe if they fucked tonight, she could finally get him out of her mind.

"Answer me. Would you let me fuck you?" Jace rubbed his thumb hard against her clit as he spoke, causing her to clutch at his shoulders or lose her balance.

"Yes."

Suddenly Jace pulled his hands from her jeans, stepping away from her. "Go home, *Venator*. You've done your good deed for the day."

Remy blinked at him in shock. He was rejecting her? "Are you fucking mad?"

"No, I'm not fucking anything at all."

Barely able to control herself, she quickly buttoned her shirt and fastened her jeans. Remy was so upset she could barely see straight. "That was…" There weren't words enough to describe how pissed off she was. "I can't believe I even allowed you to kiss me."

"Yeah, sullying yourself with a mere human, Remy." Jace's words were as cold as hers had been earlier in the day. "What ever would the boys think?"

Remy flushed. "That's not what I meant."

"Right." Jace wiped his wet hand on his shorts, as if her essence disgusted him. "You let yourself in. You can let yourself out."

With that, Jace turned and left the living room, leaving Remy staring at his retreating back.

Chapter Three

೮೧

Today was one of those days Jace wished he didn't have such a close-knit family. In fact, when the phone rang, interrupting the precious few hours of sleep he'd finally been able to achieve, he was wishing he was an orphan.

"Someone better be dead." Jace was barely able to hold the phone up as he spoke, his exhaustion wearing him out. The fact he knew it was his family before he even answered the phone spoke volumes. His house phone was only reserved for family, everyone else called his cell.

"Hey, big brother, just wanted to remind you I'll be by in an hour to pick you up." The bubbly voice of his sister Isabelle caused Jace to roll over in bed, his hand shading his eyes from the early morning light.

"Huh?"

"You didn't forget about the company picnic did you?"

In fact, he *had* forgotten about the annual Pack barbeque at the Sanctuary, advertised as the "company picnic" in order to appear more human to their neighbors. Of course Jace couldn't really be blamed for his forgetfulness. He was barely getting three hours of sleep a night and he had to wonder if the fates were laughing at him. Ever since the visit from Remy, his dreams about the mysterious blonde had increased exponentially, to the point where Jace wondered if it was cosmic payback for him walking away from the bratty she-wolf.

"Jace, you still there?"

"Yeah, sorry. I'll be ready."

"Okay, see you in an hour."

For the life of him, Jace couldn't recall why he'd agree to ride with Isabelle. She was a pest. A menace behind the wheel and she had shitty taste in music. Yet because she asked, he agreed. No one in the family could say no to her. It was a curse, and to her a blessing.

Jace rolled over, wishing he could ignore his family and attempt sleep. Realistically he knew it was impossible. Not only would his family never let him avoid Pack obligations, but the chance of him actually getting to sleep without the dreams was little to none.

"My life sucks," he thundered, giving in to the fit he so desperately wanted to throw.

He was used to having clairvoyant dreams but never had they occurred so often and been so vivid. It was getting to the point Jace was ready to start looking for the mysterious woman himself, just so he could stop dreaming about her.

Jace dragged the pillow over his head in the process, but it was no barrier against his phone, which began to ring again. After the sixth ring, Jace rolled over again and grabbed the phone. "Isabelle," he growled.

"Get up."

"I am up."

"Liar," she teased before hanging up, much to his annoyance. She knew him too well. And just as Isabelle knew he was still in bed, Jace knew she would keep calling until he got out of it. With a ragged curse, Jace fought his way from beneath the blue tangled sheets and stomped all the way into the bathroom.

He might have to be up, but it didn't mean he had to be happy about it.

An hour and a half later, after much grumbling and teasing on his sister's part, they arrived at the Sanctuary. Today's picnic was a ground-breaking event. It would be the first time the Wolves and Coyotes had joined together for anything other than to kill one another. Although from the legendary way the two Packs had of dealing with one another, a murder or two might still occur.

The weather this afternoon was sunny, an absolutely gorgeous summer day. It was too bad Jace wasn't in a better mood to enjoy his surroundings. He had a pounding headache and the annual barbeque wasn't one of his favorite events. Besides the fact he was exhausted, he couldn't participate in the evening runs like the other Weres. It was just one more example of how he was different.

"Come on, Jace, you've been in a sucky mood since I called this morning. Why won't you tell me what's up?"

At twenty, Isabelle had been shielded from a lot of the ugliness of Pack politics. She'd never experienced the horrors of the war, being one of the first few young born after the truce was called. Jace wasn't willing to allow her to give up her innocence just yet. With her mop of curly blonde hair and twinkling blue eyes, he wanted Belle to be the same fun-loving *lupa* she'd always been, if only for a little while longer.

"It's nothing, Belle, really. Why don't you find Mom and Dad while I get something to drink?" Isabelle nodded in resignation before heading across the wide expansion of grass while Jace headed for the bar. He knew alcohol would only increase his fatigue so he helped himself to a cold soda, hoping the caffeine would wake him up.

With his sunglasses planted firmly over his eyes, Jace wove his way through the crowded grounds, looking for some place to rest. It was almost too easy to pick out the different Packs from one another. Wolves and Coyotes had a different scent or so Jace had been told. The gift of differentiating aroma wasn't one he could boast. But he did have keen vision, although anyone with any sight whatsoever would be able to pick out the almost Swedish-like blond men and women of the Coyotes' *Morbauch* Pack intermingled with the cultural clash of the Wolves *Brachyurus* Pack.

Everyone was still basically sitting with their own clan, but it wasn't a segregated meet. It was a slow step in the right direction. Taking on an enemy together tended to unite people.

After bypassing several people who shouted out invites for him to join their table, Jace made his way to a quiet area at the fringe of the forest and sat in the warm grass. The land called to him, as it always had. And just like his brethren, Jace longed to be one with nature. He loved the feel of the air on his skin and the earth under his feet. The only difference was he couldn't embrace it as they did, he could only appreciate it.

Eyes closed, Jace leaned against the tree trunk hoping to get a few more minutes of sleep or at the very least some peace and quiet. But serenity, like the rest, was not forthcoming.

"I've been *instructed* to invite you over to our table." Remy's voice was filled with as much anger as it had been three nights ago.

Good.

The temptation to egg her on further was just too damn good to resist. "Well, you can trot back over to your owner and tell him thanks but no thanks."

"Fine." Jace opened his eyes in time to see Remy stomp away from him but stop only a few feet away. In anger, she looked damn good, especially from the back. Her long, lean brown legs were on display today, thanks to the denim shorts she was wearing like a second skin. Jace was willing to bet beneath those tight-fitting shorts she was wearing another pair of lacy goodness. His cock stirred at the thought, but before he could let his mind wonder further, Remy cursed aloud.

Fists clenched, she abruptly turned back around and faced him like the proud, beautiful woman she was. "You have to come with me."

"Have to?" Jace crossed his arms over his chest and raised a brow mockingly. "Remy, sweet Remy, I don't have to do anything."

"Nico commanded you…"

"Nico doesn't command me to do dick, she-wolf. You're his lackey. Not I."

"Oh, you think so, do you?" Remy's head snapped back and her eyes narrowed menacingly.

"I know so."

"Think again, Watcher Boy." Now there was the sassy woman he adored. Jace was still sore about her nasty attitude from the other day and he was just asshole enough to keep her in whatever trouble she'd gotten into with Nico.

"No need."

The green T-shirt she wore raised a tad as she placed her hands on her hips, displaying a quick flash of chocolate skin to his hungry gaze. But just as quickly as it popped into view, it was gone again.

Damn.

"Why do you have to be so obstinate?" The frustration was obvious in her tone and the look on her face. He wondered how long he could push her before she either exploded or gave up. He bet she'd explode before giving up since no one could accuse Remy of quitting a fight.

"No reason." Jace smiled and bent his head back, closing his eyes again. It was a strategic move since he was leaving himself essentially blind to an angry, seething woman. He had left her on the brink, after all. Nothing like a woman scorned and all that bullshit.

"You're purposely trying to make me look bad and I don't appreciate it."

Jace opened one eye briefly to see Remy standing right over him, hands on hips, jaw clenched. He wished he could snake his hands into those tight jean shorts to see if her pussy was as wet as it had been the other night. She seemed to get off on confrontation.

"No, I'm not. You do well enough on your own. Not that I owe you an explanation or anything, but I'm here with my family. So run along, lapdoggy."

Jace could practically see her nose flaring at his insults.

"If you think you can get away with—"

"Hey, Jace." Isabelle came running behind Remy, cutting off her tirade in midstream. "I found Mom and Dad, are you ready to eat?"

Jace stretched and stood, extremely pleased with himself. Remy looked dumbstruck as she realized he'd been telling the truth and his refusal had nothing to do with her. Walking around Remy, Jace slung an arm over Isabelle's shoulders. "Tell your boss I'll stop by for an audience later."

As he walked away, Jace could practically feel Remy's eyes burning into his back. He knew he'd have to smooth things over with Nico later, but it felt damn good to give Remy a hard time. Maybe he got off on the confrontation as much as she did.

"Jace, why do I feel like an excuse?"

Damn, his sister was more perceptive than he realized. "No reason, brat. The *Venator* wanted me to play at the royal table, but I'd rather hang out with you and the folks."

"Yeah, right. I may be young but I'm not as dumb as you assume." Isabelle shrugged off his arm and stomped away toward their parents. *Oh goodie, now I get to explain why I pissed off baby sister.* Today was turning into a real treat.

"Jace McClellan, come give your mother a hug." Rayne McClellan pulled him into her arms, hugging him tightly before releasing him and stepping back for a moment. "My God, you look terrible."

"Thanks, Mom, love you too." Jace smiled sardonically.

"I'm serious, young man. Webster," Rayne turned toward her husband, "take a look at this boy and tell me I'm wrong."

"Of course you're not wrong." Webster McClellan came over and kissed his wife briefly. Reaching out, he hugged his son before stepping back to observe him. "She's right, you know. You look like hell."

241

"I knew something was wrong when I picked him up, but he refuses to say anything. Daddy, make him tell you what's wrong." Isabelle had always been Daddy's little girl and Jace knew he was about to be interrogated by the elder McClellan.

Pulling Jace away from the women, Webster dragged him over to the barbeque. "I've seen the same look before on my grandfather's face. Is it the visions?"

Jace nodded shortly. "Yeah, I've had a recurring one I just can't figure out." Jace looked across the open field as he spoke and saw Remy standing at attention near Nico and the *Elitario* but staring across at him. Webster noticed Jace's look and smiled.

"Maybe it's not just the visions keeping you up at night."

"I have no idea what you're talking about."

Webster raised his brows. "Yeah, right."

Across the field, Remy could see Jace speaking with his father. If there hadn't been so many people here today, she might have even been able to hear what they were discussing. She noticed he looked up once and stared across at her, but since then, he'd been completely involved with his family. There was no reason she should even care or notice what he did, but of course it didn't stop her.

Ever since Jace had unceremoniously told her to leave his house, she'd been supersensitive to any thought of him. Although anger was the one usually topping her list, lust was a close second. He had gotten her to the point of letting down her guard and she'd never forgive him for rejecting her. On the other hand, if she could somehow tie him down and have her way with him, she'd be willing to try to fuck him out of her system.

"You know, you could sit if you wanted. The daggers would be just as sharp."

Bewildered, Remy looked down at Nico. He was her *Benandanti*, Alpha, best friend, all rolled into one. But it still

242

didn't mean she understood him. They had known each other since they were seven when she had been brought to the Pack by Franklin Russell after her parents perished in a car accident. After their death, the Pack had become her whole world. And Nico her constant companion. She would give her life for him, even though there were times when she was tempted to take his own herself.

"What are you talking about?"

Nico gestured casually toward Jace and his family. "I think you know what I mean."

"If I did," she growled, "I wouldn't have asked, now would I?"

"I don't know. You would if you were trying to play dumb."

"So while mine is an act, yours is the real deal." Remy was one of the few people who could get away with talking to Nico so boldly.

Instead of becoming upset, Nico grinned. He, like the *Elitario*, was used to her bad attitude. In fact, it seemed as if they all encouraged it. They were one big happy dysfunctional family with Remy in the role as younger bratty sister and the rest of them as her overprotective knucklehead brothers.

Derek, who was sitting next to Kimberly, leaned forward so he was in Remy's line of sight. "Did you just call our *Benandanti* dumb?"

Remy refused to answer. She stewed instead, which of course was the wrong thing to do because it just left her open as an easy target.

"Of course she didn't," Harrison jumped on the bandwagon. "Her reply was a highly intelligent version of 'I'm rubber you're glue'. But because you yourself, kind sir, are dumb, you missed it altogether."

"Me, dumb?" Derek placed his hand to his chest as if he were offended. "I'm hardly that, ol' chap, yet even if it were the case, I'm still pretty. And pretty beats dumb hands down."

243

"You'd have to be dumb to think so," Harrison fired back with a grin.

"Well, to quote you, kind sir, I'm rubber you're glue."

"And I'm annoyed," Remy interrupted. They were like big kids. Big, furry, chase- after-their-own-tails kids. "Somebody tell me this."

"This." Harrison and Derek chimed in at the same time, much to her annoyance and everyone else's amusement. She was going to kill them all. Then make matching rugs for in front of her fireplace.

"Why does Watcher Boy get to ignore a direct order?"

"It wasn't an order," Nico stated, and not for the first time. "I simply asked you to invite him over to our table."

Was he kidding? "You didn't ask."

"I did."

"Please, you don't know how to ask. You order."

Nico opened his mouth to disagree but was stopped by Kimberly, who placed her hand on his arm to garner his attention. "I do feel the need to chime in here. Remy is right. You don't ask for anything. You take. You demand. You instruct, but you don't ask."

Frowning, Nico glanced at his wife of three months. "You make me sound like a tyrant."

"Then my work here is done." Kimberly sat back in her seat and grinned.

The more Remy learned about Kimberly, the more she liked her. When she first met Nico's mate, the brunette Were was everything Remy herself was not. Remy initially assumed Kimberly hadn't experienced much hardship in life as evidenced by her shy demeanor. Of course looks could be deceiving and Kimberly soon proved herself an admirable mate for the *Benandanti*. The soft-spoken Were wasn't as delicate as she first appeared, and she, like Remy, didn't take Nico's shit. It was a quality Remy greatly admired.

"Be that as it may, it was just an offer. Who wouldn't want to sit with their family?"

That was a question Remy didn't have an answer for. She hadn't been privileged enough to be reared with one. The little she did remember of her own parents wasn't enough to fill a thimble. And Franklin, well, no one could ever accuse the older Were of being overly paternal. He had provided a roof over her head. He clothed her, fed her and taught her about loyalty to the Pack, but it ended there.

Remy respected him greatly, but to be honest, she didn't know jack about him. As usual, when talk about family came up, Remy's eyes sought out Derek, who sent her a little wink. He and Kellen both grew up in dysfunctional and sometimes in parentless homes as well, and only they knew the emptiness she felt.

"You have met my family, haven't you?" Jackson asked dryly, moving behind Remy. He had a plate stacked high with food and a telltale stain on his shirt. "I'd rather eat with the Coyotes."

"Then isn't it a blessing I came when I did," replied Rachel Santana, the *Benandanti* of the *Morbauch* Pack, as she strolled to the table. The petite blonde wore a look of amusement on her pixie-like face, which was a vast contrast to the look of "oh shit" creeping up on Jackson's.

"I didn't mean any disrespect," he muttered, shamefaced.

"Of course not." Rachel rounded the table with two beefy *Rahu* at her heels and took her place of honor to next to Nico. It was the seat Remy would have normally occupied if it weren't for the fledgling merger taking place.

But with the way the two Packs still sat not intermingling with one another, she didn't see the blending of their happy little families taking place any time soon.

Rachel daintily picked up her napkin and laid it in her lap. She was a tiny little thing, and it never ceased to amaze Remy how a woman apparently so delicate ruled a clan as fierce and bloody as the *Morbauchs*. There was a story there, she was sure, but Remy hadn't had the opportunity to delve into it.

Rachel nodded to her two *Rahu*. "Roman, Doc, please don't feel the need to hover. Go help yourself to some food." The two men studied one another briefly and then nodded, some sort of silent communication passing between them. One stood stationed at Rachel's side while the other wandered over to the food tables.

Rachel glanced around the gathering as she took a ladylike sip of her water. "Everything appears to be flowing smoothly."

"If by smoothly you mean at least no one's died yet, I couldn't agree more." Nico's dry tone brought a quick smile to the Coyote's face.

"That's exactly what I meant."

"It will take time for everyone to warm up to one another," Kimberly noted.

"For the record, I'm going to do my best to warm up as many of your females as possible," Derek offered solemnly to the sedate group.

"Your prowess precedes you, *Rahu*," one of Rachel's *Rahu* said. The massive man's voice was as deep as his muscles were large. Remy didn't know they made Ken dolls so bulky. "Your legend has spread even to our clan."

"Did you warn the women?" Derek asked, his over-inflated ego on high alert.

"No," Rachel said warily. "We warned the men."

Rachel's comments broke the stiff mood. Laughing, Remy finally joined the rest of them for dinner, content to let sleeping Weres lie, if only for the moment. Sitting next to Kellen, she realized how quiet he'd been through the entire exchange. Nudging him, she jerked her head, silently asking what was up.

"I don't like how Jace subverts authority any more than you do. He shows little respect for our *Benandanti* and none to you. It shouldn't be allowed."

She basically agreed disrespect shouldn't be overlooked, but she knew only too well where some of Jace's resentment came from. Their confrontations had him as heated as her and she still believed his refusal, although cloaked under the guise of family togetherness, had something to do with their attraction to one another. Unfortunately Remy worried Kellen was taking her side for one reason and one reason only, because he was interested in renewing their relationship. And it was something long dead as far as she was concerned.

"It's not our call." Remy's defense of Jace had Kellen frowning slightly.

"Remington."

Remy looked up as Nico called her by her full name. "Yes, my lord and master?"

"Kimberly has convinced me I need to be a tad more flexible. Instead of waiting for Jace to come to us, why don't we visit him and his family?"

"I don't think she meant the Pack *Benandanti* should be groveling to the *Rakshasa*."

Nico chuckled, not allowing himself to be drawn into her verbal tennis match. "Come on, *Venator*. Let's go."

Remy sighed but stood, ready to guard Nico, no matter what foolish ideas he had.

"If you'll excuse us, Rachel."

"But of course," she replied with a nod fit for a queen.

Kimberly decided to join them and the three Weres walked across the field, stopping to talk to various groups along the way. Remy noted Nico took extra pains to make sure he talked to as many *Morbauch* as *Brachyurus* groups. He was the ultimate diplomat.

Eventually they made their way to the table where the McClellan family was sitting. Rayne and Webster immediately jumped to their feet to welcome Nico into their midst. At least Jace's parents realized the importance of the *Benandanti*. As Nico and Kimberly spoke to the elder McClellans, Remy walked over to where Jace was sitting.

She couldn't help it. She had to annoy him. "What are you doing?"

Looking up, Jace frowned as her presence cast a shadow over him. "Trigonometry, now move, you're in my light."

Remy frowned back and then looked over his shoulder to see what he was doing. With a pencil in hand, Jace was furiously sketching something on a napkin, but to her eyes, it looked no better than a faceless blob.

"That's not very good."

"Thanks."

Isabelle, who was sitting next to Jace, stood and placed her hand on his shoulder. "I think it looks just fine."

The venom in her tone surprised and amused Remy. She was standing up for her brother. How cute. "The pup has teeth."

Jace paused and looked over at Remy, pride for his sister beaming from his face. "She might be tiny but she's wiry."

"I'll keep it in mind."

"Isabelle, come here for a moment please." At her mother's call, Isabelle left Jace's side, but not before letting loose a low growl.

Grinning, Remy watched her leave then turned to Jace, who was concentrating once more on his drawing. "I like her."

"I don't think she likes you."

"Yeah, that's why I like her."

Jace snorted. "Of course it is."

Unable to resist, Remy peered over his shoulder once more and stared at the drawing. Something about it just wasn't right. Jace was moving too fast. He was messing it up. Remy wasn't sure how she knew, she just knew it to be true and it was bugging the shit out of her.

When Jace went to add another line, Remy knew she had to stop him. "No, like this."

Without thought she reached down and slowed his hand. Instead of immediately berating her for the interruption as she expected, Jace allowed her hand to guide his to slower and more deliberate motions. An electric-like surge seemed to pull them together until she was leaning against his back with her hand intertwined with his.

Everything around them ceased to exist for Remy. She didn't know how long they stood there together, one focused force of energy, but ever-so gradually a face began to emerge under their dual efforts. Before long the drawing was completed and the force dissipated. She could breathe again. Although no major work of art, Remy could definitely tell it was a woman.

"She's beautiful." Even though it pained her to admit it, the words slipped out before she could censor them. Remy was certain this was the mystery blonde in Jace's dreams. If she hadn't been jealous before—and she hadn't, she tried to convince herself—she certainly would have been after seeing this picture.

Why would Jace be interested in a soldier when he could have a woman?

"No more than any other." Jace ran a shaky hand through his hair and Remy realized she still covered his other hand with her own. Hastily she went to draw back, but she wasn't fast enough and Jace caught her hand, pulling her down beside him. "Thank you. I'm not sure what you did, but...now we have a picture to find her."

Remy wasn't sure what she had done either. She only knew she had felt an urge too strong to deny. The feeling scared her as no other. It was more than just the sexual connection she'd felt with Jace in the past.

"What's going on over here?" Nico walked to the table as Remy pulled back from Jace. She felt out of her element. Instead of analyzing her feelings, she stepped back into her familiar role. Standing, she moved to Nico's right flank. Jace cocked an eyebrow at her retreat and she knew if Nico hadn't been there, he would definitely have had something to say.

"I think I've been able to capture the face of the woman in my vision. If we can reproduce these for the Pack, we'll have a better chance of finding her."

Kimberly joined her husband, wrapping an arm around his waist. "Hi, Jace." Reaching down she picked up the napkin. "Hey, do you know Cassandra?"

"What did you say?" Nico pulled the napkin from her hands, closely examining the picture. Remy wasn't sure who Cassandra was, but it was obvious Nico did. And although pleased, he also looked confused.

"Okay, I'll ask. Who's Cassandra?" Remy queried.

"My boss," Kimberly replied.

Chapter Four

∞

The howling of the Weres who had changed to wolves echoed across the fields. Jace leaned against the glass, watching the various members of the Pack change into their wolf forms and head out in small groups. This was the one part of the annual get-together he always avoided like the plague. Nevertheless, he really didn't want to be where he was either.

Inside Nico's office was a grim group, unable to take pleasure in the freedom of the run the rest of the Pack enjoyed. After Kimberly revealed the identity of Jace's mystery dream blonde, Nico had immediately called his *Elitario* together for a meeting. Some of the members of the *Maggiore* noticed the flurry of activity but none were invited to join the meeting.

Jace figured Nico wanted to keep the news with those he trusted at this point rather than risk a leak to the *Maggiore*, who still battled the *Benandanti* on every decision he made for the Pack. No one knew exactly what this development would mean. How a human, Kimberly's boss no less, could be such an integral part of Pack politics was beyond Jace, but he was sure he was going to learn more before the night was out.

"*Zingaro*, did you know Cassandra was pregnant?"

"Honestly, Nico, I had no idea. Although now that I think about it, she looks like she's put on a few pounds. But I didn't even know she was seeing anyone, so I never would have suspected."

"I still don't see how this relates to the Pack. Was there nothing else in your dream that could help us?"

"I've told you everything." Well, everything not including Remy. He didn't want to include her part in this mystery until it made more sense to him. Jace ran a weary hand over his face. He wondered if his dreams would change tonight now that he knew the identity of the woman or if he would continue to receive the same obscure messages.

"Kellen, Derek, I want you two on Cassandra day and night. Start at Lewis and Sinclair and find out where she lives. Then go there and find out every other damn thing about her," Nico ordered. "Watch her, but don't let her know you're there."

The two *Rahu* nodded and left the room.

"We're not going to just go talk to her?" Harrison questioned.

"No, not yet. I'd like to know more about what her connection is before we approach her. This is damn coincidental the woman in Jace's dream is Kimberly's boss. I don't believe in coincidence. There's more going on here than meets the eye. And I'd like to know what it is before we confront her. I hate being in the dark."

"I'd love to help you, Nico, but as I've explained to your *Venator* on numerous occasions, I can't turn on the premonition pop-up feature to explain what the hell is going on." Jace knew the frustration he was feeling came across loud and clear, but it was getting damn tiring trying to explain this over and over again.

"I'm still trying to catch up here, but how did we figure out who this woman is?" Jackson joined the meeting late and hadn't seen the drawing.

Everyone looked over at Jace, who handed him the napkin and explained how Kimberly recognized Cassandra from the drawing.

As he returned the sketch to Jace, Jackson asked, "So why didn't you just draw her right away?"

"I tried, but I wasn't having much luck. Not until..." Jace suddenly stopped and turned to look at Remy, who surprisingly was doing her best to fade into the background.

"Until what?"

"Until Remy came over to help and suddenly it was as if I were inspired."

Nico turned a thoughtful gaze to Remy, who by now looked fighting mad. Hands on her hips, she stalked over to Jace. "You just *had* to open your big mouth, didn't you?"

Hands raised, Jace shook his head. "I'm only telling the truth. You saw my previous attempts, they all sucked."

Jackson cleared his throat loudly, drawing everyone's attention toward him. "I think I might have an answer to what plagues you all."

Remy turned eyes of fury toward the speaking Were. "Share then, why don't you."

In a move averse for the quiet man, Jackson pushed his glasses back up the bridge of his nose with his middle finger, in essence giving Remy the bird. "As I was saying, there are stories in the histories of *aiutante*, those who are conduits for the *Rakshasa*."

"I've never heard anything about an *aiutante*." Jace thought if anyone would know, it would be him. His family history was rife with *Rakshasa*.

"You're clueless, imagine that." For once, Remy's snide comments about his calling didn't annoy him. In fact, it was the polar opposite. If he were to understand correctly, she would be playing a small role with his gift from now on. Vengeance had never been so sweet.

"This is ancient Were history we're talking. Nothing in the last two or three hundred years." As the Pack historian, Jackson had knowledge most of them didn't.

"I'm not any conduit. It was a fluke, okay?" Remy actually looked flustered, a state Jace had never seen her in. The perverse side of him loved it.

"I just said I don't believe in coincidence. This may mean something and we need to explore it." Nico sat for a moment in thought as the rest of the room stared back and forth between Jace and Remy. Jace had no idea if Remy was really an *aiutante*, but he was certainly enjoying her discomfort.

"Jace, Remy, I want you two to spend some time together to explore this idea of Jackson's. Let's see if Remy's presence helps your vision."

"No fucking way." Remy's outburst was followed by complete silence. Nico's eyes flared menacingly for a moment and Kimberly's soothing touch was the only thing that finally seemed to calm him.

"What. Did. You. Say?" The air in the room crinkled with tension and electricity. Even Jace, who was unable to turn, could feel the presence of the Wolf in the room. The animal they all kept just below the surface was a highly dangerous beast, one which needed little provocation to burst free. And with all the other wolves baying in the distance, it was only a matter of time before everyone else gave in to their Wolf.

"I'm sorry, *Benandanti*. Forgive me. I...I spoke without thinking." No one had ever seen Remy back down, but then no one had ever seen her respond to Nico in such a defiant way either.

"You'll go with Jace and you'll like it. Now, leave before I do something I regret." Nico turned from the group, staring out his observation window.

Remy's eyebrows rose and Jace could all but swear he could smell the blood from the wound in her tongue she made to stop from speaking out. Everyone knew there was no one Remy respected or followed more loyally than Nico, but it didn't mean she didn't have a mind of her own.

Hell, even to him, the way Nico had spoken to her was a challenge, and he waited to see what she would do. To his surprise and maybe a bit to his disappointment, Remy didn't argue.

"Yes, *Benandanti*." Remy's words may have been amicable but the way she uttered them hadn't been. She made it very clear she would do what he wanted, but she didn't like it.

Without another word, Remy turned on her heels and stormed out of the room, her gait angry and bitter. When her steps could no longer be heard, Nico turned back around and faced the rest of the group. His face was a mask of indifference, but his eyes were a different tale.

Jace could see it bothered him to have to address Remy in such a manner, but in this he wouldn't allow friendship to intercede with what he considered his duty. Jace respected his decision and despised it all at the same time.

"Do you really expect me to get anything accomplished now?"

"I expect you to do your job and for Remy to do hers." Nico's menacing stare didn't have the same effect on Jace it apparently had on Remy.

Jace wasn't his subordinate. He was a *Rakshasa* and he didn't answer to anyone, not even the *Benandanti*. Nico needed Jace a hell of a lot more than Jace needed him. "I'll do my job, but don't you make it any more difficult than it needs to be."

"And pray tell, how am I making it more difficult?"

"If Remy is my *aiutante*, then I'm going to need her to be cooperative, not there by duty."

"At least she'd be there."

Jace shook his head in wonderment. Was Nico really so dense? "When it comes to my job, let me do it my way. I'll handle Remy."

Nico laughed. "Do you really think you can?"

"I think I'm the only one who can." His comment halted Nico's amusement.

Good. Let him howl on that.

On the way over to his house, Jace continuously checked his rearview mirror. He wasn't sure if he was checking to make sure Remy was still there or to make sure she didn't speed up and ram him off the road. When he reached the

255

parking lot at the Sanctuary she'd already been in her car, waiting patiently for him like a good soldier.

Compliant Remy was just as annoying as bitch Remy. But he preferred the latter. At least then Jace knew she was acting off emotions, being herself, as irritating as it was at times. When she turned into Robo Remy, he had to resist the urge to grab her by the shoulders and shake her until the light appeared in her eyes once more.

She was a warrior, sure, but she was also a woman.

His woman.

Once they reached his house, she meekly followed him up the steps to his porch and inside, all without uttering a word. Before he had the chance to turn on the lights, she made her way into his living room where she sat stonily on his couch and stared at him. Ever the predator, her dark eyes peered at him in the dark, following his every step as he made his way in after her.

Grimly, Jace flipped the switch, filling the room with light. He was tired of her good-solider routine. "You can leave if you want."

"The hell I can."

"Go ahead, say it."

"Say what?"

"Thanks to me, right? You blame me for this."

"I blame no one. I'm here to do my duty."

"I'm not your goddamn duty," Jace thundered. "In fact, get out."

"No." Remy stood and slowly walked toward him. "Nico told me—"

"Fuck Nico."

"Don't speak of him in such a disrespectful way."

The hell he wouldn't. Jace was sick and tired of Remy fighting a never-ending war. There would always be leaders. There would always be crazy Weres fighting for control. But it didn't make any sense to him why she had to be entangled in their war. "And don't you speak of him that way to me."

"What way?"

"As if he's some fucking god. He's just the *Benandanti*. Not some infallible being. The way you follow him around sickens me."

He shoots, he scores. Remy's eyes roared to life as she stopped in front of him. His comments had obviously pissed her off.

Good.

"Why is that?"

"Because you're better than that. Better than all of them."

Remy's eyes widened a bit, as if she were shocked by his words. "I'm just a solider, Jace."

"You're more than just a soldier."

"Nico is my Alpha, my *Benandanti*."

"Nico isn't here."

"What do you want from me?" Her eyes betrayed her uncertainty. For once his she-wolf was thrown off balance.

Jace pulled Remy into him, pressing her flush against his body. "I just want you."

Remy's emotions were in a tailspin and her mind was going ninety miles an hour. She felt as if she were being pulled in two different directions at once, and instead of making a decision, she just wanted to run away and hide. Which really pissed her off since she was no coward.

Nico was her *Benandanti*, and although they'd been friends for years and she could question him at times, she always ultimately deferred to his wishes. At the same time, Jace was asking her to forget about being a soldier. And as much as she wanted to, it wasn't in her. She just couldn't shut off that part of her. On the other hand, she could take what was being offered now and worry about the consequences some other time.

Wrapping her arms around Jace's neck, Remy pressed herself into his embrace. "I want you too, but—"

"I'm not going to throw you out tonight."

She'd like to see him try. "Ah, no, that wasn't what I was thinking, but thanks for the reassurance."

"So why the 'but'?" Jace smoothed his hands down her back, distracting her thoughts. His hands were no different than they'd always been, but she could almost swear she felt an energy coming from him.

Where to start? Remy had never been one to mince words before, especially not with Jace, so there seemed no point in starting now.

"You want to fuck, don't you?"

Jace's lips twitched as he fought back a smile. "It would be agreeable to me, yes."

Damn. "We can't."

Jace placed his hand on her ass and pushed her pelvis into his. The evidence of his ability to prove her wrong was hard to ignore. "Trust me, she-wolf, it won't be a problem at all."

"Why don't I just suck your cock and you go down on me?" Remy couldn't believe herself sometimes. She usually had a better filter, but there were times when the words in her brain made it out of her mouth with no thought process in between.

"Do you mean as well or instead?"

"Instead."

"Are you kidding?"

Remy shook her head in lieu of answering. Saying it once was bad enough.

Jace stepped back, although he didn't completely release her. "I couldn't have just heard what I thought I did."

Since she didn't have a time machine handy and she couldn't erase his memory, Remy decided to try to brazen it out. "I just thought it would be better, to you know…" Her words trailed off miserably.

"No, I don't know. Why don't you explain it to me?"

Remy pulled away from him and began pacing across the living room. She should have gone for a run before she came over. Something to calm her down. Her Wolf was antsy. She could feel it beneath her skin, waiting to come out.

She wasn't in heat, but she damn near felt as if she were. Her skin felt too tight, her senses on overload. It was fucking crazy.

Remy had been perfectly fine this afternoon until she'd made the mistake of touching Jace as he was drawing. The connection they'd forged while completing the picture hadn't dissipated. She felt drawn to him now. More so than ever before. Mindful of his every move, she'd watched him as if he were her prey, and it worried her.

Her Wolf was marking him, but her human half knew better. This attraction between the two of them could never go anywhere, physically anyway. Not the in-depth penetrating way he wanted.

How could she explain her fears without totally pissing him off? One of the reasons she'd never allowed herself to think of being with Jace was because he was *Rakshasa*. It wasn't the visions that bothered her, it was the lack of his ability to change. Which sounded totally prejudiced.

When she and Kellen were together, they often felt their beasts struggling to emerge in the heat of passion. Were sex was rough, especially since the participants had extraordinary strength. Even though she'd never admit it to anyone out loud, she didn't want to hurt Jace if her beast decided it wanted to get free.

"I just think we should be careful."

Jace nodded his head, but the look in his eyes was anything but complacent. "Careful, I see. And just what is it we're trying to be careful of?"

Remy sighed, realizing not only was she not getting any tonight, she was probably signing her death warrant. Because as soon as she told Jace, he was going to go back on his word and throw her ass right out the door. And then Nico was going to kill her for not following orders.

"Look, I don't want to hurt you, okay?"

Jace grinned at first, as if he thought she were kidding, but when Remy didn't add anything to it, his grin slipped away and his face became an empty mask of nothingness.

Then all of a sudden he threw back his head and laughed. But nothing about it sounded the least bit amused. Oh no, he was extremely pissed off. With lightning speed, he shot across the room, grabbing her by the arm and twisting her around until her back was pressed against his front.

Damn, she'd forgotten he could move so quickly.

"I think I've just been insulted."

Remy could feel his cock, iron-hard, pressing into her back. In fact, his whole body felt hard and the strength in his grip was radiating off him in waves. She'd seen a few examples of his strength, but she realized she had no idea what his true abilities were. Everything she believed had just been an assumption, one she was rapidly discovering was possibly an error.

"I don't know if my beast might get out of control."

"What's wrong with losing control, Remy?"

"Nothing, but—"

"If you say you're worried about hurting me again, Remy, I'll be highly upset."

"As if I care." Remy had had just enough of being pushed around for one night. She made a move to break his hold upon her, but Jace tightened his grip and lowered his mouth to her ear.

"You care, she-wolf. More than you're willing to admit."

Remy didn't say a word. What could she say? He was right, and those were words she'd never let slip past her lips.

When her silence became deafening, Jace sighed and Remy could feel some of the tension leaving his body. "I guess I should be happy to know you actually had thoughts about us being together."

Too many times to count.

"Maybe I've imagined what it might be like."

Jace's hand crept up, cupping her breast through the thin cotton T-shirt. He rubbed across her nipple, already standing at attention. Remy bit back the moan in her throat. She'd already admitted to too much. Jace didn't need to know just how much he affected her.

"Tell me."

It was as if he were a fucking mind reader. The one thing she didn't want to do.

"No."

"Let me guess then." Jace's head bent and he nuzzled her neck, nipping at the soft spot just below her ear before licking at the mark he most likely made. The idea of him marking her as his had the cream between her thighs flowing within seconds. She should be irritated, but instead it was arousing that he wanted everyone to know what they had done, or were going to do as the case may be.

"Did you think of us in bed, under the covers with the lights out?"

"No."

"Good, because that's never going to happen. When we fuck, and we will fuck, I want to see every inch of your skin. I want to see the sweat on your brow. I want to see your nipples hard and aching and begging to be touched. I want to see your sweet pussy opening for my tongue."

The moan she'd been holding in escaped, unable to be repressed any longer. His words were like a siren's cry, making her want to turn and rip off his clothes.

"You like the idea, don't you, she-wolf?"

"The tongue thing," Remy closed her eyes as the image filled her mind, "we can do. But nothing else."

"We'll do everything else," he growled, a sound she met with one of her own.

Despite his inability to turn, Jace was showing some serious signs of Alpha Wereness. "I'm going to slip my cock in your mouth, in your pussy," Jace pressed his erection forward, "and into this sweet ass of yours."

His words made her quiver. "Think so, do you?"

"No, baby. I know it."

"You're so full of it."

"And you'll be stuffed full of me." Jace nipped at her ear.

The sharp pain startled her and Remy broke out of his embrace to face him, hand to her ear. "Watch it or I'll make you eat those words."

"I'm eating something and it's not words." Jace stepped toward her, as if all of a sudden he were the stalker and she the prey. "Heed my words, Remy. I'm going to fuck you and mark you."

"Mark?" *Talk about delusions of grandeur.* "That's never going to happen."

Jace grabbed the hem of his shirt and pulled the blue material off. He dropped it so casually on the floor, it was as if undressing in front of her were a daily occurrence. Wolves had no problem with nudity, yet Remy was having a hard time keeping the fact in mind as he kicked off his shoes and began to unbutton his jeans.

"Did you hear me, Jace?" Remy backed up, needing to put as much distance between them as possible. "Never."

Still he didn't reply. His pants and boxers soon joined his discarded shirt and shoes on the floor. As well as Remy's mouth, figuratively of course. Despite her best attempts at keeping her eyes above his chin, when his clothes dropped, so did her gaze, and it landed smack-dab on his cock, which was an impressive figure all on its own.

She unconsciously licked her lips, which brought forth a masculine chuckle from Jace. "Like what you see?"

"It'll do." Her words might have had more of an impact if she hadn't had to clear her throat twice before getting them out.

"I'm sure it will." Jace stepped toward her, to which she once again backed up. "Do I have to chase you, Remy? Is that what you want, she-wolf? Me to track you and pounce? I'm all for role-playing."

"It's not a role for me, Jace." There, it was out. "I might claw you, bite you."

"God, I hope so." He grinned and moved forward again. This time when Remy went to step back, she came in direct contact with the wall.

"I might change. In the middle. Afterward. Who knows?"

"My entire family is Were. I won't freak out if I wake in the morning and you've changed."

"But will you if I do in the middle of sex?"

Jace tilted his head to the side and gave a light shrug of his shoulders. "Bestiality isn't on my kink list of things to try before I die, but I won't go running to the hills. I know what you are. I'm not afraid of the unknown or of getting hurt. If you think you can, I say give it your best shot. You're my mate, Remy. Nothing you are can scare me."

"Mate…" Why was he making this so damn hard? "You won't be able to…"

263

"Knot." He finished for her. Knotting only occurred in mates, which was something, as far as she knew, he would be unable to do.

"Yes."

"My cock, though impressive," he added with a wink, "is one hundred percent knot free. But I don't need a growth to prove a damn thing to me."

"That's because you're stubborn. We're not mates, Jace, but we can be fuck buddies. Kellen and I—"

Jace reached out, grabbed her shorts with both hands and yanked them down her legs. The ripping material startled her almost as much as the fierce look in his eyes. Jace moved in closer to her until they were just inches apart and reached down, ripping her panties off as well.

"Damn it, I just bought those."

"Don't *ever*," Jace stressed the word "ever" as if it were a holy name, "mention you and Kellen in a sexual way to me again. Do you understand me?"

Remy couldn't resist. "No. Maybe you need to use smaller words."

"Or maybe actions speak louder than words." Jace dropped to his knees in front of her and pulled her leg over his shoulder, placing her pussy at mouth level.

Remy knew what he'd find there. With her bottom half bared, she could already feel the wetness on her thighs. His words and actions since they'd arrived at his home had been affecting her to the point she would probably come with one swipe of his tongue over her clit. If she could get him to be satisfied with this and her sucking him dry, then perhaps the discussion of intercourse would become a moot point.

Jace chuckled at the evidence of her desire and nibbled at her thighs, licking and sucking at the dampness. He avoided her clit however, parting her succulent folds with his fingers and running his tongue along her opening. Remy tried to brace herself against the wall, already sensing this was not going to be quick. Jace was planning to take his time and enjoy himself.

His teeth on her outer lips, pulling gently, had her eyelids popping open. "What are you doing?"

"Eating you up, baby. I want to learn every inch."

Jace was true to his words, licking and kissing every inch of her slit. But he continued to ignore her clit until she thought she'd scream.

"Jace, please."

"Please what?"

"Pretty please with sugar on top."

"No, you have to say it. Tell me what you want."

Remy sighed, her head thrown back, her clit aching for his touch. "Suck my clit, Jace, please, I need it."

"All you had to do was ask." Jace spread her lips wide, exposing her clit to the cool brush of air, causing her to suck her breath in quickly. When leaning in, he covered the sensitive bundle of flesh with his lips, sucking the hardened little nub into his mouth. At the same time he thrust two fingers deep inside her. Remy bucked against his hand, the dual sensations causing her nerves to go into overdrive.

"Oh shit, harder, harder." Remy braced her legs in anticipation of her oncoming orgasm. Her hands, previously balled into fists, grasped his head, holding him tight. Jace was relentless, never letting up. Remy's scream caught her by surprise. She'd never been one for screaming, being more of a low-growl-in-the-throat kind of girl. But the cry was ripped from her throat as the wave flowed through her.

Jace finally released her and Remy began to slide down the wall, her legs unable to support her any longer. Her pussy continued to pulse with the aftershocks of her orgasm.

"That's just the beginning, Remy."

Chapter Five

ॐ

As he watched Remy slide to the floor, her mouth slack and her eyes dazed with passion, Jace felt a deep sense of contentment. She may have thought she was in control of this situation, but he'd been able to prove her dead wrong. There was no way in hell she was getting out of here tonight until he fucked her into submission.

Standing up, Jace leaned down and pulled Remy into his arms, carrying her toward the bedroom. She'd finally started to recover and was struggling, but not really putting any effort into the fight.

"I can walk, you know."

"And I can carry you, which is what I wanted to do."

Jace kicked his bedroom door shut as he strode through the doorway. Approaching the bed, he tossed Remy into the center, satisfaction filling him at seeing her lying sprawled there. She looked like an odd combination of sensuality and innocence as she lay there, her legs spread and pussy open while her T-shirt still covered her breasts.

"Why don't you take off your T-shirt so we can continue with tonight's festivities?"

"I don't need to take off my top to suck your cock." Remy sat up and got to her knees, crawling over to him.

"Darling, as much as I'd love for you to suck my cock, we're going to save it for another time. We are going to fuck, and we can spend the next hour arguing about it, or we can spend the next hour enjoying ourselves. Either way, we will eventually fuck."

"Jace, I don't think…"

"It's okay, Remy, you don't have to think about it. I already have. If you're so worried about hurting me, I've come up with the perfect solution."

"What?" The suspicion in her voice made him want to laugh.

"I'll restrain you."

Remy frowned. "You do realize I'll be able to break free?"

"I know. It's not the physical bondage as much as the mental."

"What do you mean?"

"Neither one of us is naïve." Jace walked purposefully to his oak nightstand. He picked up the cordless phone handset from the base and laid it on the table next to the extra cell phone he always kept there. "I'm strong. You're stronger. Not by much, but you are."

Remy snorted but didn't interrupt. It was a start.

"What you need to realize is," Jace grabbed the phone base and pulled, ripping the telephone cord from the wall, "I don't care. Nothing you can do, with the exception of saying 'no', is going to stop me from stuffing your pussy full with my cock. You can growl at me. You can get all furry. But you and I are going to fuck."

Jace stood at the side of his bed, slowly winding the twelve-foot cord around his hand. Remy had jumped when he ripped it from the wall, but she hadn't made a move to leave and she hadn't said no. It was good enough for him. "If push comes to shove, Remy, you can get free, but both you and I know you really don't want to. You're going to stay bound to my bed because it's where you belong. And you're going to love every second of it."

Remy sat back on her heels for a moment, obviously pondering Jace's words. He knew she ultimately needed to accept she wouldn't hurt him and if the idea of being restrained was what it took, all the better.

"I guess we can try."

"Oh, we're going do more than try. Now take off the T-shirt."

Remy grasped the hem of her shirt and pulled it over her head, exposing a purple lacy bra. She must own of a collection of the frilly things. Without being told, she reached behind her, unhooked the bra and let the lace cups fall forward.

Her breasts were high and firm, and the sight of them made Jace want to take a taste. He steeled himself against the temptation however. Once he had her restrained to the bed, he could take his time and enjoy her to his heart's content. Until then, he needed to keep his mind clear and not get distracted.

"Now what?"

"Now the fun begins. Lie back down."

Remy lay back on the bed, her head turned toward him as he approached her. Grabbing two of the pillows, he put them under her head, making her as comfortable as possible.

"I'm ready." Remy thrust her hands out in front of her.

Jace chuckled and slowly wound the cord around her wrists, looping them together. Pulling Remy's arms over her head, he wrapped the cord around the heavy oak crossbeam of his headboard. When he finally had her secured to the bed, he stepped back to observe his handiwork.

"God, you look so hot."

Remy snorted, but his comment had broken the tension he'd seen in her muscles.

"You don't believe me."

"Of course I believe you. I've seen me naked."

"As have I, and let me assure you, up close, without the rest of the brat pack, your body is very impressive."

"As a Wolf, we're trained to overlook nudity."

"As you've pointed out before, she-wolf, I'm not one of you."

"Yes, you are." Remy's eyes lost the teasing glint it had just mere seconds before. "I'm sorry if I ever made you feel as if you weren't."

"Of course you're all repenty now that I have you at my mercy."

Remy lifted her head and focused her dark eyes on him. "I'm serious."

"I know, but you were right."

"What do you mean?"

Jace climbed onto the bed and lay beside her. "I'm not like you. I'm something much more."

Before Remy could question him further, Jace covered her mouth with his. Licking at her lips, he coaxed her mouth open, slipping his tongue inside. Instead of the fight he was expecting, she met his tongue with her own, matching his ferocity.

Breaking the kiss, Jace pulled back and gathered himself. He felt ravenous, as if he weren't capable of controlling himself. He wanted to sink balls deep inside her and pump her full of his cum until every Were for miles around would know she belonged to him.

With a calming breath, he centered himself. This was only the first of many times he would lie with her. There was no need to rush.

Jace cupped her cheek in his hand, loving the feel of her soft brown skin under his. Remy's eyes were still closed, but it was fine with him. He wanted to be able to explore her fully.

Slowly, with a gentleness even he didn't know he possessed, Jace traced his index finger across her full bottom lip. Remy growled softly then snapped at his finger, much to his amusement.

"My little she-wolf."

From her mouth, he trailed his finger down her chin to her neck, slowly moving it between her breasts. Unable to resist the sweet temptation before him, Jace cupped her full mound into his hands.

Her breasts were softly rounded, topped with nipples that looked as good as chocolate kisses, and Jace was addicted to chocolate. Leaning down, he licked at each nipple until the turgid little points were wet and glistening then pulled the hard peak into his mouth and teased it with his teeth. When he increased the pressure, Remy moaned and arched toward him.

"Harder," she moaned.

And he complied. He twisted a nipple, pinching tightly as he suckled the other one between his lips, adding a bit more force for his she-wolf. He could spend all night pleasuring her breasts but there was more of her he wanted to discover.

Jace pulled away from her chocolate-kissed peak and moved his hand away from her breast to her torso where it came to rest on the first of many scars. Without saying a word, he traced scar after scar, ten in total, one thin one longer than the palm of his hand. Her body was marred but still beautiful.

"Still think it's impressive?"

Jace lowered his mouth and let his lips follow the trail his hands had made until he'd kissed every badge of honor he saw. When he looked up, he could have sworn her eyes were glassy for a moment. His little warrior. "You're flawless."

Remy blinked for a moment then smiled. "And you're blind."

"Not so, I see only too well." Jace trailed his hand down her lithe frame and watched as she reacted to his stroke, shivering at his touch and bending to his hand.

Remy quivered at his attention and opened her legs. "Are you going to stop talking and fuck me?"

It was a tempting sight, but Jace wasn't ready to climb onboard just yet. "In due time, she-wolf, in due time."

The open valley of her legs made it all the easier for Jace to enjoy the scrumptious feast of her smooth-shaven pussy once more. The smell of her arousal filled the room as he moved his hand down between her legs and caressed her damp lips.

Even though he had gorged himself on her sweet caramel taste mere moments ago, Jace's mouth watered from the desire to do so once more. Remy's body lurched up as Jace traced his fingers against her slit. He feathered his fingers across her clit before dipping them into the sweet recess of her body.

"Jace…"

His cock twitched, dying to be buried where his fingers were held in her snug, wet body. "Yes, Elizabeth," he dared calling her by the first name.

Remy's growl of protest made him chuckle. "Don't call me that."

"When you're dressed and in the field, you're Remy." Jace withdrew his fingers and plunged them forth, silencing any protest she might have made. "But when you're naked and wet for me, I'll call you Elizabeth." For Jace, Elizabeth was just a term of endearment. In his mind, she'd always be Remy, his she-wolf warrior and his mate.

His fingers dove deep within her heat over and over. Remy was so fucking hot she almost seared his fingers off. The hair on his arms rose as he felt the metaphysical essence of her Wolf clawing to get out. "How long has it been since you've changed, Elizabeth?"

"A few days." Panting, Remy pumped her hips up, meeting his fingers thrust by thrust. "I warned you…"

"I'm not worried. I just want to watch you come."

"Then get inside me and stop this madness."

He could see she was on the verge of climaxing, but as selfish as he was, Jace wanted to feel her trembling around him when she came this time.

"Anything you say, Elizabeth." Jace pulled his fingers from her tight pussy and brought them to his mouth for a taste.

271

"Stop calling me that."

"Anything but that." Jace chuckled and reached over to the bedside table, pulling open the drawer and tearing the foil packet he found there before quickly sheathing his cock.

"My strength has never been a question with me. It's always been an ability I had. I can't see for miles around. I can't change. And until this moment, I thought my sense of smell was on par with humans. Boy, was I wrong."

"What do you mean?" Her voice was shaky and filled with need.

"The smell of your arousal is imprinting itself in my brain. Even poets would be at a loss for words if they tried to describe it. All I know is," Jace placed himself at the head of her sweet entrance and pressed forward, engulfing his cock with her burning heat, "it smells like home."

Seated deep within her, Jace rested his head on her forehead, trying to regain his breath. Remy was no innocent, but as her soft flesh yielded to his invasion, he swore he'd never felt someone so snug and tight before. For just an instant he wanted to stay like this forever, locked together with his woman.

Of course Remy had to rock his world at that very moment, drawing her legs up and wrapping them around him. Impossibly, he sunk even deeper into her.

"Oh God, Jace, move, please move."

Pulling back, Jace began to thrust into her, pistoning his hips and driving her deep into the bed with every forceful drive. Remy wrapped her hands around the cord binding her to the bed, her head thrown back as she growled in response.

"That's it, baby." Although Remy was afraid of her beast, Jace had no fears where that was concerned. He wanted her to feel free with him and he wanted to have all of her. But it wasn't as if he wanted her to change during sex. He didn't want her to hide part of herself from him either. Only then would she realize she could truly be herself with him.

"I need... Oh God, Jace, please." Remy was bucking against him now. Her legs had dropped from around him and she'd braced her feet against the bed, pushing back as he continued to press into her.

"I'll please you, baby." Reaching down between them, Jace grasped her clit between his thumb and finger, pressing hard on the engorged core. "Come for me, Elizabeth. Come for me now."

Remy's eyes dilated as her orgasm hit her and her body arched off the bed. The clasp of her pussy around his cock was all it took to for him to join her in ecstasy.

"Fuck. Damn. Fuck." The words were ripped from his soul as his own orgasm rode over him. A burst of energy shot through his soul and into his mind, blinding him for a moment.

The pleasure was so intense he could hardly breathe. He felt dizzy and hurt everywhere. Jace took a few deep breaths as he began to recover from his orgasm. He realized Remy was struggling with her restraints, her nails digging at the cord surrounding her wrists. Her skin was shivering, almost as if something were forcing its way out.

"Jace, let me up!"

"It's okay, baby." Rolling from the bed, Jace ripped the cord from the headboard, demonstrating the true power of his strength. Before he could unwind the cords, Remy sat up and her body began to transform. Even though the changing process was quick, it was still a merging mess of bones, flesh and fur. Yet it wasn't anything Jace hadn't seen before and soon the beautiful ebony warrior was no more and in her place was a silver gray wolf.

And yet, she was still beautiful.

Opening the French doors to the outside patio, Jace stepped back and allowed Remy to leap from the bed and out into the night.

* * * * *

The cool, brisk wind rippled through her fur as Remy raced around Jace's property. The land was large and plentiful with enough room for her to run about. Yet no matter how far she ran, his scent beckoned to her. Still, she resisted the call and darted throughout the woods.

Remy could smell the markings of other wolves throughout the terrain. The scent was of her Pack so she forged on, dodging through underbrush and leaping over logs. She became one with nature once more, as free in her fur as she was in her own skin.

The forest surrounding Jace's home was empty tonight of other wolves but not of prey. Rabbits darted away from the running wolf, and though she wasn't hungry, Remy couldn't resist the chase.

She would only scare them a little. Enough to see their furry little butts dart into the burrows beyond. It was the forest's version of cat and mouse.

When she grew tired of her game, Remy trotted back to Jace's house, amused he'd left the light on and door partially open. With her nuzzle she pushed the door farther apart so she could slip in.

A loud rumbling sound drew her attention to the bed. Jace was sound asleep. His arm hung from the mattress and Remy couldn't resist padding softly over to him and licking his hand.

Despite the shower he'd obviously had, Remy could still smell herself on him beneath the refreshing smell of the soap and the crisp scent of the water.

Yet as appealing as a shower sounded, a quick nap sounded even better. Remy jumped onto the bed and lay at the foot. Crossing her one paw over the other, she lowered her head and closed her eyes.

A quick nap and she'd leave.

* * * * *

Remy was running through the woods, but instead of the carefree jaunt from earlier in the evening, she had a sense of urgency, of a need to get somewhere and quickly. Breaking through the trees, she reached a clearing.

A small brook loomed ahead. Fun. Remy took off at a run, intent on playing in the stream, but then froze as her mind caught up with her body. How the heck did she get here? One moment she was curled up on Jace's bed. The next she was about to go splashing through some water. What the hell?

As she sat back on her haunches to rest with her tongue lolling out of her mouth, Remy looked around. Everything was too bright, too clear to be reality. She realized she was in a dream. But this was no ordinary dream. Something else was going on here. She could practically feel the energy crackling around her.

Damn Nico and his dream-walking.

Nico's annoying ability to infiltrate the dreams of those with whom he had a connection with was downright maddening. He was the only one in the Pack who possessed this gift and he wasn't shy about using it.

With the image of her human body planted firmly in her mind, Remy stretched and transformed from wolf back to her womanly form. Looking down, she realized she was naked.

"Damn it, Nico, you have a mate now. Why are you pulling me into your stupid dreams?"

When there was no immediate response, Remy shivered, although she tried to tell herself it was due to the cold, even she wasn't entirely convinced. Something odd was going on here. When they were younger, Nico would sometimes play tricks on her, invading her dreams. But that had been years ago and suddenly Remy wasn't feeling too confident this was Nico.

"Easy now, *lupa*, don't be frightened."

Remy twirled at the voice, dropping to a crouch in an effort to defend herself. Squinting she stared at the man in front of her with faint recognition. "Jace?"

"No, I am his ancestor Vladimiro. There is no reason to be afraid."

As if his assurances meant a hill of freaking beans to her.

"Why am I here?" Remy continued to stay crouched, not willing to assume she was necessarily safe from him.

"Jace needs your help."

Before she could interrogate him further, he faded into the woods. Remy stared after him for a moment before standing and turning back toward the clearing. The scene in front of her had changed. Gone was the brook and in its place was a large, human-sized chessboard with Nico and Kimberly in the positions of king and queen. Cassandra was standing directly in front of them, a baby in her arms. Most surprising of all was the image of herself, also standing on the board, right next to Cassandra.

Suddenly, from the other side of the chessboard, a number of wolves swarmed out from the woods, yipping and growling at the figures on the chessboard. Remy realized with shock she recognized many of these wolves as members of the *Maggiore*. With his back to her, Remy noticed a crouched figure studying the scene intently.

Stalking over, she squinted her eyes, trying to see whatever it was he was seeing. "What's going on?"

Jace swiveled his head, starting to lose his balance before catching himself. "Remy?"

"Yeah." *Jeez, you have sex with a guy and he forgets who you are?*

"Why are you here?" Jace stood. He appeared more surprised to see her than she was to see him.

"That's what I'd like to know. But you know what I'd like to know more? How come you *forgot* to mention I was in this little dream of yours?"

Jace frowned. "I didn't think it was pertinent."

"Oh really? Well, maybe you should let someone else decide for you because you're obviously impaired. How did I get here?" Remy squinted at him, suspicion clouding her mind. "Did you have something to do with this?"

"Look, I'm not really sure why you're here. I've never had anyone show up in my dreams except for Vlad."

"I talked to him." She decided not to mention what he said about Jace needing her help.

"You did?"

"Yeah, old guy who looks like you."

"Yes."

"Then yep." Remy walked across the chessboard and stopped in front of herself. Leaning forward, she peered into her own face. Index finger out, Remy poked herself in the forehead and giggled. "Okay, this is pretty freaking cool. I'm a sexy bitch, aren't I?"

"He actually spoke to you?"

"Did I stutter?" Remy turned back around and faced Jace, her doppelganger no longer of interest. "And stop changing the subject. I want to know what's going on here."

Jace clenched his jaw. "How the hell would I know, I'm only the Watcher Boy, remember? You're the *aiutante*. Why don't you figure it out?"

"I don't mean I want to know what's going on *here*," waving her hand at the chessboard, "I meant I want to know what's going on *here*," tapping his forehead. "Why would you neglect to mention someone who was in the dream?"

"I didn't seem to have a bearing on figuring out who Cassandra was. And I was right, you'd never met her."

"But I'm here for a reason." When he opened his mouth to respond, Remy held her hand up to shush him. "I don't mean me here, I mean that me here."

"What?"

277

"Her." Remy pointed to her other self. "She-me is here for a reason. You don't have to be one with the ancients to figure that out."

"Yes, I know."

"So what is it?"

"We have a theory."

"And?"

"How much do you know about chess?"

"Dick." Remy placed her hands on hips. Her bare flesh quickly reminded her of how undressed she was. "Watcher Boy, give me some clothes."

Jace lowered his gaze until it ran the entire length of her body and back up again. Gone from his eyes was the wary look, in its place was the look of passion. "Sorry, she-wolf, it's not that type of dream."

"Excuse me."

"I have no power over what happens here."

"How convenient." His lustful leer was beginning to annoy her. Even though she was used to being nude in front of others, this was different. Jace wasn't looking at her as a fellow being. His look was purely sexual, especially when he lowered it down to her breasts. "At least avert your eyes."

"I'm a seer, Remy, not a saint." Jace returned his gaze to her face and smiled a slow, sexy smile that made her think all things were right with the world.

Damn it. When did she become so damn girly? She needed to hit something. Or kill someone. Only then would her mind get back on track.

"So tell me, in chess, what would I be?"

The smile slid away and the seriousness of the situation came forth once more. "A pawn."

"A solider." Remy nodded her head. It made sense.

"Not just a solider, Remy. An expendable piece."

278

With a shrug of her shoulders, Remy faced the pieces once more. "That's all a solider really is, Jace. Someone who can be risked. Someone who is willing to die."

"Are you really so willing to die?" Jace grabbed her arm and spun her around. His face was filled with anger. Whether it was with her or with the situation, Remy couldn't tell.

"We all have roles, *Rakshasa*. I'm just more comfortable with mine than you are with yours."

"Or I am with yours." Jace's grip tightened on her arm.

She could tell he was at war with his vision and it touched her. "I'm not suicidal, Jace. I'm a good soldier."

"You're more than a warrior."

"I'm—" Remy's words were cut off by Vladimiro, who strolled onto the board.

"Much more than even you know."

To Remy's amusement, Jace pulled her behind him, shielding her body from his ancestor's view. Even more amusing, she was instantly covered by the same white T-shirt Jace had worn earlier in the day. It only reached the top of her thighs, but it was enough.

The funny thing was, Remy wasn't uncomfortable with nudity. Most Weres weren't. They felt as at home in their skin as they did in their fur, but it amused her Jace felt the need to clothe her, especially after he'd lied and said he couldn't earlier.

"What is she doing here?"

"You tell me, *nipote*, you brought her here."

"The hell I did."

"Maybe you need to show her the whole dream. She is the *aiutante* after all."

"Hello, this is the whole dream. And by the way, why didn't you mention the whole *aiutante* thing?"

Vladimiro sighed. "Things are revealed in the time they are meant to be. Remember, the beginning is significant to the end, *nipote*."

"Oh my God, now I know where you get the fortune-cookie crap," Remy said with a laugh.

"Ha, ha, ha."

Remy watched as the scene changed again. Cassandra was surrounded by the wolves nipping at her heels while Nico and the *Elitario* stood in another group. Remy saw herself standing between the two. But this time it wasn't the vision of herself that caught Remy's attention. Rather it was Cassandra's inability to catch the attention of a certain wolf standing with Nico's group.

"Hey, I know that wolf. It's David, Kimberly's brother."

Chapter Six

৶

Getting ready for work, Cassandra grimaced as she slipped on her shoes. She couldn't continue to handle these twelve-hour days for much longer. This baby was draining every ounce of energy she ever thought she had and then some. In fact, she'd been so tired last night, she hadn't even checked her messages. Which was surprising, considering the fact she was desperately waiting for a call. Unfortunately, pressing the button only informed her she had no messages waiting.

This was getting past the point of ridiculous. Cassandra dialed David's cell phone for the fifth time in two days, but this time, she was going to do what she swore she wouldn't do. Cassandra was going to let him know over the phone he was going to be a father, even if she had to leave a message with the news.

The previous times she'd call, she'd only left a "This is Cassandra, please call me back" message along with her phone number. Despite not hearing from him in over four freaking months, she had always been cordial, never leaving a "Call me back, asshole!" message the way she truly wanted.

Cassandra wasn't one to push herself onto anyone. If David didn't want to be in her life, then fuck him. She damn straight didn't need his money or his help to rear her child. If her mother had done it, she could too. Yet the little bit of soul she had refused to have a child with someone and keep him in the dark. Even if the father in question was a furry one-night-stand asshole like David.

The Metallica song David had for a ringer burst through the earpiece of her phone, setting Cassandra's nerves on end.

Up until she'd begun her search for David, she'd been a fan of the group, now she wished they, along with David, would fall into a pit of fire.

When the digital recording came on instructing Cassandra to leave a message for the umpteenth time, she blew her cool. "David. This is Cassandra. The woman you picked up in a bar and took home to fuck about, oh, four months ago. Well, surprise, surprise, I received a bit of startling information from my doctor's office, and it wasn't that I have the clap. I'm pregnant, asshole. Call. Me. Back."

Cassandra slammed the flip lid closed, more upset now than she'd been when she called him. "Asshole!"

"Tsk, tsk, tsk. Is that anyway for a mommy to talk?"

Hand to her heart, Cassandra spun around and faced her surprise guest. Out of the dark hallway her father walked, a sick, twisted smile upon his handsome face. With the phone still clutched tightly in her hand, Cassandra backed away, wanting to put as much space between her and her mother's sperm donor as she could. "How did you get in here?"

"And look at the way you speak to your father. For shame."

"You are not my father."

"Deny it all you want, daughter, the proof is, as they say, in the pudding." Similar to the devil himself, Franklin was a handsome man with dark black hair and eyes as blue as her own. When she'd found him, she knew instantly he was her father, his DNA ran rampant throughout her body. She was a fair-skin version of him without the wolfy gene. He was right, the proof was there, but she'd die a painful, tortured death before she'd call him father again.

"You aren't welcome in my home. How did you get in here?"

Franklin calmly sat on her ivy-patterned sofa and made himself at home. "Since when did I need an invitation?"

"Since the day you started drugging me."

"You should thank me."

"Thank you?" His words set her temper ablaze. "I should kill you."

"You're welcome to try." Franklin grinned at her comment, as if she amused him, but there was no amusement lurking in his eyes. Neither was there much humor to be found in the lengthening canines, which slid into view.

"And take the pleasure away from Nico when he finds out what you've done." Nico was her only ace in the hole, but even that threat was growing thin.

"Such as…"

"Drugging me."

"As if he'd care."

"Trying to use me to break up him and his mate."

Franklin waved his hands in front of him as if it all didn't matter. "Yet he and his mate are as happy as can be. Besides, all I did was *suggest* you get to know him. Nothing more. Nothing less."

He made it all seem so simple. "You are an evil man."

"You flatterer you."

"Stop it!" His condescending tone was driving her insane.

"Cassandra dear," Franklin bound to his feet and walked over to her side. This time Cassandra didn't retreat. She held her ground, refusing to show him any weakness. Like the wolf he was, she knew he would pounce, and Cassandra wasn't going to give him that opportunity until she had a knife in her hand ready for him to land on. "You seem all out of sorts. This can't be good for the baby."

"Leave my child out of this."

Franklin placed his hand across her womb and smiled. "My grandchild, dear one."

"Go to hell." Cassandra placed her hands across his wrist and tried to push it off her stomach but without luck. He was eons stronger than her and the battleground was her stomach. Not exactly what she'd call a level playing field. "Release me."

"You, gladly." Franklin chuckled and stepped back. With an evil little smile, he bent forward and brushed a kiss across her forehead. "I'll show myself the way out."

"Finally," she couldn't help but add, much to his amusement.

When Franklin reached the door, he paused and turned back around to face her. "You know, dear heart, if this child is so much of an inconvenience, I'll gladly take him or her off your hands."

"Over my dead body."

"Funny," Franklin opened the door, "I was thinking the same thing."

Franklin shut the door behind himself, pleased when he heard something hit the wood and shatter. His daughter, despite the horrible human DNA coursing through her system, was very similar to himself. Even if she didn't want to believe it. He'd prefer not to kill her, wanting her around merely for breeding purposes, but he'd do it anyway if forced. His grandchild would rule his Pack with or without her for a mother.

He'd reared one motherless child and he could do it again. This time of course, he'd start from the very beginning, molding the child in his own image. Remy had turned out well, but a child from his own DNA, started on the correct path from the very start, would be unstoppable.

As he walked toward his car, his pocket vibrated, reminding him the phone had a message. Pulling out David's cell phone, Franklin punched in the code and listened to his daughter's angry words with a smile.

Deny it all she wanted, his blood ran through her veins.

* * * * *

Across the street, Kellen turned to Derek, who was watching Franklin get in his car. "What the hell is that all about?"

"I have no idea, but I'm willing to bet Nico is going to want to know about this little meeting." Derek reached into his pocket and dialed his *Benandanti*. The shit was about to hit the fan. "On a bright note though," he added as an afterthought, "it looks as if we might get to kill someone soon."

* * * * *

Slowly waking from the intense dream, Jace rolled over and opened his eyes. Remy was lying naked at the foot of the bed, obviously where she'd collapsed after her run the night before. Jace was still amazed about her appearance in his dreams and how she was able to affect his visions. Deciding he might as well take advantage of both their naked states, Jace crawled over to join Remy. He was sure he could discover a few delightful ways to wake her.

Remy was lying on her side, her hands tucked under her head and her legs slightly drawn up. The curve of her hip called to him and Jace reached out to touch the expanse of skin. He stroked along her hipbone, grazing his fingers over the cheek of her ass as he trailed his hand down her legs. His she-wolf made a sound deep in her throat, rolling over to her back, exposing her luscious body to his gaze.

"Remy, don't you want to wake up?" Jace's softly whispered words were followed by his fingers stroking their way back up her leg until they rested high on her thigh.

"Hmm, don't stop." The husky order caused a smile to break out across his face.

"Happy to oblige." Jace parted her legs, caressing the tender flesh of her pussy. "Are you sore?"

"Please. Last night was a good workout."

"We need to put you on a regular exercise schedule." Finding her already starting to become wet from his attention,

Jace pressed a finger inside and watched as Remy's hips arched to take the digit. "I think the idea appeals to you."

"Maybe I need some convincing." Remy cupped her breasts and for a moment, Jace forgot everything else. Watching his woman touch herself in such an intimate way was a big turn-on for him.

"Maybe you need to do some more of that." Jace nodded toward her hands.

Remy grinned as she lightly pinched her nipples. "Do you like this, Watcher Boy?"

Somehow the previously derogatory name now had a sexual overtone as he watched her pleasure herself.

"I more than like. Pinch them harder."

Jace returned to fingering her gently as he watched her tweak her nipples to sharp little points. Remy's breath was coming in short, panting gasps and she parted her legs to allow him better access to her pussy.

"Jace." She spoke his name in a shaky whisper as he continued to pump now three-fingers deep inside her.

"What is it, baby?" He knew what she wanted, but he wanted her to ask for it.

"Touch my clit. Please."

Jace rubbed his thumb lightly over her clit once and then returned to thrusting his fingers.

"Damn you. Harder. I want to come."

"Okay, baby, I want you to come hard too." Moving his thumb back over her clit, Jace rubbed back and forth with constant pressure. Her first orgasm hit quickly but Jace wasn't backing down and continued to tease the sensitive flesh. "Come on, baby, ride it out."

"I can't."

"Yes you can. Do it for me."

Remy had released her breasts by this point and was clutching at the comforter as the second orgasm rushed through her.

Jace collapsed across the bed, his cock rock-hard and begging for attention. Grasping his shaft, Jace began to stroke the turgid length. He could hear Remy's breathing slowly begin to return to normal.

"Want some help?" Remy's breath drifted across his thigh as she spoke.

The ringing cell phone caused them both to jump for a moment and Jace groaned at the interruption. Grabbing the phone from the bedside table, he hit the talk button. "What?"

Remy moved with him, but stopped at his waist where she leaned forward and engulfed his cock in her warm, wet mouth. The feel of her lips sliding up and down his cock damn near took his breath away. Jace pushed his fingers through her hair, anchoring her head to his body. She looked up at him, her dark eyes promising.

"Good morning to you too, *Rakshasa*."

Shit, shit, shit. It was never good news when the *Benandanti* called at seven o'clock in the morning.

"Nico, what can I do for you?"

Remy's eyes widened as Jace spoke and she immediately released him. *Damn it all to hell.*

"There have been some developments with Cassandra. I need you to come in for a meeting."

Remy had risen and was standing next to the bed. She had gone all soldier on him at the mention of Nico's name and now his soft, teasing woman was nowhere to be seen.

"We have news as well."

"Remy's still there?" Nico's voice held a bit of wonder.

"Yeah, we'll be there in about an hour." Jace ended the connection, throwing the cell phone on the bed.

"I should take a shower."

"Worried the rest of the Pack might find out something?" Jace knew he shouldn't be so bitter, but it galled him to realize she was so willing to jump as soon as she knew it was Nico on the phone.

Remy clenched her jaw. "Not at all. In fact, I was going to invite you to shower with me. But now I think I'm going to rescind the offer." Stomping into the bathroom, she slammed the door.

An hour later as they were driving to the Sanctuary, Remy still was barely speaking to Jace. He knew he'd pissed her off with his comments and her subsequent one-word answers after she'd emerged from the bathroom only proved she still was mad. He was surprised he'd been able to convince her to ride along with him in the car rather than take her own. Much to his disappointment, Remy insisted on stopping by her place to grab some clothes. Jace had been looking forward to everyone's reaction when she showed up in one of his T-shirts and a pair of his boxers.

"I guess Nico was right about you being able to help me with my visions. Do you think he'll be surprised by his brother-in-law's involvement?"

Jace could practically feel Remy's stare as she turned her head to look at him.

"I have no idea."

Reaching out, he grasped her hand, wrestling with her for a moment as he continued trying to drive. "Look, I said I was sorry. I said it more than once. Can we please get past this?"

Remy sighed and he could feel a minute relaxation of her hand in his. It was something at least. "I have a hair-trigger temper."

"I've noticed."

"It's a carry-over from my childhood. React first, ask questions later."

"I've always been jealous. When my parents had Isabelle, I asked them when she was going back."

Remy laughed. "I bet you get teased about that all the time now."

"Oh yeah, my family loves to pull out the old stories."

"You're lucky. I don't really remember my parents."

Jace was amazed Remy was opening up to him. As far as he knew, she never talked much about her childhood and he was honored she was willing to share anything with him. "That must have been tough."

"Franklin was good to me. Hell, I'm *Venator* because of him. He reared me to be strong, something a lot of Weres never did for their female children."

"You're right."

"What about you? Did you always know you were going to be the *Rakshasa*?"

"No, not right away. Although my great-grandfather told me before he told my parents. I was so disappointed. I wanted to be able to turn into a wolf and getting premonitions seemed like a poor substitute."

"Yeah, especially since you don't know what they mean."

Jace tugged her hand playfully. "Poking fun at my abilities again, huh?"

"Maybe." Remy could barely keep the laughter out of her voice.

"I ought to take you over my knee."

"I'd like to see you try."

"You're on."

Remy shook her head but Jace was totally serious. He could only imagine her spread out over his lap, her ass waiting for his hand. Jace shifted in his seat to try to relieve the erection he was developing at the image.

"I've wanted to ask you something."

"Shoot."

"Have you had dreams with me in them before?"

Jace chuckled. "Baby, you've been in my dreams more than you'll ever know."

Pulling her hand from his grasp, she smacked his arm. "You know what I'm talking about, perv. I meant have you ever had premonition dreams about me?"

Remy wasn't the first one to ask him this type of question. Sooner or later everyone wanted to know if he knew something about their future. He tried to explain his dreams were often too cryptic to give exact information.

"You know what the dreams are like. I can't always tell what they mean."

"I take it that's a yes then."

Pulling into the parking lot of the Sanctuary, Jace parked the car and turned toward her. "Yes, I've had dreams of you. One especially keeps coming back over and over."

"Tell me. Please."

"It's just you and a small child. And you're smiling and happy." Jace had always loved the vision because he enjoyed seeing Remy as something other than a soldier.

Remy gasped and Jace turned to her. "Is everything okay?"

Remy's voice was hard as she spoke. "You need to work on your skills, *Rakshasa*. Your powers of perception suck." Grasping the handle, she opened the door and then jumped out of the car before slamming it and striding into the building.

Remy stood silently to the side as Jace filled Nico in on what had occurred in his vision, including their belief that David was the father of Cassandra's child. Although after his bombshell in the car, Remy was beginning to wonder once more if his stupid dreams held water.

Her — with a child. A scenario on par with him turning into a wolf. They were both examples of things neither of them would ever be able to do.

"What did you think of the dream, Remy?"

Nico's words pulled her attention back to the matter at hand. From the looks on everyone's face, he'd asked her more than once. Shrugging her shoulders, Remy moved to the black leather couch in his office and sat in what was known as her spot.

It was really funny how territorial they all were. Even though it was Nico's office, all of the *Elitario* had their designated spots. The only person who was not sitting now that Remy had was Jace, who was leaning against the bar next to the door. His demeanor might have been causal, but Remy could feel the irritation steaming off him.

What he said had upset her and he knew it. The only problem was she knew he had no idea why.

"Well." Nico tapped his fingers on his desk in a sign of impatience.

"It was a dream. People walking, talking. Strange old guy checking out my nude bod."

"You were naked in the dream?" Derek, who was sitting next to her on the couch with his feet propped on the coffee table, revved his eyebrows in a leering manner at her. The flirt even went as far as to reach across the couch and run his finger along her leg. "Do tell."

"Completely." Everyone was used to his teasing manner, and Remy knew it meant nothing more to him than it did to her, but Jace was of a different mind.

"You want to remove your hand, or do I have to do it for you?"

His comment cut short any further remarks that might have been made when everyone turned surprised looks his way.

Of course Derek being Derek didn't know how to leave well enough alone. He tightened his grip on Remy's leg and smiled. "Now what are my options again?"

"Let me show you." Jace stepped forward and Harrison, who was sitting closest to him stood, blocking Jace's way. "Get out of my way."

"No can do."

Jackson eased forward in his chair as if he were trying to get a better view of the action. He was a man of few words but there wasn't much he missed.

"Fine, I'll move you." Jace went to grab Harrison but was stopped by Nico slamming his hand on his desk.

"Can we get through one goddamn meeting without one of you assholes pulling out your cocks and waving it around?" Nico thundered, standing now as well.

"Don't you mean Were-damn meeting?" Derek piped up, ever the fool.

"Remy." Nico's tone was tired but his meaning was clear.

Without taking her gaze away from Jace, Remy removed Derek's hand from her thigh and bent his fingers back until he yelped, "Uncle."

"It's 'Auntie'," she reminded him as she raised a brow at Jace in a "better now?" way. He nodded once and took a step back, much to Remy's amusement. He might not turn furry, but he was as possessive as his brethren about his "territory". Remy wasn't sure how she felt about his marking her just yet.

"Auntie! Auntie!"

"Much better." Remy released Derek's hand and watched as he shook his fingers to alleviate the pain. "Pussy."

"You're mean."

"You're welcome."

"Can we please get back to the matter at hand?" From Nico's tone he was growing agitated at their byplay, which was extremely unusual. He sat once more in his chair and leaned back wearily.

"What's the deal?" Remy asked, kicking up her feet until they mirrored Derek's on the table.

"Tell her," Nico ordered Kellen, who during the entire Jace episode had sat back and watched quietly.

Remy had avoided looking his way until now. It wasn't as if she felt she had anything to be ashamed of. Kellen and she were long done, and to be honest, should have never gotten started. But hurting him would be as painful as hurting a brother, which should have told her something from the start. *You don't fuck family.*

There was a heavy look to his gaze but not an accusing one. "Derek and I spotted Franklin leaving Cassandra's house."

"Franklin?"

"Yes."

Franklin had been in the dream in his wolf form, along with other members of the *Maggiore*.

Damn it, what was he involved in now? Remy turned her head until she was facing Nico once more and met his gaze steadily. "Have you questioned him?"

"About?"

"About his relationship with this woman?"

"Do you think he'd tell me anything?" Nico asked.

"No." Franklin despised Nico. He'd made his position very clear in that regard over the years. He had always hoped Remy would fight for the position of *Benandanti* but her heart wasn't in it. Something he'd never understood. To Franklin, the only reason Remy had never gone for the position was because Nico had, and Franklin had never forgiven Nico. "But he'd tell me."

"No," Jace said from the sidelines. "That's a bad idea."

"Why?" Nico templed his fingers, awaiting his reply. "Do you know something you're not telling us, *Rakshasa*?"

"I know you don't send a child to question her parent."

"Remy isn't Franklin's child."

"And hello, Remy is in the room." Just in case anyone had forgotten, Remy felt the need to point out the obvious. "Also, I'm not a child."

Neither man paid her the least bit of attention. "It's wrong. She's not a freaking pawn," Jace spewed.

"Of course she's not. She's my *Venator*. And she knows her duty."

"Is it always about duty with you?"

"Yes."

"Who's waving their dick around now?" Derek murmured to Remy, his gaze glued to the ongoing debate.

"If the dick waving keeps up, I'm going to bring my plastic one from home to wield about. Maybe then someone will listen." Clearing her throat loudly, Remy stood. "Excuse me, boys. The pawn has something to say. I don't mind speaking to Franklin."

"Of course you don't." Jace's sarcasm was palpable.

"Enough. I don't really care about all the *personal* issues going on right now. Deal with them on your own time. This is Pack business and we need answers. Remy, you talk to Franklin and see what you can find out. Jace, you're coming with me and we're going to talk to Kimberly. I want to see if she's heard anything from her brother." Nico's edict brooked no argument.

Remy stared across the room at Jace. He looked as if he wanted to refuse, but she quickly shook her head at him. She knew Nico's moods and this wasn't the time to push him. In fact, she had a feeling he had some of his own personal issues going on right now.

Chapter Seven

ജ

The meeting couldn't have ended any sooner as far as Jace was concerned. He stood in front of the elevator watching the numbers light up as they neared his floor. Every last person in Nico's office was officially on his shit list, Remy included. There had never been a question in his mind about where her loyalties lay, but the fact she was willing to do anything, even something that could be to her detriment, was in-fucking-sane.

The more Jace thought about it, the more he realized Remy wasn't just a pawn to whoever was behind the whole Cassandra thing, she was a pawn to everyone who wanted to use her for something. Including their "oh-so-fearless" leader.

Remy's position in the Pack hadn't changed since they slept together, but his had. He wasn't just the Pack's *Rakshasa*, he was also the man in love with the *Venator*, and Jace wasn't just going to sit back and watch her get hurt.

The closer the elevator came to his floor, the better he felt. He had to get out of there before he said or did something he'd regret.

"You ever hear the saying about a watched pot?" Remy's voice from behind him dashed away the little bit of peace he'd manage to acquire since leaving the meeting.

"Not now, Remy."

"Still upset, I see."

Jace refused to answer. The doors slid open and he stepped in and turned, facing the controls. He hoped his silence would speak for itself, but as usual, Remy wasn't listening. She stepped in right beside him with an annoying little smile on her full, sexy lips.

He was so not in the mood for this shit.

"Did Nico send you to chase after me to make sure I don't leave the grounds?" Jace pressed the button to the ground floor harder than necessary, but it felt damn good.

"I'm not Nico's lapdog."

"Since when?"

Remy moved until she was behind him, and leaning into his back, she reached around Jace and pressed the button to shut the doors. The feel of her body pressed against his back was almost enough to make him rethink his pissed-off position. Almost.

"I'm surprised at you, Remy."

To Jace's surprise Remy's arms wrapped around his waist. "For?"

"I never thought you'd be the type to use your sexuality to get over on someone."

Instead of getting upset as he thought she would, Remy laughed. "I'm amazed you think I'd think I would be able to. I'm not exactly all known for my girlish charms."

"Then what are you doing?"

"Thanking you?" Remy nuzzled her head against his back.

"For…"

"Caring."

"Fat lot of good it does me."

"It means," Remy's arms tightened around him for a moment, "something to me."

"Then how could you—" Jace turned in her embrace until he was facing her and pushed her back so he could look into her face. "Why do you take that bullshit from him? From any of them?"

"This job, as pointless as it may seem to you, means a lot to me. Nico and the rest of them are the only real family I have.

I could never forgive myself if anything happened to any one of them when I was sitting at home being the good little girl, especially when I know I could have done something to prevent it."

"They're not the only people who care about you, Remy."

The elevator dinged as they reached the ground floor. Remy stepped away from him just as the door opened. "I know it now."

"So did you two get everything worked out?" Jace's irritation returned twofold as he turned and to see Nico and the rest of the *Elitario* standing in the lobby. They must have taken the stairs and taken them quickly.

Damn interlopers.

"Just about." Jace pressed the button to close the doors once more, much to Remy's amusement.

"You know they can still hear us, right?"

"I'm going to pretend as if they can't." And just to make things a bit more interesting, Jace hit the emergency stop button, which set off an annoying alarm. "Now where were we?"

"I don't remember."

"Sure you don't." Liar.

Remy shrugged her shoulders and smiled. Jace didn't doubt for a second she remembered exactly where they'd left off, but like him, Remy realized everyone in the lobby would be able to hear them, despite the alarm. She might have been ready to open up to him but not in front of her crew.

"I'll make this easy for you. Tonight, after we both do Nico's bidding, we take a step back and do things a bit proper."

"Proper." Remy looked amused at his turn of phrase. "And proper means what exactly?"

"I want to take you out."

Remy raised her eyebrows as if the concept were totally foreign to her. "Out?"

"You know, a date. You put on a dress. I come to the door. We go out to dinner, maybe a little dancing. Then you take me home and let me have my wicked way with you."

"I don't do dresses."

Jace shouted with laughter and he wasn't the only one. He heard a few chuckles from behind the elevator door. "Of all the stuff I said, 'I don't do dresses' is your only response?"

"I don't own a dress."

"I suggest you go shopping then." Jace turned back to the control panel and hit the emergency button once more. "And while you're at it, why don't you buy some thigh-high stockings?"

"Why don't you stick your foot up your ass?" Now there was the Remy he adored.

"Because it wouldn't be as sexy as seeing you in a dress, stockings and heels." Jace waited until the door opened and Remy stepped forward before he slapped her on the ass. "I'll pick you up at seven so you better be ready."

Remy glanced over her shoulder at him and murmured, "You're going to pay for that."

"Promises, promises." He was feeling better already.

Jace stepped off the elevator and stopped in front of Nico, who was staring at him as if he wanted to have Jace's spleen for dinner. The sick, sadist side of Jace loved how he'd infuriated Nico. It was about time someone took him down a peg or two. "You ready?"

"Let's take my car." Nico's offer was more of an order, but despite his irritation with the man, Jace knew better than to decline it. "I need to discuss a few things with you on the way over. I'll drop you back here so you can get your car."

They all headed outside to the parking lot before Remy stopped Jace.

"By the way, Watcher Boy, how the hell am I getting home when my car is parked at your house?"

Pulling his keys out, he tossed them to her. "Easy. You take my car, go back to my house and switch them and Nico can drop me at home instead of here."

"I can, can I?" Nico asked snidely, but Jace refused to rise to the bait. Instead he pulled Remy into his arms and kissed her in front of God and country, not caring who saw or why. To his delight, instead of pulling away, she leaned in to him for a moment, giving back as good as she took.

When the catcalls from the *Elitario* grew ear-piercing, Remy pulled away with a slight stain to her cheeks. His she-wolf blushing? He could die a happy man now. "Until later, Elizabeth."

Remy's eyes narrowed but she didn't reply. Not until she walked away and Derek added, "Did he just call you what I think he did?"

"Shut up," she replied with a fist to his arm.

Problem solved, Jace watched as Remy drove away in his car before climbing into Nico's.

"Why is it you're under the impression I won't kill you?"

Jace shook his head. "I don't believe you can't or won't kill me. What you don't seem to understand is, I think Remy's life is worth whatever you may do to me."

"She's my *Venator*."

"She's my mate." Nico's eyes widened at Jace's words but he kept silent. "And I don't see you allowing your mate to put herself in danger. Let alone allowing anyone else to do it."

"I don't purposely put Remy in danger, you know." Nico slammed his hand on the steering wheel. "Goddamn it, Jace, she's my best friend in the entire world. I love her like a sister. We grew up together and there is no way in hell I'd let her do something she wasn't capable of doing. This is what she does, what she's been trained to do. I don't need someone thwarting

299

my authority right now, Jace. The *Maggiore* are just itching to find a way to take me down. I need everyone together on this."

"I respect you and what you've done for the Pack. But I can't change how I feel."

"Keep it to yourself then. I want a united front. Even in front of the *Elitario*. Do you understand me?" Nico's words, although spoken softly, held a world of meaning. Jace could feel the tension in the car and he knew Nico was barely holding a leash on his beast.

Jace knew he needed to do what Nico asked and keep some of his concerns just between him, Remy and Nico. He nodded his head, and thankfully, Nico accepted his acknowledgement.

"You have it bad, Jace. Just be careful not to hurt her or I'll have to do something about it."

"No worries. I plan to keep her very happy." Even if he had to hogtie her to do it.

"How does Remy feel about this whole you being her mate thing?"

"She loves it."

Nico's burst of laughter was deafening. "I'm sure she does. You know she's not going to be easy to tame."

"I don't want to tame her. Just housebreak her."

"Good luck with that."

"I don't need luck."

Nico looked as if he wanted to say more, but instead he started the car and they headed over to the law firm where both Cassandra and Kimberly worked.

"So you still don't want to confront Cassandra?"

"Not yet. It's not exactly as if I can tell her that while I had surveillance on her, I happened to see a known Werewolf visiting. I'm not sure Cassandra knows anything about the Were community. On the other hand, if David really is the

300

father of her child, she's going to have to be brought in on the secret at some point."

"We still don't know why her child is important."

"I think I know." Jace wasn't sure why Nico didn't sound happy about the awareness.

When he didn't elaborate, Jace couldn't hold it in any longer. "Are you going to share with the rest of the class?"

"You know about the Were infertility issues. I think Cassandra getting pregnant by a Were is where our Pack is destined. Humans may be our only hope to continue the species. I'm just worried about all the current Were couples who aren't having children."

"Yourself included?"

"Very perceptive, *Rakshasa*. Once desperate to avoid pregnancy, Kimberly now worries she won't be able to have children. And I have no hope to give her."

Unfortunately Jace had no words of comfort either. Sometimes being the man with useless brain-numbing visions really sucked. The rest of the car ride continued in silence and Jace was actually happy when they arrived at their destination.

As they approached Kimberly's office, she spotted their arrival and stood to meet them. "What's wrong, Nico?" Kimberly could read her mate like a book and obviously sensed his unease.

"Nothing's wrong, *Zingaro*." Nico brushed the hair away from her face. "I just wanted to ask if you'd talked to David recently."

She shook her head. "No, in fact I haven't been able to get a hold of him for a couple of weeks now. I've left a zillion messages on his cell phone." Kimberly's gaze cut to Jace. "Have you seen something bad?"

"No, nothing of the sort, Kimberly. He was in one of my dreams but he was fine. We were just hoping to talk to him to see if he could shed any light on the vision."

"Why would he be in any of your visions?"

"That's what we want to know, *Zingaro*." Nico looked at Jace, his eyes filled with the same trepidation that traveled through Jace's soul. "That's what we want to know."

Unseen by the small group, Cassandra stood in the doorway separating her office from Kimberly's. She'd heard someone arriving and had come to see who it was right when they mentioned David. Leaning her head against the doorjamb, she curled her hand protectively over her stomach. *Dear God, what had Franklin done to David?*

* * * * *

As she stared at herself in the mirror, Remy cursed yet again. Now she knew why women were notoriously late. This girly thing was hard work. Checking her hose one last time, she thanked the Lord the package she'd bought had come three pairs to a pack because she'd already run two of them. Of course at the time she hadn't been happy about it, wondering why she was paying for three pairs when she'd probably never wear them again.

In fact, her entire shopping trip had been a major chore. She had no idea what type of dress to buy and had finally let the saleswoman pick out a few for her to try on. It was the last dress she tried that she eventually bought. Picking up the dress, she was actually hoping Jace liked it. Compared to the others it was relatively plain, a simple black wrap dress with a subtle pattern.

But she liked the material and it was actually comfortable when she tried it on. Even the saleswoman complimented her, telling her how good it looked. She'd fallen for the trap and purchased the dress, happy to finally be done with the entire shopping extravaganza.

The doorbell ringing had Remy glancing over at the clock. It was only six-thirty. *Damn, Damn, Damn.* Jace was early. The man was going to die. Pulling the dress over her head, Remy stalked to the door, ready to do battle.

Remy started speaking before the door was fully open. "You are in so much trouble, Mister—"

She blinked in surprise as she saw Franklin standing in her doorway. Although she had left several messages throughout the day, she had been unable to reach him. Remy never expected him to show up at her door. In fact, she couldn't remember a time when he'd ever visited her apartment.

"I think you've mistaken me for someone else." Franklin looked her up and down, taking in the dress, hose and high heels. "And maybe I have too. I came to see Remington, the fierce fighter of the Pack. Instead I see a young woman." Leaning in, he kissed her cheek, something he hadn't done since she was a girl.

"Ah, sorry about the greeting. You're right, I was expecting someone else." Remy stepped back, allowing him entrance into her apartment before closing the door. She watched as his gaze studied the surroundings, feeling like a child again and hoping for his approval. Unbelievable when one considered they hadn't exactly been close in the last few years.

She tried to see the room as he would. It was decorated very simply with nary a knickknack in sight. The walls were painted a dark chocolate color and the furniture was soft beige suede. There were even a few nature prints on the wall, something she'd only added in the last month. The entire theme of the room was comfort.

Taking a seat on her couch, Franklin made himself at home. "So, Remington, to what do I owe the massive number of messages I received from you today?"

Never one to play politics, Remy wasn't going to beat around the bush. "I know you've been visiting Cassandra Adams. Do you want to tell me what's going on so I know if I

303

should kill you, defend you or try to do a combination of both?"

"Remington, would you really kill me?"

"Of course I would."

Franklin smiled with pride at her words. He'd reared her to be a warrior and was obviously proud of what she'd become. "Ah, my dear, you do this old man's heart good."

"Old man, my ass. You're just as strong as you ever were. Maybe even stronger. And stop avoiding the question."

"No avoiding, I'll be happy to tell you about Cassandra. She's my daughter and your sister."

"What?"

"You heard me. She's the product of a youthful dalliance. I never knew she existed until she found me three years ago. Belinda was still alive then so I didn't want to acknowledge her publicly. But now she's pregnant and I want to know my grandchild."

Knowing Franklin had a biological child was shocking enough. Knowing he'd known about her for three years was devastating. Although they never had an overly loving father-daughter relationship, Remy felt distraught to realize she'd always thought she was special to Franklin.

Now that he had another child, his real child, who was going to give him grandchildren. Remy reached for the chair and sat, unable to take in the grief that was overcoming her. She thought she'd come to terms with the fact she couldn't have children after the battle five years ago that almost took her life. But first Jace revealed his vision this morning and now with Franklin's disclosure, Remy realized she never cared so much before.

"Remington, are you okay?"

Remy nodded, unable to speak for a moment. Clearing her throat, she tried for a semblance of order. "I'm sorry. It was the shock of it all. I was never expecting this. She's human, isn't she?"

Franklin grimaced in distaste. "Yes, unfortunately. The Were gene is recessive." He waved his hand dismissively. "No matter. The child will be Were."

"How do you know for sure?"

"The father is the young pup David Brenin, our own *Benandanti's* brother-in-law."

"But the child could still have the recessive gene, like Cassandra."

"I have faith this child will be Were. He will be the leader of this Pack someday."

As Remy listened to his words, she realized what he was saying. Not only was he trying to ensure his line went on, but he wanted his grandchild to hold the ultimate power within the Pack. The position of *Benandanti* wasn't hereditary, it was held by the strongest Were and Franklin wanted to be in that position. He couldn't best Nico himself so he was doing the next best thing.

"Sounds as if you have it all worked out."

"If only, dear child, life were so simple."

"Oh really."

"Yes, Cassandra… Well, I'm thinking she's not going to be as moldable as I was hoping."

"You mean manageable, don't you?"

"That too." Franklin chuckled. "Also, she seems a bit…off."

"How so?"

"Skittish. To be honest, I don't think she'll be up to the task of rearing a young pup."

"No." Remy watched Franklin with a mixture of bemusement and wonder. "And you think you'd do a better job?"

"I did all right with you."

"Yes, you did." *All right* wouldn't have been the way she would have worded it, but she was alive and semi-normal, so Franklin must have done something right.

"See?" He smiled. "But I have to say, that in this, I don't think I'll be up to the task. I'm getting on in age and not familiar with the new ways of things."

"As a fan of the old ones, that seems a bit right."

"This pup is going to need something neither I nor Cassandra can offer it."

Insanity-free DNA. "Which is?"

"A strong mother." The smile Franklin had been wearing as if it were a suit of armor from the moment he entered Remy's face dropped. "A warrior of unlimited proportions."

"You have anyone in mind?" Remy asked, even though she knew the answer.

"You of course."

That's where she thought he was going with this. Remy rose from her chair without a destination in mind. There was so much she wanted to say, yet she had no idea where to begin.

"Before you say no, think about this. This could be your chance at a child." Franklin rose as well and crossed the room until he was standing in front of her. In a disturbing violation of personal space, he placed his hand on Remy's flat stomach. "You will never know how I mourned the loss of your womb. I had such plans for you."

"You did, did you?" Her words were cold, as was the feeling creeping over her skin. He spoke as if her womb belonged to him and not her. "Then let me express my sorrow for you."

"No need, my child." Franklin waved away her words. "I know who is to blame."

Not this again. "It was a battle, Franklin. Nico wasn't at fault."

"He had you in the battle."

"I had me in the battle. It was a lucky passing blow. Nothing to be done."

"See, this is why I admire you so much. You'd give anything for this Pack. Hell, you did. You gave your womb. It was a sad sacrifice but a noble one."

"If I had to do again, I think I might have given a toe instead."

Her sarcasm was lost on him. "As you said, it's all water under the bridge in retrospect. I thought we'd lost everything, but I see now, it was only a small stumble in our path."

"*Our*?"

"Yes, our." Franklin patted her tummy then stepped back. "If you met her, you'd understand, Remington. She's weak, disgustingly so. I can't tell you of the war I've waged inside myself about allowing her to carry my grandchild."

"Was there another option?"

"Isn't there always?"

"Yes."

"It should have been you."

"I agree." To an extent, she did. It should be her pregnant.

"I can give you the chance again."

"Can you grow a womb for me?"

"No, but I can give you this child to rear."

"Give? Don't you think she should have some say?"

"Not really, but I can tell from your expression you think she does."

"Maybe just a little." This was getting out of hand. "You think we should just take her child. I think I'm going to need you to explain this to me a bit more."

"Another time perhaps, child." Franklin glanced at his watch. "Looks as if your beau is here. A bit early still, isn't he?"

Remy had been so enraptured with Franklin she'd missed the sound of Jace coming up her stairs. "A bit, yes."

"Not that it matters because you look lovely. I don't think I've ever seen you in a dress before. If we have a girl, you'll have to wear more of them. Nothing wrong with being a warrior and a lady, is there?"

"No," her voice was wooden.

"I agree." Franklin walked over to her door and opened it as Jace, hand raised, was about to knock. "Jace, well, well... Is this the way the wind the blows?"

"Evening, sir." Jace's voice was even and cool, as if he expected Franklin to answer. "It's a pleasure seeing you again."

Franklin held out his hand and took Jace's in a firm grip. He was a stickler for formality, even when he was plotting to take a child from its mother's arms. "You as well. Don't keep Remington out too late."

"Of course not." Jace grinned at the joke, much to Franklin's amusement.

"I like this one." Franklin winked at Remy as he patted Jace on the shoulder. "I'll be in touch, Remington. Think on what I proposed."

"I will." As if she could think of anything else. "Take care."

"Always."

Jace waited until Franklin headed down the stairs before he shut the door and let the smile slip from his lips. "What was that all about?"

"Franklin at work." Remy sat in her chair again, her legs having lost all feeling.

"What are you talking about?" Jace walked over to her and crouched in front of her until they were eye to eye. "Did he say anything or do anything to hurt you?"

Hurt? She needed to be able to feel in order to recognize pain. "No, he just offered me the chance at immortality."

"How so?"

"He offered me a child."

Chapter Eight

∞

Unbelievably for the first time in his life, Jace watched as Remy had an emotional breakdown. She didn't wail or gnash her teeth, but instead bent her head and wrapped her arms around herself. He had no idea why the idea of having a child caused her such pain, but he did know he couldn't stand to see her like this. Standing, he pulled her out of the chair and into his arms.

She felt stiff, like a cardboard replica of Remy instead of the vibrant, sassy woman he'd fallen in love with. Jace knew he needed to break through whatever barriers she'd raised and get her to open up to him. Sitting back in the chair she'd just vacated, he settled her on his lap.

"Come on, baby. You have to talk to me."

Remy raised her head and looked at him. Although there wasn't a tear in her eye, the anguish he saw there tore him up. Jace wanted to race after Franklin and beat him to a pulp for hurting his woman this way.

"I...he..." She shook her head. "I don't know where to begin."

"Let's start easy. Explain how he offered you a child."

Remy sighed, as if preparing for a chore. "He's Cassandra's father. And not only does he know she's pregnant, he thinks the child has the Were DNA. He wants to take the child from her and let me rear it."

Jace absorbed the information. Knowing the significance of a human having a Were child, he knew Nico wouldn't be pleased it was of the *Polda* line.

"Why would he take the child from his own daughter?"

Remy eyes flashed for a moment and Jace could have kicked himself.

"I'm his daughter too."

"I know, baby." Jace tried to stroke her arm but she shrugged him off. "I was just wondering why he would think she wasn't capable of rearing the child herself."

"Because she's human. And according to him she's unstable, although that's debatable, knowing the source."

"He can be a really cold bastard, can't he?"

"You have no idea. He wants this child to rule the Pack someday."

"And the hand that rocks the cradle rules the world. Well, he has high hopes, that's for sure."

"We have to let Nico know what his plans are." Remy looked as if she wanted to jump up right then and find Nico, but Jace wasn't letting her go so easily. Wrapping his arms around her, he drew her back against his chest, holding her close until he could finally feel the tiniest bit of relaxation in her body.

"The woman hasn't even given birth yet, baby. I think we can wait a couple of hours to inform Nico."

"You're right."

Jace stroked Remy's thick hair, little by little trying to get her to let go. There was more to this story but he was unsure if he should push her at this point. He had never seen her as fragile and he worried if he continued to question her, he might actually find her breaking point. On the other hand, he had the feeling this was the time and place to finally discover the true depths of this woman who was his mate.

Surprisingly, he never had to make that step.

"I can't have children."

Remy's announcement was stated matter-of-fact, as if she were telling him the sky was blue. But it explained so much. Her resistance this morning in the car and her devastation at

Lena Matthews & Liz Andrews

Franklin's offer. Jace knew she had every right to feel the hurt and pain of never carrying her own child, but he also knew it didn't matter. Not to him.

Jace hated to ask, but he needed to know. "What makes you believe you can't?"

"The lack of a womb for starters."

The long thin scar that ran underneath her bellybutton came to mind. Jace moved his hand down her stomach until it came to rest upon where he thought the scar was. "Was it an accident?"

"No, I think the Cougar's aim was dead-on. Although I'm sure he was hoping to take out more than my flesh and womb."

"When did this happen?"

"Five years ago."

Jace's grip tightened as he pulled her closer into him. He remembered stories about the battle for the Silver Mines. It was a deadly mini-war that had taken place soon after Nico took over as *Bendanti* for their clan. The fight had been unprovoked and swift, but the *Brachyurus* had fought hard and after dismantling most of their opponents, had won the right to the land.

A battle over barren land had cost Remy her ability to bear pups. How fucking ironic.

"Remy, look at me."

Remy slowly lifted her head, staring at him. She looked almost apprehensive, as if waiting for his reaction, steeling herself against the perceived blow.

"I hate the fact that you can't have children. Not because it matters one iota to me but because it causes you pain. And I hate to see you in pain. It kills me. I want to hurt someone or something. I want to fix your problem and make the pain go away. But I can't do that. I can only be there for you."

Remy nibbled at her lower lip as he spoke, her nervousness a palpable presence in the room. When he finally finished, he could actually see tears shining in her dark eyes, although her formidable will would not allow them to fall.

"Damn you. Why'd you have to go and say something so sweet? I don't want to cry, dammit."

Jace wanted to tell her she could cry in front of him, but he knew it would do no good. His little she-wolf was a warrior not a crier. "Then don't. You don't have to do anything you don't want to do."

"Why?"

"Why what?"

"Why me? You can have any Were you want." Remy glanced over her shoulder at him and peered at him from her big brown eyes. "I don't want this to go to your head or anything, but you're a very attractive Were."

She called him a Were and not a man. Would wonders never cease? "You think?"

"In a Ken doll sort of way, yes."

Always the fighter. "Thanks…I think."

"I know you've been with other Weres, just as I know you could have the pick of the litter from the Coyotes. So why me? I'm not exactly overloaded with the womanly charms. I'm more at home in a brawl than at the mall. What gives?"

Did she really not know? "It's because I want the best."

"I'm the best at fighting."

"And loving."

"I don't know how to love."

Unable to help himself, Jace burst out laughing. *Was she for real?* At the annoyed look on Remy's face, he quickly gathered his senses and took control over his mirth. "Remy, that's the biggest load of crap I've ever heard. You love beyond reason, fiercely, loyally and deeply. And if you don't believe me just ask, Nico, Derek or Kellen."

"That's different."

"Not really. There is no wrong way to love. I'm just hoping I can cash in on the love bandwagon because, Lord knows, I love you."

"You do?"

"Without a doubt."

Remy opened her mouth then promptly closed it with a frown. Jace could tell she so badly wanted to say the words, but couldn't. The fact she would try meant more to him than he could ever explain. When she went to speak again, Jace placed his fingers over her lips, silencing her. "I didn't say it so you could return the favor. I said 'I love you' because I wanted you to know. I'm not looking for you to say it back now because I know you will one day and I'm okay with that."

Remy closed her hand around his and pulled it away from her mouth. "You are insane."

"I'm willing to concede the point."

"Make love to me."

Jace lifted his hand again and stroked a finger along her jawline, watching as she shivered in reaction to the slight touch. Tracing a path down her neck, he stroked along the tops of her breasts. They rose and fell with her every breath, which was definitely becoming shallower with his attention.

"With pleasure."

"Mine or yours?"

"Both. I'm here to please."

"Does this mean I get to have my wicked way with you?" Remy was twisting the button on his shirt as she spoke, the teasing lilt in her voice a balm to his heart.

"Whatever my lady wants."

"Oh goodie." Grabbing his shirt in her hands, she pulled at the material, tearing it open. Buttons flew as they were ripped off his shirt. "I hope this wasn't your favorite shirt."

Jace laughed. "No, I couldn't care less."

314

"Good, then let's get rid of it." Remy pulled the white shirt from his body, leaving his chest bare to her hungry gaze.

"Like what you see?" He was certainly enjoying the view he was getting. The fierce warrior he fell in love with was in full attack mode and he couldn't be happier.

"Oh yeah." Running her hands over his chest, Remy's touch was causing his cock to strain at the confines of his pants. When she leaned down and licked at his nipple, Jace had to grip the arms of the chair to stop himself from grabbing her and pushing her to the floor He had promised to let her control the evening and, by God, he was going to do it, even if it killed him.

Remy shimmied to the floor in front of him and peered up from between his legs. If Jace hadn't already been hard, his cock would have stirred to life at the sight before him. His beautiful she-wolf on her knees before him. "Damn."

"What?" Remy removed his shoes and socks and ran her hands from his knees to his thighs then up to his belt buckle, all the while wearing a little seductive smile.

And she thought she wasn't woman enough for him. "You take my breath away."

"Not yet, but I will." His pants came apart as quickly as his shirt did in her firm grasp.

Jace lifted his hips so she could pull his pants off. "You keep this up and I'll have nothing to wear when I leave."

"You speak as if I'm going to let you leave."

"You speak as if I'd fight you to leave."

Remy took a bit more care with his boxers. When she moved them past his hips, his cock sprang out, hard and aching for her touch. "Looks as if someone is happy to see me."

"I agree. Why don't you come over and say hello?"

"I think I just might." Remy rose to her knees and grasped his cock tightly in her hand. The pre-cum, which glistened on the head of his shaft, was used as lube as she stroked his cock.

"Tighter, baby."

"I thought I was in control."

"I lied. And when I said I wanted you to say 'hello', I didn't mean with sign language."

Remy grinned as she leaned forward and blew softly on his cock. When he hissed, she looked up at him and batted her eyes. "Whatever did you mean then?"

"I meant suck my dick."

"Gladly." Remy opened her mouth and slid his cock between her full lips and into her warm mouth. *Home at last*. Eyes closed, Jace buried his hands in the thick strands of her ebony hair and guided her in a ritualistic dance of oral sex. He directed her, teaching her with the pressure of his hands in her hair how he liked to be pleasured, groaning deep within his throat as she soon found the rhythm he craved and moved from student to teacher.

She moved her hand in time with her mouth, stroking his shaft as she slid his cock in and out of her lips. "That's right, baby. Suck me."

Remy moved with such fierce devotion and skill she soon had Jace gripping her hair tighter and fucking her mouth as he wanted to fuck her pussy. When the familiar tingle in his balls began, Jace pulled a reluctant Remy away from his cock. "Stop, she-wolf. I don't want to come in your mouth."

"Then where do you want to come?" Her lips glistened with the evidence of his desires, making her look all the more tempting to Jace. He wanted to fuck her while he feasted on her mouth.

"So many choices."

"You can pick one." Remy rose to her feet, pulling the black dress off in the process. Her glorious body was encased only in a matching black lace bra and thong set, thigh-high stockings and the sexiest heels he'd ever seen.

Good Lord, she was trying to kill him.

Licking his lips, Jace rose as well and pulled her flush against him. His erection was pressed up against the rough texture of the lace and it felt great. "Anywhere."

"Yes."

Jace slapped his hand on her behind, and Remy's eyes widened in understanding. "Then how about your sweet ass?"

For all her supposed experience, Remy hadn't slept with many Weres. In fact, she could count on one hand the number of men she'd been with. And although Were sex was formidable, she'd never experienced anal sex. It had always seemed too personal and intimate. She'd never been willing to give up the control and let a man take her that way.

Her thoughts must have been revealed on her face because Jace put a finger beneath her chin and tilted her head so he could look her directly in the eyes. "Have you ever…"

"No, never."

Jace's satisfied smile made her want to slap the smirk right off his face. At the same time she reveled in his possessiveness. The dress must have warped her brain because she was definitely acting more girly than she ever had in her entire life.

"You are such a perv."

Jace didn't contradict her. In fact he didn't say anything at all. Instead, he stepped forward, causing Remy to retreat. Something she never thought she'd do. But she was enjoying his pseudo stalking, playing the game of cat and mouse. With her being the mouse.

"You have me at a disadvantage. I'm wearing heels."

"And looking damn fine in them too I might add. I knew when I told you to wear heels and thigh-highs I made the right call. They make your legs appear as if they go on forever."

Remy could actually feel her body flush at his words. When she'd asked him why he wanted her, she'd been dead serious. She was scarred, flawed, damaged goods. But he didn't care. He saw her as beautiful and he made her see herself as such.

"Are you thinking about it?"

"About what?" Remy eyed her surroundings. He probably thought he had her boxed in but she had some moves. She was just waiting for the right moment to unleash them.

"Delay all you want, she-wolf. I'm going to have your ass. But we can play your game first."

Jace strode forward another step. Remy held her position this time, but barely. She felt the need to run, to play the game he accused her of. Letting her Were chase her and take what she so obviously wanted to give.

It was time to make her move.

Leaping over the couch, Remy sprinted down the hallway toward her bedroom. She could hear Jace, hot on her heels, her surprise move not slowing him a single bit. Just clearing the doorway, she was tackled from behind, Jace's body cradling her own as they both landed on the bed.

"Are these your favorite?" Jace fingered her thong.

"No, why?"

"Time for payback." Bunching the material in his hand, he pulled, ripping the lace confection from her body. Her arousal was evident on her thighs and she was aching. Remy groaned in relief as his hand settled on her pussy, cupping her weeping flesh so lovingly. "Don't worry, baby. This kitty won't be lonely."

"Stop teasing me."

Jace rolled her over, pushing her onto her back and began kissing his way down her body. He pulled off her bra, paying special attention to her breasts, nibbling and sucking at her nipples until they were glistening with his saliva. Continuing his way down, he licked along the scar across her belly, staring up at her as he placed each loving kiss before finally moving lower.

"Did you change today?"

"Yes, before I came home." Remy didn't want to risk changing this time around.

"Good, she-wolf."

"I got your wolf."

"No, baby. I have yours."

Pulling her thighs wide, Jace licked at her clit, sucking it into his mouth. Remy gasped at his immediate assault on her sense, spilling forth her juices in response. Finally releasing her clit, Jace licked along the seam of her pussy before pushing his tongue deep inside. Remy grasped his head in her hands as she arched her hips toward him.

Jace paused in his sensual assault for a moment, gathering the moisture at her opening and dragging it across to her rosette. Rimming the hole with his finger, he ignited the nerve endings there, causing her to gasp at the sensation. Returning to her pussy, he gathered more of her essence to tease at her forbidden hole, finally pushing a finger deep inside.

The sensation was different from any she had ever experienced. Simultaneously she felt full yet wanted more. Jace returned his mouth to teasing her pussy, licking and nibbling at the swollen flesh, lightly grazing over her clit. At the same time he began to move the finger in her ass, loosening the tightness there. The overwhelming feelings were too much for Remy and as Jace sucked her clit into his mouth, she came with a scream, her body ricocheting back and forth between the dual sensations of Jace's mouth and teasing finger.

Vaguely returning to an awareness of her surroundings, Remy felt as if she were floating for a moment. Her orgasm had blinded her to everything for a brief moment and Jace had taken advantage of her euphoria. Her ass felt full and she realized he had added a second finger.

"Jace, it's too much. I can't take it."

Jace chuckled. "Are you telling me the big, bad *Venator* is felled by two fingers?"

"No, but you're too big. It's never going to fit."

"Oh, it'll fit, baby. We're just getting warmed up."

So saying, Jace began to thrust the fingers in her ass, moving them back and forth, slowly at first but with ever-increasing speed. Eventually Remy realized she was pushing back as he thrust forward, whimpering with need. Ever so easily he slowed his hand, letting his fingers slide from her ass. She felt empty at the loss.

"I don't want to hurt you. Do you have any—"

"The drawer."

Pulling it open, Jace found the lube and a box of condoms she had there. "Well, well, well. We'll have to play with some of these toys one of these days."

He grabbed a condom and the water-based lube before shutting the drawer. Jace tore into the wrapper with his teeth and then sheathed himself. After quickly coating his latex-covered cock, Jace returned his fingers to her ass to briefly lubricate the entrance before pushing her legs high and wide and kneeling between them. Staring into her eyes, he told her without words how much he loved her. Remy only wished she could return the words to him, but he said he could wait and she could only pray he would.

"I'll go slowly."

"I trust you."

Holding his cock in one hand, Jace pressed forward slowly until the head of his cock popped through her anal

320

ring. He stopped for a moment, allowing them both to catch their breath. Remy reached down and began fingering her clit, purposely taunting Jace to hurry. Her ministrations garnered the response she was looking for when Jace growled and pushed forward, firmly seating himself deep inside.

The fullness was unbearable at first and Remy wondered why she had been begging him to rush. But eventually her muscles relaxed and she felt the need to move. Never stopping the slow, soft strokes between her thighs, she anchored her heels on the bed and lifted her ass, pushing his cock unimaginably deeper.

"Jesus, woman, are you trying to kill me?"

Remy laughed and then gasped as Jace pulled back, almost pulling free of her ass before sinking deep once again. He began a slow, steady thrusting, and she pushed back with every plunge, giving as good as she got.

"Rub your pussy harder for me, baby. I want to see you coming on your hand."

Happy to obey, Remy continued to stroke her clit, strumming at the swollen bundle of nerves. Her body was on fire and she knew she couldn't hold off her orgasm for much longer.

"Not yet, Elizabeth."

"Why?" she moaned, holding back as he commanded.

"Because I don't want you to come yet."

"What makes you think you get to make the rules?"

"This." Jace punctuated his words with a deep thrust, which damn near brought her off the bed. "And this. And this."

He matched every word with a plunge, fucking her ass with as much vigor as he had her pussy. "Say the words, Elizabeth."

Dazed, Remy tried to focus on what he was saying and not what she was feeling. It was a difficult task. Her pleasure sensors were on overload and she was having a hard enough time remembering to breathe, let alone think. "Say…what?"

"You know what I want to hear," he growled, leaning forward until his chest was against her breast. "Tell me what you are. Who you are."

From the dominating way Jace was powering into her and lording over her, Remy didn't doubt for a moment his Wolf lived and breathed inside him. He may not change, but he was truly her Alpha in every way that counted. "I'm…"

"Say it," he ordered seconds before he sunk his teeth into her nape.

"Your. Mate!" Remy's answer roared from her lips as her orgasm swept through her body, blinding her to everything around her except for the intense pleasure washing over her body.

She came over and over, her body jerking, her pussy weeping, her ass taking every stroke from Jace's hard shaft. The pleasure was maddening and Remy didn't want it to ever end.

Jace's own release wasn't far behind hers. "Mine!"

Remy couldn't have agreed more. She was his and whether she said the words aloud or not, she knew in her heart she loved him.

They were mated. Bound for life, and Remy wouldn't have it any other way.

With a heavy groan, Jace pulled from her trembling body and plopped down next to her on the bed. Their labored breathing was synced and for a moment neither one of them said a word.

The silence was a first for them.

Of course it couldn't last forever. "Damn, you're good."

Remy chuckled at the satisfaction lacing Jace's words. "Funny, I was thinking the exact same thing."

Jace stood and headed into the bathroom, disposing of the condom and returning with a warm cloth. After cleaning Remy, he returned the cloth to the bathroom before rejoining her in bed.

"So…" Jace propped himself up on his arm and leered at her. "What's for dinner?"

"If you think I'm getting back in that dress—"

"Fuck the dress."

"Now you want to fuck the dress. My ass wasn't enough?"

"No, she-wolf, your ass was just the beginning." Jace took her hand in his and brought it to his mouth. He slowly took the fingers she had masturbated with and licked them free of her essence.

Once done, Jace placed her hand down and ran his fingers up her arm to the nape of her neck, caressing the mark his teeth had imprinted into her skin. "Does it hurt?"

"Does it matter?" she teased.

"Of course. I wouldn't hurt you for anything in the world." There was a seriousness to Jace's tone that spoke volumes about his feelings for her. Remy had felt kinship before, even love from one friend to another, but she had never felt this before.

The love of a man. The love of *her* man.

Remy had to clear her throat twice before she could speak again. Gone was the teasing tone in her voice. "I know."

"Do you?"

"Yes."

"The answer is…"

"Yes." When Jace's face clouded over, Remy reached up and caressed his check. "But I'd hurt for you, gladly. I think you're worth it."

"I feel the same way."

"I believe you." And for the first time in her life, she did.

Chapter Nine

ဘ

There was no doubt in Jace's mind when he opened his eyes where he was or why he was there. In fact, if he had slept through the night without a vision, he would have thought something was wrong. The only complaint he had was he had to walk through all the freaking underbrush to get to where the true vision lay.

As he continued to walk, the trees seemed to get larger but also closer together. The branches were bent, providing a blanket over the forest below and blocking out any semblance of light. Jace peered into the shadows, pretty sure he'd passed this way earlier, but it was hard to believe he could be walking in circles.

So far not so good. The sound of the babbling brook rang out through the silent night, but no matter how far he walked, the reverberation didn't get closer. He stumbled, he pressed forward, he fought his way through greenery that appeared to grow from every angle in every direction and over logs larger than most trees, and still he remained nowhere.

The dark night sky filled the empty spaces of the low-hanging trees and it was becoming increasingly obvious the reason he couldn't get anywhere was because the fates didn't want him to.

"Vlad!" Jace called out between curses as he battled bushes and low-swinging limbs. "Get your old ass out here."

There wasn't a reply. Not as if he thought there would be. There was something about calling his great-grandfather old that made him not want to appear.

Imagine that.

Frustrated, Jace refused to take another step forward. "A hint would be appreciated about now."

This was beyond stupid. If the fates wanted to show him something, then they better get on with the get on because he was so done with this *George of the Jungle* routine.

When his request was once again met with silence, Jace threw up his hands and flipped whoever was in charge of the dream-weaving bullshit the bird and leaned back against one of his tree oppressors.

Why couldn't he be normal and dream about Angelina Jolie? Even Rosie O'Donnell would be a welcomed break from this mumbo jumbo. A tree branch tore at his shirt and sliced his skin. Grimacing in pain, Jace looked down through the ripped yellow fabric and saw blood rise up.

What the fuck?

Jace had never bled before in a dream. Hell, he'd never felt pain before in a vision. How in the world was it even possible?

"Vlad!" he bellowed once again. "Either get your ass out here—"

"Or what, *nipote*, will you moon us next?" Although Jace could hear his great-grandfather, he couldn't see him. Which by the way he was feeling right now, was a good thing for the old man. "Your father would be so proud."

"He just might," Jace muttered, prodding at his injury. "Just tell me what I'm doing wrong."

"You're not seeing?"

"Because it's dark as hell in here."

"Darkness is not the reason why."

If Vlad were alive, Jace would have killed him. "Then why?" He added "smart-ass" silently to himself as he crossed his arms over his chest.

"Do you know the old saying, *nipote*, about not being able to see the forest—"

326

"For the trees?"

"Yes, that is the one. Take it to heart. What are you missing? What's stopping you from getting through to the vision?"

"You mean besides a flashlight and a machete?"

"Yes." The dry reply was telling.

As was Jace's aggravated sigh. What was he missing? Trees. Forest. Logs. Pain. What the hell was Vlad referring to?

Dropping his arms, Jace glanced around the crowded woods, trying to let his irritation flee. He couldn't think when he was riled. "You'd think this shit would get easier," he muttered to himself.

"Wasn't it?" Vladimiro's words whispered through his mind, clearing away the cobwebs that had gathered in the darkness.

The last time he dreamt things had been so much clearer and the difference between then and now was Remy. As soon as Jace thought her name, the forest disappeared and the chessboard once again appeared before him. This time it was minus all the pieces.

"I worry about you sometimes." Vladimiro walked up from behind Jace, frowning. "That took much longer than it should have."

"I get it. Remy is my *aiutante*. When she's here, I see things better."

"Right."

"So..." Jace looked around, waiting for Remy to appear, just as she had the last time they had fallen asleep together. When nothing happened, he glanced over at Vladimiro, who was watching him as if he were waiting for a light bulb to go off. "Well, where is she?"

"You tell me?"

"We went to sleep together."

"Yet you woke up here alone. What does this tell?"

"She's not here anymore?" *Where the hell did she go?*

"If you want an answer, *nipote*, look closer."

Suddenly Cassandra and the child appeared on the board again. But this time she was completely alone. The night air was still and calm but Jace recognized it as the calm before the storm. He looked around, waiting for the danger to appear. The silence was split by the howl of an animal on the hunt, but it wasn't a Wolf. It was a Coyote.

A small group of Coyotes broke through the trees, slinking along the ground, their bellies almost dragging as they made their way toward the chessboard. Their eyes gleamed yellow and Jace could see their lips unfurled, exposing sharp teeth. Leaping onto the chessboard, the Coyotes nipped at Cassandra, pushing her to her knees. The terror in her eyes was palpable.

"Where's Nico and the *Elitario*? Or Remy and the *Rahu* at least?"

"I thought you didn't want Remy to fight?" Vlad's words stung because in the end, he knew as much as he wanted to protect Remy, she was a fighter, a warrior who protected others who couldn't defend themselves.

"Shut up, old man."

Jace heard the howl of the wolves, but instead of the cavalry arriving, the *Maggiore* wolves appeared, circling the chessboard. They seemed willing to observe the byplay between the Coyotes and Cassandra, waiting to see who the winner would be.

Cassandra was trying to hold the Coyotes at bay but swiftly losing the battle. She curled herself over the child, attempting to shield it from danger. Jace wondered again at Franklin's assertion of her inability to rear the child. Cassandra may not be a Were, but she was protecting her child as any other mother would. Unfortunately, her human body gave out and she eventually collapsed.

As the Coyotes moved in for the kill, Nico and the *Elitario* suddenly appeared, battling against the smaller group. The fight was over in minutes, the *Elitario* obviously more experienced, although a few of the Coyotes were able to escape.

The *Maggiore* continued in their role as observers, watching as the *Elitario* attended to Cassandra. Intent on Cassandra and the child, Jace almost missed as one of the wolves broke away from Nico's Pack and headed toward the *Maggiore*.

Turning to Vlad, Nico asked the one question that had been paramount in his brain since the vision had begun. "Where's Remy?"

"You tell me, *nipote*, this is your vision."

Jace could feel his fury rising at the cryptic response. "Tell me, damn you. She's here somewhere, otherwise I'd still be stuck in the forest. So she has to be okay." He wasn't sure if he was trying to reassure Vlad or himself.

"I have no answers for you, *nipote*. Only you can find those. But you must remember to open yourself to the visions. Look beyond everything in the light and into the shadows. Because it is in the shadows you will discover the truth."

Jace wanted to ask more but a hammering was beginning in his head and it wouldn't stop. Sitting up suddenly, Jace pounded his fist on his thigh as he realized someone was knocking at the door. As he stood, he spotted his boxers laying over a chair in the corner. Remy must have brought them in from the other room. Quickly pulling them on, he made his way out to the living room to see who had the death wish.

Without checking the peephole, Jace swung the door wide. "What?"

The grim visage of Franklin greeted him. Great, Jace had slept with his daughter, who was conspicuously missing, and now he was being confronted by Daddy Dearest.

"When I said get her home at a decent hour I didn't mean I expected you to stay here."

Jace's eyes narrowed at Franklin's insinuation. "Are you having me watched or Remy?"

"Neither, my dear boy. Guilty conscience?" Jace wasn't sure if Franklin was referring to Nico having Cassandra watched or the fact Jace and Remy had obviously slept together, so he just remained silent, waiting to see what Franklin wanted. "Nothing to say?"

"Just wondering why you're here."

"Can't a father visit his daughter?"

"Twice in so many days? It's just not like you. Besides, she's not home."

"I'm worried about Remington. She is a sensitive soul. Not many see that side of her."

Jace stood back in amazement. As evil as he knew Franklin to be, the show of paternal concern and caring made Jace respect the man, if only infinitesimally.

"It's nice to see you care about one of your daughters at least."

Franklin cocked his eyebrow. "So, Remington shared our news."

"I just find it interesting you would wrestle a child from one daughter's arms to hand it over to another. Didn't you hear it's not a good idea to show favoritism?"

"You must realize I have both their welfare at heart. Cassandra is weak, a human, with no concept of the needs of a Were pup. How could she attempt to teach him all the history of our Pack with no knowledge of it herself?"

"That's bullshit. We have teachers and historians. She could learn if you gave her the chance."

"What about protection of the child? Remington is ideally suited. She was born to protect leaders."

Jace was surprised Franklin was so willing to reveal his avarice for power. But truly, what did he have to hide? The man never backed Nico, it wasn't a secret. And if he could rear a child to a position of power, what of it? It wasn't as if it were against Lycan Law. In fact, just the opposite. The strongest ruled. Nico became *Benandanti* by force, not by birth.

"Remy is more than the *Venator*. She is a woman, my woman and my mate. I won't allow her to be a pawn in your game." Jace wasn't above stating his own ambitions.

Franklin smiled. "I like you, my boy. Protecting my girl so fiercely. But remember, you will never allow Remington anything. She is her own woman and makes her own decisions."

Franklin turned to leave and Jace watched as he headed down the stairs. As he closed the door, he muttered, "You keep it in mind as well, old man."

* * * * *

Derek pulled in front of Cassandra's townhouse and shut off the engine. He adjusted his seat back until they could both peer out the tinted driver's side window. "So do you want to tell me why we're here?"

He probably wasn't the right person to call for a stakeout mission, seeing as how his Hummer didn't exactly shout "Don't look at me", yet Derek was the first person Remy thought of to bring.

In truth she could have asked any of the *Elitario* to come with her, but of the four men, Derek and Kellen were the ones she was closest to. And since, despite her shower, she still wore the scent of Jace on her skin, Remy thought it best to bring the friend who wouldn't be pouting because she wasn't giving him any.

"Recon."

"On whose orders?"

"Mine."

Derek laughed. "Just like I thought."

"Then why did you ask?" Remy focused on the floor of the building Kellen had said Cassandra lived and stared at the main door, praying the woman would come out. Even though she saw the blonde in Jace's vision as well as the drawing they'd completed together, it wasn't the same thing. She needed to see Franklin's daughter in the flesh.

"Because I wanted to hear you admit you were insanely jealous out loud."

"I admit nothing."

"You don't have to." Derek's voice lost some of the teasing quality. "She's not your competition, Remy."

"As if she could be." Even though her words were haughty, Remy's bravado was forced. She unbuckled her seat belt and turning, muttered to herself, "She's just a human."

"Who happens to be Franklin's biological daughter and carrying his grandchild." Remy had filled Derek in on the demented father-daughter chat Franklin and she had the night before in her apartment. Yet hearing him call Cassandra Franklin's child bothered her.

"It doesn't matter to me."

Remy never considered herself to be a possessive person, not when it came to Franklin anyway, yet she couldn't help the hurt coursing through her veins. This interloper was everything she wasn't and everything she could never be.

"*Right*." Derek dragged the word out as if he didn't believe the shit she was shoveling any more than she did as the words fell from her lips. "Which is why we're here at eight in the morning watching her place."

"I just want to see what all the fuss is about."

"You mean besides the *pregnancy* and the *Franklin DNA*?"

"Yes."

"Liar."

"Eat me."

When Derek didn't reply with his usual smart-ass remark, Remy tore her gaze away from Cassandra's door and looked into the knowing eyes of her friend. "What?"

"I would follow you blindly into a collapsing burning building or into battle with nary a weapon between us, but one thing I will not do is follow you down this path of bullshit."

"I don't know what you mean."

"Then let me clarify it for you. Your parents died. Mine were too consumed with the death of my brother to pay much attention to me. They let their grief rob them of their ability to parent, to love, to live. I buried them when I was sixteen, but they'd died long before then, and there wasn't a moment of my childhood where I didn't wish I could have traded places with Kai if I could have. If there is ever anyone you needn't explain wishing for more to, it's me."

"I know, it's just..." Remy did know, she just didn't know how to explain her whacked feelings to anyone. They didn't make sense to her, how could she possibly expect someone else to get it? "It's not as if I want to be pregnant right now. I just want the option. And it's not as if I wish Franklin were my birth father, I just want. I just want..."

"A family."

Sadly, Remy nodded her head. "Yes."

"You already have one." Derek reached out and took her hand in his. "Sure, I have all the looks, you have all the strength, Harrison has the brains and Kellen has all the charm. No wait, I have the looks, the strength, the brains and the charms, which just leaves you with the really good tan."

"Asshole."

"That's brother asshole to you," Derek teased. "You also have Jace. And from those teeth marks you tried very unsuccessfully to hide, I'm willing to bet he's not going anywhere for a while."

"So he thinks." Remy could feel her cheeks heating. She wasn't trying to hide Jace's mark, which surprisingly hadn't healed. Apparently the only Wolf mating ability he lacked was the knotting because the love wound was branding her skin just as surely as if he had fur.

"I don't think he's the only one."

"Shut it."

Derek chuckled. "Consider it shut. Now can we get out of here or what?"

Remy glanced longingly at Cassandra's door once more before nodding her head in agreement. "Sure."

"Good, I'm so hungry I could eat a sixth grader."

"You are so nasty. I hear those human kids don't bathe." Remy sat back in her seat and began to buckle up again when she spotted two men in a black van parked across the street. "Wait a minute."

"What?"

"I bet you five dollars we aren't the only stalkers out today."

The two blond men exited the van in sync and headed toward Cassandra's building. Their stealthlike moves combined with their musky scent screamed of their Were heritage.

"Coyotes."

When it rains it pours. "Either she's the world's biggest Were slut or they're up to no good."

Derek revved his brows in a leering manner. "Oh, I'm hoping for the former."

"Not in the mood to kill today?"

"I'd take a slut over a dead body any day."

"Good to know." Remy shook her head. Boys.

"You think Franklin has something going on the side with the Coyotes?"

"No. I seriously doubt it."

"You think she does?"

"Probably not."

"So we're thinking kidnapping."

It looked as if she were going to get to kill someone after all.

"Kidnapping." She sighed, shaking her head in dismay. *You truly just can't fix stupid.* "Do you think the idiots noticed it was daytime? It's almost as bad as staking someone out in a Hummer."

"Leave Lucille out of this." Derek opened his door and bound to the ground with Remy close on his trail. They crossed the street quietly, doing their best to stay downwind and to appear inconspicuous.

They paused next to a brick wall along the walkway and watched as one of the Coyotes knocked on the door. When Cassandra opened it, her face was set in a polite smile, which soon disappeared as the two men pushed their way into her home.

"Did you hear a 'please come in'?"

"No, I didn't." Remy started across the lawn with Derek by her side. "See, this is why I was against joining with them. No manners."

"And we all know Emily Post is your middle name."

"Exactly."

"So do we have a plan?"

"Kill the bad guys."

"I love your plans."

When they came to a stop at Cassandra's front door, Remy raised her hand and knocked. "Domino's Pizza."

"It's too early for pizza," Derek chided.

"It's never too early for pizza."

There was a muffled noise from behind the door quickly followed by silence. Just as they had caught the Coyotes' scent, Remy knew they must have caught their wolf scent as well.

Without waiting for a reply, Remy shoved her shoulder into the door, breaking the lock in the process. The red door gave under her strength and the jamb splintered as she burst into the room.

Releasing the door handle, Remy dusted off her shoulder and smiled. "I really don't know my own strength."

"You have to lay off the Wheaties," Derek said as he stepped into the room.

"I know, but I'm a growing girl." As they bantered back and forth, Remy's honed senses surveyed the room. Cassandra, the frightened mess she was, huddled behind a leather armchair, as if the dead cow could protect her from anything. The two Weres were standing just a few feet apart in front of the chair, looking like two dumb-as-a-stump statues.

The whole scene was ridiculous yet telling at the same time. There was no question Derek and she could handle these two Ken dolls.

"I'm going to give you to the count of three to turn around and get out of here before I rip you a new asshole," ordered the brawny Coyote.

"Can you count so high?" Derek calmly began to unbutton his black silk shirt and take it off. He hated to wrinkle his clothes when he changed. "And I can't speak for you, but I happen to like the asshole I have."

"One." The Coyote growled as he began to crouch lower to the floor "Two."

"Three," Derek finished for him, and pounced across the room, taking the counting Were to the floor in one fell swoop.

Remy could feel the swell of bloodlust rush over her as she charged the remaining Coyote. With the image of her beast in her mind, Remy changed into her wolf form mid-leap, knocking the transforming man to the floor. The weight of her clothing didn't slow her down as it puddled around her merging form. She was used to it. Remy had learned to adapt. Besides, she wasn't wearing clothes around her mouth. She plowed into him before he had a chance to fully change and her teeth clamped on his throat. With a powerful shake of her head, her teeth slashed through his skin, deep into his arteries.

The metallic taste of blood filled her mouth as she chomped down on him. The overwhelming urge to feast clouded her mind for a moment before reality came pouring back in. Cassandra may know about her Wolf heritage, but it didn't mean she was up to watching them eating someone in her home.

Reluctantly Remy opened her mouth and watched in glee as the Coyote's body twitched on the floor. It sometimes took a while for the body to catch up with the brain. Nevertheless, he was dead, even if his legs wanted to do a farewell dance.

Glancing over her shoulder, she saw Derek still toying with his prey. The man was almost dead. He was bleeding out from a wound in his stomach. Cassandra was going to need new carpet.

Remy trotted over to Derek and snapped at his hind legs. *Finish him already.*

Don't get pissy with me because you killed yours too quickly.

Remy glanced over at Cassandra who looked as if she were about to throw up. Apparently sister girl wasn't into gore and carnage. So much for Thanksgiving at her place.

Don't kill him just yet. I want to ask him some questions.

Fine. Derek's lips curled back as he stood guard over the injured Coyote.

Satisfied Derek would do as he was told, Remy trotted over to Cassandra and sniffed at her leg. Squealing, Cassandra pulled back as if she didn't want to get wolf hair or Coyote blood on her black slacks. Wimp.

With the image of her human self in mind, Remy transformed, stretching her body to get the kinks out. Cassandra's eyes widened as she took in Remy's bloody appearance. Her outerwear had puddled around her when she changed, but her undergarments had remained intact.

Unfortunately, they were now covered in gooey death gore, but they weren't the only things. The artery had been a gusher and spilled out, not only onto the floor but onto her pile of clothes.

"Do you think I could borrow some clothes?"

Cassandra nodded and Remy shook her head in disgust. The human was useless.

"I'm going to go find something in your closet. I'll be right back." Remy wasn't sure if she should leave her alone, but she couldn't stand there nearly naked all day. Scouring through her closet, Remy realized finding something to wear was going to be no easy task. The woman was a midget. She finally grabbed a T-shirt that was going to show off every curve and then some and a pair of shorts with an elastic waist.

It was better than nothing, she thought, as she headed back into the living room. Derek had turned back as well and was dressing.

As she made her way over to the dying man, she spotted Cassandra looking as if she were about to pass out at any minute. "Hey, are you okay?"

"I don't know. My baby…I'm pregnant. I'm not sure, but I think something—" Suddenly Cassandra cried out and doubled over in pain.

"Shit. We have to get you to a doctor."

"My ob-gyn, the number's on the fridge." Cassandra could barely speak as Remy rushed to the kitchen and grabbed the number. Snagging the phone, she dialed the doctor.

"Hi, Cassandra, what's up?" This was obviously no doctor's office.

"This isn't Cassandra. I'm at her house, but I think I have the wrong number. I need her doctor."

"This is Dr. Osterman. What's happened?"

"I don't know. Something's wrong with the baby."

Chapter Ten

ஐ

Slowly coming awake, Cassandra took stock of herself. Definitely in a hospital, she thought, looking down at the ugly green gown she was wearing. Glancing up, she sucked in her breath as she recognized the African American woman standing in the corner staring at her.

Cassandra had known who Remington was from the moment she stepped in her townhouse. Franklin had told Cassandra all about his adopted daughter, how she was an important member of the Pack and Nico's special bodyguard. Just looking at her made Cassandra feel inadequate.

Everything Cassandra wasn't, Remington was, something Franklin had pointed out to her time and again. Now looking at her, Cassandra knew why. She would never be able to compete with the dark beauty in her father's eyes. No matter how many children she birthed.

Lifting her hand to her head, Cassandra moaned as she realized there was a needle stuck in her arm. She pulled at the needle, trying to dislodge it from her arm.

"Stop it." Remy was at her side in the blink of an eye.

"I don't want any drugs. The baby…"

"According to your doctor the baby's fine and it's only a saline drip, nothing but IV hydration."

Cassandra settled back against the bed, praying Remy wasn't lying to her. "Where is Felic…Dr. Osterman?"

Remy shrugged her shoulders as she returned to her post in the corner of the room. She stood like a solider, overlooking Cassandra yet seeing her and everything in the room at the same time.

The silence was maddening and it made Cassandra feel uncomfortable in her own skin. "Thank you for bringing me here but you can leave now."

"I can, can I?"

"Yes." Clearing her throat, Cassandra ventured forth with a question that had been plaguing her since Remington and the other Were showed up at her place. "What did those other…things want?"

That got her attention. "*Things*," she sneered, adding more emphasis to the word than Cassandra had intended.

"I didn't mean it like it sounded."

"Sure you didn't."

She was definitely Franklin's daughter. "Let me rephrase, what did those Wolves want?"

"They weren't Wolves. They were Coyotes. Couldn't you tell the difference?"

"Apparently not." So there was more to the other world than Werewolves. Cassandra really wanted to find out more but she doubted Remington was in the mood to share with her. "Well?"

"We don't know. We were going to question one of them, but you got all sick and we had to kill him so we could rush you over here."

"You make it sound as if it were an inconvenience to bring me here."

"It was."

Bitch. "Why do you hate me?"

Remy cocked an eyebrow, a slight smirk on her face. "I don't."

"Please. It's written all over your face." Cassandra couldn't believe she was confronting this woman. Franklin adored her. Had lorded Remington over Cassandra in fact.

"I don't think you know me well enough to know what I'm thinking." Remington's eyes were hard as flint as she spoke, although the smirky little smile still hovered over her lips.

"I know more than you think. You're Nico's *Venator*, the greatest warrior of this generation. You believe in Lycan Law and the only thing you hold more dearly is personal loyalty. The epitome of a true Were, I think, was how Franklin put it."

Although quickly masked, there had been a look of surprise from Remington when Cassandra repeated Franklin's accolades. He must have never told Remington what he thought and now she had revealed everything.

"If you're so smart, tell me what I'm thinking."

"You see me as weak. A puny human who is so far beneath your attention you would ignore me, just as you would ignore an ant on the ground. Which is why I can't figure out why you helped me today."

"I step on ants."

Cassandra sighed with regret. She was completely and utterly alone. Franklin certainly couldn't be a refuge, he only wanted her as a baby-making machine. She was afraid to go to Nico, her complicity in Franklin's plans too big a stumbling block. And David was nowhere to be found.

"Oh for God's sake, stop feeling sorry for yourself."

"I-I'm not."

"I-I think you are." Remington's mocking imitation of her stuttering answer was the last straw and she could feel the tears gathering in her eyes.

"Don't. You. Dare," Remy ordered harshly.

Shocked, Cassandra stared back at her in horror. What would Remington do to her?

"Stop staring at me as if you're Goldilocks and I'm the Big Bad Wolf come to eat you."

"A lot you know, smart-ass. Goldilocks was eaten by the three bears. The Big Bad Wolf wanted to eat Little Red Riding Hood."

Remy burst out laughing. "Damn girl, you may actually have a backbone yet. Not crying anymore, are you?"

"No, I'm getting mad."

"Good. Get mad, get angry, just don't cry. I can't stand it."

Cassandra clenched her jaw, determined to prove herself in Remy's eyes. She didn't know why, but she had a sneaking admiration for her. It was easy to see why Franklin was so taken with her.

"So, are you ever going to explain why you helped me today?"

"You don't fuck with family. Even if it's family you barely knew you had."

Remington called her family, Cassandra hadn't been expecting such a admission. "I never had a sister. It was always just me and Mom until she died five years ago."

"My parents died when I was seven. I can barely remember them. Franklin took me in and reared me as his own. I was never really close to his mate Belinda. Really, sometimes it just seemed like me and Franklin in the house."

Cassandra wanted to ask her more but the door opened and the attractive Asian man who had come to her townhouse with Remington walked in carrying two cups of coffee.

"Hey, you're awake. Cool, I'll let Felicia know."

"It's Felicia now, is it?" Remington's tone was filled with humor.

"Oh yeah." Derek handed Remy one of the cups before bounding out of the room like a puppy.

"He's awfully cheerful."

Remington snorted. "He's in lust with your doctor friend."

"What?" Hell, she had barely thought of Felicia and what she would think of these two. Cassandra realized she may have to reveal her secret. Unfortunately she had no idea what

Franklin or even Nico might think of such a plan. The idea of explaining the reality of Werewolves to someone, even someone she considered a friend, was not high on her list of things to do. In fact, she had hoped to avoid the issue all together.

"Yeah, it was a real surprise for me too. Sure, Derek loves the humans. But she's not exactly his style, you know."

"Felicia is a beautiful woman." Cassandra felt the need to defend her friend. She was beautiful, even if she wasn't the type of woman who graced magazine covers.

Remington held up her hand. "I'm not saying she isn't. All I'm saying is he usually goes for six-foot model types with legs up to here and no boobs in sight. Dr. Osterman is practically the exact opposite of that."

Cassandra couldn't dispute facts. Felicia was short, well-rounded. About as far away from runway model as a person could get.

"So what's this I hear about my patient being up?" Felicia popped her head around the corner of the door, a wide smile across her face.

"Hi. Guess you didn't expect to see me again so soon."

Felicia walked into the room, quickly followed by Derek, who looked for all the world like a besotted loon.

"That's for sure. When your friend called to tell me you'd been attacked and there was something wrong with the baby, I practically freaked."

"Remington is my sister." The words just fell out.

Both Derek and Remy recoiled in shock at Cassandra's declaration, but Felicia took it all in stride.

"Well, thanks to Sis here, both you and the little one are doing well. You have an incompetent cervix."

"What the hell is an incompetent cervix?" Remington asked, recovered from her earlier shock.

"Unfortunately Cassandra's cervix is weak and has been gradually opening during the course of her pregnancy." Turning back to Cassandra, Felicia continued. "If you hadn't been attacked, you might never have known about the problem until you went into premature labor."

"Oh my God. So what now?"

"Bed rest."

"For how long?"

"The rest of your pregnancy, sweetie. Unless you are coming here for appointments, I want you flat on your back and your feet up in the air."

Derek snorted at Felicia's description and she turned to frown at him. "This is no laughing matter. She could put the baby's health in serious jeopardy."

Derek sobered quickly at her admonishment. "Sorry."

Felicia turned from Derek to Cassandra, who was still having a hard time processing the news.

"I'm serious, Cassandra. If this baby means as much to you as I think it does, you're going to follow my instructions to the letter."

"But…" Cassandra held her hands up in confusion. "I live alone. How can I possibly be on complete bed rest?"

"Can't you find someone to stay with you?"

Her mother was dead, her father was crazy and her baby daddy was nowhere to be seen. It wasn't as if she had a lot of options. "No one I can think of."

Felicia gestured over to Remington. "Well, what about your sister?"

"What about her sister, what?" Remington questioned, stepping forward with a frown.

"Can't she stay with you?"

Cassandra and Remington both answered at the same time. "No!"

"Why not?"

"Yes, why not, big sister?" Derek teased, leaning against the wall with a big smile.

"Because she… Because I…"

Cassandra glanced over at Remington, looking for help.

"The child's life is at stake." Felicia picked up the chart at the end of Cassandra's bed. "So whatever little family tiff you two have going on needs to be squashed now."

Without another word, Felicia walked out of the room.

"Hey, Felicia, wait a minute." Derek headed out after her, leaving Remington alone in the room with Cassandra.

Cassandra picked nervously at the nonexistent lint on her sheet. Part of her wanted to get to know Remington, but this wasn't exactly the way she wanted to go about it.

"I can hire a home-care nurse."

"Or you can just go to your house and pack your shit."

"Why do I have to move?" Cassandra asked confrontationally.

"Because I'm bigger, stronger and there's no blood on my floor." Remington turned on her heel and left the room.

Maybe having a big sister wasn't so great after all.

* * * * *

After Franklin left, Jace snuck out of her place wearing only his boxers and headed back to his house to shower and change. He just emerged from the shower, wrapping a towel around his waist when he heard his front door open.

"Hey, honey, I'm home." Remy's lilting voice rang out loud and clear.

Jace smiled in anticipation. Even though she'd abandoned their bed this morning, she'd shown up at his home, which he considered a good sign. Walking down the hallway, he stopped to admire the vision standing in the middle of his living room. Jace didn't know what he had done in life to deserve this, but whatever it was, he was damn grateful. Remy, his too-sexy-for-words mate, was wearing a tight T-shirt pressed against her body like a second skin, outlining her pert lip-licking-good nipples and a pair of running shorts, which made her long, brown hot-as-hell legs seem as if they were never-ending.

It was enough to make a man howl in appreciation. There was a God.

"Nice outfit, but did you wear it out in public?"

"Ha, ha," Remy snarled at him, and Jace just chuckled at her mock anger.

"No matter, I can rip it off in three seconds flat." Jace headed toward Remy, intent on following through with his words. The sound of a throat clearing stopped him in his tracks.

"Uh, hi." Cassandra stepped through the open door, rolling a suitcase behind her. Looking around, Jace realized there were a lot of suitcases in the room.

"Want to tell me something?"

"Jace, this is Cassandra. I think you've seen her around. Cassandra, this is Jace…my mate."

Damn Remy all to hell. Hearing her call him mate made him want to pull her to the floor and pound into her, mark her as his over and over again. She had to announce their status when he couldn't do a damn thing about it.

"Okay, what's she doing here?" Ever since he'd begun dreaming about Cassandra, Jace had wanted to meet her. But not like this and not with so much luggage. This was not going to end well.

Cassandra glanced from him to Remy with a worried expression on her face. "I don't think—"

"Shut it. You're not allowed to think. In fact, you shouldn't even be lugging a big suitcase around. Sit." Remy was ordering Cassandra around like one of her soldiers. The poor woman looked as if she'd been through the wringer. But she dutifully shut the door behind her, left the suitcase where it was and headed to the couch.

"Feet up. You heard the doctor."

Doctor? What the hell did I sleep through?

Cassandra rolled her eyes but twisted around on the couch until she was lying flat with her feet up on one arm. "I feel ridiculous."

"Too bad."

"Hello. Anyone want to tell me what's going on?" As much as Jace was amused by their banter, he was interested in the home invasion more.

"We're moving in for a bit. Hope you don't mind."

We? Since when was Remy a package deal?

"Cassandra, please excuse us." Jace shackled Remy's wrist in his hand and dragged her to the kitchen. Before he could begin to cross-examine her, she started to speak.

Rapidly.

"I'm sorry, but I didn't know what to do with her. Since we're mates now, you're stuck with my sister, just like I get stuck with yours."

There was the mate word again.

All of a sudden, the whys and the hows didn't matter one little bit. She acknowledged *them*. Who cared about suitcases? Pressing her against the counter, Jace let Remy feel the evidence of what her words did to him. "I love it when you call me mate." He licked at the mark on her neck, happy to see it still remained, a clear sign of his possession of her.

"You have a bigger place than I do and she needs help. I'm not good with people, you know that." Remy was babbling away about the hospital and doctors as Jace licked the curve of her ear and bit down on her lobe. Pushing his hands up under the T-shirt, he cupped her breasts, pinching her nipples lightly. "Shit, Jace, that feels so good."

"You can move in anyone—sister, brother—I don't care. Just not your father."

Remy started to laugh but it quickly turned to a moan as Jace snaked his hands past the elastic band of the running shorts.

"Hmm, no panties. I like."

Remy widened her stance as Jace's fingers found her moist opening. But before he could delve deeper, she grabbed his hand. "Jace, we can't. Cassandra's right in the other room."

"If you're both going to be living here, she better get used to seeing and hearing some stuff. Understand? There is no way in hell I'm not making love to you."

"Well, that's good, because I'm not giving you up any time soon." Remy grabbed Jace's ass. "I just think we should get Cassandra moved into her room before we start fucking in the kitchen."

Jace pulled back, realizing the truth of her words. "Fine. But as soon as possible, I want you out of this outfit and spread-eagle on my bed."

"Out of it?" Remy cocked her head to the side. "I thought you liked it."

"Like isn't even the word." His feelings on the outfit were more of deep-hungered gurgling noise from the pit of his throat. The sound a hungry man made when he spotted food. It was nowhere in the vicinity of like.

"I might have to keep it then."

"It's not yours."

"Do you really think I'd own something so…tight?"

"A man can hope." But now that she mentioned it… "Who does it belong to?"

"Malibu Barbie in there."

"And you're wearing it, why?"

"Because I changed and my clothes were bloody."

348

Jace closed his eyes and took a deep breath. His she-wolf was going to be the death of him. "Do I even want to know?"

"Do you follow the belief couples should be open and honest with one another?"

He shouldn't have asked. "Yes."

"Then Derek and I killed two Coyotes."

"Two."

"But it was self-defense. Sort of."

"Sort of?" Jace knew he sounded like an idiot repeating everything she said, but he couldn't help himself. This whole thing was beyond comprehension by anyone completely sane.

"Well, it's not as if they really stood a chance against us. So it was more of a slaughter — but for a worthy cause. We saved Cassandra and her little messiah."

"I never said her child was the Wolf messiah."

"Yeah I know, it just sounds a lot cooler than I saved my adoptive dad's daughter knocked-up and her out-of-wedlock kid."

"You are so right." Jace laughed as he leaned his head against her neck. "So how long do you think the two of you will be here?"

"She's here until she drops the kid and I'm here, well, I guess it's up to you."

Jace pulled away and looked deep into her eyes. God he loved this woman. Crazy family and all. "How so?"

"I'm here for as long as you'll have me."

How his she-wolf warrior could be so fierce yet so vulnerable all at the same time amazed him. Remy was so guarded, it was remarkable she even brought up the issue of moving in. The fact she felt comfortable enough to show up with her suitcases was a step in the right direction. "How does forever sound to you?"

* * * * *

349

Remy eased out of bed and padded softly down the hall toward the guestroom. Or not-so guestroom, seeing as how Cassandra was now occupying it for at least another five months. Despite everything she had gone through in the last few days, she was still having a hard time comprehending how she ended up babysitting the woman who not only haunted her mate's dreams, but who was also her adoptive father's birth daughter. In addition to being the woman carrying the hope for the next generation of Weres all wrapped up in one person and now in Remy's very own care.

Talk about an overload of facts.

Remy opened the bedroom door quietly and peered inside. Still asleep, Cassandra snored softly, which earned the sleeping woman a frown from Remy. Could she be more cute? Even her snoring was ladylike.

This shit was going to get annoying real fast.

Closing the door, Remy made her way back into her new bedroom and closed the door. This time the faint noises coming from sleeping blonde didn't bother her in the least. It made her smile. Jace's snoring was cute, and not in an I-have-to-gouge-my-eyes-out way. Almost as cute as every other aspect of him.

The exact moment Remy realized she was standing in the dark naked staring at the former bane of her existence with a stupid smile on her face, was the exact moment she realized she was a goner.

Damn it. She was in love.

This was all Jace's fault.

Walking back to the bed, Remy joined Jace under the covers. He turned toward her immediately, wrapping his arms around her lovingly, even in his sleep. As much as she loved the snuggling, she was ready for something more. Which was surprising when she considered how thoroughly Jace had loved her just hours before.

Leaning forward, she nibbled at his neck and laved the love mark she'd given him in return. Sometimes she felt as if they were a couple of kids making out and wanting to show off to their friends what they had done. But it was true. Remy wanted to let the Pack know Jace was hers.

Remy's hands stroked over the muscles in his chest before snaking down between their bodies to find Jace's warm cock.

"That's right, baby. Keep going."

"You're awake."

Jace rolled over until Remy was flat on her back, her core cradling the cock she had just been stroking. "Uh-huh, and a very nice way to wake up it was."

"You're insatiable."

"Who was the one teasing whom here?"

"Okay, we're *both* insatiable." So saying, Remy wrapped her legs around Jace's and using her Were strength rolled him over until she was lying over him. "This is better."

"Any way I can have you is good for me." Jace pulled her head down for a kiss, wrapping his fingers in her hair.

The ringing cell phone broke them apart. Jace groaned as Remy grabbed the receiver and checked the caller ID. "Nico," she said, as she handed it to him.

Jace hit the talk button. "I think you do this shit on purpose, man. Do you have some kind of bias about somebody besides yourself getting some?"

"This is no time for jokes. I finally reached Rachel Santana and we've set up a meeting."

Jace sat up, all sense of enjoyment draining from him. "Did she know about this?"

"She's not talking, but this issue with the Coyotes needs to be resolved immediately. The *Maggiore* are biting at my heels about this treaty with the *Morbauch*. This could either make or break us. I need you both here as soon as possible."

"I understand, *Benandanti*. We'll be there."

"I guess I better leave a note for Cassandra."

"Don't think you don't owe me a good time, mate."

Remy smiled. "I won't forget."

Chapter Eleven

ɞↄ

Jace and Remy walked into the boardroom at the Desert Sanctuary to find the room already full. Every head turned toward them expectantly. Nico was sitting at one end of the table, the rest of the *Elitario* flanked behind him. At the other end sat Rachel.

She had brought two of her *Rahu* with her, yet they stood to one side, leaving her looking slightly alone, in Jace's opinion. He wondered how telling it was in regards to the situation at hand. Glancing at her face, he noted she looked more haggard and drawn than she had a few days ago.

As Jace and Remy walked to the other end of the table to join Nico, they received a number of speculative looks from their Pack. It may have had something to do with the fact they were holding hands, but since Remy didn't seem to mind, Jace was going with it. Remy released his hand and stepped behind Nico, taking her usual spot directly to his right, while Jace went and stood behind her. Up until this point, he hadn't had a specific spot, but from now on this would be it. He would have her back no matter what she did and to hell with the rest of the world.

"Can we get started?" Rachel's voice, although low, resonated throughout the room. From the annoyed look in her green eyes, apparently she didn't relish getting out of bed in the middle of the night to answer Nico's summons any more then he did.

"Derek, Remy. Please tell us what happened earlier today."

Derek and Remy began to describe the incident at Cassandra's townhouse. Although they kept strictly to the facts, Jace was amazed by their daring. His she-wolf was one audacious Were. The room was silent, listening to the story until they began relating the fight scene. Then the Coyote Weres exploded, disputing the events.

"You must have come on them unaware, to take down two of our Coyotes so handily."

"I assure you they were aware. Right until they drew their last breath. In fact it was quite pathetic. I'd been under the impression your Pack knew how to fight." Remy had her hands on her hips but her body was coiled and ready to spring into action at any hint of a threat. For the first time, Jace didn't begrudge Remy her position. She was a warrior and a damn fine one.

The Coyote looked as if he were going to speak, but with a wave of her hand, Rachel shut him down. "Enough. It doesn't matter…"

"It damn well does matter. I don't need any advantage to kick your ass. I won't allow us to be accused of being cheats or liars just because your Pack doesn't know how to fight."

"Are you sure they were ours and not rogues?" Rachel questioned.

"Why don't you tell us?" Nico turned to Kellen, who stepped forward with a black garbage bag in his hand. Reaching inside, Kellen withdrew a severed head, one after the other and placed them on the table in front of Nico. The bloodless bobble heads stared lifelessly toward Rachel and her *Rahu*.

The Coyote woman gave the display a passing glance before looking back at Nico with a grim look on her face.

Nico grabbed the closest head to him and held him up by his blond hair. "Do they look familiar?"

"Yes." Rachel nodded her head in annoyance. "Unfortunately."

"Why were they there?" Nico asked coolly. Jace could practically see the wheels turning in his head as he watched the reactions of the *Morbauch*.

"I guess we'll never know, since they were killed in battle." A blond *Rahu* crossed his arms over his chest and sneered at them defiantly.

Jace noted Rachel's jaw clenching tightly for a moment before she spoke. "I can assure you I did not send them. In fact, I have no idea who this human woman even is or what they would want with her."

"Your assurances are most kind but difficult to accept when we examine the evidence in front of us."

"I have no proof to give you of our innocence. There is only our mutual history since the treaty began. We have been friends to you in your time of need."

Rachel reminded Nico of her Pack's assistance four months ago when Kimberly had been kidnapped by a member of the *Maggiore*. Without the added strength of the Coyote, they may not have been able to save her.

Nico nodded. "I know you have appeared as friends, but there is the old saying, 'Keep your friends close and your enemies closer'. Perhaps you are just drawing us in to determine if we have any weaknesses."

Rachel threw up her hands as if she were annoyed. "I cannot make you trust us. Only time will tell if we are truly your friends and eager members of this alliance. If you are unwilling to give us the time to prove ourselves, I don't know what else we can accomplish here. You aren't the only person who's had to deal with rogue Weres. There are members of my Pack," Rachel glanced coolly to the Coyote who had spoken, "and of my own inner circle who disagree with my decision to merge with your Pack."

"Then why did you?" Nico inquired.

"Because like you, *Benandanti*, I too see the hungry look in the eyes of our women for children who have not come. I too realize fighting only ends in death, not in peace. And I too am tired of the ways of old. Change is a necessity, not a luxury."

"Then why the attack?"

"It is a question I cannot answer. Who was this woman?"

"My sister," Remy said, speaking up. If any of the *Elitario* were shocked by her claim, they didn't show it. Cassandra was living in his house and Jace was still having a hard time coming to grips with it.

Rachel shook her head. "Sorry, but it means nothing to me."

"Maybe you should ask someone else who apparently knows more about your Pack than you do." Kellen spun one of the heads on the table like a top. "Because you seem a bit left out of the loop."

"Fuck you, dog boy." The *Rahu* to her left stepped forward menacingly but halted when Rachel held her hand up.

"Let him be, Doc." Her words said one thing; her angry eyes said another. "He has balls. I wonder how they'd look adorning my rearview mirror."

"Come find out." Kellen smiled, rolling the head he'd been toying with toward them.

"May I make a suggestion?" Harrison stepped forward.

"Why not? Everyone else has," Rachel responded as she grabbed the head and tossed it to Doc as if it were merely a ball. "Bane's mother might want his head."

"I think we don't trust one another because we are such strangers. Historically our Packs used to intermingle and it was only right before The Great War when we became so secretive toward one another."

"They came to the barbeque," Derek noted.

"Okay, fine. But we need to learn more about each other to truly learn to trust. I suggest we have an exchange of sorts, with one of the members of our Pack working together with the *Morbauch* and one of the members of their Pack coming to work with the *Brachyurus.*"

"I think it's an excellent idea," Rachel said.

"Of course you would," sneered Kellen. "Especially if you were trying to spy on us. You've just gotten one step closer."

"We would have the Coyote in our midst. It's not like we couldn't watch him," Harrison noted.

"I agree. It's a sound plan." Nico stood. "And Harrison, since you thought of it, I think you should go learn about the Coyotes."

"What?" Harrison's shocked rejoinder echoed through the room.

"Scared?" one of the Coyote *Rahu* asked.

"Not at all." Harrison crossed his arms in imitation of the man.

"Good, now that we have the situation settled, who do we get?" Remy asked, eyeing the two *Rahu* like fresh meat.

"I think Roman would be a good candidate," Rachel said, indicating the now-shocked and reluctant-looking *Rahu* to her right.

Stepping forward, he laid his hand on her arm. "*Benandanti*, I don't think—"

"Then it's a good thing I didn't ask you." Rachel's voice never changed tone but she glanced down pointedly to her arm. Roman removed his hand and stepped back, standing as if carved from stone and looking at neither Pack.

"So it's decided then." Rachel smiled across to Harrison. "I guess I'll see you tomorrow."

Harrison nodded, still looking slightly dazed about his new assignment. Rachel gathered her coat and stood. "Roman, gather Zed, if you would."

Reluctantly Roman walked to the end of the table and scooped up his departed comrade's remains.

"And Blondie," Remy called out, "you can report here tomorrow."

Roman nodded, turned back around and followed the Coyotes out the boardroom. Kellen followed them out, making sure they left the building before returning.

"So what's the plan?" he asked.

"What do you mean?" Nico looked as confused as Jace felt.

"Come on, *Benandanti*, you have to have something else in mind, right? I mean you're not really just sending Harrison to them without a plan."

"I truly believe in this treaty, Kellen, and think this exchange is a good idea. I have no ulterior motive."

Kellen shook his head in disbelief. "I think you're making a mistake."

Jackson, who had remained silent through the entire exchange, spoke up. "I agree, *Benandanti*. History has shown us we cannot trust the Coyotes. We shouldn't be so eager, especially now they've started to show their true colors."

"What true colors?" Jace asked, taking a seat finally. All the bickering and finger-pointing reminded him a bit too much of schoolyard shenanigans. Nothing had been resolved concerning the whys of Cassandra's would-be kidnappers, if that was even what they were there for. "Rachel said she knew nothing of the plan, and I for one believe her."

"Well, now I feel reassured," Kellen sneered.

Jace refused to rise to the bait. The Were was bitter, and after lying in Remy's arms, he could understand why. But she was his mate and Kellen was just going to have to get used to it.

"Are your feelings dream related?" Nico asked.

"No," Jace admitted. "Just a gut feeling. I can sense she wants this to work."

"As can I," Remy spoke, adding her support. "I mean, I don't trust them, but I trust her."

Everyone around the room nodded their head as if in agreement.

"We will see this plan through to the end." Nico's tone brooked no disagreement. "Harrison, are you prepared to learn and report back to us?"

"Yeah, but now I'm wishing I kept my mouth shut," he grumbled, sitting with a pout. It was amusing to see a six-foot-tall muscular man act like a three-year-old.

"See? This is why I don't raise my hand in class," Derek teased. "That's what you get, teacher's pet."

"What are we going to do about Cassandra?" Remy asked, cutting the teasing men off. "I mean, she can't stay with us forever."

"Us?" Derek raised a brow at her wording. "You're an us now?"

"Shut up." To Jace's surprise, Remy blushed, much to the amusement of everyone in the room.

"Oh my gawd!" Harrison placed his hand over his heart and rolled his eyes. "Do my eyes deceive me or did Rem-fastest-ass-kicker-in-the-west-ington just blush?"

"I do believe you're right," Derek replied in the same falsetto tone. "Next thing you know, she'll be wearing pink and doing her nails."

She did have a set of pink panties, but Jace figured he'd keep that bit of information to himself for now.

"Even I'm at a loss for words." Kellen stared at Remy as if he were seeing her for the first time. "My Remington blushing."

"No, *my* Remington," Jace felt the need to point out the obvious.

"I guess," Kellen conceded.

"Can we get back on track here, people?" Remy, still battling the heat in her cheeks, turned her gaze toward Nico. "What are we supposed to do with Cassandra?"

"Watch her. Protect her but don't trust her. Not fully."

"I don't," Remy said softly. "She's hiding something, I just can't tell what yet."

"Give it time." Nico stood. "Remember, what's done in the dark will always come to light. Secrets and shadows never remain for long."

* * * * *

It was very, very early in the morning when Remy and Jace finally made it back home. Already she was thinking of Jace's house as home. She might as well just end her lease and move in because she couldn't imagine going back to her apartment now. Not after he'd asked her to stay forever.

The only thing marring her happiness with Jace was her inability to tell him how much he meant to her. Remy wasn't the kind of girl who could say "I love you" easily and since Jace had already said it first, anything she did would be anticlimactic. On the other hand, she wanted to let him know she cared.

Kicking off her shoes, Remy picked up the note she'd left for Cassandra on the kitchen counter, crumpled it in her hand and tossed it in the trash. "Probably didn't even know we were gone."

"It was still nice of you to do."

"Ugh, don't use nice and me in the same sentence. It gives me the chills." Remy opened the refrigerator and grabbed a bottle of water for herself and one for Jace. She was really starting to make herself at home here. Handing him the bottle, she bit her lip in thought.

"Okay, what is it?"

"What is what?"

"The question you want to ask me but don't know how to ask me."

"I'm losing my touch. I used to be able to hide all my telltale signs around you." Remy tipped the bottle back taking a swig of the water. "Now you can read me like a book."

"Is it so bad? We are mates."

"Yes, I guess we are. It just seems so…weird. I mean, I never imagined myself with anyone permanently."

Jace crowded her up against the counter. "You're stuck with me now. Hell, you announced it to the *Elitario*. Can't go back on your word. Wouldn't look good in front of the guys."

"Maybe I don't want to change my mind." She wrapped her arms around his shoulders and pulled him down for a kiss. "Just remember, this is a two-way street. You can't change your mind either. Even if you want to."

Jace stepped back, looking down into her face intently. "What's that supposed to mean?"

"Look, I know this thing between us happened kind of fast. And I know you said you didn't care I can't have kids." Jace started to interrupt her, but Remy held up her hand. "All I'm saying is, I hope you don't change your mind down the road because I'm a natural-born killer and I don't share my stuff."

"I ought to spank your ass."

"For speaking my mind?"

"No, for doubting my word."

"It's not as if I doubt you. It's just I don't want you to regret something later you said in the heat of passion."

"Fine." Jace placed his hands on her hips and picked her up. Startled, Remy dropped her water bottle and grabbed hold of his shoulders, quenching the girly squeal rising in her throat.

"What are you doing?"

"Proving a point." Jace carried her the few feet to the marble counter and sat her down. But he didn't release his hold on her. "Elizabeth. Dear sweet, fierce, loyal, deadly, sexy-as-all-hell Elizabeth, listen to me. If you never in your life believe anything else I say to you, believe this. I love you, and whether or not you can bear my child has little to do with it."

Blinking, Remy fought back the tears swimming in her eyes. "But with Cassandra being pregnant now, we know somewhere out there is a cure for our infertility. It's only a matter of time before the rest of our Pack is able to breed again."

"You're not listening to me. We will have a child. One day. It may not grow in your body or come from my seed, but I swear to you, you will be a mother. A great one."

"Promises, promises."

"It's a fact, she-wolf." Jace brushed his lips across her cheek, kissing away a fallen tear. "Besides, look who you're talking to. I'm the watcher, the seer of our clan. Don't you go doubting my gift."

"I thought it was a curse."

"Do you always have to have the last word?"

Remy tilted her head to the side as if she were pondering his question. Jace tightened his grip on her hip and gave her a warning growl, forcing Remy to smile at the sound. She'd make a Wolf out of him yet. "What a silly question, Watcher Boy. Of course I always have to have the last word."

"Then get on with it, she-wolf."

Jace nuzzled her neck, his breath whispered across the mark she wore proudly, causing Remy's body to shiver in his embrace. "I love you."

Jace froze in mid nuzzle and slowly pulled away from her. Her words didn't exactly get the reaction she'd been expecting. It wasn't as if she'd been expecting balloons and a parade or something, but she had expected him to look as if he were happy.

"What?"

"Nothing."

The hell it was nothing. "Is that all you're going to say?"

Jace slyly smiled. "I thought you wanted to have the last word."

"Ass." Remy grumbled as she pushed at his shoulders. She didn't push too hard though, she didn't want to actually move. Just to put up a bit of a fight. She may not be all that feminine, but she wasn't stupid.

"Say it again," Jace teased.

"Gladly, ass."

"Oh sugar," Jace picked her up and spun her around. "You and your sweet-talking. No wonder all the boys fall at your feet."

Remy wrapped her legs around his waist and tightened her grip around his shoulders. "No, it's because I knock them down."

"You're so fierce."

"You know it."

Jace began to walk out of the kitchen with Remy firmly attached to him. "I know you love me."

"Allegedly," she teased.

"Oh no, she-wolf." Jace fumbled with the doorknob to the bedroom and pushed it open with his knee.

"If you let me down, this would go a lot smoother."

"You want down?" Without further delay, Jace placed his hands under her arms and lifted her up off him then dropped her on the bed.

The jarring fall startled Remy into laughing. "Fool."

"For you, baby. Just for you. I suppose I better close this, we don't want to scare your sister." Jace closed the bedroom door.

"Then I guess you'll have to learn how to keep the noise level to a minimum."

"It's not I who does the howling, she-wolf."

"Sure you're not." Yawning Remy rolled over and stretched out on the bed, her body sinking into the cerulean comforter as she wiggled her toes.

"Tired?" Jace massaged her shoulders, releasing the knots in her muscles.

Remy nodded. "Hmm, that feels nice. Much more and I'll be out like a light."

"Too bad."

Remy glanced back over her shoulder. Although Jace's touch was soothing rather than sexual, his face was a different story. As tired as she was, the hungry look in his eyes made her perk up and take notice.

"Aww, did Watcher Boy want some loving?" Remy teased, using her old familiar taunt in a whole new way.

"You know, I always hated when you called me Watcher Boy, but now, it's kind of like our thing."

"You are so twisted." Remy rolled over on her back, stretching her arms high above her, causing her T-shirt to rise. She had worn her own clothes to the meeting, but had taken her bra off in the car on the way home. Her nipples were stiff under the thin fabric. Just having Jace in the same room made her feel excited.

"But you like me this way."

"No, I love you this way."

"Getting used to saying it, aren't you?"

Joining her on the bed, Jace held her arms above her head and took a nipple in his mouth. He sucked on it through the thin material of her T-shirt and Remy hummed in appreciation. He held both of her hands in one of his and pushed her top until it was up around her neck.

Her nipples begged for attention and Jace nibbled and licked at them until they were hard little points. Finally releasing her hands, Jace pulled her T-shirt off, throwing it over her shoulder. Getting up on his knees, he stared down at her.

"What?"

"Just looking."

Licking her lips seductively, Remy ran her hands over her breasts and down her stomach to the waistband of her jeans. Slowly she unsnapped them, pulling the zipper down. As she braced her feet against the bed, Remy raised her hips and tugged at the material until she could kick off the pants. She started to slip her hands inside her jade silk panties but he grabbed her wrist.

"No, let me."

Jace hooked his fingers on the sides of the panties and gently slid them down her long, brown legs. His hands caressed her thighs and calves as he moved lower, drawing out the anticipation. No matter how many times he touched her, it always felt as if it were the very first time. "Jace, please."

"I love it when you beg so prettily."

Remy whimpered as Jace finally bent his head and his tongue parted her soft folds to taste her. With eyes closed, Remy surrendered her body to his delicious torture. Arching her hips, she tried to push her heated flesh onto his talented tongue, but Jace wasn't having it. Pulling back, he blew on her sensitive nub. "I don't think so, she-wolf."

"Jace." She growled. "Don't tease me."

"Teasing implies I'm not going to pleasure." Jace swiped his tongue against her clit. "I'm simply delaying your pleasure."

"Bastard."

"Let's see what other naughty words I can get you to say." Jace toyed with her clit, licking it, teasing it with his teeth, nibbling her erect bundle of nerves until Remy thought she would go insane.

With every stroke of his tongue, Remy's breath quickened and she grasped the comforter in a death grip. Still Jace forged on. He suckled the tight bud into his mouth and intense pressure bordering on pain, yet feeling so damn good, tore through her body. Remy couldn't keep her cries muffled any longer. "Fuck...yessss...Jace..."

Chuckling, Jace began to double his efforts to drive Remy out of her mind with pleasure. It wasn't enough for him to just torture her with his mouth, the bastard had to get his fingers involved in the action. Sliding his fingers deep into her pussy, Jace began to finger-fuck her as he licked her clit.

Her hips gyrated as he fucked her with his fingers. Thrust after thrust brought her closer to her release. "Jeeze...yes...Jace...yes..."

Suddenly Jace withdraw his fingers from her soaked pussy and placed them against her rosette. His fingers, wet from her juices, slid into her ass, sending Remy over the precipice and her body began to shake uncontrollably as she came hard. Jace continued his assault of her senses, exposing her clit to the air and blowing across it, sending shivers throughout her body. He withdrew his fingers, much to her dismay, and began to kiss his way up her stomach. When Remy finally opened her eyes, she saw Jace kneeling over with a cocky grin on his handsome face.

"Now it's my turn." Remy sat up and pushed Jace down until he was lying flat on the bed.

"So you want to be in control, huh?"

"Oh yeah."

"Who am I to stand in your way?"

Remy began trailing kisses down his chest to his stomach. Jace sucked in his breath when she reached his groin, but she just laughed lightly and stroked down his thighs and calves, ignoring his cock but for the brief wisp of hair she trailed over the tip. As his cock was leaking pre-cum, she knew Jace was close and wanted to tease him at little.

Finally, she reached up and grasped his cock in her hand then leaned down to swirl her tongue around the head. Holding his balls in her other hand, she fondled them gently, eliciting a welcoming growl from her mate. Jace had wrapped his hands in her hair, guiding her head as she took him deep in her throat. But just as she started to suck his cock in earnest, he pulled her back.

"I want you to ride me, baby."

Chapter Twelve

ဢ

Remy looked up at him, her hand still around his cock and her full lips wet from tasting him. She smiled at widely. "My pleasure."

"No, both our pleasures."

Jace hissed with delight as she licked across the head of his cock one last time before scooting her body up to straddle him. Taking his cock in her hand, she rubbed it between her legs, coating him with her juices. Although he enjoyed her touch, he wanted to feel the grasp of her warm, wet pussy squeezing him tightly.

Remy's eyes were closed and her body was moving in countermotion to her stroking, her hips rocking against his hardness. Grasping her ass in his hands, Jace halted her motions and she opened her eyes in question.

"Now, Elizabeth. I need you now."

"So much for me being in control," she pouted.

"How about the illusion of control? Back up, baby." Jace waited until Remy moved off him before reaching into the nightstand table and pulling out a condom. As he tore into the package, Remy touched his hand.

"Uh, Jace, honey." Her voice was filled with humor.

"Yes."

"No womb, remember, so no chance of kids." Even though there was humor in her voice, it didn't quite reach her eyes.

Jace tossed the condom back on the table and sat up so they were eye to eye. "There may not be a chance of you carrying our child, but you will mother our child."

"Whatever." Remy pushed him back down and straddled him once more. "I'm healthy. Blood test and all that jazz."

"As am I."

"Then no condoms. It's just you and me from now on."

"It's been just you and me for a while now, Remy."

"What can I say, I'm a slow learner," she teased.

"Well, welcome to Jace's remedial class of fucking. Please grab the nearest cock and climb aboard." Reaching down between her legs, Remy spread her lips wide and guided his cock into her waiting entrance. Bit by bit she slowly lowered her body. Jace could feel her muscles yielding to the pressure as her pussy clasped him snugly.

"How am I doing, Teach?" Remy's words were halting, as if she were having a hard time speaking. Jace knew the feeling well.

"You're a bright pupil. I might have to move you to the head of the class. Now you're in control. You set the pace, she-wolf."

Instead of immediately moving, Remy leaned down to brush the tips of her breasts across his lips. Jace opened his mouth to capture one of her nipples and sucked it into his mouth. Remy's nails were digging into his shoulders as she braced herself and her low moan was one of delight. Releasing her breast with a pop, Jace turned his head to its mate, swirling his tongue around the berry-brown nub.

"Jace, I don't think can I stand any more."

Jace gently bit at the tip of her breast one last time before reluctantly allowing her to sit back for a moment to catch her breath.

"Move for me, baby."

Remy began circling her hips, rising on her knees and experimenting with finding a perfect a rhythm. Jace held on, stroking his hand over her curves. Just seeing his pale hand

369

move against her dark flesh had Jace's cock aching. She was beautiful. She was sexy. She was his.

Finally setting a pace, Remy began rocking back and forth, her pussy working his cock as if it were a fulltime job.

"Damn, baby." Jace gripped her hips in his hands, breaking his word to let her set the pace. She just felt to damn good. Jace moaned as her body contracted around his cock.

So tight. So hot. So wet. Her pussy was a virtual wonderland of pleasure. "You fuck so good, she-wolf."

"You're…not…bad…" Remy's nails dug into his skin as she rode him, "yourself…fuck, Jace…"

"You want it, baby. You got it." Jace gripped her as hard as he could and turned her rocking motions to straight up and down fucking ones. His cock, so hard and thick, drove into her wet, tight pussy over and over. The vision was breathtaking. Her body taking his offering, swallowing his shaft time after time until their rhythm was just a blur of motions.

"Yes! Yes! Yes!" she cried, her voice rising to glass-shattering levels.

Mindful of their guest, Jace reached up and covered her mouth with his hand, ceasing her muffled cries but not the low moans drifting out.

She was an animal. So wild and primitive in her passion. Head thrown back, Remy's hand left his shoulder and cupped her breasts, squeezing her erect nipples between with her fingers.

"That's right, baby, play with your nipples for me."

Bearing down on him, Remy ground against his cock as she exploded around him. Her legs tightened around his hips as she rode her orgasm to completion. The walls of her tight pussy contracted around his cock, milking him as he pounded into her. The tight sensation and muttered moans had Jace spiraling out of control.

With a savage groan of his own, he pulled her down onto him and came pouring into her heated core.

Jace clasped Remy's collapsed body in his arms and listened as her labored breath slowly regulated as they lay there. He could stay with her in his arms like this forever and thankfully would be able to.

"Do you need to go for a run, she-wolf?"

Remy lifted her head, shaking it in denial. "No, too tired."

"Poor baby." Jace rolled her over and pulled the comforter, which had been kicked to the bottom of the bed, over her rapidly cooling body. Remy mumbled her thanks but was already half asleep from exhaustion.

Closing his own eyes, Jace recalled the hurt look in Remy's eyes when he had again mentioned their child. If only she could see what he did.

* * * * *

Jace found himself back in recognizable territory, walking through the forest. Unlike the last dream he had, the pathway was clear and the reason why was the woman walking by his side. They soon heard the sounds of the babbling brook through the clear night air and found themselves in the familiar clearing. He watched as she looked around her surroundings before turning back to him.

"Do you always dream this same scene?"

"Not exactly, she-wolf. This is the tableau for my dreams, the actual scenes change often."

"Hmm, interesting. So, what's the movie tonight?"

"Just watch and see." Jace grimaced as he realized he was starting to sound like Vlad with his cryptic answer.

The air around them shimmered a bit before finally coming into focus. Remy was kneeling on a blanket spread over the ground. Instead of her usual uniform of jeans and a T-shirt, she was wearing a poppy-colored halter dress and the loose waves of her hair were tied back with a ribbon.

"Are you fucking kidding me? As if I would ever dress like that." Remy pointed at the image of herself. "Change it."

Jace laughed at her indignation. "I can't change it, she-wolf. This is the vision."

"Pretty damn convenient for you." Remy crossed her arms, giving him a hard glare.

Jace watched as the dream Remy began pulling food out of a hamper and spread it out as if setting up for a meal.

"Oooh, a picnic, what's for dinner?" Her sarcasm came through loud and clear.

"Shh, you're supposed to be watching."

Remy rolled her eyes. "It's not as if she can see or hear me. In fact, she is me. A disgusting version of me, but me nevertheless."

Jace pulled Remy into his embrace, wrapping his arms around her. Leaning close to her ear, he whispered, "Pay attention."

Remy sighed dramatically but stayed silent and watched the scene unfold.

There was rustling in the woods and a small toddler came running out, quickly followed by an image of Jace himself. Although he'd seen many images of Remy with this child, this version of the dream was one he'd never experienced before. In fact, it was the first time he'd ever seen himself in one of his visions.

The child had spotted Remy and, with a leaf in one hand and a twig in the other, raced toward her at breakneck speed. Holding her arms wide, Remy caught the young girl as she barreled into the hug. The other Jace joined them as Remy dutifully looked at the treasures the child presented to her, oohing and ahhing over them.

"She doesn't look anything like me," Remy whispered, her taunting about how she couldn't be seen or heard forgotten.

On one hand, Jace had to agree with her. The child had sandy brown hair, which at one time looked as if it might have been braided, but several strands had escaped and now hung loosely around her face. He couldn't tell the exact color of her eyes from this distance, but they were a lighter color, gray perhaps. Most telling, however, was her pale skin, a stark contrast to Remy's cocoa features.

On the other hand, he could see Remy's fierceness and strength of character in the child's face, her love of life. "I stick by my story. This is our daughter."

"I didn't think you could control your dreams."

"Normally, I can't. In fact, I'm not really controlling this one. But I've had many visions of you with our child and when I went to sleep last night, I remember thinking I wanted to show this to you."

Jace didn't know if she realized it but Remy was softly stroking his arm as she watched their little family picnic. He wondered if she was going to say anything more about the vision.

"We look like we do right now. Well, almost, except for the crazy clothes I'm wearing."

"Let it go."

"You're not the one who looks like a Stepford wife."

"You don't look like a Stepford wife. Besides, I think dresses are sexy."

Remy turned in his arms, her lips pursed. "No, you think dresses are accessible."

"That too."

"My point is," Remy poked him in the chest as she spoke, "this could be us tomorrow for all we know."

"Exactly." Vlad's voice startled them both and they broke apart.

"I should have known you'd show up," Jace said dryly.

"Of course I'd show up. I'm your guide, aren't I?"

Remy stepped forward. "So what do you mean 'exactly'?"

"Just like you, *nipote*, your *aiutante* wants all the answers handed to her."

"Damn right I do."

"You must prepare for the arrival of your child at any time. You don't know when or where it will happen. Just as in life, you must be open to all possibilities."

Remy turned to look at Jace. "He really sounds like a fortune cookie sometimes."

"I know. Annoying as hell, isn't it?"

"If you both weren't so..." Vladimiro shook his head before continuing. "Just remember what I told you before, *nipote*. This isn't over yet. There is much more to come and sometimes the answers are there, just hidden in the shadows beyond our regular vision."

"Mumbo jumbo," Remy grumbled as she turned to look back toward the dream version of them. "She looks happy with us."

"But of course." Jace took her hand in his. "You're her mother. How else would she look?"

"I'm a mother." Her voice cracked as she spoke. Surprised, Jace looked down at her and watched as tears poured down her face.

"Remy." Pulling her into him, Jace held tight to his little warrior woman. "I didn't show you this to hurt you."

"I'm not hurt," she denied, pulling back so he could see her face. Though tears stained her cheeks, a smiled graced her lips. "I'm happy, Jace, and in love."

"With our daughter?"

"And with you."

"Sweet-talker." He would never grow tired of hearing her say she loved him. And for the first time in his life, Jace didn't consider his visions a curse. It was a blessing, just like the

374

woman he held dearly in his arms. "This is only the beginning, Elizabeth."

"I know, Watcher Boy. I know."

* * * * *

The cool air whipped through Franklin's beige fur as he ran over his land. The winter weight of his fur was long gone now, which permitted him to enjoy the brisk morning air. While others enjoyed running at night in Packs, Franklin preferred the solitude of first light. Away from the masses, he could be one with nature and with himself.

His morning ritual would have to change soon though. At least the solitary part. He had a cub to think about, to show the way as he had Remington when she was just a child. Except this time he would mold the newborn from the beginning. With Remington, he had to work with a semi-blank slate, erasing all memories of her family along the way.

This child would be completely moldable and all his.

With his backyard in sight, Franklin sprinted faster. The rolling green of the untouched land gave way to flat plains. His modest brick home belied the largeness he strived for, instead presenting an unpretentious face.

Suddenly he noticed he had a visitor waiting for him, reclining on his lounge chair as if he didn't have a care in the world. Ballsy.

Franklin skidded to a stop in front of the lounging Were and growled. Much to his amusement, the man stood and rounded the deck, opening the back door for him. With a skill developed over time, Franklin eased out of his wolf form and into his human one, all within a blink of an eye.

Stretching, he worked out the lingering kinks in his shoulders before reaching over to the barstool and retrieving his robe.

"Did you have a good run, sir?"

"Always." Tying the stash, Franklin turn to the young Were and eyed his protégé speculatively. "And you, did you have an interesting meeting?"

"The Coyotes failed, sir."

"Did they?" Franklin raised a brow as he rounded the bar and made his way to granite counter. Without asking, Franklin poured himself and his visitor a cup of coffee. "I think not."

"But they didn't capture her as you wanted."

Franklin chuckled. People would never learn. "I assure you, young pup, things happened just as I intended."

"You knew Remy would show up and stop them."

"But of course." His visit with Remington couldn't have gone any smoother. Franklin knew dropping the bombshell of Cassandra would send Remington scurrying over there to check out what she would consider her foe. As if Cassandra could ever hold a candle to her. "Just as I knew the forged medical records would ensure Cassandra would need to be on bed rest, which would entail…"

"Remy inviting her to live with her?"

"But of course." After handing the Were his cup, Franklin, his own cup in hand, walked into his pantry and activated the hidden switch to slide the far wall back, opening the entry to his cellar. "Remington has never been good about leaving well enough alone."

The two men made their way down the stairs into the dark underground room. Even though the former wine cellar was now a prison, didn't mean it had to lack class. It had all the comforts of home with taupe walls, leather chairs and a bar with a dash of something extra, such as prison bars. And of course what good was a prison without a prisoner?

Pausing in front of the cell, Franklin took a sip of his coffee and sighed. He loved mornings.

"I see he's given up on changing."

"I'm not sure if he's given up or just worn out." Franklin admired the sedated man's drive. Despite being held captive for four months, David hadn't given up his fight for freedom. It was commendable. Foolish, yes, but still commendable.

"They know he's missing."

"It took them long enough." If he had to have opponents, the least Franklin could hope was they'd be worthy foes. "It doesn't matter now of course. Cassandra will be nearing her fifth month soon. We now know the fertility drug is a success."

"What are you going to do with him?"

"Well, release him of course. I'm not a monster. Just a proud grandfather."

"And what do you want me to do now?"

Franklin turned to his apprentice and smiled. "What traitors do best of course, blend in."

"I'm not a traitor." The yellow eyes of his apprentice widened in delight. "I'm a revolutionary."

"Long live the revolution," Franklin toasted, amused at the Were's words. A revolution. How delightful.

Why an electronic book?

We live in the Information Age—an exciting time in the history of human civilization, in which technology rules supreme and continues to progress in leaps and bounds every minute of every day. For a multitude of reasons, more and more avid literary fans are opting to purchase e-books instead of paper books. The question from those not yet initiated into the world of electronic reading is simply: *Why?*

1. *Price.* An electronic title at Ellora's Cave Publishing and Cerridwen Press runs anywhere from 40% to 75% less than the cover price of the exact same title in paperback format. Why? Basic mathematics and cost. It is less expensive to publish an e-book (no paper and printing, no warehousing and shipping) than it is to publish a paperback, so the savings are passed along to the consumer.

2. *Space.* Running out of room in your house for your books? That is one worry you will never have with electronic books. For a low one-time cost, you can purchase a handheld device specifically designed for e-reading. Many e-readers have large, convenient screens for viewing. Better yet, hundreds of titles can be stored within your new library—on a single microchip. There are a variety of e-readers from different manufacturers. You can also read e-books on your PC or laptop computer. (Please note that Ellora's Cave does not endorse any specific brands.

You can check our websites at www.ellorascave.com or www.cerridwenpress.com for information we make available to new consumers.)

3. *Mobility.* Because your new e-library consists of only a microchip within a small, easily transportable e-reader, your entire cache of books can be taken with you wherever you go.

4. *Personal Viewing Preferences.* Are the words you are currently reading too small? Too large? Too… ANNOYING? Paperback books cannot be modified according to personal preferences, but e-books can.

5. *Instant Gratification.* Is it the middle of the night and all the bookstores near you are closed? Are you tired of waiting days, sometimes weeks, for bookstores to ship the novels you bought? Ellora's Cave Publishing sells instantaneous downloads twenty-four hours a day, seven days a week, every day of the year. Our webstore is never closed. Our e-book delivery system is 100% automated, meaning your order is filled as soon as you pay for it.

Those are a few of the top reasons why electronic books are replacing paperbacks for many avid readers.

As always, Ellora's Cave and Cerridwen Press welcome your questions and comments. We invite you to email us at Comments@ellorascave.com or write to us directly at Ellora's Cave Publishing Inc., 1056 Home Avenue, Akron, OH 44310-3502.

erridwen, the Celtic Goddess of wisdom, was the muse who brought inspiration to storytellers and those in the creative arts. Cerridwen Press encompasses the best and most innovative stories in all genres of today's fiction. Visit our site and discover the newest titles by talented authors who still get inspired - much like the ancient storytellers did, once upon a time.